A REMEDY FOR FATE

M.A. Kuzniar

HODDERSCAPE

First published in Great Britain in 2026 by Hodderscape
An imprint of Hodder & Stoughton Limited
An Hachette UK company

The authorised representative in the EEA is Hachette Ireland, 8 Castlecourt Centre, Dublin 15, D15 XTP3, Ireland (email: info@hbgi.ie)

1

Copyright © M.A. Kuzniar 2026

The right of M.A. Kuzniar to be identified as the Author of the Work has been asserted by her in accordance with the Copyright, Designs and Patents Act 1988.

All rights reserved. No part of this publication may be reproduced, stored in a retrieval system, or transmitted, in any form or by any means without the prior written permission of the publisher, nor be otherwise circulated in any form of binding or cover other than that in which it is published and without a similar condition being imposed on the subsequent purchaser.

All characters in this publication are fictitious and any resemblance to real persons, living or dead, is purely coincidental.

A CIP catalogue record for this title is available from the British Library

Hardback ISBN 9781399737241
Trade Paperback ISBN 9781399737258
ebook ISBN 9781399737265

Typeset in Baskerville MT by Hewer Text UK Ltd, Edinburgh
Printed and bound in Great Britain by Clays Ltd, Elcograf S.p.A.

Hodder & Stoughton policy is to use papers that are natural, renewable and recyclable products and made from wood grown in sustainable forests. The logging and manufacturing processes are expected to conform to the environmental regulations of the country of origin.

Hodder & Stoughton Limited
Carmelite House
50 Victoria Embankment
London EC4Y 0DZ

www.hodderscape.co.uk

A Remedy for Fate

For Rory Croucher, Ben Humphrey, Aidan Littlehales, Alicja and Jake Shellard for being my found family.

CHAPTER

One

Prague, 1769

THEA HURRIED DOWN a winding street, her pockets stuffed with handfuls of rosehips and fresh thyme, a single crow's feather tucked behind her ear. The basket of blackberries she had hooked over one elbow swung with every step, her velvet cloak billowing behind her like a spectre. She was late. Too late to stop and admire her surroundings.

Prague, with its glittering spires and dreaming domes, felt like an enchanted city. The cobbled paths and buttery pastries made it feel like there was a snap of magic in the air. And there was . . . But only if you knew where to look. Most people had no idea that magic existed, let alone that there was a secret Magic Quarter hidden underneath their noses in Prague.

Thea dashed over Prague Bridge and headed straight to the oldest statue standing sentry: St John of Nepomuk. There she paused, sweeping a look over the bridge. A few shoppers were dashing off on errands, a couple of carriages clattered by, a child dropped a biscuit. But just as Thea pressed a hand against St John's stone base, she caught a stranger's piercing, emerald gaze.

As the protective ward – an invisible shield of magic that kept out any unwanted visitors or trouble – recognised Thea as one of its own, she was enclosed in an invisible whisper of magic, removing her, and anything . . . *unusual* from view.

The woman's eyes widened, looking around the now empty spot. Thea winced, hoping the woman would put her disappearance down to a vivid daydream or a moment of dizziness – it was remarkable how little most people noticed.

St John's stars glittered, whirling around his head like a galaxy, as with a deep groan, the base of the statue snapped open, revealing a spiralling set of stairs.

They should have led to a dark, subterranean chamber beneath the city streets. And they would have, if the world marched along to logic and reason. If it wasn't a glorious web of magic and whimsy. Instead, when Thea's foot touched the last step, she was ushered out into a tangle of narrow streets with dagger-sharp twists and turns: the Magic Quarter, the heart of all enchantment in Prague. It was wreathed in mist and framed with old, watchful oaks that bore a parliament of time-telling owls. A weather-witch was busy extinguishing the flickering witch light from each street lamp, and messenger ravens, some carrying tiny packages, flew in all directions.

Thea beamed, filling her lungs with the scent of caramel and hot chocolate. *Home.* The Magic Quarter was one of a handful of safe havens for magical folk in Europe, where there were no exorcisms for ghosts, nor a wooden stake for the solitary creaky vampire who lived in the attic of his antiques shop, the Crypt. Empress Maria Theresa might have outlawed witch-burning and torture last year in 1768, but witches – *real* witches – still preferred to stay hidden. And their quarter was protected with wards that kept almost everyone out: magic was a secret most people couldn't be trusted with. Those that could, found their way to it – magic seeks those who deserve to know.

An owl nestled into one of the oaks hooted the time at her. Thea groaned and rushed past a line of shops, their pastel-painted stonework like a box of sugarplums: the Gingerbread House, Zdenka's Fortunes, Fleur's. Their signs shimmered as Thea passed. Fleur waved, happily ignoring her waiting customers as she battled a voluptuous gown in her window display. An autumnal gust of wind sent crisp leaves scuttling over Thea's boots like beetles.

Halfway down the street sat Stiltskin's Apothecary, a three-storeyed building in mint green with a curved mansard roof, an abundance of windows, and a gilded weathervane perched on top that bore a different animal each time Thea looked. Today, it was a hare.

A long line snaked from the door. The hare-weathervane twitched its nose anxiously. With a wince, Thea hurried faster. Sunrise had found her strolling along the Vltava, gathering fresh ingredients for her potions, along with little curiosities she'd found along her early morning walk. Her fingers purpling from picking wild blackberries, the time had seeped away until she'd realised with a jolt that she was late.

'My apologies.' Greeting the grumblers with her sweetest smile, Thea rummaged through her cloak pockets, pulling out delicate bird bones and an oval polished stone she'd found along the riverbank, before she finally located her key.

It was dim inside, lit only by a large moon. It hung from a bronze chain down the centre of the apothecary and echoed the phases of the real moon; currently, it was a sharp crescent. Thea ran a discerning eye over the gleaming wooden floors, the spiral staircase that wove up to the mezzanine, and the banisters she'd polished yesterday. Shelves huddled into every nook and cranny, from floor to ceiling, hugging each slanted floorboard, each crooked wall, each wooden beam, groaning under the weight of rows upon rows of glass bottles. Against the dark wood, the walls were a soft spring green, hand-painted with wildflowers.

Thea set down her basket and scurried from lamp to lamp, illuminating the thick gloom with buttery candlelight as shoppers crammed inside, jostling for space and gossiping. Some days, the apothecary smelt like a salt-rimmed shore. A flower-strewn meadow. The crackle of an incoming storm. Today, it smelt like rain. Rain and lilacs. Thea inhaled deeply before sliding behind her thick, oak counter, tucking her golden hair behind her ear and smiling at her first customer of the day. Smiles cost nothing, but spreading happiness was priceless. Removing her cloak, she hung it on a brass hook her side of the counter, smoothed down her emerald-green dress, and strung an apron around her waist.

'My son's got a bad case of boils,' a large, frazzle-haired woman announced, pushing the boy in question forward. 'Show her, Geoffrey.'

'That's not necessary—' Thea began, but she was too late; the boy's shirt was whipped off, the nearest shoppers backing away as if it would catch. A couple of pixies darted behind the counter.

Paní Dagmar, an elderly witch who Thea hadn't realised was also standing in line, peered closer at Geoffrey. 'I would pay excellent money if you allowed me to lance one of them,' she offered brightly. 'A good ingredient oughtn't to be wasted, you know—'

'Here's an ointment,' Thea interrupted as the customer's expression curdled like milk, plucking a jar of healing cream from the nearest shelf. 'It should clear that up straightaway.' She narrowed her eyes at Paní Dagmar in warning.

The customer eyed the glass jar. The contents were a benign beige colour, studded with calendula petals, though it did emit a faint glow from the dash of ghosts' luminescence Thea had added, to make said boils vanish. 'Is this really magic?' the customer whispered.

Thea smiled; it must have been their first visit to the Quarter. There were few non-magical folk who were allowed past the warded entry. Only those who truly had need of the Quarter, whose motives were pure, could enter the spelled bubble of protection. 'Yes, it is.'

'Are you a witch?' Geoffrey piped up. 'Everyone says there's no such thing as real witches, but this street appeared out of nowhere when we were crossing the bridge today!'

Before Thea could explain where they'd found themselves, Paní Dagmar poked her nose in. 'No, no, dears, Thea is no witch.'

The customer looked up from the jar. 'You're not?' Her brow wrinkled.

'No—' Thea began.

'Oh no,' the elderly witch chuckled. 'She's much worse than that!'

The customer's confusion thickened like fog. Thea rubbed her forehead. 'Really, Paní Dagmar, you're not help—'

'She's *human*,' Paní Dagmar confided with an outlandish wink in Thea's direction.

'You're in the Magic Quarter,' Thea said loudly, deciding to ignore Paní Dagmar. 'It revealed itself to you because you were found worthy to enter, but if you're not sure you're ready to try magic, you could try the apothecary in the Old Town.' Thea hesitated; she wasn't one for boasting of her own abilities, but she was a firm believer in not shrinking yourself down for the comfort of others. 'Though theirs is made with scorpion oil and pigeon dung, which I can assure you will not work faster than mine, if at all.'

Geoffrey gagged.

'There was a reason you were allowed entrance to the Magic Quarter,' Thea continued in a softer tone. 'The wards only permit those who need our services to enter, those who bear us no ill will. The last thing I would ever wish is to sell you something harmful. Trust me, you are safe here.' She offered a warm smile.

The customer nodded and parted with some hellers, dragging Geoffrey through the crowd as he gaped at the shelves stacked with potions and elixirs. The next shopper stepped forwards to unburden their woes. Magical folk flocked to Thea's apothecary, and whether they were sad or sick or just fancied a chat, she made sure to smile at each and every one of them. Everyone had their own story and you never knew what page they might be on that day. It was why she'd painted the walls with a meadow of wildflowers: daisies and daffodils, lilacs and snowdrops. Even in autumn, when the nights were drawing closer, entering the apothecary tasted like a mouthful of sunshine.

Thea dispatched a visiting vampire with a bottle of storytelling ink concocted from the ashes of a fire that she'd read her favourite stories aloud to in the thickest part of the night, and a single feather from a firebird. Each sentence, penned in the charcoal ink would lend the writer the skill of a poet. She served Paní Dagmar a thick cream drenched in honey and friendship lilies that softened the skin and invited flowers to bloom as you walked by, then shooed a couple of sneaky pixies out from behind her counter. Their long fingernails were coated with the honey she kept there to sweeten her teas.

Then she spotted her: a girl, somewhere in her late teens. Her gaze was furtive, her eyes shadowed. Haunted with more than a lack of sleep. They always looked like that, the ones who come for something only Stiltskin's Apothecary could provide. The ones desperate enough to pay the price Lord Stiltskin demanded.

Thea's heart grew heavy – or it would have done, if she had a heart. Instead, a spell lived in her chest. She could feel it when she pressed a hand there: it fluttered like the wings of a paper bird. Thea might be one of the few humans in the Magic Quarter, but she herself was bound together with magic.

The girl entered the shop, making a pretence of examining a bundle of rowan berries on crimson thread. Thea tried to ignore her, busying herself with a string of customers instead. Thea knew what she would see if she caught her eyes: the hope that would glimmer there. But her trust in Thea was misplaced.

From the corner of her eye, Thea watched the girl slink closer. She was wearing a maid's livery, starched and pristine, her hair neatly pinned back, though she kept worrying at her bottom lip with her teeth. Her hands were red, too coarse for her age. Dread crawled into Thea's stomach; she'd seen too many people like this before.

Eventually, the morning crowd eased to a trickle, the apothecary emptying until the hanging crescent moon gleamed across the bare expanse of dark oak floor, bathing everything in pearlescence as though they were standing inside a seashell. Enough for the girl to meet Thea's concerned gaze over the counter.

'I was told that you could help me,' she whispered, twisting her hands together.

She was young. Too young to pay the necessary price. Thea's pulse thudded with sympathy, her smile wavering for the first time that day. 'You heard wrong.'

The girl blinked. Once, twice, before shaking her head and pursing her lips. Determination turned her voice stronger. Louder. 'Please. I need help with my place of work, and I was told this is the place to get it.'

'Look . . .' Thea glanced around, ensuring they were alone. There wasn't a customer nor honey-sampling pixie in sight.

'Al—' the girl began.

'No names,' Thea almost snapped. Closing her eyes for a beat, she leant closer, the counter pressing into her stomach, nausea rising in her throat. 'I can help you, but the price is steep . . .'

The girl dug in her apron pockets. 'I have savings . . .'

'It's not your money that I need,' Thea said sadly. 'Not for this. You will need to pay with time.'

The girl's determination wavered.

'Think on it. Try to find another solution. Because amending fate isn't something I stock on my shelves, it isn't as simple as drinking an elixir.' Thea stared at her, imparting her words with the severity they required. 'This is a last resort.'

The girl's throat bobbed up and down as she swallowed. 'And if I still wish to go ahead?'

Thea sighed. 'Return after the sun has fallen, when the apothecary is closed and the night is still. Two sharp knocks on the back door.' The rest of the Quarter might have been aware that Thea used Jasper's borrowed power but she preferred to operate under the cover of darkness for the privacy of her customers and her own safety with some of the services she offered.

The girl nodded and scurried away, sending the bell ringing as she stepped back into the street and left quickly. Hopefully, she would never return.

After the girl departed, there was a quick flurry of business; an assortment of magical folk who had travelled from across Prague and the Quarter itself passing through, and Thea's third new customer of the day, though they were giddy enough from voyaging into the Magic Quarter for the first time, their need that granted them admittance through the wards seeming simply to be their desire to have a little magic in their life, which proved as much a treat for Thea as them. She dispatched them with a bottle of dream-bubbles: a gorgeous teal elixir that promised both the bubbliest baths and the sweetest dreams. Her good mood blossomed with the entrance of one of her favourite non-magical city regulars, Alena Böhmová, an opera singer as fabulous as she was lauded.

'Rehearsals have been brutal this week. Please tell me my throat drops are ready?' Alena rasped, resting one hand on her neck, shrouded from the autumnal chill with a silk scarf, ruby-red to match her dress. Though she hadn't applied any cosmetics, her hair was piled high with dove-grey powdered curls, and a tiny beauty patch remained affixed to her forehead – a little star, which Thea had never seen her without.

'I have enough to last you all winter.' Thea retrieved a handful of small glass jars, filled with hard-boiled sweets in a curious shade of blue that shifted and deepened in the light, like river water. 'Though I also recommend drinking honey and lemon and trying not to talk outside of the theatre,' she added, wrapping the jars in paper and exchanging them for the hellers Alena had already deposited on the counter.

Alena took the jars eagerly. 'Yes, yes, I will be a saint. A silent saint,' she declared, speaking with her hands as much as her words, each as emphatic as the other. 'You are magic, darling Thea, as magical as these.'

Thea smiled. Alena was a woman born to the stage. Nobody could ever silence that voice, least of all Alena herself.

'Whatever do you put in these that sweeten my voice so beautifully?' Alena fixed Thea with a shrewd look.

'Marshmallow root, a fairy's tear and the song of a nightingale, captured in honey,' Thea told her, with not a small glow of pride. She had concocted the recipe herself. She may not be a witch, but anyone could make a potion, provided they got their hands on the right ingredients – those with a little sprinkle of magic – and Thea happened to have a knack for hunting them out.

Alena gave a dramatic, heaving sigh. 'That sounds as lovely as a song.'

After Alena left, Thea pulled on an apron and walked through her backroom and further back, until her darkly atmospheric apothecary gave way to verdant wilderness. Flowers, herbs, ferns and mosses, even trees, stretched up to a high glass ceiling, which revealed a bowl of endless blue sky that did not match the clouded grey outside the apothecary windows.

This was Thea's haven. Her sanctuary. The trees waved their branches in greeting and the ferns rustled with excitement on seeing her; this wall of Stiltskin's Apothecary nudged against the Rose

Basket, shop and home of Rose, her neighbouring garden-witch, and the reason why Thea's jungle had just a little more personality than most plants she'd come across. Magic didn't believe in keeping tidy borders.

Emptying the basket of blackberries she'd picked earlier onto her work bench, her hands fell into routine, letting her mind fly free and wild. Thea loved making potions, but she was no witch. Paní Dagmar had been correct in that.

Sometimes, she wondered what would it be like. To have the hum of innate magic at your fingertips. To be able to conjure a ball of witch light at a whim, or grow trees that danced, or rule over the skies. There were so many kinds of witches, each born with an affinity, like weather-witches or kitchen-witches – she'd always thought she'd be a garden-witch, if she were one.

But no. Thea was human. A human caught between two worlds.

She absent-mindedly crushed the berries with a mortar and pestle. Seven years ago, she had been just like the girl from today. Hopeful. Trusting. She had found her way to this apothecary's back door and knocked on it, trading everything she had for a new life. Trading away her very heart, leaving her unable to ever love anyone.

And now she couldn't even remember why.

She pounded the blackberries harder, turning them to pulp, then liquid as her first memory resurfaced. Seven years ago. Standing in front of the apothecary with a stranger. Lord Stiltskin, owner of Stiltskin's Apothecary, as devastatingly handsome as he was cold.

'Our deal is concluded, then,' he had said, as shock rendered her silent, unresponsive. 'As per the contract we have forged, you will be my new apprentice and must reside on the premises to manage both the day-to-day running of the apothecary, and the deals in fate you have agreed to handle on my behalf while I devote myself to my other business affairs. You will find everything you need to be comfortable in the rooms upstairs. I will leave you now to acquaint yourself with everything, and will return in three days to begin your training. Fate is a tricky mistress, but in time I am confident you shall be able to shape her to your will. After all, my power runs through your veins now. Do not disappoint me.'

'I don't remember who I am,' she'd managed to whisper.

He'd inclined his head. 'That was your condition for this ... arrangement.'

She'd frowned. 'And if I no longer wish to adhere to whatever bargain I made that I can't remember? I need to see this contract.'

'I promised that if you guessed your true name,' he said, locking his dark blue eyes with hers, 'I would return your memories and heart, and you would be free to leave.' He unspooled a leaf of parchment that bore signatures, but Thea was too panicked to read it properly. She clamped a hand to her chest, an unfamiliar sensation unmooring her. Where once there must have been a rhythmic thudding, now there was a flutter that felt too light, too insubstantial. 'What did you do to my heart?'

His eyes drifted to the heart-shaped box he held like lost treasure. 'I promise you, Theodora, that I will take great care of it. You may not remember, but you asked for this as well. The spell woven here is a masterpiece. It will not fail.'

With that, he'd handed her the keys to the apothecary and walked away. Leaving her reeling in place. 'No, *no*,' she shouted after him. 'You cannot leave me here, I have no memory of making this deal!'

'A deal is a deal, and I never renege on a deal,' he said without turning.

A spurt of blackberry juice hit Thea's cheek now, distracting her from her memories. Wiping it away, she blinked hard. Filtering the juice from the pulp into a little copper pan, she set it above a flame to simmer, adding water, a sprinkle of salt and a splash of home-made vinegar, fermented under the watchful eye of a wolf who was not always a wolf, and muddled in some fresh mint.

She loved crafting potions: the process soothed her, made her feel calm and in control. A sharp contrast to the power that coursed through her veins: fate's power. The power of bargains and balances, which had been given to her by Lord Stiltskin, along with the apothecary itself. Both for the small price of Thea's heart, memories, and her name. If that girl returned, this would be the power Thea would wield to grant her wishes, requiring the girl to pay for the service with time.

'That smells divine.'

Thea startled, glancing up from her blackberry potion. 'Sorry, I didn't hear the bell ring.' Wiping her hands on a nearby cloth, she smiled at the stranger by habit, though her mouth was tight; he'd intruded on her sanctuary.

The stranger's embroidered blue waistcoat and matching jacket and breeches whispered of wealth; his light, tawny features peered out from under pomaded and powdered hair. The apple tree in the corner blushed, its green apples glowing red. Resting an elbow on Thea's work desk, the stranger peered into the pan. 'What are you making?' He turned his gaze back onto Thea, his close attention sending warmth rushing to her cheeks. How ridiculous. She was a grown woman around five and thirty, not a young girl harbouring a secret affection. Or a flighty apple tree.

'I'm making ink,' she told him. 'A rich purple ink, imbued with protection and luck and love. It's for writing beautiful letters that will arrive safely.'

Thea longed to write something lovely to send to a distant friend, or relative. But without her memories, she didn't know if there was anyone out there in the world for her. Anyone who pined for her, as she pined for the idea of them. Instead, she made this ink, to help others connect with their loved ones, even if she couldn't find hers.

Sadness pinched her. Shaking it away, she added, 'Is there anything that I can help you with?' She ran an eye over him, realising that he was her fourth new customer of the day. How unusual.

'Ah, yes.' He straightened. 'I'm having some trouble sleeping.' His rueful smile revealed a single dimple on his smooth, clean-shaven face. Thea couldn't help staring at it. It looked like it would perfectly fit the tip of her finger.

'I have just the thing.' Tearing herself away, she led the stranger back to the shop floor and up the spiral stairs to the mezzanine, where the moon hung like a suspended jewel.

When she glanced up from a velvet-lined drawer of sleeping potions, their silvery light playing over her face like starlight, the stranger was standing at the top of the staircase, staring around in wonder.

'This is quite fascinating, Paní . . .?'

'Thea will be fine,' she said, a little shyly.

'Malek.' He canted his head. 'A pleasure to meet you.'

Suddenly, the scent of blushing apples filled the apothecary. Hiding her secret smile, Thea removed a sleeping potion before easing the drawer shut. She tilted the glass bottle, watching the potion slink to one side. Liquid moonlight. It gave off a soft lilac shimmer. 'Add two drops of this to a cup of tea an hour before you wish to sleep. I recommend brewing this as an accompaniment.' Crossing the mezzanine to a shelf lined with baskets, she ran a finger over the labels she'd penned with her favourite quill and sapphire-bright ink. 'Happiness, Love, Luck . . . Ah, here, Sleep.' Plucking a handful of sachets packed with her signature blend of valerian, lavender and camomile, strung out to dry beneath a star-spangled night, she handed both the brew and the potion to Malek, who was distracted.

'Love? Can you truly brew a tea to make someone fall in love with you?'

'No, you cannot. It's one of the hardest things to do, even if you have magic coursing through you, to steal someone's heart.' Thea absent-mindedly touched her collarbone. With a start, she smiled at him. 'That you'll have to do the old-fashioned way.'

He slowly smiled back at her, flashing that dimple once more. This close, she noticed the bags under his eyes, the bluish cast beneath the white powder he'd attempted to conceal them with. 'No more than four drops per night,' she cautioned, making her way back down and over to her counter, writing down the purchases and taking his coins.

'Until next time, Thea.' He lingered over her name, giving her pinpricks of delight. 'I am certain we shall meet again soon.' That dimple made another appearance before he strolled out into the gloaming hour. Around him, the Magic Quarter was settling, with shoppers hurrying back for dinner, and the scent of cooking and potions – and perhaps a spot of rain – twining down the cobbled street.

Thea gazed after Malek. The ghost of her heart gave a solitary thump.

CHAPTER

Two

A LOUD RAP ON the window made Thea jump.
Outside, a petite, well-rounded woman with chestnut curls escaping in every direction, her russet dress and apron dusted with flour, waved at Thea, pointing to the cake she was holding, then in the direction that Malek had just departed. *'Who was he?'* Zofka mouthed.

Five minutes later, Thea and Zofka were ensconced in the Lantern, the bookshop where Talibah, the third woman in their trio, lived and worked. Hundreds of lights in gemstone colours dangled from the ceiling, sending rainbows skittering around the room, which was filled with squashy sofas and armchairs.

'And a dimple?' Zofka asked, cutting her apple and cinnamon cream cake into generous slices, which she arranged on three plates. Rich, autumnal spices seeped into the air, making Thea's mouth water.

'And a dimple,' Thea confirmed, taking two of the plates and leading the way to their favourite spot, where three cups of hot chocolate were gently steaming on the table, thick enough to stand a spoon in. Lashings of whipped cream melted on top.

Outside, the shops and stalls were closing for the night, the wide main street and crooked alleys emptying of anyone who didn't live there. Messenger ravens criss-crossed the navy sky and Rose, the garden-witch, and Zdenka, the fortune-teller, were either gossiping or bickering nearby, Thea couldn't tell which.

Thea wrapped her hands around her cup of hot chocolate and sank back into her favourite purple chair as Talibah entered from the little old wooden door embedded in her back wall that led to the books. 'Whose dimples are we discussing?' She joined Thea and Zofka, resting a few books on the table.

Thea craned her neck to read the titles. *Serenading Vivian*, *Eudora and the Ship's Captain*, *The Adventures of Georgina*, all by one Arabella Wildgoose, whom she'd never read before but thought the most magnificent nom de plume.

'Thea met a man,' Zofka whispered conspiratorially.

'Oh?' Talibah sat down with the elegance of a ballerina, her ebony hair falling over one shoulder in a curtain of silk. All three women were in their middling thirties, but where Zofka had been born and raised in Prague, to a long line of witches with baking in their blood, Thea's English accent was her only clue to her past. No stranger to travel, Talibah was an Egyptian woman with the gift of second sight and a penchant for exploration. She'd spent her twenties hopping from one ship to another, joining expeditions until she'd ended up in Prague. She still occasionally vanished for a month or two, shipping back crates of books and new lanterns in fantastical prints and colours. Thea often daydreamed about joining her – imagining the wind in her hair, all the new sights and smells – but she was bound to the apothecary, and they were just that: dreams.

Besides, she told herself, adventuring would mean relinquishing her creature comforts for far longer than she'd ever desire. Even if she had had a choice, she'd stick to the romance novels she devoured instead. As a bonus, those tended to come with dashing captains or seductive pirates.

'Do tell me more,' Talibah continued. 'Have all these romances I've been supplying inspired you?' She grinned at Zofka, who was smirking behind her cup.

'I'm going to ignore that, since you brought me these.' Picking up the books, Thea hugged them to herself. She'd been in desperate need of something new to read; there were only so many times she could lose herself in *The Lost Love of Iris Pearl*.

Zofka swatted Thea's arm. 'Don't you dare – we need to hear every single detail. Immediately!'

Thea filled her mouth with cake in a moment of petty rebellion. Zofka narrowed her eyes impatiently as Talibah chuckled, her amber eyes gleaming.

'He was just a customer.' Thea shrugged. 'I don't have anything more exciting to tell you.'

Zofka's resulting sigh was dramatic. 'Maybe he'll return.' She brightened at the thought and, loath as she was to admit it to herself, so did Thea. Well, he had been rather handsome.

'Aren't you forgetting something?' Thea toyed with her fork. 'I have no heart. I can never fall in love.' Her lack of heart was a snarling pit; as much she tried to fill it with smiles and kindness and laughter, still it yawned inside her chest, open and raw. It had to be the reason that sadness and fear and loneliness skulked into her thoughts, her dreams, the quietest part of the day when she was alone. It was that pit, that lack inside her. Her body knew something was missing.

Zofka cut her a second slice of cake. 'Who said anything about love? You don't need to fall in love to have a little fun.' She raised her eyebrows suggestively and despite herself, Thea laughed.

'We had some theatrics of our own today.' Talibah rested her cup on her knees. 'Apparently, a couple of men were spotted snooping around just before the shops opened this morning. Rose saw one of them trying to sneak inside the Rose Basket. She said the same pair were lurking around Fleur's hours later, and they were still wandering about, writing something on scrolls, after closing, when she watered her window boxes.'

'It could have been a shopping list.' Zofka's voice was tinged with hope.

'Were they witches or vampires, or . . .?' Thea let her question hover.

Talibah's mouth thinned with disapproval. 'Rose wasn't sure. They could have been shape-shifters or fate-weavers, perhaps.' Her gaze flicked to Thea, who tensed.

Fate-weavers, like Lord Stiltskin. Like the borrowed power Thea was swimming in.

Zofka gave a delicate shudder, her eyes turning fearful. 'Fate-weavers are rare; they tend to stick to their own realm rather than interfere with ours.' For good reason; magical folk tended to distrust beings who could alter the path of their destiny with a flick of their fingers.

'Lord Stiltskin owns an apothecary in our realm,' Thea reminded her.

'He is the exception, not the rule,' Zofka countered. 'And he makes himself scarce here.'

Talibah looked thoughtful. 'Well, whoever they were, Rose overheard them talking amongst themselves. Something about reporting back to someone. She believes they were there on behalf of someone else.'

'It sounds like Rose managed to overhear a great deal.' Thea's lips twitched at the thought of the older woman creeping along behind her window boxes, eavesdropping.

Zofka barked a laugh. 'You know she's an interfering wretch,' she said fondly. 'Though if she's right, I'd like to know who's paying off magical folk to do their underhanded work for them. The Quarter is a secret for a reason. I know it's been a while since witches were burned at the stake, but there are still Magic Hunters out there that would have us all run out of town if they knew we existed.' Her hot chocolate began bubbling. Thea gently nudged her. 'I know, I know,' Zofka sighed. 'I'll rein it in.'

Thea forked up another mouthful of cake, rich in nutmeg and cinnamon, the thick vanilla cream a delight against the sharp notes of apple that sang through the slice. And, it being a cake baked by Zofka, with each bite came emotion; memories that were pleasant and gentle and not her own. Of baskets piled high with rosy apples and an orchard groaning with ripe fruit. It warmed her in ways that had nothing to do with the temperature.

'I didn't see anyone, and I was up at the crack of dawn, heating my stoves.' Zofka continued, unable to help herself. She looked as if she needed a taste of her own medicine. Her hot chocolate bubbled over, sputtering cream over the nearest lantern.

Talibah removed Zofka's cup before it shattered, and Thea lay a reassuring hand on Zofka's arm. 'I'm sure it will come to nothing.'

Zofka nodded, stealing the last of Thea's hot chocolate and sinking back into her armchair with a sigh of contentment. Talibah met Thea's eyes with a note of concern.

'Would the wards guard against anyone snooping around?' Thea asked quietly. 'Do they not protect against people spying on us?'

Most people didn't believe in magic; it was a secret known only to those who could be trusted, along with a handful of those who could not, whose families had passed down the information, or who had learned of its existence by happenstance. Magic was power and that kind of power was often misunderstood or disliked, particularly by those already in positions of power, who would do anything to cling onto it. Insecure kings and emperors kept Magic Hunters in their employ to shut down and banish anyone who might threaten their rule. It was why the Quarter had been warded in the first place. At some point, centuries ago, someone with immense power had crafted the magical protective shield to keep everyone with magic safe. A handful of those residing in the Quarter were not magical – like Zdenka, the fortune teller, or Talibah with her second sight, who were both human like Thea – but the Quarter had called to them and the Quarter protected its own. Nobody who intended harm could enter, and even if one of the residents suddenly developed a hankering for violence, the magical wards would swiftly remove them from the Quarter. Thea had seen it happen only once, when a witch attempted to steal a shopper's purse. The witch couldn't breathe until she'd fled the Quarter: the magic pushed her out, rejecting her. It was why nobody feared Wojslav's appetite for blood; he was forced to hunt outside the ward's bounds.

'Not if the people spying didn't have malicious intentions,' Zofka told her. 'If someone sent people to snoop on their behalf, they knew what they were doing. They removed themselves from the situation enough that the wards failed to pick up on anything. Maybe we could try and strengthen the wards with some additional spells . . .' She trailed off, turning to Talibah. 'Can you *see* them with your second sight?'

Talibah nodded, answering every one of Zofka's questions as fast as they tumbled out – yes, she could see the wards, though they were invisible to everyone else; she could see the magic rippling like sunlight glancing off water with a rainbow flash. No, she couldn't see the moment someone was granted entry, nor how the wards encouraged those who needed the Quarter to enter. And no, she couldn't see Zofka's magic in action, though she could tell which cakes were enchanted – they glimmered.

Thea smiled into her cup. After Lord Stiltskin had left her new and vulnerable and alone, a flame of rebellion had sparked. Rather than obeying the man who had carried away her heart and bound her to the apothecary, Thea had marched into the Lantern, lured by the promise of books. But as she'd ventured deeper and deeper, into the mustiest, farthest shelves, she'd grown so lost she couldn't find her way back. She'd spent the night there, waking with a crick in her neck and Talibah kindly peering down at her. That same morning, she'd barely taken her first step inside the apothecary, encouraged by Talibah, who had remained at her side, when Zofka had entered, bearing cake.

Together, they had told Thea stories of Lord Stiltskin's previous apprentices, and had stayed for dinner, cooking goulash and pouring glasses of Madeira as they navigated Thea's new home together. When the second bottle was opened, Thea had confessed she was held together with a spell, her mind whirling with thoughts instead of memories. Near seven years later, Talibah and Zofka had never made her feel lesser for her lack of heart. Never made her feel anything less than cherished. They were the heart of her new life.

The three women enjoyed the comfortable quiet now, interrupted only by the scrape of forks against plates and the occasional squeak emanating from the stacks: fanged bookworms.

'Aren't you worried that they'll gnaw your books into shreds?' Thea asked idly, admitting defeat and surrendering her plate. 'I can't imagine anything worse than turning the page, expecting a delicious first kiss, only to be met with rows of tiny teeth marks instead.'

Zofka snorted.

'They're fine.' Talibah waved a dismissive hand. 'I just leave them a handful of crumbs every night and I haven't found a single nibble in any of my books.'

Some hours later, Zofka kissed them both on the cheek before hurrying back to the Gingerbread House and Gretel, her partner. Talibah retired for the night, leaving Thea to stroll back to her apothecary, weighed down with her new books and leftover cake. Trees lined the street, each one crowned in gold. Autumn was Thea's favourite time of year in the Magic Quarter, when the air chilled enough to pull out her velvet cloak and butter-soft boots, and every gust of wind crackled with leaves.

Thea dragged her feet, savouring the crunch of leaves beneath her boots and the cold biting her fingertips, hoping against hope that the girl from earlier wouldn't be waiting outside, too eager to pay a price she could never reclaim.

A shadow swept behind the building next to Thea's. Thea slowed, tightening her grip on her borrowed basket. All seemed fine. No, *there*. The dark silhouette reappeared, peering through the windows of the Rose Basket next door. Thea very much doubted that, whoever this stranger might be, they wanted a bouquet of unusually out-of-season peonies or roses that smelt like your favourite dream. Talibah's earlier news filtered through her thoughts in a crimson wash of panic; was this one of the pair who had been spotted snooping through the Magic Quarter all day? Who were they and what were they doing? If Zofka's fears proved right, they could be spying on behalf of someone else in order to sneak around the wards. Though Thea was safe from anything malicious, thanks to the wards, she couldn't let them learn whatever it was they were digging for. The Quarter *must* remain a secret.

The shadow moved to the door. 'Who goes there?' Thea called out, loudly enough that a few candles flared in windows. 'Show your face,' she demanded.

The stranger fled.

A window squealed open. 'Are you all right there, Thea dear?' Rose, fellow Englishwoman, elderly owner of the Rose Basket and notorious eavesdropper, peered out with a candle that illuminated her nightcap.

'Yes, thank you, but there was someone nosing around out here. Make sure you lock your doors and windows tonight,' Thea called back. Though Rose was English too, they conversed in Czech, the language of the Quarter.

Rose made a disgruntled sound. 'They must have caught wind of the daffodils I was selling today. Mighty popular, those were. Tasted like the creamiest butter you've ever had. You could pull off a petal and spread it right on your toast.'

Thea hid her smile. 'You could be right,' she said seriously. The window closed with a rusted scream, sending a shiver down the back of her neck. She didn't relax until she'd hurried back to her apothecary and locked the door behind her, melting with relief.

In the back room of Stiltskin's Apothecary, a narrow set of stairs led to Thea's home. It perched in the roof of the shop, with sloped ceilings and dormer windows along each side. Half the windows peered out into the sky, where the moon hung like a scythe. The other half overlooked the Quarter's oak trees, their branches tapping on the glass like gnarled fingers. A hunting owl swooped past as Thea set her basket down and lit candles.

She had a neat table with two dining chairs, a couple of overstuffed armchairs, a copper bathtub that took forever to fill unless you enlisted the help of a friendly, passing weather-witch, and a big bed. Though it was just one large, open space, she had added layers of thick carpets, and every surface was covered with jugs of wild flowers and candles. She'd even painted violets that looked as if they were blooming straight out of her headboard. Stacks of books threatened to topple over next to Thea's bed, which was mountained high with plump pillows and blankets that Zofka had knitted for her. Each blanket was a different shade of yellow. 'Because you're like sunshine,' Zofka had explained, each time she'd presented her with a new one. They were thick and lumpy, with an abundance of dropped stitches thanks to Zofka's impatience, and Thea couldn't appreciate them more.

But the best part of her home was sitting on said blankets, twitching his fuzzy little nose at Thea: Cinnamon. Thea scooped up her brown rabbit with floppy ears, holding him close as she brewed a cup of her own night-time tea. There were worse places to be bound to stay. She could come and go from the building as she pleased, but if she ever attempted to leave forever, the doors would refuse to open, or her path would wind straight back to the apothecary. Jasper Stiltskin had expertly tied her fate to the apothecary and since it was impossible to change the past, she could not unpick the bargain he had woven.

Depositing Cinnamon on her bed, Thea changed into her nightgown and snuggled down into her pillows and blankets, with Cinnamon cuddled up on her lap. Sipping her tea, Thea opened *Eudora and the Ship's Captain* with a pleasing creak of the spine and began to read.

She'd only made it to the end of the first line when it came: two sharp knocks on the apothecary door.

CHAPTER

Three

It was a tale as old as the gods and every bit as cruel. Thea brewed a pot of lavender tea as the girl poured out her story. Of a master of the house whose attentions she did not want but could not refuse for fear of losing her position and the salary that she and her bedridden sister relied upon. Still in her livery, she twisted her apron in hands which were reddened and raw, either from washing clothes or dishes, Thea wasn't sure, but she slid a jar of thick calendula and night-blooming rose cream into the girl's pocket. It was the least she could do.

The back room of the apothecary, huddled between the shop floor and Thea's jungle of plants, was a witch's cave of ingredients and trinkets. Herbs and flowers hung from the walls to dry, feathers were stuffed into glass jars, and everywhere you looked, you'd be sure to find a curious object. River stones polished smooth as glass, a bird's skull that stared directly at you, a twig shaped like a crooked finger. And, in pride of place, a large tome, propped open to a double spread of recipes for ink-making. But Thea didn't need to consult her Compendium of Magic for this. 'I can make you unappealing to him,' she said when the girl had finished speaking.

The relief that passed over the girl's face was intense. It made her look younger than the seventeen years she'd claimed, piercing Thea with fresh guilt. She stared at the girl, wondering if she had a daughter herself out there somewhere. *What if I had carried her in my womb for months and months, feeling her quicken and dart about like a quick-silvered fish, slippery with life and all my hopes and fears? What if now she was almost a woman, standing in the back room of an apothecary, begging for help? What then?*

The girl clasped both of Thea's hands in hers. 'Really? Are you serious?'

'Yes. He'll be discouraged from pursuing you,' Thea told her.

The girl gnawed at her lip, in a manner so similar to Thea's own, she jolted, automatically searching the girl's face for her own features. They both bore hazel eyes, and perhaps there was something in the shape of her nose – but perhaps she was just searching for the impossible. 'But what if he dislikes being around me and I lose my position that way?' She sat heavily down on a wooden stool.

'There's no need to worry.' Thea smiled at her. It was bittersweet. She wrapped the cloak she'd pulled on over her nightgown tighter around herself. 'He won't find you distasteful – he won't think of you at all, in fact. You'll blend in with the house as if you were part of the furniture.'

'Thank you.' The girl smiled back. 'Our mother left us seven years ago, it's been just us since then. I don't know what we'd do if you didn't help us.'

Thea froze. Seven years – surely that was just a coincidence? Surely, she couldn't be this girl's mother? Surely the girl would have recognised her? But memories faded and people changed, and the possibility that they were linked in some way rattled in Thea's head.

'I will help you.' She forced the words out over the lump in her throat.

Her vision blurred as she tapped into her weaving power. Became a conduit for fate itself. The air in the apothecary vibrated, shimmering as threads appeared all around her, visible to her alone, in every shade and hue she could name and thousands more she could not. Revealing the tapestry of the world in its infinite connections and possibilities. Present and future; the past was not available to fateweavers, much as Thea wished it was, so that she might glimpse the life she'd lived but could not remember. Thea located the girl's thread, a rich auburn, here and there lanced with scarlet where a second thread entangled it. Her master's, Thea presumed. As the knowledge of what to do slid through Thea's thoughts like scissors through silk, so did the price that such a service would necessitate. Only, this thought was sharp and hard, the shearing edge of the scissors, forcing itself into the forefront of her mind like a particularly nasty headache: shaping fate interfered with time, so in order to maintain a balance, to stop the strings of fate and time from collapsing in on themselves, Thea took time from her customers. Sometimes it came in the form of memory, sometimes a dream. But for this untangling, such delicate work would cost more. An entire year.

The girl seemed to sense Thea's shifting mood. 'And the payment?' she asked, her nervous energy returning threefold.

Thea swallowed thickly. 'One year of your life.' She braced for the girl's reaction; this was the worst part of Thea's contracted service to Lord Stiltskin. The part that prowled through her sleep, nightmares coming thick and fast in the deepest part of the night.

On hearing their price, some cried. Some bargained, others raged. And some, like this girl, gave a stoic nod. 'Will it hurt?' Her voice trembled, betraying her fear.

'You won't feel a thing,' Thea assured her. None of them did. They only missed what was taken when they needed it most; then, it would return to haunt them. If she'd taken dreams, they would be remembered when at their lowest and loneliest. If they'd paid in memory, they'd spend the rest of their lives prodding that blank space like a missing tooth. Had it been a lost love? A great passion? A talent that they could no longer recall? Then there were those who needed more. Who paid in years. Whose regret would fester when their deathbed loomed closer than it ought. Fate gave and it took. Thea was not a master of fate, only the holder of the scales. And this strange power she'd borrowed from Lord Stiltskin determined the price. She didn't know how she knew, only that she knew it as certainly as she knew that grass was green and the sun would rise tomorrow. An innate knowledge. Perhaps other people would find it magical, but for Thea, it was more akin to a curse.

'Then take it, quickly.' The girl stood, bravely facing Thea, all big hazel eyes and pointed chin and one large freckle perched beside her nose. With a nod, Thea placed one hand above the girl's heart. Silvery strands, luminous as lost starlight, emerged from the girl's chest. Thea pinched them between her fingers. Pulled them out. The girl inhaled sharply, not with pain, but with knowledge; agreeing to pay a year of your life was a different matter to seeing that life dragged from your body. Thea pulled harder, sweat sliding down her collarbone.

The girl whimpered. Had Thea made a similar sound when she'd stood in this room and allowed Lord Stiltskin to take her memories? Had it hurt when he'd removed her heart? Had this girl, with those familiar mannerisms, been someone she'd walked away from? Had she done something terrible that had necessitated her paying such a steep price? Could this girl be a daughter or a niece or someone she'd forgotten?

Thea's hand shook. And she let go.

The silver strands snapped back into the girl's chest as Thea slumped back against the table.

'What happened?' the girl whispered.

Thea closed her eyes. She'd never broken her agreement with Lord Stiltskin before, never not taken a price to tweak another's fate. Fear turned her palms slick, but whatever consequences she might bear for this, she knew she couldn't take a year of this girl's life, not now that she'd noticed something familiar about this girl with a missing mother. *Seven years ago.* 'Don't ask questions,' Thea whispered back, her heart-spell thrashing in her chest.

She reached into the tapestry of fate, disentangling the thread that kept strangling the girl's lifeline, until it ran clear and unhampered, into the future.

The girl made to thank her.

'Do you know where your mother might have gone?' Thea interrupted, sweat running down the back of her neck. No consequences seemed to have occurred yet, but fate could be tricksy like that.

The girl's hazel eyes turned sorrowful. 'She died. Tuberculosis.'

'Oh,' Thea managed. She'd broken her agreement and risked

upsetting the delicate balance of fate for nothing more than a coincidence.

Night had advanced by the time the girl departed. Thea blew out the candles, save for a single lantern, which she held.

Before Thea turned around, she knew that *he* was standing behind her.

His presence was impossible to ignore, even when you weren't looking at him. The apothecary crackled with his energy, with the ancient dark power of the fate-weavers rippling through his veins. She hadn't heard him enter the apothecary, she'd been so immersed in her own thoughts, but now they halted. She turned and set eyes on the man who'd taken her heart. Her name, her life.

Jasper Stiltskin stood in the centre of the back room, shadows falling over him like a cloak. He was tall, imposing in a quiet way that drew the attention of a room, somehow sensing his silent strength. Lanternlight illuminated the planes of his face as if he'd been sculpted to life, with a sharp jawline and sharper gaze, his eyes an almost unnatural shade of blue. Thea couldn't remember ever seeing the sea, but Jasper's eyes looked the colour she imagined the sea would, a blue so potent and wild it could not be tamed. A cold depth rippling with danger.

'I'm here for the records.' His voice was deep, dark. It sent shivers down the back of Thea's neck. Owing to the late hour, he had forsaken the neat, powdered wig he sometimes wore, revealing his natural hair, curled above the ear, in a rich brown that appeared near-black. She wondered what fashions he kept in his own realm, the entrance to which was buried somewhere in the forest and was inadvisable for anyone who was not a fate-weaver to pass through. Though if he ever visited his own realm, she did not know. Only that he had a grand residence in the Old Town where she presumed he spent most of his time, though that too, was a guess. Jasper was unknowable.

'Of course.' Without another word, matching his succinctness, she reached for the leather-bound tome she kept below her workbench and opened it to the latest page, spreading it on the table Jasper was idling against. 'There.'

Jasper scanned the record of Thea's dealings with fate and their subsequent prices.

Thea acted unbothered by his presence, closing her Compendium of Magic, ready to carry it upstairs and perhaps read a little with another cup of lavender tea. She caught Jasper's mouth pursing in displeasure from the corner of her eye. *Did he know she hadn't taken that girl's price?* 'Something the matter?' she asked, unable to mask the thrill of satisfaction his disappointment gave her. Even if he knew what she'd done, it had been worth it. She was prepared to bear the consequences for letting the girl's price go unpaid.

Jasper ran a finger down the listed entries. Some noted a single dream, others, like the year she'd failed to take from the girl, detailed amounts of time. The rest held more ephemeral records: memory. Thea had taken more memories than she cared to dwell on, but never more than one at a time: a beloved memory, a worst memory, an old memory. She had never taken every memory from one person before, which made her wonder what on earth she could have asked for that had demanded a price high enough to reforge her entire existence. *What happened to me?* Sometimes she was scared to find out.

'There is less than I expected here.'

Good, Thea thought fiercely to herself. *That means fewer desperate people have been prepared to sell a sliver of their souls.* Keeping her thoughts tucked firmly inside her own head, she shrugged. She needed to distract him. She was contracted to stay at the apothecary, to take these prices and pass them on. If he discovered she hadn't taken one, she didn't know what might happen.

Jasper looked up, appraising her.

Thea's face heated. *Did he know?* She stared back at him. There was something about the man that never failed to burrow under her skin. Perhaps it was that he was the only person who knew what had happened to Thea before he'd taken her memories and heart. It needled that Jasper, of all people, knew her the most. Knew her true name. Her identity.

'Anyway,' she declared, desperate to distract him. 'Something seems afoot. There have been suspicious people lurking around the Magic Quarter; I spotted one of them myself tonight. Magical folk, I presume, but it bears keeping an eye on.'

Jasper's spine tightened. He drew himself to standing, his jawline rigid as he looked at her. She shivered again despite herself, her body reacting to his height, his presence, towering over her. 'Why did you not send me a raven immediately? Must I remind you that one of your duties is to report anything unusual or troubling directly to me, the moment it happens?'

Thea refused to bend to him. 'Perhaps my *heart* just isn't in it,' she said wryly.

A muscle ticked in Jasper's jaw. He closed the records, his twitching muscle the sole clue that Thea had provoked him. And oh, how she enjoyed provoking him. It was one of life's little pleasures, up there with the first bite into a cream cake or rereading a favourite book. Sweet and satisfying. 'I shall return in a few days,' Jasper said, somewhat stiffly.

Thea bristled with alarm. 'A few days? You usually only come once a week.'

'Whilst I am sorry that my company causes you such distress, I must remind you that this is my apothecary, and you work for me. If somebody is lurking around either my shop or you, that bears urgent investigation.'

'I do not belong to you,' Thea said softly. Dangerously.

Jasper's stare collided with hers. He looked as furious as she felt. Every time they exchanged words, it felt as if they could raze the apothecary down to ashes. 'I am more than aware of that,' he snapped. 'I can assure you that I dislike these . . . meetings every bit as intensely as you do.'

'Then why do you insist upon them?' Thea folded her arms, glaring at him.

Jasper glared back. The edges of Thea's vision flamed. 'A deal is a deal,' he said at last, before stalking from the room without a backward glance. The bells did not ring when he left the shop.

Thea half collapsed against her workbench with muddied relief and frustration and some other feeling she couldn't place that left a bitter, brackish taste on her tongue. *He didn't know that she hadn't taken a price.* And if he didn't know ... did that mean she could try it again? She so hated taking these prices that a tentative hope sparked.

Until she recalled what she hadn't asked him.

Running out of the apothecary, remembering too late that she hadn't put any shoes on since the knock at the door had disturbed her reading, Thea chased Jasper down the street. He cut an enigmatic figure, striding away in his navy-blue breeches and coat through the silence. A lone pixie, strolling through the trees, let out a squawk of alarm on spotting the fate-weaver, and hid beneath a pile of leaves.

'Wait!'

Jasper turned, frowning as Thea drew to a stop, breathing hard. 'What is it?' He glanced at her bare feet, that tic in his jawline giving a single pulse.

Distaste, Thea thought, for her lack of decorum. Well, she didn't care. What she had to say was more important than what he thought of her.

'A deal is a deal,' she echoed back at him, a little breathlessly. 'You didn't wait to hear my guess today.'

Jasper's frown hardened. 'Very well.'

I promised that if you guessed your real name, I would return your memories, your heart, he'd told her. Thea's hope struggled in her chest, her missing heart giving a ghost of a thump as she looked up at Jasper. Perhaps tonight would be the night she guessed right, that she would discover her true name and her long-lost memories would come flooding back like patient old friends. Setting her free from the apothecary. 'Adela,' she whispered, her heart-spell fluttering in her mouth.

Jasper looked inscrutable.

'No.' He walked away without another word, and for once Thea couldn't fault him; what more was there to say?

It didn't stop her loathing him, though.

When Thea marched back into the apothecary, she locked the door with shaking hands. Something creaked, as if the apothecary was shuddering in fury, too. She winced at the sound, glancing up. And freezing in place.

A crack was running along the ceiling, splintering the paint.

CHAPTER

Four

THE FOLLOWING DAY brought a hive of activity. Each time Thea had a spare moment to glance out of the window, the Magic Quarter was thronged with customers. Was it her imagination or were there more non-magical folk than usual? Not even a sudden rain shower that fell in brilliant violet drops and fizzed on the cobblestones managed to deter the shoppers. Everyone was hungry for a taste of magic. And if the rain spattered their wigs and silks with purple, well, that only added to the enchantment of it all.

Thea wrapped orders in paper and took coins, working her way through the queue as she dragged her tired bones through the day, pointedly ignoring the crack along the ceiling.

A raven flew through the open window and landed on the counter in a rustle of night-black feathers. Thea's latest customer, a young shape-shifter with a frightful cold, waited as the raven hopped over to Thea and stretched out one leg with a caw. Thea quickly untied the little note affixed to its leg. With an inky glimmer, the words revealed themselves.

> *Is there a holiday coming that I don't know about? Run over when you've got a minute, I've made you lunch.*

Zofka never added her name to any of the notes she sent via the Magic Quarter's messenger ravens, but Thea read the note in her voice anyway. Lunch. She cast a wistful glance outside as the raven flew away, past the street lamps struggling against the gloom. Fog was setting in, thick enough to be a lost cloud. Perhaps it was. Rose occasionally dragged a cloud down from the sky when she was feeling overwrought. Zofka too, had bouts of the weather becoming inextricably linked with her emotions; either one of the witches could have accidentally conjured the violet rain, not to mention the cackle of weather-witches who dwelled in a windmill the far side of the Quarter.

A loud sneeze drew Thea's attention back to her customer. 'Here.' She thrust a jar of lemon and moon-mothwing pastilles at him. 'Chew two immediately.'

'Not so fast!' Paní Dagmar squeezed herself to the front of the queue. She wore a traditional patterned headscarf, tied beneath her chin, and her face wrinkled like parchment as she beamed. 'Sneeze into this vial for me, young man.'

Thea pinched the bridge of her nose. 'No. You cannot possibly have a potion that requires a sneeze—' Paní Dagmar opened her mouth. 'Stop pestering my customers!' Thea took a different tack in a hurry. 'My apothecary is not your hunting ground for spell ingredients!' Nobody knew what kind of witch Paní Dagmar was but it was rumoured that she was well into her second century. Though she herself claimed that she was at least twice this age.

The young man sneezed into his sleeve. Paní Dagmar sighed and shuffled away.

An hour or so later, when the storm of customers had relented to a quiet drizzle, Thea flipped the sign on the apothecary door to *Closed* and ran across the street to Zofka's.

The thick walls of gingerbread that had given Zofka's café and bakery its name were iced and glossy. Icing sugar puffed from the chimney. Thea entered the darling door and crossed the floorboards – planks of hardened biscuit – and weaved between packed tables – also a rich brown biscuit – to the sugar display cases. When it came to cake, Zofka was unparalleled. Blackberry torte and apple pies with cinnamon-dusted crusts, biscuits baked in the shape of leaves, *trdelník*, a sweet pastry wrapped around a stick and cooked on Zofka's fire and chocolate mice with pink sugar noses. And, of course, gingerbread. Slabs of richly spiced gingerbread cake, preening under a thick layer of icing, and rows of gingerbread people, happy and sad and everything in between.

Behind them stood Gretel, willowy in a way that called to mind long walks beneath the stars and lace-trimmed gowns, her beauty ethereal in her soft brown eyes and long, curling eyelashes, cream skin and dark hair. 'Thea!' Gretel smiled warmly at her. 'Isn't it busy today? I've never seen this many non-magical folk here before.'

'It's heaving.' Thea couldn't help returning Gretel's smile, though her own was marked with dark shadows crawling under her eyes; she had been up all night, and it was wearing on her. She mourned those years when the tiredness wouldn't have shown. She scanned the café, not glimpsing Zofka, though she noticed Rose had somehow managed to secure an entire table for herself. 'Is Zofka baking in the back?'

Gretel softened with affection, and Thea felt an ungrateful pang. What was it like to have someone in your life who melted when their thoughts wandered your way? Thea often hoped that if she ever got her heart and memories back, she would discover a great love gracing the tapestry of her life. Other times, she hoped not; what did it say of that great love, if Thea had willingly surrendered her heart to a monster?

'She is.' Gretel interrupted Thea's spiral. 'A batch of apple strudl. She also made goulash and freshly baked rye bread that's being kept warm in the stove for you.'

Before Thea could thank her, a slender man with wiry spectacles and an impressive, powdered wig forged a path to the front of the café, stepping in front of Thea as he addressed Gretel. 'Am I to understand that since this establishment is housed in these . . . conditions' – he eyed the café dubiously – 'that these confections contain magic within them?' He stared at the cakes and biscuits in their sheer sugar cases. A gingerbread person took it into its biscuited-head to leap up and begin pirouetting.

The man stared at Thea and Gretel. 'I see,' he murmured. His face was painted white, his lips and cheeks reddened, and this close, his wig gave off the distinctive whiff of bergamot oil, though it couldn't distract from the lice crawling between his curls, attracted by his beef-fat pomade.

Thea inched closer to Gretel, misliking him at once.

'As you can see, they do,' Gretel said. 'Is there anything in particular that catches your eye?'

Gretel had a good dash of woodland spirit in her ancestry, but her greatest gift was her serenity. Gretel kept Zofka grounded and together; the pair were in harmonious balance.

'You may address me as Pan Novak. I am a court-appointed Magic Hunter and I, along with several others, have been instructed to investigate this . . . curious sector of the city. Do you know, I am not sure I have ever been here before?'

Ice ran down Thea's spine. 'This isn't possible,' she breathed. The snooping around was one thing, this was another entirely. The wards should have protected them from this, as they had any other time Prague had become infected with intolerance. Why must people be so distrusting of that which they did not understand? The folk of the Quarter made easy prey for those who were only concerned with lubricating the wheels of society and stuffing their own coffers with gold.

Someone dropped a fork as the magical folk sensed the disquiet spreading through the café.

Gretel remained calm, though her fingers, resting atop the counter, slowly turned white.

'I beg your pardon?' Pan Novak asked crisply.

Rage uncoiled in the pit of Thea's stomach like a dragon awaking from slumber. How dare this man bring his political machinations into the Gingerbread House? She had to know how he'd slipped past the wards' magic.

'I only wondered how you stumbled upon us . . . We are in such a quiet spot.' It took effort not to betray her fury, but if Gretel could maintain that calm demeanour, she could emulate her. Keep her voice steady.

Pan Novak's smile was slow and creeping as fog. 'Then you admit you were hiding. How curious indeed.'

'Not at all,' Thea protested.

'We have no reason to hide,' Gretel added calmly.

Pan Novak's lack of words spoke volumes.

'What could you be investigating here?' Thea asked, not without bite. 'This is only a café; there's nothing more harmless than a piece of cake.'

Pan Novak surveyed Thea over the top of his wire-rimmed spectacles. 'I am afraid I must disabuse you of that notion. These products are being imbibed; I have been sent to ascertain exactly what they contain and if they provide any adverse reactions in those who consume them.' His gaze fell to the pirouetting gingerbread man, a frown worming across his forehead.

How had he managed to cross the wards? Thea glanced past the Hunter to the rest of the café. There were an extraordinary number of non-magical folk seated there, including a family whose children were happily biting the heads off chocolate mice, laughing with glee at the resulting squeaks. They were oblivious to the current of alarm rippling through the magical folk. Some tables had silently emptied, leaving plates of half-eaten cakes and untouched hot chocolates. Others remained, though their heavy-lidded, vacant looks suggested they were tapping into a myriad of magical abilities, readying to fight or flee. Rose, who was mid-munch through a slice of blackberry torte, was lost in thought.

'Pan Novak, all of our wares are freshly baked here each morning and I can personally assure you that we would never wish harm on anyone,' Gretel said, clear and firm, wisely refusing to raise her voice to a pitch which might alert Zofka in the back. Zofka was a whirlwind that could not be contained and if she unleashed herself on this man, the consequences could be devastating for all involved.

The glazed sugar windows gave a menacing rattle. Pan Novak's attention flitted to them, and back. 'As that may be, my directives are clear. I must take a sample of your wares away for further investigation.'

Gretel gave a curt nod. She reached towards the nearest sugar case, but Pan Novak was already shaking his head at her, that intolerable smile hovering about his mouth. 'I shall select them myself.' Without asking, he replaced Gretel behind the counter, taking a large selection of their day's offerings and packing them into the biggest box he could find. Gretel stood beside Thea, the pair watching in a mire of helplessness and frustration as they'd been set aside, silenced.

He walked away with the box without deigning to say another word.

'He didn't compensate us for the loss.' Gretel stared at the emptied cases. 'There's no time left to restock, we'll just have to close early today.' She offered Thea a weak smile, a ghost of her earlier happiness. 'At least it will be lovely to have a longer evening off.'

'Gretel—' Thea began.

'Hold that thought.' Rose materialised, giving the scarce offerings a despondent sniff before turning her attention to Thea and Gretel. 'That *man*' – she gave another desultory sniff – 'managed to breach our wards with no whisper of a reason why or how he might have managed it. I'm calling an urgent Magic Quarter meeting at once.' Bringing her fingers to her mouth, she let out an ear-shattering shriek of a whistle.

The last of the non-magical customers took that as their cue to leave. Zofka ran through from the back just as a volley of messenger ravens flew inside and settled on the empty counter.

'What in the goddess is going on here?' Zofka was pink and flushed from baking, her hair glittering with escaped sugar. Gretel filled her in as Rose addressed the unkindness of ravens. 'Fetch every resident of the Magic Quarter and bring them to an urgent meeting in the Rose Basket at once.' She thought for a moment before adding, 'Wojslav will need more encouragement than the others, don't be afraid to give him a good peck.' With that, Rose clapped her hands, and the ravens departed like a bad omen.

Rose led the way to her flower shop, tailed by Zofka and Gretel, who were deep in conversation, and Thea, whose thoughts kept straying back to Pan Novak and the sardonic twist of his mouth as he'd exerted the full power of his position over her and Gretel.

The Rose Basket looked less like a florist and more like a living jungle had sneaked inside. Everywhere you looked, there were plants, lush and green and vivacious, perfuming the air with a verdant freshness. Rose's ceiling had been magically extended, allowing her trees to grow as tall as they fancied, and though it was rumoured to have once been propped up with wooden beams, these were now impossible to see under vines that hung like rope swings and ivy embroidering the walls. The floor was a thick carpet of moss and lichen and now and then a fern scurried past on its roots, trailing soil. And then there were the flowers. Protective roses that hissed and bared their thorns, sunflowers that crooned at you, and lilies that blushed and tickled your earlobes.

As Talibah joined the growing huddle, her raven-note still clutched between her fingertips, Thea filled her in on Pan Novak's incursion. More and more magical folk appeared, crowding the door, as Rose coaxed an outcropping of toadstools to grow big enough to seat them all. The shop groaned as it shifted in its foundations, stretching to fit everyone inside.

Zdenka, the fortune teller who, being human, never foretold anything of note, wore vibrant robes in seven different shades of blues and purples and pinks. Zofka and Gretel settled beside Thea and Talibah. A few minutes later, after another crop of toadstools grew into seating, Paní Dagmar perched nearby. 'How exciting,' she whispered, louder than if she'd spoken, 'I haven't seen such dramatic goings-on in the Quarter since my secret lover met my first. They duelled over me,' she told Thea, with no little pride. 'That was why the wards were first conjured, you know.'

Zofka buried her laugh in a cough.

'When was this?' Thea asked politely.

Paní Dagmar tapped her creased cheek, thinking. 'Some five hundred years ago now.'

Zofka coughed harder, ceasing only when Talibah nudged her.

Fleur, their resident modiste, sat beside Zdenka. They were joined by a skulk of men who shape-shifted into foxes at will, and a cackle of weather-witches. A group of pixies darted inside, making themselves comfortable on a bed of pillowy snowdrops.

'Are we all here?' Rose stood on a toadstool, surveying them all.

The bluebells arcing over her door tinkled. Wojslav, the vampire, slunk inside. Casting an appalled look at everyone sitting in one big clump on Rose's toadstools, he opted for lurking next to the door. Thea had no doubt that the next time she glanced his way, he'd have vanished. For someone who required human blood to exist, he hated spending time with people. Thea often wondered how he managed to carve out a living, though maybe he'd lived enough years that he required very little income these days; the Crypt was closed more often than it was open, and when someone did manage to wander inside, they were met with a disappointed sigh when Wojslav realised he had company. She was impressed he was here at all, until she noticed the beak-shaped chunk missing from his hand. It seemed the ravens had taken Rose's instructions to heart.

'Now that our latecomer has arrived,' Rose aimed a disapproving look in Wojslav's direction, 'Gretel, dear, would you mind coming up here and sharing what happened today?'

Gretel floated to the centre of the shop. In her ethereal voice, she described the events that she and Thea had just witnessed, the veiled threats that had spilled from Pan Novak's mouth. They were met with a fragile silence.

It shattered almost at once.

'How can a Hunter have entered?' Zdenka cried out, fussing with their robes. 'We are supposed to be protected in this Quarter.'

'Obviously,' Wojslav cut in, each word deep and measured, 'there is a problem with the wards. I myself have observed that my antiques shop is missing a windowpane. I am disturbed from my slumber all hours of the day by those frightful ravens.' He cast a dour look at his wounded hand.

'The apothecary ceiling has cracked, too,' Thea pointed out. 'Could this all be connected?' She had a sudden, terrible thought:

what if her refusal to take a price had triggered all this? 'When did you notice your missing windowpane?'

Wojslav gave a tortured sigh. 'Last week.'

Thea slumped back in relief. It hadn't been her, then. Perhaps her missing price would reveal itself another way soon.

'You know, now that you mention it, I have seen that the wards hold a misted area,' Zdenka suddenly declared, interrupting whatever Rose had been on the verge of saying. 'A spot that is obscured from view. Perhaps that could be the point of weakness?'

'Maybe your crystal ball needs a clean,' Rose muttered under her breath.

Before the pair could leap into another of their arguments – last time that had happened, they'd set fire to one of the tables in the café – Talibah interrupted. 'Then we are all in agreement. Something worrying is happening with the wards, which may not be the cause of our recent troubles, but if fixed, would definitely prevent us from being bothered again?'

She was answered by a slow, rattling snore: Paní Dagmar had fallen asleep.

'I believe so,' Thea said instead.

There were murmurs of agreement, spiked with a few whispers of discontent.

Rose, still standing on her toadstool, clapped her hands, summoning their attention. 'Then I propose that all witches join me in investigating the wards and everyone else can can—' She looked to Talibah.

'Research,' Talibah finished, adjusting her headscarf as she stood. 'There are countless texts at the Lantern, not to mention each witch here has their own grimoire; Wojslav—' she stopped. Wojslav had vanished. 'Well, Wojslav has a collection of old reference books at the Crypt, and Thea, you have your Compendium of Magic. I suggest we all consult our own resources and combine our knowledge. We might not be able to control the Hunters' suspicions but we can prevent them from entering our Quarter again.'

Rose nodded. 'Excellent. Well folk, you have your marching orders,' she called out as people began to drift out the door. 'We'll meet again soon!' she hollered, ensuring that half the Magic Quarter could hear her.

Paní Dagmar woke with a snort.

Zofka didn't bother hiding her chuckle this time and Gretel swiftly ushered her away. Talibah left on their heels, but Thea hung back; she needed to speak with the elderly witch. She had a burning question for Paní Dagmar.

CHAPTER

Five

ANÍ DAGMAR, MIGHT I have a word?' Thea asked, now that the elderly witch had re-entered the world of the living.

She beamed at Thea, her bark-brown face seasoned with laughter lines. 'Of course.' She shuffled over, looping her arm through Thea's as Rose began shrinking her toadstools back down. 'You know, you are welcome in my haberdashery any time if you fancy a pot of poppy tea. Gives you the most wonderful dreams, you know.'

'Oh, er, thank you,' Thea said, thrown for a moment. 'Actually, you mentioned having lived in the Quarter for centuries – you must have known so many people with so many names and I was wondering if there were any names that you think would best suit me?' She was running out of inspiration for her guesses.

'Of course, dear!' Paní Dagmar lowered her voice to a confiding tone. 'I am over five hundred years old, I have seen every name there is stroll through this Quarter.' She laughed brightly, squeezing Thea's hands as she spoke loudly and clearly: 'The name that best suits you is *Theodora*.'

Thea stood there as Paní Dagmar left. 'Thank you,' she said automatically, hating how hope had brushed against her, just for a moment.

'You're lucky she calls you by your name, even if it isn't what you were after,' Rose told her dourly. 'She keeps calling me *Daffodil*.'

*

Thea pored over the Compendium of Magic on her bed in a nest of sunshine-yellow blankets. It was thick and sturdy, bound in taupe leather with its title pressed on in neat letters. When you opened it, you stepped inside a portal to another woman's life. It burst with colours and thoughts and potion recipes, conjuring an old memory.

'I can't do this any more,' Thea had told Jasper, her nails cutting into her palms as she heaved the words out.

'You are making it more complicated for yourself,' he had shot back, his frustration mounting as another of their lessons in fate-weaving ended in glares and clipped tones. 'Your predecessors at this apothecary did not have half the difficulties you're displaying in understanding my instructions.'

'Then perhaps you made a mistake the day you set the terms of our bargain,' Thea fired at him. 'Perhaps you should tell me my true name now and set me free. I have no wish to work for you and even less to take these prices.'

Jasper's face shadowed like a portent. Thea held her chin high, refusing to show neither a lick of fear nor the wobble in her left kneecap.

'Fine.' Wordlessly Jasper stalked from the back room of the apothecary into the glass-roofed room next door, empty apart from an apple sapling that had been a gift from the sharp-tongued garden-witch next door, and was given to dramatic outbursts. As Jasper passed the sapling, it dropped a handful of leaves with a noise that sounded like a gasp. Jasper ignored it, flexing his long fingers and performing a series of motions that he'd spent the past three days trying to teach Thea.

As she watched, the threads of fate rippled alive around him, leaving Thea unable to tear her eyes away as Jasper expertly untangled a curious knot, revealing a large book that had been hidden from sight, perched on a shelf. 'Here.' He handed the book to Thea. 'I've taught you enough to fate-weave, now. One of your predecessors kept this; the others found it useful, too. Send a raven if you have any questions.' His voice had been the sharp cut of glass, his eyes averted as if the very act of looking at her irritated him.

Now, Thea flicked through the book's well-worn pages, past potions for memory and recall that she'd tried in her more hopeful days, searching for something that might bolster the Magic Quarter wards. Or explain why they were faltering. She dipped a slice of rye bread into the bowl of goulash Zofka had dished out for her after the meeting, packed with garlic, marjoram and caraway, careful not to splash any on the book. Some of the potions were simple remedies, like how to make fire-ginger, which burnt away any threat of an incoming cold. Others delved deeper into magic, like how to track down a magical ingredient or how to reverse a shape-shifter's transformation if they became stuck in their second form.

But more than magic, Thea was captivated by love stories, and the slow-brewing one penned into the margins of this compendium was the most delicious she'd ever read. Giving up on finding a solution to the faltering wards for now, she indulged herself with rereading the first entry in the Compendium, which was every bit as comforting as the second slice of hot buttered toast she munched while reading:

I met someone yesterday. He was dark and quiet and charming, and he looked at me as if he couldn't believe his luck. I was gathering dream bud flowers; the tiny pale pink blooms are forever locked inside a bud unless you open them in your dreams. Each one was the size of a teardrop. They were growing like lichen over the escaped roots of the blackwood trees and their flowers are so hardly seen, they felt like treasure. He was walking through the forest and we fell into step together. My basket was already full when we stumbled on the largest outcropping of dream-buds, but he removed his cloak, offering it as a makeshift sack. We picked flowers together and talked about everything until the moon rose and I took his cloak home.

Last night, I dreamt of picking dream-buds with him. When I awoke, I was surrounded by flowers.

*

Several days later and Pan Novak had not yet reappeared. Nor had Thea had a single knock on the back door of her apothecary come nightfall. Nobody had emerged from the darkness, keen to surrender their time, memories or dreams for a tweak of fate's threads.

As Thea pondered, she tested her batch of blackberry ink, doodling on a scrap of parchment: *Briar, Anastasia, Caliope, Juniper, Araminta.* She didn't realise she had a customer until they were standing in front of her counter, regarding her with amusement.

'Oh!' Thea wiped purple ink from her hands.

'My apologies, did I startle you?' Malek's single dimple made an appearance, flustering her further.

'Not at all,' she lied. 'What can I do for you today?'

'I happened to be passing by and couldn't resist coming in. You made such a lovely picture, immersed as you were.'

'Oh,' Thea said for the second time, noticing how his crisp white shirt set off his olive-toned glow, how his eyes were the shade of oak leaves in autumn. She buried herself in the pages of love stories every night, yet her own story would have been nothing more than a couple of footnotes; in the years since losing her heart, she had only kissed a couple of men, the latest of which, she'd discovered, had also been kissing Zdenka and Fleur. 'You've got to kiss a few frogs before you find your prince,' Talibah had told her after the recent disaster, after which Zofka had unhelpfully chipped in, 'Try to avoid the toads, though.' Both were infuriatingly hopeful on the subject considering Thea didn't *have* a heart, but still, she made little attempts here and there. Things got awfully lonely if you cut yourself off from even the possibility of falling in love.

Malek's smile was slow, sensuous. 'I wish I could see the thoughts dashing across your face.'

Thea laughed. 'No, you don't, they're more of a nuisance than anything else.'

'I confess I'm intrigued.' Malek raised an eyebrow, lending him an impish look. 'What are your thoughts whispering about me?'

Was he interested in her? Thea couldn't tell. Surely not; she was already five and thirty and there were many other women in Prague, ones who came with dowries and youth on their side. Ones who were not indentured to an apothecary. 'Now that would be telling,' she said lightly.

'Hmm,' Malek said. He cleared his throat, his attention sharpening.

'I have rather a strange request, and after my first visit, I understand that this is the place to make it.'

Thea's stomach clenched. Disappointment set in like an unexpected storm. He hadn't come here for her as he'd claimed, then. She'd suspected as much, but surely he wasn't going to—

Sweeping a glance over his shoulder, Malek leant over the counter, dropping his voice to a warm whisper that would have filled Thea with delight if her every nerve wasn't standing on edge.

'I need a key that will grant me safe passage into a locked room without a single soul knowing that I have entered it. I must leave no mark behind, not a smudge of my fingerprints nor a scuff of my boot, nor,' he whispered, 'a single memory in the mind of any other person who might witness my entry.'

Oh. Oh *no*.

'I can assure you that I am an honest man,' Malek said as if he had read the doubts coursing through her, his tawny eyes shining bright and true. 'And that I would not ask if I did not have considerable need of such an item.' Pain flashed through him. 'Only, it is not for me, but my sister. She has found herself in an . . . undesirable situation and I must protect her. She is all the family I have left and if I were to lose her too . . .' he trailed off, clearing his throat. 'Well, I could not forgive myself had I not tried everything in my power to save her.'

Thea reached for his hand. 'I understand. Family is a gift to be treasured.' Although she had no family of her own that she knew of and could not love them if she had, without her heart, she knew what it meant to wish to protect someone. There was nothing she would not do if Talibah or Zofka needed help.

He looked down at her hand, pressing his. Slowly, he turned his hand palm up, clasping her hand within his. 'Then you will help?'

'Well, it would help if you could tell me more about the situation,' she hedged. But to make a physical, tangible magical object that not only amended the fate of those who held it, of one or two named souls, but any person's memory . . . it was more than she had ever endeavoured to craft before. She didn't know how to approach such a task and feared it might be beyond her Compendium's reach, too. Usually when a person made a request, both the action and price needed wove through her own thoughts, but this time, nothing happened. The path forward was unclear. Perhaps she ought to refuse. 'Nothing you feel uncomfortable with sharing, but if I could know more about what you intend to use the key for—' She spread her hands.

Malek gave a solemn nod. 'Jana has always been more free-spirited than I—' He took a hefty breath. 'Seeking adventure, dissatisfied with a small life. It started with a wager from a man she admired.' Malek's sigh was rough. 'I confess she has not admitted the finer details to me; she is my sister, you understand,' he said uncomfortably as Thea gave him a sympathetic smile. 'From what I have pieced together, she lost the wager and as forfeit has signed her life away to this man.' A note of anger sang through his voice. 'She must work for him, carry out his bidding . . . live with him.' He shook his head, staring out the window for a beat.

Thea prickled with anger on Jana's behalf.

'I need that key so that I can not only enter their dwelling but search for the relevant legal documents. Their house is well guarded and I do not wish for my sister's captor to learn even a hint of my intentions, lest he move her somewhere less accessible to me. If I can get my hands on those documents, I can hire solicitors, begin to unpick this . . . *bargain* between them.'

It all sounded uncomfortably familiar. 'It might be easier if I were to speak with your sister herself . . .' Thea began, thinking hard. Surely there *must* be a way she could craft such an object. Fate was ephemeral, amending it an invisible project, but Thea had spent the past seven years stocking Stiltskin's Apothecary with all manner of potions and elixirs; vials and jars brimming with tangible products. What if there was a way to combine the two – fate-weaving and potions – to forge a physical object with fate-weaving properties?

'No.' Malek looked directly at her. 'My sister cannot leave or receive visitors. I would fear exacerbating her situation.'

'Leave it with me,' Thea said with determination. 'Though it will not come without cost, a price that cannot be paid with coin,' she warned, her chest constricting at the thought of asking for the kind of price that those services would require, a world apart from the way he was regarding her now, tender and soft and relieved. She could have bottled that gaze and sold it as liquid happiness. Still no price presented itself in the usual manner. Thea was intrigued; did this mean this key could not be done, or that it was going to be harder than she'd imagined to make it? She couldn't remember the last time she'd been challenged like this.

'I understand what I am asking for. You have my sincerest gratitude.' Malek did not surrender her hand. Nor his gaze. Thea's pulse scudded. 'Though I do not wish for Jana to pay whatever price this demands. If I ask you for help, it is my price and I can at least spare her that.'

Thea softened. 'You are a kinder man than most.'

'Am I interrupting something?' Jasper's dry, disapproving voice punctured Thea's happiness.

Realising she was still holding onto Malek's hand, the pads of his fingers pressing her palm, Thea released him, straightening behind the counter. 'Just serving my customers.' Thea smoothed her apron down, wishing she could smooth her emotions down as well.

Jasper was dressed in mercurial grey, a dark cloud to Thea's sunshine, his mood stark against Malek's good-natured manner. A flock of pixies entered the apothecary, their tiny elfin faces freezing as they spotted Jasper. With a small squawk, they darted back out of the door. Even magical folk feared people who could work the strings of fate like a puppet master. 'Why are you here in the day?' Thea frowned as a weather-witch also decided against coming inside, though her gaze panned over Jasper's face once, then twice. Thea scowled at her; if she was going to ogle Jasper, she might as well have just entered the apothecary.

'There is apothecary business I must discuss with you. At once.' Jasper's pinched stare flitted to Malek. 'Privately.'

Malek glanced between Thea and Jasper. 'Stiltskin's Apothecary,' he said slowly. 'Then you, I presume, are Pan Stiltskin?'

'Lord Stiltskin,' Jasper corrected.

Malek gave him a gentlemanly nod. 'Malek Jaromir.'

Jasper stared as if Malek was a fly in need of swatting. Thea glared at him from behind Malek's back until Jasper sighed and doffed his cocked hat, folded at the brim. 'A pleasure to make your acquaintance,' Jasper said stiffly, and not at all sincerely.

Malek's smile was fading fast. Yet not to be deterred, he turned his back on Jasper, leant an elbow on the counter and dropped his voice, eking out a moment of intimacy between them to tell Thea, 'I must leave now but I shall return shortly.'

Thea's gaze drifted over Malek's shoulder onto Jasper. Jasper, who looked as if he was trying to set Malek alight with his stare. If Malek was summer, bright and airy with that irresistible smile that dimpled his left cheek, then Jasper was winter. Dark and cold. Cold enough to burn. It was a wonder Malek could not feel Jasper's gaze burrowing between his shoulder blades like a dagger. Thea rewarded his patience with her brightest smile, the one that Talibah had once told her was as golden as her hair, gilded like a sunset.

Malek blinked for a moment. Then he fumbled out a goodbye and left, barely acknowledging Jasper, who stood there, glowering.

'You ought to be careful or you will give him a false idea of your feelings,' Jasper ground out.

'Have you not considered that perhaps I gave him the exact measure of my feelings?' Thea shot back.

Jasper's nostrils flared. It was the sole sign she had rattled him and Thea clung onto it, secretly delighted.

'It's bad business to become involved with our customers.' Jasper's voice knotted over the word *involved* as if it physically pained him to speak it.

'He isn't a customer,' Thea lied. 'He came here for me. To visit me,' she amended, flushing.

Jasper tracked her flush as it travelled down her neck and over her collarbones. His fingers flexed at his side. 'I see,' he said at last.

'I do not allow my missing heart to keep me from courting who I wish.' It was an untruth but she would not give him the satisfaction of seeing how their bargain affected her.

Jasper looked disbelieving. Perhaps her face was disobeying her again; Thea's thoughts tended to run away with themselves and write her emotions across her face for all to read.

'What a relief,' he said, in a tone that sounded anything but relieved. 'After all, we would not want you to miss out on any . . . romantic opportunities, Thea.'

Her name sounded like a shadow on his lips. A dark promise, a sharp hatred. It roused her temper, that slumbering dragon within her. If anyone was no friend to her, it was Jasper. Jasper, who had continued speaking while she'd been lost in thought. Impatience rolled from him. 'Are you that infatuated with the man that you cannot hear?' Jasper's eyebrows pulled up with his disbelief.

Thea ignored his mood; it was nothing new. Jasper was grumpy as often as there were clouds in the sky. 'What did you come to tell me? We are alone, thanks to you scaring off any customers, so speak your mind.'

He scowled. 'I came to warn you. I have learnt that a band of Magic Hunters are sniffing around. They must have heard rumours of the Magic Quarter and decided to investigate for themselves. I've done some investigating of my own and they're headed up by one court-appointed Hunter, Pan Novak, who is as notorious for his cruelty as he is his hatred of magic. He is an ambitious man, and I fear he sees this as his chance to rise to power. The wards ought to prohibit him from entering the Quarter, but should he worm his way through, do not bring his ire upon you – you must comply with anything he asks of you. I will deal with him myself, do you hear me?'

'I'm afraid your news is coming a little too late for that.' Thea caught herself before she winced. 'Pan Novak came into the Gingerbread House yesterday while I was there and—'

Jasper let out a pained sigh. 'Why did you not send me a raven?'

Thea winced, remembering his request.

'What did you do?' he continued.

'Why do you assume I did anything?'

'Because I know you.'

'Barely.' Thea relented. 'I may have been on the defensive and . . . drawn his attention more than I intended to. Rose called a meeting of all residents to try and figure out how he managed to break past the wards and—' She swallowed, her heart-spell shifting behind her ribs as Jasper focused on her face, waiting for her to continue. 'And his entry wasn't the only sign that something's wrong with the wards.' She glanced at the crack running across the ceiling.

Jasper followed her gaze. With a grace she hadn't expected from him, he sprang up the spiral staircase and leapt up onto the mezzanine railing to inspect the ceiling more closely. He was more lithe than Thea could have guessed; the fabric of his breeches taut across his thighs as he balanced on the railing. His fingers wove in the pattern that Thea had come to recognise as fate's skeins were revealed to them both. He deftly examined the threads binding the Magic Quarter in protection, preventing its older buildings from crumbling, and keeping everyone safe. 'This will hold for now, but it is related to a much greater problem,' he said solemnly, jumping down from the railing and walking back down the stairs.

Thea kept her gaze averted as he adjusted his tailored jacket and breeches.

'You're right; the wards are malfunctioning. I must investigate this further.' There was something in his voice that Thea didn't recognise. She disliked it at once; if Jasper could not fix the wards, what chance did the rest of them face?

Shifting his attention back to her, Jasper drew himself out of his own thoughts. 'Are you certain that you have been taking a price for all of your workings with fate? The balance—'

'Must be kept, I know,' Thea said, shoving her guilt away before Jasper read it on her face. 'It was nothing I did; Wojslav's window-panes went missing days before our ceiling cracked.'

She looked up, checking the crack hadn't split further. That the apothecary wouldn't come raining down on her.

Jasper's frown was more impressive than she'd seen in a while. 'I see,' he said, glancing back at the ceiling. 'Well, the day Pan Novak sets foot in here, you must send me a raven at once.'

'I will.' She would not; she could handle herself. 'Though I presume you were invited to attend the meeting along with the rest of us? If you wanted to be kept updated, you ought to have attended.'

'I have other means of keeping updated.'

'Right,' Thea said sceptically, unsurprised that Jasper hadn't come.

Jasper remained standing in place, waiting. Thea stared back at him.

'Are you going to make today's guess, or must I wait here until sunset?'

Oh. 'Gisela.' Today, it lacked hope.

A softer frown wandered across Jasper's brow. 'No.'

Thea nodded. 'Would you even tell me if I guessed correctly?' she asked bitterly.

Jasper looked uncertain. For once, his height seemed an encumbrance as he stood there, awkwardly considering her. Usually he delighted in stalking about, tall and dark and imposing. 'Of course,' he told her. 'A deal is a deal.'

'And you do love your bargains, don't you?' Thea snapped back.

'Is there—' Jasper cleared his throat. 'Is something the matter?'

'Why would anything be the matter?' Thea swung an arm out, impassioned. Too impassioned, for an apothecary stacked with delicate glass bottles and jars. She sent the nearby display of blackberry ink crashing down. Purple ink spattered the floorboards. Jasper eyed the mess warily. 'I have no heart, no memories and no name. I can't leave this apothecary permanently.' Whatever she'd signed in that contract had her bound to stay there until she guessed her true name.

'You do have a name.' Jasper bent to one knee and started gathering the broken bottles, piling shards together on one palm. His hands were strong from years of fate-weaving. A sudden image of him reaching for Thea's hand fell into her head. She shook it straight back out.

'Right.' Thea snorted. 'A name that I cannot remember. A name before you looked at me that first day, standing outside this apothecary, missing my heart and memories, and called me Theodora with no rhyme nor reason, simply assigning it to me as if I were a butterfly you had pinned to a cork board.'

Jasper paused, looking down at the pooling ink. His dark curled hair was tied at the nape of his neck with a black velvet ribbon. An intimate view. For some reason, she found herself unable to look away. 'I happen to like the name Theodora,' he said quietly.

'Did it ever cross your mind that I might not?'

Jasper rose to his full height, dwarfing Thea once more. In silence, he placed the broken glass on the side, withdrawing into another of his moods, his attention drifting like smoke. 'Perhaps I'd better take my leave.'

'Fine, go.' Thea huffed out a weary sigh.

With a doff of his hat, Jasper left. As the door swung shut behind him, a damp misty scent leaked through the apothecary. It smelt like mouldering book pages and broken promises. It smelt like sadness.

There was something about starting a new journal, being confronted with that first blank page. As impressionless as a fresh snowfall. Thea balanced her inkwell and quill beside the new journal she'd opened on her bed, and consulted her Compendium of Magic. If she was to make the key Malek had requested, she needed to make a start as soon as possible. If Jasper wasn't such a pain, she'd ask his advice, but she'd become quite adept at potion-making over her years at the apothecary and the idea of combining that with fate-weaving was more exciting than handing out bottles of fire-ginger to sneezing witches in cold season.

She flipped through the pages of ingredients. Some couldn't be found in this world, others were found deep in the forest, where the strangest and most magical ingredients tended to grow. Others could be procured in the Rose Basket or Paní Dagmar's haberdashery. She ran her finger down the text:

Fungi are connected, forging a living, breathing map through the forest. If your intent is to locate or find something, then a mushroom or toadstool will enhance your potion. None are more potent than the silver spot-dapples.

*

This was accompanied by a rendition of said silver spot-dapples. Thea carefully copied both the text and the drawing into the second page of her journal. On the first she wrote: *Silver spot-dapples? Excellent for locating and finding – like a key that draws you to the correct spot.*

After skimming through another few pages, she jotted down – *A firebird's breath? Could remove all trace of being there?* – then scribbled it out on discovering that it would also remove Malek without a trace. Yawning several times in succession, Thea put her inkwell and quill on her bedside table and curled up in her blankets to read another snippet of the Compendium's love story before she slept:

> *Storm season is setting in, hard and fast. Mother and Father are bolting the shutters and casting stronger wards over our sprawling roof, lest a tree comes crashing down. Such are the perils of living this deep in the forest. Worse will be surviving the season trapped inside with them, an atmosphere that promises to be colder than the forest.*
>
> *I ought to stay inside. Though I am haunted by my dreams of him. Making a last dash to the market before our doors lock and do not open for the rest of the season, I took his cloak and ran through the squalling wind and hunting birds, searching for a glimpse of his face.*
>
> *He was not there. I am bereft.*
>
> *At least his cloak still smells of him.*

CHAPTER
Six

HE MAGIC QUARTER was lined with gourds. Hollowed ones, snarling in carved faces that glowed with a dark green flicker not even the rising wind could snuff out. Witch light. Zofka was not the sole witch living here that felt the cold threat of persecution breathing down her neck. It had been a hundred years since the height of the witch trials that had scourged Europe, but all witches lived with that legacy. Magic Hunters still existed. These modern-day Hunters were not fuelled by paranoia and religious fervour, but a mission to keep power sitting on thrones and ruling empires, stopping magical communities from forming and growing too powerful. Becoming a threat to the way they liked their world run. This was why magic needed to remain a secret.

The gourds growled a warning as Thea passed them. Something told her that Pan Novak would not take this new addition to the Quarter well. They needed to shut him out before he shut them down or had them arrested for treason. The Magic Quarter was a tinderbox and Pan Novak had just struck a flint.

A nearby tree howled a lament as Thea pulled her velvet cloak tighter around herself, hurrying back to her apothecary. She'd been for a long walk through the woods, ruminating on Malek's strange request, on Jasper's concern over the wards, as if he was out of his depth for a change, and her head was full, her thoughts wheeling like gulls through a storm.

Thea kept seeing the girl's face. She had refused to take time from her, and nothing had happened. All those dreams and memories and life she'd taken to balance the scales while fate-weaving . . . Had she ever needed to take them? Or was Jasper hiding something? She needed to test this theory. The next time she fate-wove, she resolved not to take a price again.

Buckets of roses hissed at Thea as she passed the Rose Basket; usually Rose removed their thorns, but these were spiteful. Even the weathervane perched atop the apothecary roof was keeping a wary eye out in the form of a hunting eagle: the Magic Quarter was raising its shields.

A curl of parchment pinned to Thea's door distracted her. Could it be a note from Malek? She had not heard from him in several days, and she kept dwelling on him and his dimple in pockets of idle time.

Her smile hardened as she neared. In the darkness, she hadn't seen what was beneath the note: a raven had been nailed to her door. Thea froze in place, horror seizing her body and mind.

The raven's eyes sprang open.

Thea wasn't aware she'd made a sound until Talibah came running across the street and was suddenly at her side, holding her.

'It's still alive,' Thea whispered hoarsely, unable to look away from the poor creature. Voicing this aloud made Thea snap out of her own nightmare and rush to support the raven, murmuring soothing words as Talibah slid out the long, jagged nail.

They took it inside the apothecary, locking and bolting the door as Talibah bustled about, finding a suitable box and soft cloth to keep the messenger raven comfortable while Thea sat on the bottom step of her spiral staircase and cleaned its wound before bandaging it up tightly. It was a small puncture, but deep; the nail had run straight through its fragile body, piercing gods knew what in its path. Determination bled through Thea's sadness: she *would* save it.

As Thea felt for the threads, the apothecary glimmered, alive with the tapestry of fate. The raven's threads were worn thin, ragged. Thea twined more threads around them, reinforcing them until the raven's fate shone brighter, taking a memory of her own as payment:

the memory of reading the first chapters of *Eudora and the Ship's Captain* last night.

'Have you read the note?'

Talibah's voice summoned Thea back to the present. She placed the raven into the box Talibah was holding out, tucking the creature under several layers of soft cloths to keep it warm. 'I have.'

Talibah ripped the note into pieces. '*I am coming for you.*' She scoffed. 'Drivel. Written by weak people who detest anyone with greater power than them. There was a reason this was pinned to your door and not said to your face. A reason why they inflicted their hatred on a poor, defenceless creature.' Talibah sank onto the step beside Thea. Weariness was etched into the fine lines around her eyes. Thea reached for a nearby slab of soap, filled with plump mallow root, lavender flowers and fallen starlight, and slipped it into Talibah's pocket. 'This means the wards are failing us.'

'I agree,' Thea said.

Talibah rested her head on Thea's shoulder. They both looked down on the raven. Its eyes were closed but the shallow rise and fall of its chest marked it as sleeping. Thea softly stroked its beak. It was beetle-black and shiny as enamel. 'I came to Prague because I'd heard rumours about this place,' Talibah said. 'That there was a Magic Quarter who welcomed magic and magical folk. People who were different. Now I wonder if we've been naïve all these years, if the threat had been here all along, biding its time. A wolf snapping its jaws at a paddock of sheep, patiently salivating until it finds a way through the gates.'

'I'd pay to hear you call Rose a sheep to her face,' Thea said drily.

'Do you ever wonder what drew you to Prague before you lost your memories?' Talibah turned her curiosity onto Thea.

'All the time.' Thea stroked the raven's wing. 'I don't know if I'd already been living in the city or if I'd been elsewhere, searching for a new home, and found it in Prague. I don't even know if I want to know what drove me to give it all up, who I was back then that led me down this path. But we can't think like that,' she said firmly. 'We belong here as much as we do anywhere. It's the people who believe there is no place for outsiders, for magic and immigrants and people who live and love differently to them, that are the problem, not us, do you hear me?'

'I hear you.' Talibah tilted her head, considering. An echo of a smile played with the edges of her mouth. 'You can be quite fierce, you know. I hope that man with the dimple knows what he's getting himself into.'

Thea let out a surprised laugh. Then a groan. 'That's a whole other problem.'

'I did think I'd spotted him coming inside the other day,' Talibah said. 'Is it a problem that you wish to discuss?' she asked carefully.

Thea's finger stilled on the raven wing. 'He's asked me to fate-weave for him,' she admitted.

'Ah.'

'It's an unusual request; I need to figure out how I'm going to fulfil it.' Thea tugged her hair back. 'It's not important right now.' The raven's heartbeat was weak, thready. She'd never attempted to wrench something back from the brink of death before. 'What shall we call this poor fellow?'

Talibah glanced at the raven. 'He was badly wounded—'

'He's going to be fine,' Thea said stubbornly.

'And you?' Talibah tucked a loose strand of Thea's hair behind her ear. 'I would sleep better if you were nearby, safe with me at the bookshop. Whoever did this targeted you, Thea, and if the wards are faltering, you need to be on your guard.'

'I can't leave now.' Thea stared down at the raven. 'Giving into my fear would be easy, but it would make it harder to return. Besides, I refuse to be chased out of my own home.' A new, sudden fear pierced her.

'What is it? You've gone pale . . .'

Thea thrust the raven's box at Talibah, picked up her skirts and ran to the stairs that led to her private quarters. Talibah called her name, sharp with alarm, but horror was pounding a new beat through Thea's pulse, the spell in place of her heart faltering as she crashed through her door. Fear swelled and swelled, swallowing her whole, until something moved in the corner of her eye.

Thea half collapsed to the floor in relief, pulling Cinnamon onto her lap as Talibah ran in with the raven box. 'I was so worried.' Thea's voice wobbled, betraying her.

Talibah gently set the raven down and met Thea on the floor, gathering her into her arms. Cinnamon's nose twitched happily at all the attention. 'I hope you don't snore,' Talibah told Thea, 'because I'm not going anywhere tonight.'

Thea had been certain she was in for a sleepless night. But she hadn't reckoned on Talibah, who told her stories and secrets until the candles burned low. 'I lost my heart in Arabia,' Talibah whispered in her melodic voice, unwinding her headscarf and changing into one of Thea's nightgowns, as she told the tale Thea loved best. 'To a man who guided me deep into the desert, with windswept hair, whose laugh remains my favourite sound to this day. I'll never forget the look on Amir's face as he stared out across those red sands after we'd climbed a rock arch together. I loved him deeper with each passing day, but it wasn't enough to stay. It's never enough to stay.'

'When will you visit him again?' Sometimes, Talibah made the trip to Arabia. Other times, they journeyed to a different point on the atlas and met there, in places with names that tasted like spices and desert winds. Thea couldn't imagine finding the other half of her heart and soul only to spend years apart, but love worked in a hundred different ways.

Talibah hesitated. 'When I don't need to worry about leaving you and Zofka here.'

'Do you ever consider going to live with Amir?' Thea asked, even as the very notion made her chest ache.

'All the time. Each time I think this will be the last visit, that this time I will stay, that this time he will not wish to travel any more, but we are twin souls, destined to wander the world. I am only grateful that occasionally, the stars align and our ships pass in the night.'

Thea sighed wistfully. 'It's terribly romantic.'

Talibah's laugh was low, tinged with that pain, that love that she carried every day. 'All the best love stories ache the most.'

'If I get my heart back, I hope that I'll fall in love. But sometimes I lie awake at night, convinced that I gave my memories up because I'd already found love and it proved too painful.' Perhaps an old love, turned sour. Or the most painful kind of love that existed, the one that was never to be returned, leaving you with sweet agony burning in your chest each time you crossed paths.

'I'm still combing the stacks for anything that might help,' Talibah said softly. 'I want you to know, Zofka and I will never stop searching for how to return your memories.'

Thea found Talibah's hand and squeezed it. 'I know.' But it had been seven years: if they were going to find a way, they would have found it by now. Thea had long since given up. 'Maybe I've never fallen in love and my love story is yet to come. I hope it will be sweet and easy, like falling into a meadow of wildflowers.'

'I wish that for you, too,' Talibah said. She did not say that life was rarely like that, that it was big and hard and could be every bit as terrible as it was wonderful. She didn't need to voice what they both knew as they fell into silence, listening for the raven's breath, though it was too small to hear.

'Sometimes I worry that I've missed my chance,' Thea confessed as the candles guttered, leaving them at the mercy of the moon, traipsing in and out of the clouds – Thea slept with her windows flung open, to hear the rustle of the trees and count the stars. 'That maybe the opportunity to seize my heart back opened up but I didn't take that leap. Now I'm in my thirties and if I want that love, that family of my own' – she clenched her bedsheets either side of her, battling the emotion rising in her throat – 'it's almost too late.'

Talibah propped herself up on one elbow. A lost beam of moonlight fell over her face as she regarded Thea. 'There is no one right way to do things,' she said seriously. 'Life looks different for everybody and just because something you want hasn't happened yet, doesn't mean it won't. There are a thousand different stories waiting in your life, Thea, and you still have time to tell whichever one you want. Don't let anyone tell you otherwise.'

Thea relaxed. 'How did you grow to be so wise?'

Talibah laid back on the neighbouring pillow. 'It's all the books I read.'

Death stalked Thea's dreams that night. Hunting her soul with his sharp hunger and sharper scythe, her lost heart beating from its box, summoning her to find it. When Death gazed down upon her, he held her heart-box. And he wore Jasper's face.

Thea awoke the following morning to floorboards bathed in golden sunlight, Talibah's hair like spilled silk. Thea lay there, caught between the realms of sleep and waking, confused by what had roused her until she heard it once more: a soft cawing.

The raven had lived through the night.

CHAPTER

Seven

HEA HUMMED AS she changed the raven's bandage. Just one day later, he was stronger already, eagerly snapping up the worms Thea fed him. Stroking his feathers, she decided to call him Biscuit.

It was a late October day, crisp and golden as honeycomb, one of those days that made it hard to imagine that anything horrible could ever happen, let alone someone nailing a bird to her door last night. Talibah had already left, assuring Thea that she would be back to check on her soon, but Thea wouldn't show how shaken the event had left her: she wore her favourite sage-green dress, with embroidered daisies dancing down her stomacher, before adding a dab of rouge to her cheeks and lips. Painting herself with the confidence she wished she felt.

Customers were thin on the ground. A couple of pixies ransacked the shelves, searching for a truth-telling potion until Thea shooed them away. She believed they'd been unsuccessful in their mischief until an hour later, when one very red-faced pixie entered alone, begging for an antidote while confessing his undying love for honey fried cake. The crack on the ceiling remained much the same and Thea began to relax around it, no longer fearing the apothecary would fall apart around her.

Beside her, a mug of spiced apple and cinnamon tea gently steamed, and her Compendium of Magic lay open as she consulted a section entitled: Magical Creatures and the Gifts They Bear.

Beautiful drawings accompanied these pages, painted in delicate pastels. Firebirds and lake spirits, unicorns and pixies. Though even Thea scoffed at the notion of a unicorn existing, she couldn't help half hoping that perhaps one did, hidden deep in the thickest tangle of an ancient forest somewhere. She was still daydreaming about stumbling across one when something interesting on lake spirits snatched her attention:

Lake spirits are gentle creatures that only wish to live undisturbed in water. With hair like strands of algae, they can be found hiding beneath large lily pads in the richest, greenest waters. One strand of their hair, once consumed, may help cure seasickness, whilst a single fingernail, once ground to dust, will enable you to hide in plain sight. Though heed my caution! Once disturbed, lake creatures are vicious beings and will almost certainly attack.

Thea added *A single fingernail from a lake spirit?* to the list in her journal, tapping it thoughtfully with her quill.

One of her favourite little story snippets had been penned next to a prancing illustration of a unicorn and she read it again, smiling to herself:

What unexpected joy today! A ray of light lancing through the all-pervasive gloom. A single letter has made it through the raging storms and been delivered straight to my hand, through a crack in my shuttered window:

'I long for the day I might see you again.'

I sleep with it beneath my pillow and dream with a smile upon my lips, for it is from him, I am certain of it. The flowering season cannot come soon enough. Seeing him again cannot come soon enough.

The bells strung on the apothecary door jangled, making Thea look up. Malek's face had been running through her head when she'd pulled this dress from her armoire, but her hope was short-lived.

Pan Novak had returned to the Magic Quarter and this time, he was not alone. Two other men accompanied him, striding into Stiltskin's Apothecary on his booted heels. More Magic Hunters.

Thea's hands trembled; there had to be something terribly wrong with the Quarter's wards to allow this incursion. All three men were almost indistinguishable from each other with near-identical powdered wigs, painted faces, and scarlet coats and waistcoats over cream breeches.

Thea slowly slid the raven from her counter and onto a shelf below. Biscuit cocked his head at her, clicking his beak shut as if he understood the need for silence. She snapped her journal, then the Compendium shut, turning its title face down.

A couple of local weather-witches made to enter the apothecary in a whirl of sea-blue gowns and gossip when, on spying Pan Novak and his men, they swerved from the door, moving on as if the tide was sweeping them down the street.

Thea sighed inwardly. 'May I help you with something?'

Pan Novak's smile was tight and close-lipped. Perfunctory. 'I am certain that my men will find what we need.' With a jerk of his head, his companions made their way upstairs, eying the waxing moonlight that flickered as they passed.

'If I knew what you were looking for—'

'Evidence.' Pan Novak's pupils glittered as he stared at Thea through his spectacles.

She met his stare, steadying herself on the counter. 'Evidence of what?'

'I'm interested in seeing if the rumours about this so-called Magic Quarter are true.' Pan Novak did not blink. 'I will prove to the councillors that dangerous magic exists in these shops, in these products, threatening their livelihood and the health of the good people of Prague.'

Thea's hand stiffened on the counter. 'Most people don't even believe in magic,' she said softly. 'What will you tell them?'

Pan Novak leant in closer. It took everything in Thea not to step back, not to let him see how his sudden proximity affected her. 'That you're all charlatans, swindling them out of their hard-earned income.'

Thea suppressed a shiver. 'So, you'll be lying to them for your own means.'

Pan Novak's mouth curved into a semblance of a smile. 'You can think what you like, but your days here are numbered.'

'Your motives are purely political,' Thea realised. 'It doesn't matter what you find here, your mind is already decided. It has been since before you took a single step inside the Quarter.'

Pan Novak clicked his tongue. 'There you are wrong. I shall be taking the proper steps to secure the closure of this Quarter. I am nothing if not diligent.'

Alena Böhmová chose that moment to enter the apothecary. On catching sight of Pan Novak and Thea locked in a silent battle, she pursed her lips in disapproval. 'Is this man bothering you, dearest?'

A tinkle of broken glass snatched Thea's attention. Glancing up at the mezzanine, she gritted her teeth as one of the Hunters roughly swiped an entire shelf of sleeping elixirs into a box. A cloud of pearly dust swooned in their wake. Thea smelt smoke. An ashy scent was spreading through the apothecary, as if the entire building was panicking. She didn't dare imagine how her overwrought apple tree was reacting.

She rubbed her left temple. 'Must your men be so rough with my wares? Those elixirs can only be brewed once every three months!'

Alena clucked under her breath.

Hearing the soprano's disapproval, Pan Novak's stare snapped onto her, a note of haughtiness entering his voice. 'It is of the utmost importance we test a wide variety of products available here.' He peered through his spectacles at what remained of Thea's blackberry ink before pocketing two bottles, leaving one lonely bottle standing on the display.

'Yes, I understand what you are doing,' Thea said, 'but is it necessary to test the entire batch? Will you be compensating me for the expense?' Sarcasm bled through her words.

Pan Novak ran a finger down the last bottle. 'You ought to count yourself fortunate that I did not come here to detain you for questioning. You're peddling dangerous substances to innocents.'

'People come here because they trust me to help them, which I do,' Thea replied evenly, though her blood hissed and steamed. 'I do not endanger people, I ease their suffering.'

'Perhaps you should see for yourself that Thea's apothecary is harmless before you spread these lies,' Alena pointedly added, her star-shaped beauty patch travelling down her forehead with the ferocity of her frown.

'We shall be making our own judgement on that.' Pan Novak gave a single clap of his hands, summoning the other two Hunters downstairs, arms laden with a rainbow of Thea's wares.

Thea seethed. 'I believe you know very well that what is one person's cure is another's poison.' She took pains to keep her tone calm, lest she be accused of descending into hysterics. Gods forbid a woman should show any emotion. 'Might I enquire how you are to run experiments if you have no idea what these are for, nor the correct dosage?'

Pan Novak's thin lips stretched wider. Unnaturally so. 'Your objection has been noted.'

'It wasn't an objection, it was a question,' Thea said hotly. 'But you're not planning on testing them at all, are you? Not when your mind has already been decided.'

'I think perhaps you had better leave now.' Alena's voice, powerful enough to fill an entire theatre, swelled to fill the apothecary.

The two accompanying Hunters heeded her command, swiftly marching out the door. All that time and effort Thea had invested in those potions, elixirs, inks and creams and teas was carried away with them. She felt sick.

Pan Novak lingered a moment longer. 'I would suggest treading very carefully now. The eyes of the court are on you now. On all of you. Your little hiding place is out in the open now and I will uncover every last one of your secrets before I shut you down for good.'

'What a vile man,' Alena declared, the instant Pan Novak exited the apothecary.

Thea shuddered, her earlier bravado fading fast as dying daylight. 'Something tells me this will not be so easily resolved. Pan Novak has his own agenda and he's determined to make an enemy of us.'

'You must put him out of your pretty head now,' Alena said firmly. 'Come, let me take you out for a drink.'

'Oh, I couldn't possibly . . .' Thea glanced away from Alena's arched eyebrow to the crack splitting the ceiling, Biscuit and the Compendium and her notes on Malek's key, all vying for her attention. 'The apothecary—'

'Will still be standing when you return. Your problems can wait for a couple of hours.' Unaccustomed to taking no for an answer, Alena steered Thea towards the door.

Thea gave in. There was something reassuring in it; in giving someone else the reins, in simply stepping away from the encroaching sadness. Telling it, *not today*. She flipped the *Open* sign over to *Closed* on her way out.

On Thea's return, a large wooden box blocked the apothecary door. A red velvet bow and a note perched on top. The lid was stamped with the trademark golden crossed needle and thread of the Magic Quarter's resident dressmaker: Fleur.

Thea hesitated. Her thoughts rustled with bloodied raven feathers, and this box was plenty large enough to conceal a bigger animal. Talibah pulling that nail from Biscuit was a sound she'd never recover from; what if this box held something else macabre? With an unsteady hand, she picked up the note:

> *I would be delighted if you would join me tomorrow night at the opera.*
> *Yours,*
> *Malek*

'A dress from Fleur?' Rose popped her head round a new display of sunflowers outside the Rose Basket. When the wind rustled their petals, they tinkled like bells. Now and then, one turned its head and stared at the thorned roses standing guard behind them. 'Those are mighty pretty dresses; Fleur learnt her craft at Versailles before she tired of court life.' Rose fixed Thea with a knowing look. 'There's a note on it, too.'

'Yes, there is.' Thea smiled before carting the box inside. Knowing

Rose, she'd probably already read the note; the Magic Quarter was really just a nosy village.

Inside, Thea toyed with the slip of paper. It was a tempting invitation, not least because Josef Mysliveček's *Il Bellerofonte* was currently showing at the Divadlo v Kotcích, where Alena was singing the role of Argene, which Thea was desperate to see. But was Malek inviting her to sweeten the deal with this key she was making, or was he expressing genuine interest in her, when she knew she could never love him in her heart-less state?

Zofka burst through the apothecary door, accompanied by a sharp peal of the bell and a sweet almond scent clinging to her pale pink skirts and frizzy curls. Marzipan. It was a sure-fire sign that the season was growing colder and darker when Zofka began experimenting with festive treats. 'Ooh, Fleur.' Zofka joined Thea at the counter, giving the box a reverent stare. 'What did you order?'

Talibah came on Zofka's heels, the calm breeze to Zofka's whirlwind. She pressed a kiss to Thea's cheek. If Zofka was scented with marzipan, then Talibah was parchment and mint, books and tea. 'We came to check in on you, Thea dear. I told Zofka what happened last night.'

Zofka's head jerked up. 'Yes, she did,' she confirmed, her voice rising a pitch. 'A raven *nailed to your door*? You poor thing, perhaps it isn't safe here in the Quarter any longer—'

'I'm not leaving my home,' Thea interrupted before Zofka spiralled. 'It was an act of desperation, a cry for attention. Nothing more. And we have a powerhouse of magical folk living in this Quarter working on fixing the wards as we speak. I am confident one of them will manage it, then I need not worry any more about whatever or whoever sent me that message. What is it?' she asked as Zofka beamed at her.

'You called this your home.'

'Of course it's my home, I live here—'

'It was more than that,' Zofka interrupted. 'I felt it in your voice.' She tipped her head to one side, considering Thea. 'I used to wonder if you'd ever be happy here, after Lord Stiltskin left you stuck here and carried away your heart but . . . you are, aren't you?'

Thea blinked back at her. 'I guess I am,' she said slowly. 'You're both here, and Cinnamon, and I enjoy making potions and meeting people and, well, I've made a home here.' She glanced at the wildflowers she'd painted on the walls, the remaining potions she'd stocked the shelves with, the street outside with its witch light gourds and gnarled oak trees and buttery cobblestones. Happiness had been a slow creep over the past seven years, but she couldn't deny that it was present. Perhaps not as complete as it could have been with love missing from her life but there, nonetheless.

'Do you need me to stay with you again tonight?' Talibah asked.

Thea shook her head. 'I'll be fine,' she said as if she believed it herself. She hadn't realised how much she'd depended on the wards protecting them all until their defences had cracked and Pan Novak had stridden through.

'What about—' Talibah began, but Zofka had grown too restless.

'Never mind that now, Talibah.' Zofka drummed her fingers on the box lid. 'The man with the dimple has sent her a *gift*.'

Thea grimaced. 'Forget baking, you ought to solve mysteries. However did you know?' She held the note up between her fingers. 'I know that you couldn't have read this.'

'There was a note?' Zofka attempted an eager grab.

Talibah swatted her away. 'Honestly, must you force your nose in everywhere? Perhaps Thea doesn't want you reading her personal correspondences.'

Zofka wrinkled her pert nose. 'It's part of my charm,' she said mildly. 'And I knew that you,' she added, facing Thea, 'would never spend the amount that Fleur charges for her gowns. You'd much rather spend it all on books instead.'

'That's quite true,' Thea admitted, relinquishing the note.

Zofka eagerly snatched it.

Despite herself, Talibah leant in to read it over Zofka's shoulder. As one, both women lifted their gaze to Thea. 'What?' she asked, self-consciously.

'This is, well . . . this is the kind of gesture that belongs in one of those books you inhale,' Talibah said.

'It's deeply romantic,' Zofka added. Her eyes glistened.

Thea worried at her bottom lip.

Talibah looked curiously at the box. 'What did he order for you?'

'I haven't opened it yet,' Thea confessed, curling one of the ribbon ends around a finger. 'If I open it then that means this is real, and *that* means—'

'No,' Zofka groaned. 'No overthinking this. Just open the box and look at the pretty dress, Thea. Opening it does not mean that you need to make any decisions, it will only give you more options. A fuller picture. Although why you'd turn him down baffles me.'

'Perhaps because she cannot be bought?' Talibah raised an eyebrow at Zofka, who happily ignored her, seizing a pair of pruning scissors from the counter and passing them to Thea.

'Open it.'

Thea opened the box. Brocaded silk spilled over her hands. All three women let out a reverent sigh: it was a gown of deepest, darkest blue. Midnight.

Talibah lifted a panel to examine the delicate design. 'Oh, look.' Crimson roses bloomed, their petals curling before dropping from the stems, where they became autumn leaves, golden and russet and caramel brown.

'How perfectly enchanting.' Zofka gave Thea a pointed look.

Happiness, sweet and soft as honey, seeped through Thea until she glowed. Just when life was starting to harden, to make its rough edges felt, it had thrown her a shimmer of magic. A little promise that no matter what might or might not come to pass, there were still pockets of joy. Of lovely little things. That hate might exist in this world but so did love and magic. 'I think I shall go after all. I'll send him a raven tonight.'

CHAPTER

Eight

HEA CREPT THROUGH the trees by the light of the full moon, hanging suspended in the dark cloth of the sky like an orb. She paused for a second to stare at it; its glow never failed to soothe Thea's nerves, to calm her racing thoughts.

But not tonight. Tonight, for the second time, she had refused payment to change a woman's fate, biting her tongue hard enough to draw blood in an effort not to ask the price. She needed to know if Jasper had been deceiving her all these years and there were no consequences to not taking a price. Now, only time would tell.

A headache skulked across Thea's temples. She needed to focus on her task: mushroom picking. She still wasn't certain exactly what she would need for Malek's key, but she figured she might as well gather some of the easier ingredients now. Fishing her journal out of her cloak pocket, she looked over the notes she'd copied from her Compendium:

Silver spot-dapples? Excellent for locating and finding – like a key that draws you to the correct spot.

She'd copied the drawing, too. Silver spot-dapples were named for their cap, dappled with white spots that glowed as if they had been painted with molten starlight. She'd have to tread deep into the forest for them.

As Thea walked between the big hoary trees, all twisted trunks and eyes that peered back at her through their knots, she pondered the key. She still had no idea how to collect half the items on her list, nor how to create a physical object with the power of fate itself, but she was determined to try. And she would have to hurry: Malek needed this for his sister's sake, and soon.

Thea wandered deeper into the moonlight-silvered forest. A gust of wind lifted her hair, and she relished the wildness of it all as an owl hooted in the distance. She filled her pockets with some basic ingredients she needed to start restocking the apothecary: nettles, a lost wolf's tooth, shiny owl feathers, rosehips and elderberries.

But then the surrounding woods fell silent. There were no birdcalls tossed from branch to branch, no rustle in the fallen leaves of small mammals harvesting their berries, nor of the trees themselves, shifting in the wind. Realising with a start that she'd been thinking too hard to pay attention to her route, Thea turned, trying to gather her bearings, but the forest looked the same no matter which way she looked. Every view it presented to her screamed one thing: she was lost.

Footsteps sounded behind her. Thea whirled.

A white stag stared at Thea with pure white eyes. The forest began to hum, and the hair rose on the back of her neck. She could taste it in the back of her throat: oh-so similar to Jasper's power.

The Crossroads must be near. Thea scanned her environs, searching for anything else out of the ordinary, nerves clustering in the pit of her stomach. Thea usually found her best potion ingredients at the Crossroads, where other realms rubbed against theirs, their magic bleeding through, making everything grow bigger and wilder and more dangerous.

Realms like Jasper's. Thea wondered if he missed it, or if he was happy in the grand townhouse he kept in the oldest corner of Prague, nestled in the streets twining up to the castle. She'd visited only once, some five years ago, when she'd sent him a raven asking for help to unpick a moral dilemma; a man who'd asked for a woman to acquiesce to his every demand. Jasper had summoned her to his townhouse, though they met outside, where he'd told her that she should trust her instincts and never weave fate with doubt in her heart.

Pushing Jasper out of her head, Thea decided to follow the seam of the Crossroads through the forest until she'd reorientated herself. With that thought, her panic softened into intrigue: what curiosities might she find in this unexplored part of the forest? A rabbit bearing antlers of bone darted past, making her jump.

Half a step away, she noticed something peculiar: the air was misted under the moonlight. It swirled together like the eye of a storm. She lifted her lantern higher, and lowered her head to look through. Was that a – *turret*?

Thea's chest convulsed: what was she doing? Standing there in the forest, peering into another world. Yet, something compelled her to reach out a hand, and when her fingers touched the swirl, they passed straight through, disappearing from sight.

Thea gasped, hurrying back, her shoe dislodging a carpet of moss and revealing something glowing beneath. With the toe of her boot, Thea pushed the moss further back, revealing a cluster of mushrooms. Their caps were silver spotted. She checked them against her drawing with a shaking hand: a perfect match. Pocketing her journal, she plucked a handful, wrapping them in a small cloth and putting them in her other cloak pocket for safe keeping.

As she followed the seam of the Crossroads, the trees grew thicker and wilder, the undergrowth a snarl of roots and thorns that threatened to trip her, and the hum deepened. This part of the forest was thick with magic that was strange and unknown, and she was lost in the middle of it. Unease tasted like bile, creeping up her throat.

Then she heard it: voices.

'—in the Magic Quarter.'

Thea snuffed out her lantern. She crept closer, as quiet as she could manage in her old leather boots, the woollen dress she wore for her midnight wanderings dragging across ferns and brambles until she stopped to yank her hems up.

'All it took was a whisper in the ear of one of the Hunters in

Prague that magic was flourishing in his city, under his nose, and he's snapped into action.'

Thea pressed a hand over her mouth, quieting her breath.

'Pan Novak does seem positively riled,' an unfamiliar voice drawled. 'As does the other Hunter you've enlisted – and he's a city councillor as well.'

'They're puppets dancing on my strings,' a second, female, voice said. 'The wheels are turning and everything has already been set in motion: the Magic Quarter will close soon, and then it will be ripe for my picking.'

A wave of dizziness washed over Thea as all the blood drained out of her. It was unsurprising that the Magic Quarter had been targeted: magic bred power which bred greed which ran straight to resentment. It was dangerous to be different. But who were these strangers discussing the Quarter in the deepest part of the forest in the witching hour? Thea needed to hear more.

'You're lucky you found a way through those wards, I was beginning to think you'd never weave a path through,' the first voice laughed.

Were they *fate-weavers*? Craning her neck to better listen, Thea hadn't realised she'd moved until a twig cracked beneath her boot.

'Someone's here,' the second voice snapped.

Thea picked up her skirts and ran. Her heart-spell flickering, her lungs shuddering, she fled through the trees until the trees stopped humming, until the plants no longer glowed, until the forest blinked and Thea crashed to a halt, gasping for air.

Someone was manipulating fate.

A pinprick of light danced into view.

It was a blushing red-pink, the same shade as the fruit Talibah had brought back from her last voyage: pomegranate. The light was joined by a second, then a third, then more than Thea could count. She swivelled, failing to keep track of them as they surrounded her. They looked like something from a faerie story: *bludička*. Will o' the wisps. Thea had read about them in a tome she'd found on the Lantern's shelves. Some tales said they were the lost souls of those who had met an unfortunate end, others that they were members of the fae, marsh tricksters with a malevolent streak. The voices she'd heard had woven fate to send them after her.

Thea peered closer at the nearest light. It flared a deep crimson before springing forward with a hiss, its light parting to reveal a dark maw, framed with teeth. Crammed in above, a pair of empty eye sockets stared back at Thea.

Biting back a scream, she ran.

The lights gave chase. Flickering brightly, each pink spark bled red. A warning.

Clenching her fingers into fists, nails cutting scythes into her palms, Thea banished her pain and fear, looking to fate to guide her home.

Yet when she reached out to tweak the threads, they would not yield. Whoever was manipulating fate, sending those creatures after her, held a power that Thea did not.

She ran faster.

The lights burnt brighter.

With each beat of her boots against the forest floor, fear drummed through Thea. The *bludička* were on her heels now, hissing and snapping their teeth as they neared. Thea could not outrun them, so instead she stopped and turned. Thrusting out her hands, she buried them deep in the loom of fate, shrouding the forest, and *pulled*.

The forest shuddered. Leaves fell from trees, birds took wing in fright, squirrels and woodland mice and foxes fled. And the *bludička* hesitated, regarding her anew. Her fingers still entwined with those glimmering threads, Thea glared at them.

'One more step and I will crush you,' she hissed.

They retreated. Their crimson lights fading to pink, they lifted the edge of a blanket of moss and vanished beneath. Not waiting to chance anything else, Thea ran once more, the fistful of threads still in her hand leading her back onto the path out of the forest.

When Thea returned to Stiltskin's Apothecary, dawn was laying siege to night. The door was unlocked. And the apothecary's namesake was standing inside, his back to her.

Thea closed her eyes for a beat, tiredness gnawing at her bones.

Sensing her, Jasper turned. He was formally dressed tonight, his coat and breeches a rich forest green that brought to mind pleasing autumn evenings. He looked wearier than Thea had seen him before, his dark gaze distant and unfocused.

Something was clearly vexing him. Thea's stomach sank faster than a rock through water. He knew she'd been breaking their bargain. He must. And now he would punish her for it. But what punishment could be greater than the loss of her heart?

Before she could ponder what best to say, how to defend herself, he glanced at her hair. And did not look away.

Setting her cloak on the counter, Thea removed a twig from her hair, which was a tangled mess after running through the forest, though come to think of it, she suddenly wasn't sure *why* she had been running? Frowning to herself, she smoothed her woollen dress, ignoring the mud staining her hem, her boots, the leaves still clinging to her skirts. She was too aware of him, conscious of each breath she took, how the air bent and flowed around the two of them. His power was quiet tonight, reined in, but she knew what lay beneath the still surface: power enough to take her heart without killing her, to have forged the spell that sat in her ribcage in its place. Her missing heart pulsed as she looked at him.

Jasper jerked, as if coming to his senses, and dragged his eyes away. They landed on the dress box, still sitting on her counter. 'I see you have requested Fleur's services,' he commented. 'That's an expensive gown.'

'Don't fret, you're not paying me enough to fritter my earnings away there,' Thea retorted without thinking.

A frown flashed across the storm of Jasper's face. 'I did not intend . . . Are your earnings insufficient for your needs?'

'No no, they're fine,' Thea said quickly. In fact, they were more than generous considering that they came with a free home. 'It was only a joke, a bad one—'

'I shall raise them,' Jasper said at the same time, their words crossing like swords.

'Why bother to pay me at all?' Thea was seized with curiosity. 'I am contracted to work here anyway.'

Jasper cast her a baffled look. 'I wouldn't have you starve under my roof.'

'Oh.' Thea fiddled with her sleeve.

Silence rang between them, sharp enough to cut. 'It was a gift,' she told him, somewhat awkwardly. 'The gown, I mean.'

Jasper hadn't been smiling before – had she ever witnessed him smile? Such an event must be rarer than an eclipse – but he was certainly not smiling now. His habitual frown had settled deep into the planes and grooves of his face like a grudge. 'From the acquaintance I met before?'

'Yes, actually.' Thea raised her chin, high and defiant. 'A beautiful gown in midnight blue.'

'Dark blue is not your colour,' Jasper ground out.

Thea blinked. Of all the things he might have said, this would have been her last guess. 'I was not asking for your opinion.'

Jasper stalked towards her. 'You should be in gold, as radiant as the sun. As your hair.' He reached out towards her hair as if he wanted to run his fingers through it. 'Your hair looks pretty tonight.'

Thea clutched her sleeves. 'What?'

'Your hair.' He cleared his throat. 'The way the candlelight is cast across it, it looks like spun gold.'

Thea's heart-spell caught in her throat. Jasper closed his hand in the air, but he did not step away, did not reclaim the distance between them. His voice lowered, so close and intimate she could have tasted his words. 'You ought to spend your time with someone who knows you.'

Anger spiked Thea's pulse. 'Nobody can know me,' she hissed. 'Not when I have no heart nor any memory prior to the day I began working here. Not even my own name. If I don't know who I am, how can anyone else be expected to?'

Jasper's face was expressionless. It was disorientating, standing this close to him. She'd always registered his height but his shoulders were broad too, a hidden strength playing through his form that she hadn't noticed before.

'As I said, I was not asking for your opinion,' Thea added. 'And it's none of your concern who I spend my time with, romantically or otherwise.' She folded her arms and glared.

A vein ticked in Jasper's jaw. 'You're right. It is none of my concern. But this is.' He reached for Thea.

She sucked in a breath before registering he was reaching past her, towards the records log that Thea had not noticed, lying open on the counter beside the dress box. 'The entries are sparse.'

'I told you, business has been slow.' Panic tasted like a rancid wine, more vinegar than grape. It burned Thea's tongue.

'Thea.' Jasper stared at her as if he could taste it too. 'I know you ... disapprove of the payments,' he began, looking as if he wanted to say something quite different but was restraining himself. 'But let me remind you, they are necessary. You cannot simply toy with fate: each alteration requires a balance in kind. If you do not take payment, you will destroy that balance and there will be consequences—'

'Are you threatening me?' Thea interrupted.

Jasper reeled back. Horror and sadness filled his eyes. Thea had never seen him like this before. It was haunting. Like looking into a lake with no bottom, an unending ocean. Beautiful in a way she'd never considered.

Before she could muster any words, his expression froze. Shutting her out so thoroughly she wondered if anyone had ever been permitted inside. Jasper did not wear a mask but a suit of armour. He was unknowable.

'I would consider it if you were not so unbelievably stubborn that I knew it would be pointless.' His tone skated over the message but Thea received it all the same, with a lick of fear and a blaze of defiance. It swept away any sympathy she might have felt.

He was the enemy, with his own agenda, and she would do well to remember that.

'As I told you, business has been slow,' she repeated firmly.

Jasper's answering look intimated that he did not believe her one bit. 'I shall leave you to it, then.'

'Please do,' snapped Thea. 'I've already wasted too much of this morning quarrelling with you when I could have been having a much more pleasant time elsewhere.'

Jasper jerked back as if she'd struck him. 'My apologies,' he said stiffly, placing a hat atop his head. 'Of course my company is abhorrent to you.'

Guilt chased Thea's words though she didn't know why. She banished it, holding herself tall. Claiming a confidence she didn't feel, standing there in her simple dress and muddy boots, cold and tiredness and the after-effects of fear puddled in her head. She was sure that she had something she'd meant to tell him but she couldn't quite remember what, only that it had been important at the time. That something had happened in the forest. But the more she tried to recall it, the faster it darted out of reach. She put it out of mind, craving the comfort of her bed, of hunkering down with Cinnamon and a book and whatever snack she could rustle up.

Jasper turned on his heel and stalked out. He did not wait for Thea to guess her name and this time, nor did she chase him.

CHAPTER

Nine

JASPER'S VOICE ECHOED through Thea as Zofka and Talibah dressed her for the opera. *You should be in gold. Radiant as the sun.* No. She refused to allow Jasper's opinions to vex her; nothing would tarnish the enchantment of tonight. She sat in her linen shift, stays and stockings as Zofka painted her cheeks in two inverted triangles before blending the rouge, dabbing more onto the centre of Thea's lips to give them an inviting plushness, and Talibah piled her soft curls atop her head.

Now and then, Thea glanced at the books stacked beside her bed, wishing she had not accepted so that she might stay home and read.

'Shall we add a beauty patch to your cheek?' Zofka mused, opening her patch box in pale pink porcelain, gifted from Gretel last spring. 'Perhaps a heart?'

Thea winced before she could catch herself.

'Or a moon,' Zofka quickly added. Her smile turned mischievous. 'We could put it next to your lips, give Malek an invitation to kiss you.'

'She's going to the theatre, not Versailles,' Talibah laughed. 'Next you'll be giving her mouse-fur eyebrows.'

Zofka threw a cushion at Talibah as Thea laughed, feeling lighter than she had in hours. After the disquieting exchange she'd had with Jasper, she'd managed to snatch a few hours of sleep. A delicate French pastry, glittering with sugar and excitement, had practically been shoved down her throat by Zofka, who had shot a horrified look at the dark circles haunting Thea's eyes, and fed her magical treats until they vanished, which Thea had not protested.

As Zofka perused her patches and Talibah fed Biscuit, who was pointing with his wing to a bowl of berries on the kitchen table, Thea swallowed a sickly gulp of feverfew and fairy's tear elixir for her headache; she'd been expecting it to dissipate after she'd closed shop and had a nap, but it had only unfurled along the base of her skull, growing and spreading. Hopefully she wasn't ailing with anything; she already felt guilty over closing the apothecary early, but she'd suffered a distinct lack of customers in the hours leading up to her decision. There were fewer magical folk wandering through the Magic Quarter while the wards were splintering and Pan Novak's Hunters might be spotted, harassing another of the proprietors.

'You are thinking too hard again,' Talibah murmured as she darkened Thea's eyebrows and lashes with the kohl Talibah lined her eyes with. 'No wonder your head aches.'

'Nothing misses your attention.' Thea gave her a wry smile.

Talibah's smile was creased with concern. 'You, my dear friend, are an open book. I think a night out is exactly what you need. At the very least, it will distract you from whatever's going on in your head.'

Thea agreed.

'Now for the main event,' Zofka cooed, waltzing over to Thea's armoire. 'The gown.'

Thea tied a thin, simple pannier around her waist before pulling on a quilted petticoat, one that would both fluff up her gown and keep her warm. Zofka helped pin the stomacher to the front of Thea's stays before Talibah lifted the skirt and then the rest of the gown over Thea. It fell into place like a dream, and, thanks to Fleur's enchanted design, the rest of the fabric shaped and secured itself, needing no further pinning.

Thea looked into her floor-length mirror, flanked by Zofka and Talibah. Her new gown was beautiful, the fabric gauzy and gorgeous and more costly than anything she could remember owning, with brocaded vines traipsing over it, unveiling budding roses. Though the more she gazed at it, the more she couldn't help thinking that it looked as if she'd been swallowed by the night sky. It dimmed her star.

'Hmm,' Zofka began.

'It was a beautiful gift,' Talibah said at the same time.

'Very generous,' Zofka agreed.

'And you look beautiful, dearest,' Talibah told Thea as Zofka nodded beside her.

'*Very* beautiful,' Zofka added, giving Thea's satin-gloved hand a squeeze.

'It's all right,' Thea smiled. 'I can see it too, and it doesn't matter one bit.' She clipped a pair of pearl earrings onto her lobes.

'He has only just met you.' Talibah slid a matching comb into Thea's hair. 'It would have been more surprising if he'd selected something that suited you perfectly.'

Zofka rummaged in Thea's jewellery box. 'Yes, that's very true. Besides, life would be boring if everyone knew each other already. Getting to know someone, now *that's* where the fun begins.' She pulled out a gold necklace. An oval pendant hung on a simple chain, engraved with violets. 'I haven't seen you wear this before; when did you get this?'

Thea lifted her hair as Zofka fastened it around her neck. 'I don't remember, I've had it forever.' She was already wearing it the day she awoke to her new life, standing outside the apothecary with Jasper. Which meant only one thing: it had come from her previous life. Sometimes she wore it as a talisman, as if the pendant would coax her memories back. Inspire her to think of a name, the right name, the name that would unlock the key to her past.

'It's perfect for tonight.' Talibah nodded her approval.

'Sometimes I wonder if it was a gift from my mother,' Thea whispered, pressing the pendant against her chest. 'If she's still out there, not knowing what happened to me—' Her voice failed. That thought was almost worse than the alternative, that perhaps her parents no longer lived at all, and she'd missed their last days.

'Oh, Thea.' Zofka's blue eyes turned to mirrors.

Cinnamon hopped over and flopped at Thea's stockinged feet.

Before she could pick him up, Zofka beat her to it. 'Oh no you don't,' Zofka laughed. 'I am not wasting hours of primping for you to cover yourself in rabbit hair.'

'Cinnamon doesn't shed,' Thea protested, grateful for the timely interruption. She had enough clanging around in her head without bringing her missing past into the cacophony. She was being taken to the opera by a man with dimples and a charming smile. A man who'd asked her for the biggest challenge of her life as far as she could remember.

CHAPTER

Ten

MALEK CAME FOR her in a carriage.

The secret entrance to the Quarter was a clever little enchantment; it knew when to present the visitor with a staircase down into the Magic Quarter and when to stretch along Prague Bridge, opening wide enough to allow horses to trot down a stony slope instead. For such a simple, seamless process, its magic was entangled with the powerhouse that was the Quarter's wards, ensuring that not a soul on Prague Bridge would witness an entire horse and carriage vanishing.

Thea waited on the doorstop of the apothecary as two cream Kladruber horses clopped over, their hooves kicking up piles of leaves, a handsome ochre carriage clattering behind. Witch light flickered through the many gourds' faces like a hundred devilish candelabras.

'Good luck,' Zofka whispered from above. She and Talibah were hanging out of one of Thea's windows to watch; Zofka was beaming down, Cinnamon in her arms. Talibah wore an inscrutable expression.

Nerves and excitement fizzed in Thea's stomach. After the last toad, who had also been kissing half the folk in the Quarter, she had stayed in her comfort zone, oscillating between the apothecary, the forest, the Lantern and the Gingerbread House. Staying far away from any potential frogs. Thea could never fall in love without her heart, but she didn't want to close herself off to the idea of it altogether. She didn't want to be left alone if she never got her heart back.

The coachman drew the carriage to a halt, the pair of horses gently huffing.

Malek sprang down from the carriage. When he set eyes on Thea, he flashed her that dimple, setting her at ease. He was dressed as elegantly as she, in coordinating navy, his pomaded wig tied back with a ribbon that looked cut from the same silks as Thea's gown. 'You look exquisite,' he told her, extending a gloved hand.

Thea laid her hand in his. 'I've never received such a lovely gift,' she admitted as he handed her into the carriage. 'You were far too generous.' Her dress bloomed like a blowsy peony as she settled onto the velvet bench.

Malek's smile widened. His smiles came easily; conversation with Malek was no battle to be fought, there would be no trading blows tonight. Only good company and excellent music. Malek sat opposite Thea and thumped on the roof for the coachman to usher the horses away. As the apothecary receded from sight, Thea spotted her weathervane, spinning wildly in the rising wind; a wolf, howling back at her. She frowned, unsure if that was a reaction to the change in season, or a portent. Perhaps it had been howling since Pan Novak had last stepped foot over the threshold and she hadn't noticed. At least it wasn't a toad.

'You cannot blame me; how could I resist treating you?' Malek leant a little closer, giving Thea a nose of his cologne; a fashionable musky scent she recognised from some of the gentlemen who passed through her apothecary. 'You deserve to be treated like a queen.' Opening a box beneath his own cushioned bench, outfitted in russet velvet to compliment the gleaming woodwork, he withdrew a bottle and a couple of goblets. 'Champagne?'

Thea accepted a goblet. 'I've been making some progress on your request,' she told him. 'How is your sister faring? I'm afraid I need more time to make your key, it's a rather complicated feat of magic.'

Malek's smile softened. 'I did not invite you here tonight to chase you for an update. I trust your process. And my sister, well . . .' He took a hearty gulp from his goblet. 'She understands that help is on the way, but it would ease both our minds if we knew how long that would take?'

'I can give it to you in a fortnight or so. I'm sorry it's not sooner, but as I said, it's a complicated process.'

Malek leant forwards, resting his elbows on his knees. 'Please do not apologise; I would not wish for this to be rushed.' The golden champagne warmed his tawny eyes.

It warmed Thea, too. She might be unable to love but she knew from past experience that she wasn't immune to affection, or the first stirrings of a crush.

He sipped his champagne. 'Your employer, Lord Stiltskin, seemed . . . disconcerted by my presence the last time I happened by. Is there anything . . . romantic between the two of you?' Malek's question was tentative.

'Absolutely not,' Thea declared.

'Does Lord Stiltskin reside near his apothecary?' Malek asked.

'No, he doesn't even live in the Magic Quarter,' Thea told him to reassure him. 'He lives over near the castle.' And hopefully the pair would not meet again. Jasper did have such a way of repelling customers and . . . friends. Was Malek a friend? She hardly knew anything about him. 'What do you do?'

'I'm a landowner,' Malek said. 'I own a collection of enterprises in the Old Town, which I oversee. I live nearby – I can't imagine Lord Stiltskin not wanting to keep a closer eye on his apothecary, but I suppose he has no need when you seem to manage running it by yourself?'

'So, you don't work either,' Thea teased, desperate to distract him from the topic of Jasper.

'Well, you do not seem to be jumping out of the carriage so I will take that as a good sign.' His smile was playful, though a hint of concern shone through, betraying him.

Thea smiled over the rim of her goblet. 'Perhaps I'm simply waiting for us to stop in traffic before I orchestrate my escape.'

Malek groaned, clamping a hand to his navy coat, each brass button shining like a coin. 'You wound me.'

Thea laughed.

Malek lifted his goblet. 'Now I would much rather celebrate that I walked into your apothecary that day, for if I hadn't met you then, I would be a less fortunate man tonight.'

Thea's laugh was as effervescent as her wine. Being escorted through the city in a charming gentleman's carriage, wearing a gown as fine as any duchess, was a dream she did not care to wake from.

They soared up the cobblestoned hill, the Magic Quarter falling away as they approached the yawning void where the statute of St John of Nepomuk stood, and through, back onto the medieval stone arch bridge. The statue magically closed behind them, folding the Magic Quarter back into its veil of secrecy. Thea sipped champagne and luxuriated in easy conversation with Malek as they passed the dark, haunted Gothic architecture of the Old Town Bridge Tower, joining the royal route along Karlova Street, and into the treasure box of baroque buildings in lemon yellows and dusky pinks and duck-egg blues. It was a short ride to the end of Kotcích Street, where the theatre stood, half obscured by the line of carriages pulling up to its doors.

People from all walks of life were filtering through the doors, some emerging from carriages in fluttering gowns, others arriving on foot from their places of work, all united by a love of music. When it was their turn, the coachman hopped down to open the door and Malek helped Thea down, ushering her inside. 'Come with me. I rent one of the boxes here. It's a little extravagant, but I consider it an investment in culture.' He sidled a look to her as if gauging her reaction to his display of wealth, and Thea gave him an uneasy smile back; she was getting the impression that she'd walked into a fairy tale where she had been cast as Cinderella, making her wonder precisely what Malek thought of her. A couple of roses wilted on her dress.

A painted ceiling arced above them, stealing Thea's concerns away as they took their seats in Malek's box. 'My mother used to bring me here as often as she could,' Malek said as Thea took in the chandeliers dripping with melted wax, the orchestra pit readying their instruments, and the large stage that stared imperiously back at them all. 'We didn't always agree on everything, but she loved music.'

His smile was wistful, compelling Thea to rest a hand on his forearm. He clasped it in his. 'She had the most beautiful voice I've ever heard. We lost her years ago and her face is fading from my memory, but that voice—' He gave a shake of his head. 'That voice will never leave me.'

'How lovely that you honour her with coming here,' Thea told him.

With a rich brassy note, the orchestra sprang to life, making the theatre hush with expectation.

As the opera unfolded, a solitary figure entered the box opposite to theirs. 'Joseph II,' Malek murmured, noticing where her focus had drifted. 'He's in Prague for a spell, to open the annual Winter Ball.'

Thea lifted her opera glasses to peer through them. 'I heard it's to be held in Prague Castle this year.'

'Yes, which suits Joseph, since he's fond of travelling,' Malek continued. 'But he dislikes attention, so much so that he uses a pseudonym when he journeys. Count Falkenstein.'

Thea laughed quietly, bound up in the enchantment of it all. When the theatre erupted in song, roses bloomed up her stomacher, making her glad of the darkness as magic fizzed through her dress. Malek's hand lingered on hers as the music seized Thea with a power all of its own. The spell beating in her chest surged through her veins as Alena took the stage as Argene. As the theatre swelled with Alena's voice, clear and high and bright, heartstrings instead of vocal cords, Thea's own body swelled with emotion. For one bright glittering moment of panic, she feared her heart's return: if she could feel this much without it, what would she feel when she was whole again?

She caught the moment Alena noticed her beyond the flaming spotlights, as she tossed a wink at Thea without missing a note.

'A friend of yours, I take it?' Malek's lips twitched.

Thea smiled. 'Alena is a loyal customer.'

By the time the opera reached its sparkling crescendo, the garden of roses had bloomed on Thea's dress, turning to golden leaves that fluttered down her skirts and shone along her hems. She admired them on the carriage ride home and, when she lifted her gaze from her gown, she found Malek admiring her. Time slowed to a syrup as they looked at each other as Prague passed by in a drizzle of street lamps and spires.

When they reached Stiltskin's Apothecary, he jumped from the carriage and faced Thea, a question shining in his eyes. 'Thank you for accompanying me tonight.' He held out his hand.

Thea took it and hopped down in a swirl of midnight silk and golden leaves. Feeling Malek's reluctance to part with her hand, she let her touch linger, peering up at him from beneath her eyelashes. Wondering if he would kiss her.

He cleared his throat roughly. 'Could I . . .?'

'Yes,' Thea whispered.

Still clasping her hand, Malek gently pulled her towards him and pressed his lips to hers. Soft and sweet. A tender first kiss. Just as in *The Lost Love of Iris Pearl*, when Iris kissed the Marquess on the last page: it was everything their first kiss ought to have been. Until a pair of dark blue eyes, haunting and deep, materialised behind Thea's eyelids.

Alarmed at the intrusion, Thea opened her eyes, but at the sight of Malek's face so close to hers, she snapped them shut again. Kisses were not meant to happen with your eyes open. But now her thoughts had meandered, she couldn't wrangle them back, and try as she might, she could still see Jasper's eyes.

She kissed Malek harder, paying no heed to the heat rolling under her skin, ignoring the way her heart-spell ticked faster, hating that Jasper's power was inside her.

Focus on the man you are kissing, Thea ordered herself. *On his mouth, his hand covering yours, his scent.*

It was unlike Jasper's, whose scent was tinged with wildness: the salt-lick of the sea, and the mossy darkness of the deepest forest.

The kiss ended, and with it, Thea's maelstrom of thoughts. Malek smiled, his hand a light touch on hers.

Thea mirrored his smile. This was the man for her, she was certain of it. Malek was good for her, he treated her well and he was steady.

Who cared if she couldn't fall in love? Love faded, tarnished with age. Love broke hearts. It belonged in her books, along with the kind of kisses that set your soul aquiver. Malek was nice, kissing him was nice. If another man had roamed through her head while they were kissing, well, that was just her pesky brain causing trouble.

It meant nothing.

CHAPTER

Eleven

HERE SHE IS! Tell us everything.' Zofka's apple cheeks were rosier than usual when Thea walked upstairs and into her private quarters.

Home, at last.

She cast off her heeled shoes and perched on one of her armchairs, opposite Talibah, who was stitching a frayed book spine back together. 'You look like one of Zofka's cream cakes,' Talibah grinned as Thea's layers mushroomed around her.

Her home glimmered with candlelight. Cinnamon's whiskers twitched as he slept on her bed, and a rich tomato scent emanated from her little stove, making Thea's stomach groan.

'And we know Malek found you *delectable*,' Zofka chimed in, crushing herbs and salt and pepper with a pestle and mortar as she came to hover at Talibah's side, giving Thea a knowing smile.

Thea couldn't help laughing as she shook her head. 'You're incorrigible,' she said affectionately as Zofka performed an exaggerated curtsy. 'How long were you spying on me?'

Zofka's clear blue eyes sparkled with mischief. 'Long enough.'

Thea feigned a sigh. 'I regret the day I gave you a key.'

'Then who would feed you tomato soup and dumplings when you come home late at night after being out on the town with your beau?' Zofka sing-songed, dancing back to the little stove that was cranking out enough heat to warm Thea's entire home, along with Biscuit, who was sleeping in the bed Thea had cobbled together for him.

As Zofka dished out their late dinner, Talibah assisted Thea in removing her gown, pannier and petticoat, until she was sitting in her shift and stays. Zofka returned with the promised bowl of tomato soup and dumplings, sliced like fresh bread, with a side of fried cheese. 'I forgive you,' Thea said promptly, going for the cheese first.

'How was the opera?' Talibah leant forwards, intrigue radiating across her face. 'Doesn't Alena sing like a dream?'

'It was wonderful,' Thea gushed. 'I could listen to her every night. It . . . It stirred me.'

Zofka curled up at Thea's feet like a contented housecat, idly dipping a dumpling into her soup. 'And Malek?' Zofka was a relentless force. 'Did he stir you, too?'

Thea shuffled, attempting to ease the discomfort setting in.

Zofka bit into her dumpling, her voice softening, turning wistful. 'First kisses are their own kind of magic.'

'Not all first kisses,' Talibah pointed out, watching Thea's face. 'Some improve with time.'

Both women fixed their attention on Thea. 'It was . . . fine.'

Zofka winced. 'That bad?'

'Not at all,' Thea protested, squirming with guilt that she was sitting there wearing the gorgeous gown Malek had presented her with, after enjoying a beautiful evening at the opera with him but feeling . . . less than enthusiastic. It had to be her lack of heart. She was moving through life, lost in a sea of feelings that never made sense because there was only a spell holding her all together. Some days it felt as though, if someone looked at her the wrong way, she would fall apart. As though she was nothing but a collection of hopes and fears, dreams and worries, masquerading as human. 'I was just distracted. You know how I struggle to rein in my thoughts.'

Talibah tilted her head, giving Thea a pensive look that missed nothing. 'What were you distracted by?'

'It means nothing.' Thea shrugged. 'My mind races from dawn to dusk – you know I couldn't stop it if I wanted to. And I did want to. Very much.'

Talibah's pensive look grew talons.

'Fine,' Thea groaned. 'Jasper popped into my head at the most inopportune time. It was a very unwelcome intrusion and—' She trailed off, catching the significant look traded between her friends.

Zofka's hands flew up. 'I'm not telling her, she'll bite my head off.'

Talibah gave an elegant sigh and set her bowl aside. 'Thea, we love you dearly but when it comes to Lord— *Jasper*, you seem somewhat . . . blinkered.'

'Blinded,' Zofka amended with another mouthful of dumpling. 'For goddess' sake, Thea, the man looks like he was carved from marble. He's ridiculously handsome.'

Thea's spoon hadn't made it to her mouth. She put it down. It clattered against her plate harder than she'd intended. She'd been so busy loathing Jasper that she'd never considered him in that way before; when she looked at him, all she saw was the man who had walked away with her heart in a box. Now that she thought about it, she supposed there was something hypnotic about those eyes . . . She swallowed.

'Haven't you seen the way other people look at him?' Zofka continued, with no little amusement. 'Just the other week, a witch practically fell over her own petticoats to get a second look as she scurried away from him.'

'She was probably scared of him,' Thea said stubbornly. She refused to admit that she had noticed how he drew attention on the rare events he entered the apothecary before nightfall. What did it matter if he had a perfect jawline, when he was keeping Thea's memories hostage?

Zofka pointed her spoon at Thea. 'That doesn't mean she didn't notice his looks.'

'It's more than that, though. The way you two look at each other,' Talibah began, either ignoring or oblivious to Thea's incredulous stare, 'the air between you could catch fire.'

'Because we loathe each other,' Thea said. 'I can't believe you're even considering this . . . You know how often I've complained about him.'

'Oh yes.' Zofka's eyes widened. 'Often. It would seem that you can't stop thinking about him, in fact.'

Thea threw her hands up. 'Because I detest the man!'

'Tension,' Zofka countered. 'Because you have this deep, sexual tension running between you like a canyon. The day you two become *better acquainted*, well . . .' She fanned the air, throwing a mischievous smirk at Thea.

Talibah cut herself another couple of dumplings. 'According to all the great writers, hatred and love go hand in hand.'

'Like cake and books,' Zofka said.

Thea slumped back. 'You cannot be serious.'

'As a curse,' Zofka said.

Talibah's voice gentled. 'We are not telling you to pursue anything romantic with Jasper, only that it seems that there is . . . something there.'

'He took my heart.' Thea tipped her head back. 'I've spent the past seven years playing his little game, listing names that never belonged to me. I lost my heart and memories to a fate-weaver for some reason I can't remember.'

Her headache returned, threefold fiercer. She rubbed a knuckle against the bridge of her nose.

'Let's change the subject.' Talibah gathered their bowls and plates, putting them into a pail of water in the kitchen. She glanced at Biscuit. 'How is the raven healing?'

'Well,' Thea said, distracted by Jasper and her missing heart and the pain that thudded in her temples, along with the constant needling of the price she had not taken from the witch she'd helped a few days ago. Her first memory. Something within Thea kept forcing its way through her head and dreams, reminding her, chasing her to get it. It was stubborn. But she was stubborn, too. She could outlast it. It was worth it not to take any more prices.

Talibah returned with three cups of lavender tea. 'If you make him too comfortable, he'll never want to leave.'

'The poor thing was nailed to a door!' Thea whispered. 'He needs time.'

Zofka snorted into her teacup. 'Time, maybe. A scented pillow, no.'

Thea sighed. 'Fine, I'll release him in a few days.'

Zofka sobered. 'The Hunters have paid us a second visit. Gretel insists I have nothing to worry about, but it's starting to feel like a witch-hunt.' She shivered.

Thea pulled one of her many yellow knitted blankets over both herself and Zofka. 'Actually, it's the opposite.'

Talibah handed a cup of tea to Thea. 'Why? What have you learnt?'

Thea stared back at her, her headache pounding as a faded memory crept back into place. 'I overheard something. Last night, near the Crossroads. I—' She pressed a couple of fingers to one temple. 'I don't know how I forgot to mention it. I meant to tell Jasper too, but I just . . . forgot. This headache, I swear I'm losing my mind.'

Zofka stood, peering into her eyes. 'How long have you had this headache? Did it start in the forest?'

Lavender-scented steam rose like mist as Thea wrapped her hands around her cup, thinking. 'No,' she said slowly. 'It started before, I'm sure of it.'

'Then it can't have been someone meddling with your head to compel you to forget.' Zofka slid back under the blanket and took her own cup from Talibah, though her forehead was still creased.

'No.' Thea put her cup down on her blanketed knees. Half of it splashed out. Zofka twitched her fingers like a conductor, and it flowed backwards, returning to Thea's cup. 'Thank you.' Thea's voice cracked. 'I . . . I can't lose more of my memories, I—'

'We don't know that that's happening,' Talibah said. 'Your original memories were exchanged as per a bargain with a fate-weaver; you never lost them. Maybe your headache and fuzzy memories have something to do with the wards weakening. One of the weather-witches' powers has been malfunctioning, too.'

'Yes!' Zofka perked up. 'And I almost set fire to my stove yesterday.'

'You do that every other week,' Thea said, though she smiled. Maybe her head pain was just a consequence of the wards. Or maybe it was because she hadn't been taking prices and this was how fate was balancing the debt. She pursed her lips, wondering.

'What did you find out in the forest?' Talibah prompted.

Thea took a sip of tea. It scalded her throat. Ignoring it, she spelled out the whole ordeal, particularly on the person she'd overheard boasting of their involvement with the Quarter, wondering if the *bludička* had scared the memory out of her head, though she seemed to have no problem recalling their pointed teeth and empty eye sockets.

'How intriguing,' Talibah murmured.

Zofka's eyes were moons. 'Why would the fate-weavers – I presume they're fate-weavers from what they said about weaving a way through? – want to interfere with the Magic Quarter? And for goddess' sake, they have enough power to take us down themselves if that's the end game – why would they need to go through the Magic Hunters?'

'I do not know,' Talibah said. 'And that concerns me.'

'Agreed.' Thea rose, striding over to the nearest window. Pulling it down with one sharp tug, she brought her fingers to her lips and whistled. Biscuit ruffled his feathers, cawing back at her. 'Not you,' Thea told him, 'You're still healing.' A different raven materialised, spreading its wings wide as it landed on the windowsill, the night sky a curtain of stars and cloud wisps at its back. Thea reached for a nearby scrap of paper and a quill. Scratching out the names written there – *Sybil, Agnes, Margery* – she penned a quick note. Rolling it into a tight scroll, she attached it to the raven's leg strap. 'Take that next door, to Rose.'

Returning to her spot, Thea nestled back into the warmth of her blanket, shared with Zofka. 'I've told Rose what I'd overheard before I can forget again, and called for another Magic Quarter meeting. We need to fix the wards as a matter of urgency now we know for certain it was a targeted attack from a fate-weaver.'

'Good thinking,' Zofka said, reaching for a leftover piece of fried cheese. 'Let's discuss something happier now. What's going on with Malek? Talibah mentioned he'd asked you for something peculiar?'

Thea pulled out her journal, showing them the list she'd jotted down as she let them in on what Malek had told her, about his sister and how he wanted to be the one who bore the price for saving her. Of the key he had asked for and how she was unsure how to go about fate-weaving around an item, so she had begun searching for ingredients for a complementary potion. Fate-weaving was powerful, but it wasn't a tangible object in the way that magic could be. Combining them both would allow her to create something much more powerful, which was exactly what Malek needed.

'You told us that Jasper gave you this Compendium in your first week here,' Talibah remembered, opening the Compendium as if she couldn't have a book in her lap and not run a hand over the vellum of its pages. 'That it had been hidden until he'd tapped into his power and untied certain knots that revealed it?'

'Yes, of *course*.' Thea's spirits soared, recalling how Jasper had pulled the book from the wall. 'Then it is possible to fate-weave around a physical object – I am on the right lines.'

Maye she would stop doubting herself when her heart was returned to her chest.

Zofka traded the journal for the Compendium. 'I agree that you're on the right lines, with the potion and fate-weaving a physical object.'

'Interesting,' Talibah commented, looking through the journal and reading the list aloud:

> *Silver spot-dapples? Excellent for locating and finding – like a key that draws you to the correct spot.*
> *A firebird's breath? Could remove all trace of being there?*
> *A single fingernail from a lake spirit?*

'You should add a fairy's tear,' Zofka said around a mouthful of fried cheese. 'Even if you're not using it for its magical properties, it makes an excellent binder and you're going to want something really sticky so it adheres to whatever you use as the actual physical key.'

Talibah passed the journal to Thea, who added it to the list. 'At least I already have a vial of tears in stock.' It had been one of many ingredients that the apothecary had come supplied with when she first started working here, and a little went a long way. Which was useful, seeing as she'd never met a fairy in real life, only the pixies and sprites that inhabited the Quarter.

'Oh,' Zofka said on turning the page of the Compendium. 'I haven't read this bit before.' She read aloud as the three women huddled in their blankets, snacking on leftovers as the candles burned low.

> *I love the forest best when the flowers bloom. When all those endless greens and browns burst into a hundred, a thousand colours. It is a jewellery box of riches. Though this year, when the storms finally crest and blow out to ravage the oceans instead, I am searching for one thing only: him.*
>
> *He awaited me in the forest. We had exchanged more notes after that first one, until I came to know his thoughts and feelings as intimately as my own. Falling into his arms does not feel like embracing a stranger but my closest friend, my confidante. My lover.*
>
> *I could have lain in his arms, in a sea of petals, forever.*

'Oh,' Zofka sighed happily. 'How romantic.'

Talibah and Thea remained silent. Thea's non-existent heart weeped in its void.

CHAPTER

Twelve

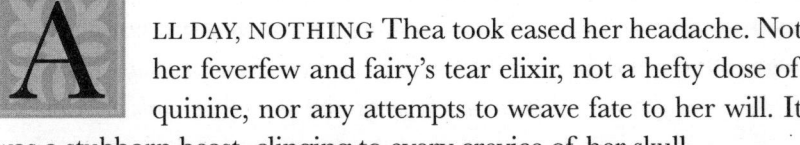LL DAY, NOTHING Thea took eased her headache. Not her feverfew and fairy's tear elixir, not a hefty dose of quinine, nor any attempts to weave fate to her will. It was a stubborn beast, clinging to every crevice of her skull.

'I heard you required a price?' The young witch standing in front of Thea peered anxiously at her. Tendrils of fog escaped their shirtsleeves, creeping down their wrists like bracelets of cloud. 'That I needed to be prepared for whatever you might ask of me.' They dragged in a breath, fog skulking around their collarbones. 'I want people to notice me. I'm tired of being the smallest voice in a room, of being constantly overlooked. I just – I just want them to see me.'

Confidence, that was what they needed. Paired with a lick of enthusiasm. Ignoring her headache, flickering in the corners of her vision, Thea focused on the power thrumming through her until the apothecary distorted and fate layered over it like a veil. Ready to be manipulated by her own hands, a flick of her fingers. The witch's threads were worn thin in places, grey and fine and insubstantial as their wandering tendrils of fog. Thea wound other threads around them, bolstering them until the witch's self-belief was strong enough to command a room.

The necessary price needled against her head: the memory of their single greatest accomplishment. She did not take it. Other than perhaps her headache, she had yet to notice any consequence from refusing prices. And if her headache was the sole consequence, well, she could withstand that if it helped others.

'There,' she said. 'I've ensured you'll be seen everywhere you set foot.'

The witch almost evaporated with relief. 'Oh, *thank you.*'

Thea held their gaze. 'But be warned, sometimes what we seek isn't what we need.'

Frowning, they adjusted their thistle-purple coat with care, another wave of fog seeping out between the decorative stitches. 'And the price?'

'It's your lucky day.' Thea didn't bother to berate them for not visiting at night – customers were still few and far apart since the wards had been damaged and Pan Novak's Hunters had ransacked her wares. It was just as well; between working on Malek's key and this incessant headache, restocking her shelves was taking time.

They looked at her as if she'd plucked the moon from the sky and handed it to them. 'Are you quite sure?'

'Go before I change my mind.' Thea rested her head on her arms with a groan. Never mind the champagne she'd enjoyed in the carriage last night, it felt like she'd downed the entire bottle.

A raven darted through the apothecary door before it closed.

When Thea groaned again, it hopped over and prodded her arm with its beak. It was carrying a little package. Untying it, Thea smiled at the biscuit it had carted over. She didn't need to read the note to know who had sent it:

> *I can hear you groaning from across the street. Eat this, close shop and go for a walk.*

Everyone needed to befriend a kitchen-witch. Thea did as ordered. The biscuit was soft and light as a cloud, and as it burst on her tongue with the taste of blueberries, her headache retreated enough for her to pull on her warm cloak and her battered boots. She slid her journal into her pocket. She wasn't sure where she might find a lake spirit in the forest, nor how to take one of its fingernails, but if she didn't start looking, she'd never find one.

Another raven swept in before she left, bearing a missive from Rose:

Urgent meeting in the Magic Quarter tonight at nine.

Thea had just skimmed it when a third raven fluttered in on the wingtips of the second.

Can we hold it somewhere else this time? Sarah has a severe sunflower allergy.

Thea sighed, wondering if the ravens were getting lost. 'You need to take this to Rose,' she told the raven as yet another bird appeared at her window. 'This can wait,' she muttered to herself, darting outside. The skies were besieged with messenger ravens, criss-crossing the street. No wonder the messages were going awry. Pulling up her cloak-hood, Thea headed for the forest.

It felt different at this time. Softer, somehow. More magical with the sun sending out its final rays and the canopy muting everything into a glow. She didn't overhear any other conversations about fate-weavers toying with Prague though she kept her senses sharp, listening out for every snap of a branch, each skitter of a creature, trying to hear anything that could be a whisper. Looking for any shimmer of water, large enough to harbour a mysterious lake spirit.

She didn't see or hear either, but she did stumble on a little meadow, tucked away in the heart of the forest.

And there was Jasper. Alone.

Thea halted, bracing herself against a spruce tree as she caught her breath, undecided whether she ought to steal away before he noticed her, or say something. She peered around the trunk at him.

He was kneeling in the earth, clenching a bunch of wildflowers – crocuses and lilies and violets – hard enough to crush their stems.

Magically out-of-season flowers for a magical spot. Seeing him sitting there, vulnerable and alone, gave Thea a peculiar feeling she could not name.

She knew she should leave. She was intruding on something private.

'Careful, you'll squash them,' she said instead, stepping free of the bracken.

Jasper started, staring up at her. Devastation was writ upon his face.

'What happened?' Thea whispered. 'What's wrong?'

His hair was untied, falling around his cheekbones, his eyes midnight-dark. Before he composed himself, there was half a moment where the forest stilled around them, when the birds hushed their songs, and the wind ceased to blow, when Jasper looked at Thea as if she was the answer to everything.

Then Jasper tipped his head back, staring up at the sky. At the edge of the canopy, where the leaves didn't quite meet, chinks of rose-red clouds were revealed, along with a setting sun that bathed the forest in a petal-soft glow.

'Today is a difficult anniversary for me.' His voice splintered, cracking wide open. Exposing the valley of hurt beneath.

For a moment, Thea forgot that this man had taken her heart. All she saw was pain.

She crossed the distance between them and laid a tentative hand on his arm. She had never dared touch him before, and he jerked as she did so, setting her heart-spell thrashing in her chest.

'I'm sorry to hear that,' she said. 'I'm here if you want to share anything. Sometimes it helps, to talk.'

'Thank you.' His voice was hoarse. 'I lost my daughter this day, many years ago.'

'Oh, Jasper, I—' Thea swallowed. 'I have no words for that. I cannot imagine the hurt you carry every day. How old was she?'

Perhaps all this time, he had been as lonely as her, had suffered the way she did when she awoke in the thickest part of the night, too many thoughts running through her head, each one a ripple in a lake, starting small, then growing and growing until she could not look away. Maybe this was why he behaved in the manner he did; he wasn't grumpy and uncaring; he was living with a great loss.

Jasper lowered his gaze to the earth and the wildflowers he still clung to. 'Just twelve.'

'I'm so sorry,' Thea whispered. 'I should never have said anything—'

She choked back her curiosity over what might have happened; over who the girl's mother had been. This was not about her. Instead, she sat beside him, not caring that her dress would stain, or that she shouldn't be showing sympathy for the man who had taken her heart and kept it to this day. All she felt was his pain.

So, she stayed with him until a fresh wash of the deepest, duskiest blue crept over the bowl of the sky.

'The sun has set,' she told him, as he seemed not to notice. 'The day has ended now.'

The corner of his mouth twisted, wry and weary. 'It always does.'

He stood, reached back and extended a hand to Thea, who took it without hesitation; after hours spent on the ground, her bones had soaked up the cold, stiffening. Jasper dropped her hand and frowned, as if seeing her properly for the first time. 'What were you doing here?'

'I was sitting with you.' Thea shot him a disbelieving look, pausing in brushing the loose earth from her skirts. 'You seemed as if you could use the company and I didn't want to leave you alone—'

'No,' he interrupted. 'Before that. You were walking alone in this part of the forest, just before sunset?'

'Yes, I do so often.'

Gone was Jasper's moment of vulnerability, the peeling back of his armour to reveal his true heart, raw with grief. His armour was firmly back in place.

Jasper's frown grew into a glare. 'Have you lost your mind?' he demanded. 'Do you realise how dangerous this forest is ?'

'Is this the part where you tell me that there are vampires in the forest?' Thea asked wryly, though the last time she'd ventured here, she'd been sent fleeing from a posse of *bludička*.

'No.' Jasper raked his hair back. 'Most vampires reside in Prague. Or in Vienna, or Paris. They have a fondness for court life; I believe the strict social structure and rules appeal to them, and their needs can be passed off as mere eccentricities among the nobility.'

'I can look after myself,' she said coolly.

Jasper drew a step closer. 'You are standing on the brink of the Crossroads. Have you not noticed the way the trees hum in this part of the forest? The peculiar things that grow around here, the deer with their white stares, the strange lights that dance through the trees?'

The back of Thea's neck tingled. 'Of course. But some of the best plants and fungi grow here. This is the perfect time to harvest them. I use them for crafting elixirs and—'

Jasper closed his eyes, pinching his nose as if she had greatly aggrieved him. 'I did not think I had to warn you of this. I never supposed you'd be running around in the forest at all hours of the night, unaccompanied.'

Thea's eyebrows shot up. 'Please tell me you are not concerned about my *virtue*?'

'Don't be ridiculous.' Jasper's eyes snapped open. His voice lowered to a growl. 'The Crossroads is the seam of the world. The point where it brushes against other, darker worlds. Worlds where demons prowl, where incubi hunt for women like you, where fate-weavers hold the fabric of the universe at their fingertips. That's why you have found potent ingredients here: it's magic from those worlds bleeding through.'

Thea folded her arms. 'I know all of this.'

Jasper's voice turned dangerous. 'Then why have you been walking right along that seam, knowing that with just one misstep you could just slip through and be lost forever?'

'Do not treat me like a child when you know well it is your apothecary I am contracted to run, to stock its shelves with magical ingredients. Where did you think I was getting them from all these years?'

The colour seeped from Jasper's face. 'That did not occur to me.'

'No, why would it? After all, you're off busy doing whatever it is you do while I'm running your apothecary.' Thea hesitated. 'What *do* you do with your time?'

'The apothecary is not my sole business venture,' Jasper snapped. He relented. 'If there are some ingredients you don't have, you should come to me. I will supply you anything you might need.'

Thea's thoughts halted. Maybe she should ask him if he happened to have a lake spirit's fingernail floating around in a drawer somewhere. But then she'd have to tell him about Malek and his key, and something about that felt very much like a bad idea.

'You can tell me anything,' Jasper added, as if he'd read her mind. 'Have there been any updates about the wards? I have been looking into it, but they are a complex magic. I'm afraid it will take some time.'

Maybe she should tell him how she'd been threatened by way of Biscuit, or what she'd overheard the last time she'd been here. 'Are you coming to the Quarter meeting tonight?'

'Absolutely not.'

'Maybe if you came, the other residents would see that fate-weavers are not to be feared simply because they have the power to alter destiny,' Thea pointed out. Although, she was about to attend to tell them that a fate-weaver had threatened their safety . . .

Jasper cut a sideways glare at her. 'If I turn up, the other magical folk will leave.'

'Perhaps if you weren't so grumpy—'

Jasper's glower deepened.

'This concerns you, too. The apothecary sits in the Magic Quarter and there's a rift through our ceiling.'

'I am looking into that myself.'

Thea gnawed at her lip. 'Since you're not coming to the meeting, I have to tell you that the last time I came here, I accidentally overheard two people talking about how they'd infiltrated the Quarter, that they were the ones who'd riled up the Hunters – they mentioned weaving, Jasper.'

Jasper stilled. A predator hiding its claws, teeth, power, lest it scare away its prey.

Thea winced, unsure if she wanted to share the rest.

'What happened?' Jasper ordered. 'Tell me everything. This instant.'

'It's fine, I'm fine,' Thea said in a hurry. 'They sent some *bludička* after me, but I escaped them, and the fate-weavers never learnt my identity. No harm done.' She smiled, ignoring the flash of crimson light that blazed through her memory, of sharp teeth and empty eyes and the way they'd crept under that moss, all long fingernails and scurrying bodies, lying in wait for their next victim. How her memory of the conversation she'd overheard had immediately vanished from her head, only returning hours, days later.

Jasper's jaw clenched. 'Then you were lucky. Though it proves my point: stay out of this forest. It is not the place for you.' He began striding from the clearing.

Thea pursued him, taking two steps for each of his strides. 'It's funny, I've been hearing a lot of that lately and I'm getting awfully tired of it.'

Jasper halted abruptly. They were sheltered from the moon here, the surrounding spruces fracturing her shine. 'What are you talking about?'

'This.' Thea fished in her pocket for the note that had been pinned to her door. Along with Biscuit. A reminder that she would not give in, would not give up. It was speckled with flecks of raven blood; bright red tears. 'I came home to it one night.'

Jasper's face was stone as he read it, his reaction unknowable. 'I will look into this.' Pocketing the note, he strode away.

Thea pursued him.

Jasper muttered something under his breath. Out loud, he added, 'I've heard that Pan Novak has you in his sights. That you were defiant towards him. Provoking him.'

'Who told you that?'

'You are not the only one I speak to in the Quarter.'

Curious. 'He deserved it,' Thea said.

Was that a suggestion of a smile crossing Jasper's lips? 'Oh, I am certain of that, but the fact cannot be denied that he is a powerful man, and you must not invite his wrath. Any more than you already have. Pan Novak may be human but that doesn't make him any less dangerous. His hatred and distrust of magic is not to be underestimated; he could outlaw the entire Magic Quarter, revoke our permits to conduct business in the city. Which is why you must stay away from him.'

'Yes, yes, fine,' Thea huffed impatiently. Jasper was pacing through the forest as if it had been set alight and her legs were beginning to burn with keeping pace. 'But if you're going to look into the threat, and the failing wards, you should let me help. I can access places which you, your *Lordship*, cannot.'

They reached the main path, well-trodden by fellow foragers and hunters. Here, the forest was placid, the creatures commonplace. The mushrooms perfectly ordinary and delicious in a stew. Finally, Jasper slowed to an agreeable pace. He gave a single shake of his head. 'I do not wish for you to be anywhere near this—'

'This is not the time to be a lone wolf—'

'It's too dangerous,' Jasper said softly, cutting a glance at her. 'I don't want it on my conscience if you come to harm.'

Well, that was unexpected. Still, Thea did not relent. 'You're powerful, are you not?' she asked, bolder in her determination.

'Yes—'

'How powerful?'

Jasper stopped, turning to face her. 'Too powerful to fall prey to whatever game you're playing here.'

Thea lifted her chin. 'Then you can make sure I won't come to any harm.'

He gave a dry laugh. 'You, Theodora, have trouble written into your bones. Every time I see you, I am reminded of what an impossible task I took on the day you became contracted to me.'

'Fine.' Thea walked away, taking another path home. 'Then I will have to attend the meeting and investigate by myself.'

'Thea,' he called, exasperation etched into her name. 'Theodora, it is *not* safe out here in the dark!'

'I am not the defenceless creature you imagine me to be,' Thea called over her shoulder. 'Do not make the mistake of underestimating me. I will not be caged for your comfort.'

He stopped following her then.

'Send me a raven when you arrive home,' he ordered. 'Do you hear me? I want to know the minute you get back safely.'

Thea waved a hand, though she had not one intention of following his orders. She needed to attend the Magic Quarter meeting and decide her next move. Because no matter what Jasper thought, she would not be sitting idly in her apothecary waiting for the wards to shatter and the next threat to land at her doorstep. She would be hunting them down herself.

CHAPTER

Thirteen

WHEN THEA RETURNED to the Magic Quarter, she went directly to the Lantern. Dusk stained the sky like blackberry cordial and a weather-witch stood in the centre of the street, holding her hands out to conjure a single flame of witch light that flitted from street lamp to street lamp, lighting each one. After exchanging brief pleasantries with the witch, Thea let herself into the Lantern. There, she was not the only one feeling out of sorts.

'What's wrong?' she asked Zofka, who was sitting in the comfiest chair, looking more frazzled than usual.

'I've caught something.' Zofka's sigh was heavy enough to loosen some of the flour in her chestnut ringlets. It dusted the table between them like a fine layer of snow.

Thea turned back towards the door. 'I'll go and fetch my lemon and fire-ginger tonic.'

'No, no, no.' Zofka waved her back over. 'I've caught a spirit.'

Talibah ventured over with a tray, upon which sat her polished silver teapot. Gifted with second sight since birth, Talibah could see traces of magic woven through the world. This gift, combined with her penchant for travelling, meant she had a habit of stumbling across enchanted objects. From a candle whose light would never die, to shoes that changed size depending on the wearer. But the women's favourite was this teapot that Zofka had poured her signature hot chocolate into one day, only to discover that the teapot returned many, many cups. More than Zofka had made by far. It was still going to this day, some four years later, and she had never needed to refill it yet. Nor was it anything other than the perfect sipping temperature. Talibah held it aloft now, pausing to consider Zofka. 'Like a ghost?'

'Not *like* a ghost. An actual once-living, no-longer-breathing ghost. A spirit, a phantom, and now the bane of my bakery.' Zofka flopped her head back, gesturing at the teapot Talibah held. 'Forget the cup, I'm going to need the biggest hot chocolate you can pour.'

Talibah obliged.

Thea flumped down in a neighbouring chair. It had been a long afternoon and her headache was creeping back with a vengeance.

'His name is Radim,' Zofka continued, shooting Talibah a grateful look as she handed her a small bowl of hot chocolate. 'And he's rather lovely, only he has such suggestions and won't stop meddling with my recipes.' Zofka pinched the bridge of her nose. 'We haven't had any hauntings in the Quarter for decades – spirits prefer human homes.'

'Really?' Thea accepted her own cup from Talibah with a smile of thanks. 'Even ghosts of magical folk?'

'The wards mostly keep them all out,' Talibah informed her, coming to sit down. 'Something about the clashing energy between the two. Now and then a persistent one slips through, though.'

Zofka groaned.

Thea exchanged a baffled look with Talibah. 'Perhaps a banishment—' Thea began.

'Oh, I couldn't! He's admitted that baking was his lifelong dream. I can't take that away from him now, he's already lost his life, the poor thing. It isn't his fault that he died in such a ghastly manner, all that blood, you know.' Zofka pulled a face, picking up her hot chocolate and taking a deep, gratifying gulp, seemingly immune to Thea and Talibah gaping at her. 'Such a shame. I really think that the customers would enjoy chatting to him if they gave him half a chance.'

'I . . . I don't know what to suggest,' Talibah said.

'Me either,' Thea admitted.

'Well, enough about me, how's your headache?' Zofka turned to Thea.

Thea grimaced. 'It ebbs and flows, but it hasn't gone yet.' She hadn't told them that she was suspicious that it was linked to refusing prices for her fate-weaving; if Jasper found out, she would incur his wrath upon herself and herself alone. What they didn't know, they couldn't be blamed for.

'Still?' Talibah frowned behind her cup.

Zofka raised her eyebrows. A fleck of cream graced her pert nose. 'Even after those biscuits I baked for you?' She *tsked*. 'You should mention it at the meeting, see if anyone has had anything similar. Ah, I see Rose already.' Looking through the window, she jumped up, knocking her bowl over. Chocolate spilled everywhere. Talibah and Thea leapt for cloths but Zofka flicked her fingers and it vanished. She pushed her bowl, now empty, towards Talibah, who refilled it automatically. 'Keep it coming; I'm going to need buckets of chocolate to get through this meeting.'

Thea, Talibah and Zofka, teapot of hot chocolate in hand, walked down the street to the Gingerbread House, where the residents of the Magic Quarter were amassing quicker than last time, as if they sensed the growing threat. Zofka placated them with endless cups of hot chocolate and Rose glowered any time someone pointed out how much nicer the café was as a meeting venue over the the Rose Basket. Poor sunflower-allergic Sarah, who could shift into a beautiful black cat with silky fur, bore the brunt of most of those glares.

'—and the *hot chocolate*,' Zdenka gushed.

'That's it.' Rose stood. 'Thea has been waiting to speak for yonks, I suggest you listen to her.' She beckoned Thea up.

Thea told the congregated magical folk everything she'd recently remembered about her eavesdropping in the forest, near the Crossroads. How she suspected the unknown bragging fate-weaver was to blame for their failing wards, and that they'd been riling up the Hunters and informing them that the Magic Quarter existed, though for what purpose she couldn't guess – and worse, how she'd immediately forgotten everything she'd overheard and didn't know why.

'By chance, did you encounter any *bludička* on your travels?' Paní Dagmar enquired, scooping the cream off her hot chocolate with a spoon and slurping it up like one of Rose's spring-cleaning tulips.

'Yes, the fate-weavers sent them after me,' Thea exclaimed. 'How could you have possibly known that?'

'Ah, they're tricksy little sprites. Some call them memory thieves.' She waved her cream-flecked spoon at Thea. 'That'll be why you forgot what you overheard. Not to worry though, their effects are temporary, they wear off with time.'

'So, they're different to my missing memories then?' Thea said dryly.

'Very,' Paní Dagmar enthused.

'Any time you'd like me to consult my crystal ball on your behalf—' Zdenka began, but Talibah shook her head at them. She and Zofka were well used to evading the well-meaning but usually unwanted offers from the rest of the Magic Quarter when it came to Thea's missing memories.

The alpha of the vulpine shape-shifters stood. 'While the wards are down, we'll be starting dawn and dusk patrols to ensure the safety of the Magic Quarter, particularly since one of our own has been threatened now, too.' He nodded to Thea before sitting back down amidst his skulk.

'Oh, thank you,' Thea said, touched. 'I haven't found anything that might help repair the wards in my Compendium,' she admitted, 'Has anyone else had any luck?'

Talibah frowned. 'Not yet, though I'm sure it's just a matter of sifting through the material. If I were to have a few volunteers—'

'I'll help,' Gretel offered.

Zdenka, dressed in viridian green, raised a hand. 'Count me in, too.'

'Thank you,' Talibah told them.

'Have any of you witches had any luck in assessing the wards?' Thea asked, though she wasn't quite certain what that might entail. Whoever the group of witches or fate-weavers had been that had conjured it into place, their magic was immense, fabricated into such an intricate lacework of stitches and knots and graceful tangles that Thea couldn't understand it one bit.

A couple of weather-witches detailed their experiments with bolstering the wards, but it seemed they'd only caused adverse weather patterns.

Zofka shrugged as she topped up Rose's hot chocolate. 'What am I going to do, throw a biscuit at it?'

'Well, Jasper's looking into it,' Thea said without thinking.

Zofka's hot chocolate ran over the lip of Rose's cup and over the table as everyone began speaking at once. Swirling her fingers, Zofka caught the escaping hot chocolate and reversed the spill's direction, pouring it back into the teapot.

A pixie hid behind one of the cups on their table, the shape-shifters growled in response, and Rose pursed her mouth. 'I don't think that's a good idea,' she said pointedly.

'For once, I agree with her,' Zdenka added.

Thea suffered an unexpected pang of sadness on Jasper's behalf. She couldn't stop dwelling on how she'd found him kneeling in the forest with a handful of crushed wildflowers, surrendering to grief. How he'd quietly stated nobody would attend the meeting if he had come. She swallowed hard. 'He's more powerful than I am, perhaps he could—'

'If your information is correct, it was a fate-weaver who got us into this mess to begin with,' Rose said hotly, Zdenka nodding along. 'They can't be trusted. Have you considered that Lord Stiltskin may be behind all of this?'

Thea's heart-spell gave a fierce flicker. 'I don't think so,' she said thoughtfully. 'His apothecary is in the Magic Quarter and that's been affected by the failing wards too, with the crack running through our ceiling. No, he'd lose a considerable investment . . . It just doesn't make sense.'

'Fate-weavers can't be trusted,' a weather-witch said. 'They walk around like gods with all that power at their fingertips, it isn't right. They're dangerous.'

Thea's cheeks were beginning to warm. She knew the other Quarter folk didn't take issue with her using Jasper's power – or if they did, they'd never voiced it, since she herself was only human, a mere conduit – but it rankled all the same. Jasper's power was *her* power and yes, it could be terrifying what he was capable of but she'd also seen how much that power had helped countless people. 'But his involvement doesn't make sense – if he meant the Quarter any harm, he never could have opened an apothecary here. This is a pointless vendetta and we don't want to waste time investigating dead ends.'

'Thea's right,' Paní Dagmar piped up. 'Jasper's a sweetheart, he wouldn't have done this.'

Thea stared at the ancient witch.

'A *sweetheart?*' Zofka asked, holding the teapot in mid-air.

'Of course,' Paní Dagmar chuckled. 'He's an old friend of mine. I've lived in this Quarter for over five hundred years, you know.'

Rose kneaded her forehead. 'Paní Dagmar, it's near impossible for witches to live that long—'

Paní Dagmar raised her cup of hot chocolate as if it was champagne. 'That's why it's a good idea to befriend a fate-weaver, dear.'

Thea's lips twitched despite herself.

'Right.' Rose closed her eyes for a beat. 'Well,' she said on opening them again, having composed herself. 'Now that we have volunteers to go through all our material, we can find the answers faster . . .'

'What about Pan Novak?' Zdenka interrupted. 'What should we do about him?'

Rose sighed. 'He's human. We repair the wards and he and his Hunters can no longer even enter. Neither can these fate-weavers. But if we fight back now, we run the risk of bringing a greater threat down on our shoulders.'

'I agree,' Talibah added. 'More research and twice-daily patrols seem our best options.'

'I could always . . . intercede.' Wojslav's hint of a smile bared his elongated canines.

'I'd let you feast away on him if I didn't think there'd be a line of other Hunters in the wings, waiting to step into his shoes,' Rose told him.

The meeting took a while to disperse as it was drizzling outside, and the magical folk were reluctant to leave the biscuit-scented warmth and endless hot chocolates of the café. Eventually Zofka retired the magical teapot and they left. Thea, Talibah and Zofka stretched out, as Zofka wondered aloud if she should bake singing gingerbread people or if that was a bad idea, if her spirit would ever haunt another café, and whether or not Talibah ought to get a cat. Sarah, the feline shape-shifter with a serious sunflower allergy, rehomed all kinds of lost animals at her sanctuary, World of Whiskers, and had recently had an influx of kittens with white socks.

But eventually, Thea's head ground back to the same worry she'd entered the meeting with. 'The fate-weaver mentioned another prolific Hunter, but we've only seen Pan Novak,' she thought out loud. 'Should we be investigating who the other one is? They claimed it was a city councillor.'

Talibah turned to her. 'You need to be careful. Those notes, that raven—'

'Biscuit,' Thea said automatically.

'Biscuit,' Talibah continued. 'Someone wants you to be afraid.'

Zofka set her hands on her hips. 'Then we won't rest until we get to the bottom of this.'

CHAPTER

Fourteen

THEA WAS READING in the bath when an idea for Malek's key popped into her head: a spirit could cross thresholds without a key. And she was certain she had just the right thing to represent a spirit. Somewhere.

She sat up, dislodging the garden of rose petals scattered in her copper tub. Periwinkle bubbles floated up to the ceiling, each one the size of her head, conjured with fresh lavender and a breath of spring air from a weather-witch. Neither had worked: her head still pounded. But she was on a time limit to forge Malek's key and it wasn't as if she would have been able to sleep anyway.

Setting *Eudora and the Ship's Captain* out of the bubbles' reach, Thea dried in a hurry and pulled on a nightgown, ignoring her hair, damp and curling at the ends. As she padded downstairs, barefoot, lantern in hand, Cinnamon hopped along at her heels, nose twitching with delight at being allowed along on her night-time secret.

The apothecary was best at the witching hour, when Thea's sole company was her rabbit and the swollen moon with its baleful glow. When the contents of her bottles and vials gently twinkled and rustled in the lantern's path. The floorboards were cold against her bare feet but there was something freeing in only wearing her soft white nightgown when all the windows peered out onto a sleeping street.

'Where did I put it?' She slid out boxes and jars in her back room. 'Ah, here.' It was at the back of a drawer, beneath a large cobalt snail shell hiding it like a coffin: a dead man's finger bone. '*You* are going to be my key.'

Perhaps she didn't need the other ingredients after all; perhaps having this as her physical key, with a little extra magic and fate's embroidery, would be sufficient. Then she wouldn't have to worry about confronting a lake spirit, let alone finding a lake in that nightmare-inducing part of the forest.

Reaching for the jar she'd stashed the silver-dapples in, Thea pulled half of the glowing fungi out, pausing to admire their light before she crushed them with her pestle and mortar. Thea's hands and thoughts fell into a dance, slow and rhythmic. When the mushrooms had been reduced to a luminous powder, Thea added rose water and a single fairy's tear and gave it a brisk stir, until it took on the consistency of melted silver. She popped the finger bone inside the bowl of liquid.

It was as Thea was watching the bone soak in that magical mix that it occurred to her: she had *power*. Her bones were soaked in Jasper's power; she should be able to do anything she set her mind to. Including solving the trouble settling over the Magic Quarter like a belligerent shadow. She did not need Jasper's help nor his permission for that; she might be his apprentice, but she had made the apothecary a success all by herself. She had friends, a life in the Quarter. And he did not live here – his townhouse was buried in the foothills of the castle.

Perhaps if she was able to make this key for Malek, to allow him to enter anywhere without trace, she could make the *inverse* for the Magic Quarter. Some kind of key that would lock them all away safely.

Pulling out her leather-bound journal, she reached for a fresh quill and a pot of her favourite sapphire ink and jotted down some notes while the bone bathed in forest magic. First, she methodically described what she was making now, before working out her thoughts on creating a key that could be used for protection.

When she'd finished spilling her thoughts and ideas across the pages of her journal, Thea pulled the bone out. It gleamed like a jewel. Now to harness fate. Sharpening her focus, Thea relaxed her gaze, waiting for fate to make itself visible.

The pain in her head surged, sending nausea writhing through her stomach, but she had to get this key forged. She'd already kept Malek waiting long enough and the situation with his sister couldn't be getting better. She couldn't wait until her headache went. No little part of her also relished the idea of having an excuse to send Malek a raven to come and collect the key in the morning; she hadn't seen him since the opera, and their kiss.

Shoving the pain into the darkest crevices of her head, Thea concentrated on the threads. They appeared and vanished, slipping in and out of view as Thea struggled to hold on to them. Gritting her teeth with the effort, she gave it everything she had, and suddenly they blazed to life. Thea wove fate around the glowing finger bone, tying intricate knots to alter its shape, turning it into a skeleton key. Her energy ebbed but she refused to stop, reaching down into that well of borrowed power pooled in her marrow, forcing the spell binding her chest together in blood and bone to tick harder, faster, to keep up with the fate she was altering.

The apothecary door swung open as if it had not been locked for hours and Jasper strode through, an argument already spilling from his tongue, 'What part of *send me a raven* did you not comprehend—' When he caught sight of Thea, elbow deep in a magic more powerful than any she'd ever conjured before, the words died in his mouth.

'What do you think you are doing?' he growled.

Thea knotted strands around the key, giving the holder the power to open any door, to remain unseen as though they were a spirit passing between walls. But when she let go, the key turned dull, returning to bone.

'It didn't work,' Thea gasped. 'Why didn't it work?' The spell holding her together gave a weak patter. 'Oh,' she said stupidly, feeling the floor undulate, as if she was standing on honey rather than oak. She staggered to her counter.

'What is it?' Jasper asked, appearing at her side, his hands slightly outstretched towards her though reserved as usual, he did not touch her.

'The spell you made me.' Thea clasped her chest. 'I think it's giving out.'

She was vaguely aware of Jasper calling her name, sharp with alarm, before the fog rose and swallowed her whole.

Something cold touched Thea's lips. She closed her mouth, refusing it entry. 'Drink this,' a familiar voice ordered.

'No,' she murmured, unsure if she'd spoken aloud until the voice sighed.

'Why must you always be so stubborn?' Jasper grumbled.

Thea cracked open an eye. She was lying on the apothecary floor with Jasper peering down at her. Her head was cradled in his lap. His large hands wrapped around her, holding her tight and safe and warm. Which was strange. If she hated him, why did he make her feel so safe? He was bent over her, his jawline stubbled. 'Drink.' Jasper lifted the cold vial to her mouth once more.

It looked like molten diamonds, glimmering with fate. It looked beautiful. It looked like something from another realm.

Her head roiled with pain. Intense, skull-shattering pain that washed over her in a wave she couldn't withstand. Clamping her hands to her temples, she screamed, arching her back as it possessed her whole. Jasper didn't wait for permission before tipping the elixir down her throat.

Liquid warmth spread through her chest, sunrise creeping through her veins. Like magic, her headache vanished at once. Sweetness lingered on her tongue. It was chased by awareness. She'd never been this close to Jasper before, never felt him wrapped around her, never stared back into his gaze and seen how deep those blue eyes ran, like an unending sky washed clean by a storm. What worlds had those eyes seen? What unimaginable horizons had Jasper been born to?

She leaped up, breaking that contact between them. The second she left his arms, she was colder. Less . . . secure. A tinge of regret chased it that she did not wish to examine. 'What did you give me?'

Jasper rose to his feet. 'You told me that business was slow, not that you hadn't been taking prices for your weaving.' Outside, a thunderclap as loud as a breaking heart punctured his words. Cinnamon came running, paws scrabbling in his panic to reach Thea. Thea wrapped her arms around him and lifted him, holding him snug against her chest as Jasper looked at them. 'Is that – a rabbit?'

'Business *has* been slow. It has been since the Hunters started investigating.' Giving Cinnamon a kiss on the nose, Thea let him back down again. He scampered away. 'But that wasn't the whole truth. I'm sick of exploiting people. I have power, I can help them, why should I have to charge them for that? You told me that it was to balance fate, to keep time intact, but I haven't taken a price in weeks and the world hasn't ended yet.'

Jasper stared silently back at her, his face set harder than stone. 'You collapsed, Thea. Fate took its price from *you*. If I hadn't entered when I did, then I do not know how much more it would have taken.'

Thea swallowed hard. 'Did I break the wards?' she whispered. If it had been her fault that the Hunters had invaded their lives, she didn't know how to forgive herself. 'I worried it was me . . .' Her eyes drifted to the cracked ceiling. 'But the Crypt was damaged before the apothecary ceiling cracked, remember? And that was before I refused my first price.'

'Really?' Jasper's stony frown was unyielding, the tension between them cut deep as a ravine. 'Then it cannot have been you.' He sighed. 'I don't understand why you felt the need to test this. I explained the balance of fate-weaving in depth many times before I gave you free rein with the apothecary.'

'It started with a girl.' Thea's throat thickened. 'There was something familiar about her. I thought she could have been . . .' She shook her head. 'I just couldn't take her price. When nothing happened, I distrusted you.'

The street lamps and candles extinguished as one, sending them plunging into darkness. Thea gasped, gripping the countertop.

'It is only a storm, it will pass,' Jasper said.

The moon dangling down from the ceiling glowed dimly, the sole lantern in this sudden night.

Iced arrows flew at the windowpane. When Thea went to look out of the window, the world was painted a fierce white, hurling snow down with a vengeance. Jasper came and stood beside her, watching the Magic Quarter slowly disappear behind a blanket of snow.

Her heart-spell gave a weak flutter; there was no way Jasper could battle through such a blizzard anytime soon.

They were trapped here together.

'Oh no,' Thea sighed bitterly.

CHAPTER

Fifteen

HEN JASPER FACED Thea, he was already scowling. 'Am I so terrible?' His voice was soft. 'Do you truly hate the very sight of me?'

'You took my heart!' The words exploded from Thea like lightning. 'I have no memories. I cannot love. I do not even know my own name. Do you really expect me to rejoice in your presence?'

Jasper stared at her, his throat working hard. The pale moonlight illuminated his cheekbones and silvered his eyes. 'We made a deal,' he said gravely. 'You may not remember it, but you chose this. I took nothing from you that you didn't want to give.'

Defiance ignited within Thea. 'That was seven years ago! I am different now. I do not want this.'

'You cannot reforge a deal simply because you have regrets,' he bit back. 'We all have regrets we must live with – it is the way of the world.'

'Spoken like a man with experience.' Thea folded her arms. This hugged her nightgown closer, making her aware of how little she was wearing and the way that the moonlight illuminated her generous curves through the thin material.

Jasper's eyes darkened. A lock of his hair escaped over his left temple. Thea's heart-spell twitched as the usually every-strand-perfectly-in place Jasper started to come unbound.

'Why must you insist on hating me?' he asked hoarsely.

'Because I do not trust you.'

Jasper gestured at the records on the counter. 'You are the one who has broken my trust.'

'Good. Then our hatred is mutual.'

They glared at each other, a question flaming between them, heating the air, demanding to be answered.

Jasper stepped closer. 'Fine.'

Thea raised her chin, her chest rising and falling faster with her fury.

'Fine,' she whispered.

Then Jasper reached for her, his hand grasping her waist, roughly clenching the nightgown she wore as if he wanted to tear it from her. Thea shivered, picturing his lips on her mouth. What would it be like to kiss him? Would he taste as wild as the scent that clung to his collar, his hair?

'Are you still seeing that man?' Jasper's voice was gravel.

'I am.' She refused to apologise. 'He's kind and caring and—'

Jasper's hand was warm through her thin nightgown. How had she ever considered him cold when there was this *heat* running through him?

'And?' he prompted, his dark stare never once leaving her eyes. He looked at her as if he never wanted to stop. As if this storm could cleave the world apart and they would still be standing there, in the blistering ruins, with his eyes locked on her. Hoarfrost crackled along the windowpanes, devouring the glass.

Thea ran her tongue over her lip. Jasper's stare dropped to her mouth. 'And he's nice to me,' she finished weakly.

'I can be nice.'

'No, you can't.' Thea's breath hitched. 'You're not nice.'

'No, I'm not,' Jasper agreed. 'But I know exactly what you want. What you need.'

'And what's that?'

'*Me.*' His hand still clenching her nightgown, he pulled her towards him and kissed her.

Thea's lips parted in surprise. She shouldn't want this. His arms wrapped around her back, pulling her tighter towards him. His mouth was softer, warmer than she could have imagined. Suddenly, she couldn't remember a single reason why this was a terrible idea. She kissed him back. Jasper moaned into her mouth as she responded, kissing her more urgently, his stubble brushing against her, sending lightning rushing through her veins, thunder cleaving the skies open outside as he broke her world apart and reforged it. She grabbed the front of his shirt, rising onto her toes as their kiss became more fervent. Jasper's hands slid up to Thea's neck and tangled in her loose hair, and she melted into his burning heat as he tasted her, seeking more, more, more, more. He was dark, wild, delicious, and she never wanted to stop.

Her back bumped against the counter. They paused, staring at each other, wide-eyed and breathless. Jasper's hair was windswept, his collar undone.

'Jasper,' she whispered, his name filled with a stark wanting that might have embarrassed her if she hadn't seen that same need reflected in him.

Quick as another flash of lightning, Jasper lifted Thea onto the countertop, her nightgown riding up her thighs. She clamped them around his hips, pulling him closer as their mouths met, their kiss turning fierce.

'Gods, Thea,' he groaned as she pressed against him, burying her hands in his hair. He braced himself on the counter as she wrapped herself around him, losing herself in his kiss.

Something clattered to the floor.

'Leave that,' Thea sighed into his mouth.

Jasper bent to retrieve it. It was her journal.

'That's not important,' Thea said quickly, breathlessly. Her lips were cold with the lack of him.

Jasper frowned as he looked at the journal, realising what she had written there: the list of ingredients for Malek's key, along with her ideas on where to procure them. Her idea of creating the inverse of that key to protect the Magic Quarter. 'When did you write this?' he demanded.

'This evening,' she admitted.

'You are still planning to go foraging near the Crossroads?' Jasper stared at Thea, his mouth swollen, his hair in disarray after she'd plundered both. 'After I just warned you to stay far from there?'

Thea's fingertips rested on her bruised lips, her breath ragged, her thoughts turned inside out by the man she hated who'd made her feel things she couldn't remember ever having felt before. 'Surprisingly, I do not heed your every word, especially when you don't bother to answer any questions I have or explain anything I should know.'

Jasper touched his temple as if she'd pained him.

Thea couldn't help laughing. 'If that irritates you then imagine how I feel, left in the dark, never knowing anything but always wondering. Who was I before I knocked on the back door of that apothecary? What happened to me that I wanted to give my heart and life in exchange for ridding myself of my memories? Every single last memory. And why were you the one to take them?' she added. 'Why not whoever was here before me?'

Jasper closed her journal, replacing it atop the counter. He did not resume his position between her thighs, nor did he move further away. They were at a stalemate. Becoming aware of that distance between them, Thea tugged her nightgown back down over her knees. 'Yours was an unusual request,' he said quietly. 'Too advanced for my previous apprentice.' He raked his hair back. 'I couldn't risk your heart like that.'

Thea's heart-spell flickered. As if it knew they were discussing it. 'Why did I give it up?'

Jasper's chest rose and fell. 'I cannot tell you that. I cannot break our bargain.'

'Will I ever get it back?' Thea whispered. 'Will I ever be able to leave?'

Jasper closed his eyes for a beat. 'When you guess your true name, your memories – and your heart – will return and you will no longer be bound to the apothecary.'

Thea took a ragged breath. 'It's been seven years. If I haven't guessed it—'

'Don't stop,' Jasper said fiercely. 'You must never stop guessing, never give up hope.'

'All right.' Thea's heart-spell flickering harder as she stared at him. 'I won't.' Either she was delirious, or Jasper *wanted* her to break the spell. Her understanding of who he was suddenly . . . shifted as all her thoughts and recollections reframed themselves.

Jasper's hand flexed on the countertop beside her. 'Good. As for your predecessor, she left shortly before you arrived needing a place to stay.' His jaw ticked. 'I am not the monster you assume I am. Each one of my apprentices came here looking for a new beginning. They, like you, needed this. But you must stay out of the forest. If you need something, you ask me, and I will retrieve it for you.' He fixed her with a curious look. 'Tell me more about this key; what were the customer's parameters?'

Thea explained how Malek had requested the key. What his wishes were. Jasper listened so attentively, withholding any judgement, that she then broached her theory about crafting the opposite to bolster the wards. 'You read my thoughts about both in my notebook, what do you think?'

'The key is a complex bit of magic,' Jasper said approvingly. 'Your skills are improving, but I'm afraid creating the inverse of it will not help the Magic Quarter; the original ward was interwoven with the buildings itself, forging a liminal space where the Quarter can expand as much as needed over the years, preserving its shops and homes and streets. Yours was a valiant idea, but we must repair the original ward.'

Thea must have looked disappointed, for Jasper apologised.

'Do you know who made the original wards?' she asked.

'They were made by a fate-weaver, centuries ago. One that I am not in contact with, or I would have reached out to them by now. It's their greatest legacy, creating a safe, secret space for an entire Quarter. We must find a way to ensure it continues.'

'We will,' Thea said softly.

The blizzard was breathing its dying gasp outside, a weakened wind rattling the street lamps, the thunder and lightning long faded away. They were no longer trapped together, and though realising that would have filled Thea with cheer not an hour earlier, now she noted the storm's end with despondence.

Jasper made to leave.

'Wait,' Thea clasped his wrist.

Jasper turned back, a pinprick of hope shining through him, one that made Thea's breath catch in her throat. She hopped down from the counter and looked up at him. 'I need a fingernail from a lake spirit.'

Jasper rubbed his forehead with a groan. 'Lake spirits are notorious for needing their own space. The only way to retrieve one of their nails is if it becomes embedded in your flesh when they attack you.'

Thea winced. 'Do you have one?' she asked hopefully. 'I need it for the key.'

'Unfortunately, I do,' Jasper said darkly. 'I'll bring it tomorrow.'

'Jasper—'

'Tomorrow.' His voice roughened. 'I swear I will bring it tomorrow, but it's growing late and—' he swallowed.

'And what?'

'And we don't want a . . . repeat occurrence,' he said, looking at her mouth. 'This should never have happened.'

Thea bit her lip, unable to help noticing how Jasper tracked her teeth sinking into her bottom lip. 'No, we don't want that.'

'We are entirely unsuited to each other.' Jasper's voice was still rough, though it lifted at the end like a question. Just enough to betray him.

'Horribly unsuited,' she whispered.

If he wasn't going to voice that he felt something, then neither would she.

He gave a sharp nod. 'Then we are agreed. Goodnight, Theodora.'

'Cassandra,' she said.

He blinked, unfollowing.

'Is my name Cassandra?' she repeated.

'It is not.'

He walked out into the softening snowfall. Thea headed to the stairs alone, pausing to lift Cinnamon into her arms, before she returned to her little home overlooking the frosted oak trees, and slept at last. The last thing she saw before she fell into a dream was how Jasper had looked down at her when she'd come round, his sapphire-blue eyes more anguished than she'd ever remembered seeing them.

CHAPTER

Sixteen

I WAS GOING TO send you a raven,' Thea said when Malek strolled into the apothecary the following afternoon.

He shivered, buttoning his thick navy coat. Everyone was feeling the after-effects of the blizzard, theorising on whose magic might have caused it. Wojslav had been overheard blaming Rose, who'd then further irked the grumpy vampire by sending an army of sunflowers marching on the Crypt in a moment of petty revenge. Sarah, who'd been shopping there for new cat beds, had run out in a flurry of sneezes. Zofka had sent several ravens soaring over to Thea, updating her on the feud.

Thea had kept quiet on her encounter during the storm, though it wouldn't be long before either Zofka or Talibah wrangled it from her. Jasper had stalked through her dreams until she'd woken sweating and confused. But, no. She refused to think of him that way. No matter how many times their kiss played through her thoughts. She had Malek. And, besides, she and Jasper were wrong for each other in every way. He had carried away her box in a heart and she had spent the past seven years hating him.

'Then it seems I had the right idea coming in here today.' Malek lifted his hand, revealing a bouquet of roses. Their petals were velvety and white as new snow. When Thea ran a finger over them, they fluttered and giggled as if she'd tickled them.

'Would you do me the honour of accompanying me to the annual

Winter Ball? It's being held in the Spanish Hall at the castle this year.'

'I would be delighted.' Thea smiled at the roses. They bore a wild sweetness with a dark undertone, one that reminded her of long, late autumnal walks. And something else, which she couldn't place.

Malek's chest puffed up. 'Then that makes two of us,' he told her. Tapping the bouquet, he added, 'Apparently these are meant to smell of your favourite memory, but all I get is freshly baked bread so maybe it's just your favourite smell.' He laughed. 'What do you smell?'

Thea's smile strained. 'The forest,' she lied slowly, placing the scent at last: the air before a storm, an evening surrendering to night. It was Jasper. Ignoring her snarling guilt, she set the roses down on her countertop, the same one that Jasper had lifted her up onto last night. No. She banished the thought, forcing herself to concentrate on Malek.

'And speaking of gifts, I have something to tell you.'

Malek's face softened with hope. 'You have finished it?'

'Almost. I need a couple more ingredients, but I am very much hoping to have it for you the night of the ball.'

Provided this second attempt actually worked. And Jasper kept his promise; she'd been waiting for him to appear all day, jolting each time the bells rang but he hadn't yet darkened her door.

'How are things with Lord Stiltskin?' Malek asked, glancing over his shoulder as if he'd heard her thinking about him.

'The same as usual. I only see him when he deigns to appear,' Thea told him.

Malek looked curious. 'Do you never visit him in the castle district?'

'No,' Thea said, frowning a little. 'Why do you ask?'

Malek dimpled at her. 'I confess that I would quite like to live there: it's a beautiful neighbourhood. I wonder if I have ever passed his house? It must be grand, if a lord lives there.' Catching Thea's frown, he changed the subject. 'Though this Quarter seems far more interesting than the rest of Prague. When I walked through today, there were kittens everywhere.'

Thea laughed. 'It is one of my favourite places. How is your sister? I am sorrier than you could know that I haven't been able to make this key faster—'

'I have been able to send word that help is forthcoming. She is . . . hopeful, for the first time in a while. As am I.' Malek's dimple deepened. 'All thanks to you.' Closing the distance between them, he cupped her face, his thumb brushing against her cheek.

Her guilt surged back as she smiled at him. 'Then I will see you at the ball?'

'I will come for you in my carriage,' he promised.

When Malek left, the apothecary descended into silence. Thea coaxed her fire to burn brighter, to chase away the lingering cold snap. Outside, the Magic Quarter was worryingly empty. Not a pixie nor a kitten wandered past. The oaks groaned under the weight of the icicles dripping from them, the cobblestones looked like Zofka's kitchen after she'd dropped a bag of flour, and the witch light gourds seemed to be snarling more than yesterday.

Thea toyed with the fraying edge of one of her sleeves, hoping that the lack of customers had more to do with the frigid air blasting down the street than – *Pan Novak*. He was back.

Stepping back from the window, Thea observed discreetly as Pan Novak marched through the Magic Quarter, flanked by five Hunters. In their solemn attire and grey wigs, they looked like ghouls.

Zofka and Rose emerged from their doors, keeping a wary eye out.

As the Hunters neared Stiltskin's Apothecary, the moon light slowly dimmed, and the elixirs, which were usually fond of glowing or chiming like bells, dulled and silenced. From the backroom came the unmistakable sound of an apple falling. But they were not the intended target today.

Pan Novak marched straight past the apothecary, past the Rose Basket, and into Fleur's lilac-painted establishment.

'She's not going to like that,' Thea murmured to her empty shop floor, watching as Zofka and Rose's postures eased. If anyone wasn't going to need back up, it was Fleur.

It began with a snap.

Lingering by her window, Thea braced, half expecting to see a bullet shoot past or the sky crack open with lightning. Instead, a Hunter ran past, yelling for help as a whalebone corset snapped its supportive bones one at a time, wrapping itself around his face. Seconds later, another Hunter fled after the first, pursued by an army of stockings and stays, lashing out with every strap, lace and ribbon. The other three Hunters cut a swift exit, amid a quartet of wide gowns charging down the Quarter, and finally, Pan Novak marched back the way he came, his scowl fiercer than the petticoats that swirled around him like belligerent clouds.

As he passed the apothecary, he turned his head and stared straight through Thea's window. His eyes were blank, shrouding any lick of emotion, though his mouth gave a single twitch of displeasure.

Thea shivered.

The Quarter descended back into chilled silence. Thea poured a cup of spiced apple and cinnamon tea. In an effort to cheer herself, she read another piece of the story in the margins of her Compendium:

Home is becoming a battlefield. More and more, I steal away to the forest, where he is always waiting. He worries for me. Wishes for us to leave, asks me when he can whisk me away to other, far-flung places. The worlds are wide, he says, and we have seen so very little of them. Imagine seeing them together. Imagine everything opening to us like a flower in bloom. Imagine being together every day and never fearing that we will be torn apart. It sounds like a beautiful dream, but I am fearful it will remain ever that – only a dream.

A tapping at the door summoned Thea back to the present moment. When she opened the door, a raven flew through, delivering a note from Zofka:

That was the most delicious thing I've seen all day!

Thea had barely finished reading it when a second raven knocked on the window with its beak, bearing Zofka's next thought:

Do you think this is the end of the Magic Quarter?

Thea scribbled an emphatic *No!* on the same scroll before dispatching the raven back to Zofka. Sipping her spiced tea, she watched as flakes of snow lazily fell from the sky to rest, undisturbed, on the near-empty street.

Thea woke with a start. The hour was late, the moonlight slanting across the floorboards, the apothecary quiet. Jasper still hadn't come with the promised fingernail, and Thea couldn't wait any longer. Impatience pricked at her.

Restless, she dashed across the street to the Lantern, in a bid to find some more reading material, since she'd already devoured half of *Eudora and the Ship's Captain*.

For once, the soft rainbow of lanternlight did nothing to soothe Thea's internal maelstrom. Talibah, luminous in a teal dress and matching headscarf, was busy with a pair of shape-shifters – a couple who changed into a hawk and a falcon and, Thea had been told, had fallen in love in the skies.

'Have you noticed anything strange in the forest when you've flown over lately?' Thea interrupted to ask.

The couple shook their heads before resuming their conversation.

Thea grabbed a map from the pile of enchanted parchments and ducked through the gnarled wooden door at the back of the shop.

With a sigh, a long row of candelabras ignited, illuminating floor-to-ceiling shelves in every direction beneath a slanted wooden ceiling. Stairs wound down to deeper levels, carved out from the liminal space in which the Magic Quarter hid.

Thea closed her eyes and took a deep breath; there was nothing better than the smell of books. New books with crisp ink type, old books with fusty pages, endless scrolls of even older tales with crumbling words.

Distant conversation echoed through the maze of shelves, interspersed with the odd squeak from a passing bookworm. Opening her eyes, Thea consulted the map. It was an aged sprawl of parchment, thick and yellowed at the edges, its enchantment carrying the scent of spice markets and faraway moons. Talibah had found these maps many years ago, slumbering in an abandoned crate of trinkets for sale in Cairo. She'd held onto them as she wandered the world, until she'd collected enough books to cobble her bookshop together.

As Thea watched the map, it revealed an arrow. 'Come on, take me to something good,' she pleaded. 'I want to read a love story that will sweep me off my feet and make me forget about *him*.'

The arrow danced forwards. And Thea followed.

Its path wended through shelves until Thea couldn't have found her own way back to the main front of the Lantern if her life depended on it. But this? The promise that the map would lead you to the book your heart desired to read above all else – that was well worth getting lost for. She followed each curve of the arrow's path, pacing past shelves, anticipation trilling in her veins as the titles blurred together. As expected, the arrow drew to a halt in front of a shelf of romance novels. Thea waited patiently.

A book shot from the shelves, landing in her outstretched hands.

'Your map is broken.'

Talibah took the enchanted parchment from Thea, giving it a cursory glance as she did so. 'Ah, sometimes it has a sense of humour.'

Thea glared at her friend. 'There is nothing funny about this.' She waved the book the map had led her to, time and again, until she'd given up ramming it back onto the shelf and brought it back into the main room of the bookshop: *Falling in Hate with his Lordship* by Clara Bell.

Talibah fought to keep the smile from her face. She failed. 'Perhaps it's trying to tell you something?'

'That,' Thea huffed, 'is painfully apparent.' Tucking the book under her arm, she dumped a handful of coins in Talibah's hand before marching out of the Lantern.

'I thought you didn't want it?' Talibah called after her.

'I have nothing else to read!'

CHAPTER

Seventeen

THE BELLS STRUNG on the door trilled merrily. When Thea lowered *Falling in Hate with his Lordship*, Zofka and Talibah were standing in front of her counter, wearing expressions as different as their outfits: Zofka in mismatched patterns, her chestnut curls escaping their ribbon as a lick of mischief toyed with her face; Talibah in teal, regarding her thoughtfully.

'What?' Thea asked, suspicious at once.

'Just checking in on you after your . . . visit,' Talibah said.

Zofka's mischief deepened. She drummed a couple of fingers on the countertop. 'Spill,' she demanded.

'Zofka . . .' Talibah's exasperation was softened by their years of friendship.

'You told Talibah you had nothing else to read,' Zofka interrupted, shaking her escaped curls back over her shoulder. 'Which can't possibly be true. And you only stockpile books when you're trying to distract yourself.'

Thea fidgeted, knowing the second she confided in them, they were going to have *thoughts*. Notions. Many, many opinions.

Zofka narrowed her eyes.

Thea groaned. 'I kissed Jasper.'

'Let's get a drink,' Zofka said at once.

Outside the Quarter, a thin rain was falling, painting Prague in shades of grey, its streets overrun with water that soaked through the women's boots and dribbled down their hair. The women didn't slow until they reached a noisy tavern, tucked away in a street off Old Town Square, with a glimmering side view of the Orloj, the astronomical clock.

Zofka brandished two goblets of *svařák*, spiced wine, and a ginger tea for Talibah, and slid into her chair, setting them out on the little table they'd snatched on entering. 'I thought we could use warming up; it's been a long day.'

The tavern was rowdy, but Thea rather liked it; it distracted from the noise inside her own head. A group of people were gambling on a game of chance nearby, and two women were roaring with laughter at the bar. The air was warm and peaty with hops.

'Drink up.' Zofka pushed Thea's goblet in front of her. Its scent tickled her nose, all cinnamon and clove and citrus, married with a rich red wine. Thea took a long drink. 'Now tell us *everything*.'

'What happened with Malek?' Talibah stirred honey into her ginger tea. 'I thought you were fond of him.'

'I was. I am,' Thea amended. She buried her hands in her hair. 'I feel terrible. It's all his fault!'

'Malek's?' Zofka asked.

'Jasper's,' Talibah countered.

A knowing light illuminated Zofka's sky-blue eyes. 'Ah. Of course,' she murmured, sipping her own wine.

'Not like that.' Thea's frustration burned hotter at the notion of having feelings for Jasper. She refused to spend any longer dwelling on the single – rather long – kiss they'd shared. The softer side Jasper had shown, grieving alone in the forest. 'It's Jasper's fault because I cannot love Malek, nor any man.'

Zofka patted her hand. 'Well, that, I quite understand. I know it takes some getting used to the idea of being different in this society, but I have trod this path before you and believe me when I tell you that you will *not* regret it.'

'I'm not sure she's telling us what you think she's telling us,' Talibah said, with no small hint of amusement.

Zofka raised her goblet. 'Well either way, I recommend it. Women smell much nicer than men and they have the softest hands—'

'You know I cannot love anyone.' Thea took another deep pull from her goblet. 'That's why it's Jasper's fault. He didn't need to take my heart, I'm certain of it. My entire life of memories must have been enough payment for whatever I asked of him. If he needed more, I could have paid in years. He could forge a new deal with me now, taking my time in exchange for the safe return of my heart. Yet still he keeps it.'

'Thea,' Talibah said gently. 'You keep telling us that you cannot love, but I can't believe that that's true.' Thea started, but Talibah continued before she could interrupt. 'You love us, do you not?'

Zofka beamed at Thea. '*That*, is an excellent point.'

Thea frowned into her goblet. These two women had waited up for her safe return from the opera, helped her puzzle through the hardest magical request she'd ever received, and listened to her every worry and concern. They were her friends, her family, her everything. And, yes, she loved them. Looking up, there was nothing but kindness and understanding reflected in their faces as they waited for her to speak. 'I do love you both, very much. But I'm not *in* love with either of you.'

'Romantic love is a different beast,' Talibah acknowledged. 'Your spell-heart might carry different capabilities. Or it is perfectly adequate, and you simply haven't met the right person yet. You were never told you couldn't love without your heart, you've just always assumed that's the case. What if it isn't, after all?'

Zofka snorted. 'You do have an unfortunate habit of kissing toads.' Her attention sharpened. 'Now, tell us about kissing Jasper.'

Thea groaned into the dregs of her goblet.

'Why don't you start at the beginning?' Talibah suggested. 'Last we spoke about him, you were adamant you hated him.'

'Oh, she's going to need more wine for that.' Zofka spun on her stool, raising a hand and an impish grin at the barkeep. 'And so am I. More tea, Talibah?'

The barkeep came over to refill Zofka and Thea's goblets with spiced wine. Steam framed her face as she poured, tossing a wink at Zofka, who blushed.

With the second goblet, it all came pouring out, as inexorable as the moon dragging the tides across an ocean. How they'd been arguing when he'd told her *I know exactly what you want. What you need.* And then kissed her.

Zofka choked on her spiced wine, her eyes moons. 'Are you serious?'

An errant giggle escaped Thea, and she laughed into her goblet, making it bubble like an over-brewed potion.

Talibah shook her head at their antics, hiding her smile.

'How was it?' Zofka asked. 'Was it better than your kiss with Malek?' She sipped her wine like a contented cat. 'I bet it was,' she continued. 'You two have that, that—'

'Energy,' Talibah finished, exchanging a smug smile with Zofka.

Thea groaned. 'It doesn't matter, it was a mistake and it's never happening again.'

Zofka's grin widened, scenting blood. 'So, it *was* good then.'

'Fine, yes, it was *good*. But we both agreed it would never happen again,' Thea told them. 'Then earlier today, Malek brought me flowers and invited me to the Winter Ball.' Suddenly things didn't seem quite so funny.

Zofka frowned. 'Why won't it happen again?'

Thea took a hearty gulp. The spices scorched a path down her throat. 'It was nothing, it meant nothing,' she said firmly, ignoring the doubt reflected back at her from her friends. 'It can't mean anything, it wouldn't be fair to Malek.' Dear, patient Malek, who was courting her like a gentleman. Who was bearing the price to save his sister from a terrible fate.

Talibah nodded to herself, sipping her tea.

But Zofka, a few goblets deep in spiced wine, leant closer. A ringlet dropped down to the table as she hushed her voice. 'What was kissing Jasper *like*, though?'

Thea flushed, touching her bottom lip before she realised and stopped.

Zofka swore excitedly, drawing the attention of the gambling table, who hooted and raised their tankards to her.

Talibah laughed. 'You raised an interesting point earlier.' Her amber eyes gleamed against the lantern-lit tavern, all honeyed stone and rosy wooden tables scarred from decades of clinking tankards. 'We haven't once considered that Jasper might forge a new deal with you.'

'Oooh,' Zofka added. 'Have you ever asked him?'

'There's no point,' Thea said darkly. 'I doubt he'd go for it.'

'If he did, would you be prepared to give him back what he's given you?' Talibah asked. 'The power, the apothecary, your home, all of it?'

Slowly, Thea nodded. Giving up her home would be challenging; she adored her cosy little hideaway with its crooked ceiling and windows overlooking the trees of the Magic Quarter, with their foliage that smelt of caramel each autumn, harbouring a parliament of time-telling owls. But home wasn't a place, it was her friends, and Cinnamon. Home was wherever she hunkered down with a book at the end of the day. And the magic? Well, that would be missed, but if it meant never again having to ask a girl for her memories in exchange for her safety, then she would be glad to lose it. 'I would return it all in a heartbeat to learn who I really am. To feel my heart beating in my chest. To not be beholden to him.'

Talibah leant over the table. 'Then ask him for a new deal, on your own terms. You've grown . . . closer recently, perhaps he'll surprise you.'

Zofka swallowed the last of her wine and slammed the goblet down, leaping to her feet, where she wobbled in place. 'Let's go.'

Thea tugged Zofka back down. 'I've asked him for my heart before and he's always refused. I need to think what he might want in exchange—'

'You overthink too much,' Zofka grumbled. 'I'll tell you what he wants.'

Thea and Talibah stared at her, waiting.

'You,' Zofka said simply, looking back at Thea.

A lump settled into Thea's throat. 'How is your spirit?' she asked instead, changing their conversation onto other matters, Zofka's spirit and Talibah's next trip, the Magic Quarter meetings and if anyone had learnt anything on the wards. They had not. Thea and Zofka drank more *svařák*. Until the tavern lanterns glowed brighter and Thea's thoughts sank into submission. Zofka won a handful of hellers from the group playing chance nearby, her ringlets escaping every last pin.

The trees slanted as they marched back through the Magic Quarter, arm in arm, Zofka singing a cheerful festive tune as Talibah shushed her and Thea cackled in delight. Until they saw who was standing outside the apothecary, impatiently waiting.

'Jasper,' Thea uttered.

'Let me speak to him.' Zofka swung her cloak back and pushed her dress sleeves up.

Talibah held onto Zofka's cloak, stopping the inebriated witch from lunging at Jasper. 'I wouldn't,' Talibah said mildly.

Footsteps echoed down the cobblestones. Gretel arrived, slightly breathless. She wore a simple gown that nipped her narrow waist, and her large brown eyes softened when she saw Zofka bumbling around.

Talibah cleared her throat delicately. 'They've, er, had a long night.' She handed the bottom of Zofka's cloak to Gretel.

'Thank you, I'll take her from here,' Gretel said, holding onto Zofka's cloak and taking it all in stride as if this was a typical scenario to occur in the middle of an autumnal night.

Zofka sang all the way back home. Loud and cheerfully out of tune.

Jasper stepped into the light under a nearby street lamp. Snow dusted his dark hair like sugar. Thea wished she could sink her hands into it. She shook the intrusive thought from her head. 'I will take Thea off your hands.' He was dressed in black, as if he knew he belonged in the shadows and darkness.

Talibah hesitated.

'It's fine, I'm safe with him,' Thea told her.

'Send me a raven before you go to sleep,' Talibah said, loud enough to make certain that Jasper also heard. 'I want to know that you're safe and well.'

Thea flapped a hand in agreement. 'Of course.' She brightened. 'Did I tell you that Biscuit took his first flight earlier? All the way across the apothecary.'

Talibah's smile was gentle. 'That is good news indeed.'

Thea smiled back. When she blinked, Talibah seemed to vanish across the snow-strewn street. The witch light blazing through the gourds' carved faces flickered as if they were laughing.

'What are you doing here?' Thea stumbled past Jasper and into the apothecary. 'It's been a long night, I need to sleep.'

Jasper gave her a bewildered look. 'We agreed to meet tonight – I came to bring you this.' He gave her an envelope. 'One fingernail, previously belonging to a lake spirit.'

'Oh, *thank* you,' Thea gushed, opening it. 'I wanted this so very badly,' she admitted, 'Meeting a real-life lake spirit does not sound pleasant.'

Jasper's tone darkened. 'I can assure you, it is not.'

Inside the envelope was a slip of paper, folded over many times, and a lump of something slimy. 'What is this?' she wobbled in place.

'What is what?' Jasper took the envelope. A frown marred his forehead.

Thea stared at it. He frowned so often that she recognised his frowns the same way other people might recognise smiles. This particular frown was half confusion, half irritation, with a good dash of frustration tossed in for measure.

'It's rotten.' Jasper's mouth drew into a straight line. He sighed. 'I shall have to source you another one. My apologies. It might take a week or so, I am preoccupied with investigating this issue with the wards and—' He gave Thea a suspicious look. 'Why are you staring at my forehead?'

'I'm interpreting your frowns,' she told him.

His frown drew tighter. 'I think perhaps you'd better go to bed.'

'Oh, you'd like that, wouldn't you?' Thea asked. 'But I am not kissing you again, ever, never mind climbing into bed with you.'

Jasper cleared his throat, his frown contorting into something quite unfamiliar.

'Are you . . . *smiling?*' Thea gasped.

'Absolutely not.'

'Hmm,' Thea told him.

'Do you have any guesses tonight or are you too inebriated to make one?' he asked dryly.

'Is my real name *Jasper?*' Thea asked.

Jasper was definitely fighting a smile now. She was sure of it. She stared at him suspiciously. 'Unsurprisingly, it is not. Goodnight, Theodora. Please drink some water.'

CHAPTER

Eighteen

WINTER BROKE TWO days later. In the forest, each tree was encrusted with ice crystals and when a ray of sunlight cut through the clouds, it set them all a-glitter. On a day like this, it seemed impossible that anything bad could ever happen. But according to the novels Thea read, this was precisely when something bad would definitely happen, especially since she was making a beeline straight for a cursed lake.

Yesterday morning she'd risen like the undead after drinking half the tavern with Zofka, but she couldn't wait an entire week for Jasper to procure another fingernail. Her hope flurried like a tentative snowfall; if all went to plan, she should be leaving this forest with the last ingredient secured to finally make Malek's key. If it did not – no, she couldn't consider that now. She needed to be confident. The ball was drawing closer. She tried to ignore the part where she'd need to successfully steal a fingernail from a lake spirit, but Jasper's voice echoed through her thoughts: *The only way to retrieve one of their nails is if it becomes embedded in your flesh.*

Stubbornly, she walked deeper into the forest. Towards the Crossroads, where the trees hummed and white eyes watched her path. Magic buzzed in the air, this close to where the seams frayed and other worlds rubbed against this one, turning everything wild and wonderful.

Careful with each step, her nerves hammering a warning, Thea forged on, searching the forest for any sight of water. She'd sent ravens to Zofka and Talibah, letting them know where she was going and asking them to send help if she was more than a few hours. Just in case. Following the path of the Crossroads, she wandered into unexplored territory, further and further until her feet hurt and she thought about giving up. But she couldn't. So, on she marched, until at last she caught the scent of water.

Crossing her fingers, Thea cut a path through thinning trees. Through the wintry, sparse foliage, she glimpsed a lake. It didn't *look* cursed. She stepped over thorned undergrowth to examine it closer, drawn by something she couldn't voice, something her thoughts refused to shape. Oh. Oh no, it was *definitely* cursed. Its surface was dappled with light as if sunshine danced across the water, though the sun was now absent, lost to clouds that hung low as fog.

Her nerves swelled. How did one go about locating a lake spirit?

Wind skated over the surface of the lake, but the water did not move. She bent to pick up a pebble and tossed it into the lake. No ripples formed. Somewhere deep down, a thin, high laugh echoed up.

By the edge of the lake was a cluster of big smooth rocks, and Thea knelt on one to peer more closely at the water. It seemed as if it ought to be clear, but she couldn't see the bottom. A lily pad drifted by. Thea peeled it back from the water, checking beneath it. Something slinked around Thea's fingers like algae, slippery and wet.

She lurched back. Had that been a lake spirit's *hair?* 'Hello,' she said out loud, feeling more than a little stupid. 'I'm sorry to bother you, but if you are a lake spirit, I desperately need one of your fingernails for an important potion I'm brewing. It would help someone very dear to me and—'

That laugh echoed up again.

A tiny moan of fright escaped Thea.

Hoof-beats pounded the ground. They reverberated through Thea's bones as she leapt up, the hood of her cloak falling down.

'*Thea!*'

Her name was a roar of desperation in Jasper's mouth. Rounding the trees, he came galloping into sight, his hands tight on a black horse's reins. He was not dressed for the changing seasons, clad in only a shirt, breeches and riding boots. Her heart-spell flickered.

Jasper leaped from his horse, striding towards her, his chest heaving. 'Thea.' Confusion muddied his relief. He halted before her, his gaze stripping her bare. 'Are you well?'

'Perfectly, why?' Thea blinked in confusion. 'Are you?'

Jasper frowned. 'I received a raven from Zofka. She was in the apothecary instead of you. She was distraught. She informed me that you'd gone to the forest to gather ingredients hours ago and had not returned.'

Well. That was . . . untrue.

'I—' Thea cleared her throat. 'My apologies, I lost track of time. I had no wish to concern anyone.' Oh, Zofka was not going to hear the end of this. Had she been genuinely worried, or . . . Thea sighed internally, flashing back to Zofka's reaction when Thea had confessed she'd kissed Jasper. What a devious matchmaker. She gave Jasper a remorseful smile.

'And running the apothecary? Had that also slipped your mind?' Jasper's voice was harsher now, his concern fading fast. 'Regardless of how many customers we might or might not be receiving these days, you are still expected to be there, to keep everything running smoothly.'

'It is not part of my duty to create goods for the apothecary?'

Jasper glowered. 'You know well I have repeatedly warned you to stay away from this part of the forest, and I have offered to provide any ingredient you should need. What's really happening here, Thea? Last time we spoke on the subject, I left under the impression that you understood why you should not come here. I brought you the last lake spirit fingernail in my possession.' His voice trailed off as he took in where she stood. On a rock in the shallows of a cursed lake. 'No, Thea,' he said severely. 'Please tell me you did not come here to retrieve a fingernail by *yourself*.'

Thea glanced at the mist wending through the lake-edge. 'That fingernail you gave me was rotten.'

'And I said I would procure you another,' Jasper spoke through gritted jaw.

'I needed it urgently,' Thea told him.

'Must you always have a reason for everything?' Jasper growled.

'You are the sole person who seems to take issue with everything I do,' Thea shot back.

Jasper gestured at the cursed lake. 'Because you refuse to heed my warnings; it's as if you wish to deliberately court danger.'

Thea's heart-spell thrashed with anger. 'No, you didn't warn me, you *ordered* me. And I do not take orders from you.'

'Clearly.' Jasper raked his hair, glowering at her.

The last time they'd fought like this, it had ended with her wrapping her thighs around him. Thea startled; where had *that* come from? Did she want him to kiss her again? No, of course not. Her stare flitted down to his mouth for a second. The forest was grey under the ceiling of cloud and thick layer of frost, the trees shivering phantoms. Their hum low-pitched enough for Thea to hear Jasper's quick intake of breath.

'Thea,' he scratched out, his whisper rough. Deep. Sinking into that ravine of unexplored emotion that ran between them.

His horse whinnied.

Thea jumped, instinctively stepping back. The heel of her boot slipped on the stone, uprooting her. Flinging her arms out to catch at something, she yelped in alarm.

Jasper grabbed her hand, but it was too late, they were already falling.

They plummeted into the lake, tangled together.

Thea gasped as she hit the freezing water. Jasper yanked her straight back up, his hands swallowing her waist as he stabilised them both in the water, muttering darkly.

Clawed fingers wrapped around one of Thea's ankles.

'Jasper!' she managed to shriek before she was dragged straight down, through the water and into algae-slick mud, which suddenly parted, revealing that the lake shallows were in fact, not shallow at all.

Lake water roared past Thea's face, clogging her ears, nose and throat as she kicked out, trying to free herself. But the hand was unyielding, clawed fingers banded around her ankle like iron. The water turned inky as whatever had claimed Thea pulled her into the lake's hidden depths. Shivering with shock, a second fear hit Thea like a ship sailing into an iceberg: it was deathly cold. Colder than the dark expanse between stars. And it was growing colder the further down she went. Her borrowed powers refused to answer her call, too smothered in fear.

Now and then, eyes glittered as she passed. Occasionally there was a flash of bared teeth. Her heart-spell almost gave out with fright. Until a flare of light cut through the murk, sending the creatures darting away. Jasper. He arrowed straight down as if he'd been propelled, fierce determination carved into his face.

Thea reached for him, her fingers scrabbling against his as only their fingertips touched, then he was there, grasping her wrist, then elbow, then waist as he slowed her descent. Her chest heaving as she struggled not to inhale, Thea held onto Jasper's shoulders, his arm wrapped around her waist. Reeds snarled at her feet; they were approaching the true bottom of the lake, at last.

With his free hand, Jasper stretched out, snagging the tapestry of fate. The water undulated. A dark gleam rose as threads appeared all around them. Whatever was clinging onto Thea's ankle hissed. Its nails sank deeper into her skin. Thea opened her mouth in a silent scream. Water rushed in, choking her. She clung harder to Jasper, trying to kick the creature off in a panic. Jasper cast his fury at it, yanking that tapestry of fate until threads snapped, their ends floating past Thea's face as the creature who'd seized her simply . . . vanished.

Then it was she and Jasper alone. Stars spattered in her vision as her thoughts began to fade. Jasper's arms tightened around her waist.

She blinked and they were cresting the surface.

Jasper slapped her back until Thea coughed and spluttered, dredging rancid lake water up from her lungs. 'What did you do?' she gasped. 'You made it disappear . . . What did you pay to do that?'

'That's not for you to worry about,' Jasper said.

The power he'd channelled to just *snap* those threads; he had to have made a considerable sacrifice. For her. Something told her he would never forgo a price after his lectures. Thea's chest was tight, her throat raw from inhaling cursed lake water. She couldn't stop imagining it sloshing around in her stomach, wending its way into her blood.

'You'll be fine, you're safe now.' Jasper's hand remained on her back. He began rubbing it in slow circles, coaxing her lungs to relax and fill with air.

She gagged as another mouthful of lake water came up. 'What *was* that?'

'Like I said, magic from other realms, bleeding through,' Jasper said grimly. 'Sometimes more than magic slips through. You just met your first lake spirit. Though lake spirit is a nicer term than water demon.'

Thea's shiver had nothing to do with the cold. She couldn't stop imagining those long, narrow fingers snatching her ankle again, their claw-tips sinking in. If Jasper hadn't saved her . . . Remembering the other glittering eyes that had stared at her, she began ploughing through the shallows at speed.

'Slow down,' Jasper ordered.

She did not.

Lakeweed tangled around her boot, tripping her. This time, Jasper was fast enough to grab her arm before the lake claimed her once more. His hair was pasted to his neck, droplets clinging to his eyelashes. She raised a hand to one temple, dizzied. He looked like he'd walked straight from one of her more . . . dangerous dreams of him.

After a long pause, Jasper cleared his throat. 'I'm sorry?'

Had she said that out loud? Thea blushed to the roots of her sodden hair. 'Nothing,' she said quickly. Ripping her gaze from his, she gathered up her sopping cloak. Wringing it out, she stomped through the fingers of frost creeping across the lake's shallows. The cold was still sinking through her as if the lake had marked her. Leaving her feet and fingers numb and unwieldy.

'You've dreamt of me?'

As if caught in a trance, she turned back. He was slowly walking from the lake, his white, wet shirt clinging to him. Revealing a well-defined chest and sculpted lines leading down from his stomach that entrapped her, before she caught herself staring.

'No, not at all,' she said in a tone that sounded unnatural to her own ears.

'That's not what you just said.' Jasper strode towards her.

Thea's legs quivered with more than the cold. 'They were nothing,' she said, in that same unnatural tone she couldn't seem to shake. 'More like nightmares really.'

'And what do I do in your nightmares?' Jasper asked huskily.

'You, you . . .' Thea failed to think of a single word. When Jasper swallowed, she tracked the rise and fall of his throat hungrily, feeling the sudden urge to skim her teeth over him.

Jasper's hand clenched at his side. She watched it, fascinated.

'Stop that,' he ordered.

'I don't want to,' she whispered.

'Tell me what I do in your dreams,' he whispered back, stealing closer. Close enough to touch, if either of them were brave enough to cross that dangerous line. Again. 'What do I say to you?'

She closed her eyes, feeling his breath slide over her neck.

'What do I make you feel?' he continued. 'What— Thea, you're bleeding.'

Her eyes snapped open. Jasper knelt at her feet, brandishing a furious frown as he delicately lifted her left foot onto his knee, his hands wrapping around her calf, lifting her dress to examine her leg.

Her blush turned as furious as his frown.

A thin line of blood wept down her calf. A shard was lodged there. Jasper plucked it out. Blood welled. She had barely time to panic before Jasper threw up the tapestry of fate and healed her. The pain vanished at once. Before she could thank him, he was standing before her. He gave her the shard. 'I hope it was worth it.'

It was a fingernail. Storm-grey and veined with green. Thea beamed down at it. 'I got one!'

'We are not doing that again. Ever,' Jasper told her as Thea nodded seriously, attempting not to smile – though now she'd finally be able to make Malek's key and he could save his sister, and it all felt so *good*. Like she could do anything if she put her mind to it.

Jasper sighed. With a furtive glance back at the lake, he brought his fingers to his mouth and whistled. His horse came trotting into the clearing, munching on a mouthful of weeds. Jasper patted its mane. 'Good girl,' he murmured.

'What's her name?' Thea asked through clattering teeth.

Jasper frowned again, his gaze turning unfocused. The chill soaking into her bones suddenly vanished and her soaking clothes and hair dried. 'Thank you,' she said.

'Her name is Eclipse,' Jasper told her, mounting his horse. He held a hand out to Thea. 'Come.'

'Oh, I can make my own way home,' she began.

His hand remained extended as he looked down at her, waiting.

'Fine.' She gave him her hand. 'But I'm never going to be able to get up there—' Jasper gripped her wrist, pulling her up onto the back of the horse before she could worry about it. A soft, 'Oh,' escaped her.

Jasper chuckled under his breath.

Thea stared at his back, unsure if she'd really heard him make that sound. 'You're entirely too pleased with yourself for someone who just fell into a cursed lake,' she grumbled, tentatively placing her hands on his waist.

Reaching for her hands, Jasper tugged them hard, making Thea slide up flush against his back, her thighs either side of his legs. She stifled her gulp of surprise, glad he couldn't see her face, the way she was sure her cheeks had bloomed, her eyes widening as he had pulled her into position.

'Hold on tight.'

Thea clung on for dear life as Eclipse cantered through the forest, sighing in relief when they'd passed the Crossroads, and that pervasive hum of colliding realms disappeared. Jasper slowed their gait as they rode beneath a canopy blazing in crimson and burnt orange like a living ember. A flash of gold snatched Thea's attention. 'Stop!' she cried out.

Jasper halted Eclipse. 'What is it?' he asked, sharp with alarm, scanning the forest.

Thea unknit her fingers from their death's grip on Jasper's shirt and slid off the side of Eclipse. Her knees buckled and she hit the ground in an undignified heap.

The corner of Jasper's mouth twitched. 'What are you doing?'

'*Look.*' Picking herself up and dusting herself down, Thea ran into the little meadow she'd spotted, beaming with late-blooming sunflowers. Each one as golden as lost treasure. Flinging her arms back, she spun in a circle, giddy with joy. 'I've never seen this many sunflowers before, and out of season, too.'

Jasper slowly dismounted, watching her with an indecipherable look.

Thea bent to stroke the petals of the nearest sunflower. It wasn't one of Rose's; it bore no reaction to her touch. 'Did you know that sunflowers tilt their faces to the sun?'

'I did not.'

'And when it's an overcast day, they turn their faces to each other instead. Isn't that the loveliest thing you've ever heard?'

'Lovely indeed,' Jasper said.

When Thea glanced back at him, he was still watching her, something unreadable on his face. A visible hunger in his eyes. She stood, her fingers falling from the sunflower. Jasper straightened, walking towards her slowly, with purpose, his gaze locked on hers.

Without a single word, she went to him.

They met in a fiery clash in the centre of the meadow. Thea tilted her head back like she was a sunflower and he the sun, and he took her mouth as if it belonged to him. As if it was inevitable that they would have continued that kiss in their apothecary days before. As if *they* were inevitable. All the anger and frustration and loathing wound up so tightly within Thea spilled out as she tore Jasper's shirt off, pushing him down onto the long grass, before sitting on his lap and kissing him with that wild hunger ripping through them both.

He unlaced her as expertly as if he was unthreading the fates of the world, shoving her dress, her underclothes down to her waist. 'Thea,' he groaned, his gaze more black than blue as his pupils dilated with need. She wetted her bottom lip, watching him take her in. Noticing, he groaned again, wrapping his hands around her waist and bending to take a peaked nipple into his mouth. She melted under his heat, her head tipping back as she surrendered to his touch, her thoughts quieting to a whisper. When she felt him lick his way across to her other nipple, she reached down for his breeches, suddenly needing to touch him, too.

His mouth fell from her breast with one last, reverent kiss. 'Are you sure?' His stare searched hers. Looking for what, she didn't know, but she bent to kiss him long and hard and deep, losing herself in a way that felt so right, she wondered why she'd wasted so much time loathing him when they could have been doing this instead. He responded in kind, his hands skimming up her thighs and higher still, until he found that tight bud at the apex of her thighs and pressed it firmly, making her cry out for him.

She untied him hungrily, bracing a hand on his shoulder as he continued working between her thighs and she eased herself down onto him. Thea paused, staring wonderingly at him, at how they had ended up here after everything that had raged between them for years. Then Jasper sighed, whispering, 'I have been dreaming of this.' His other arm wrapped around her, supporting her, his thumb stroking her waist. She watched his throat move as he swallowed, his hand steady but tender between her legs, coaxing more heat from her until she felt as if she might die from wanting. Instead, she lost herself in him.

They moved as one until Thea's hair was a wild tangle. Until she was clinging onto Jasper's arms, his muscles tightening and flexing as he moved her with ease when she tired, until their breaths turned ragged and mingled together and she could no longer distinguish where his ended and hers began. Until they came undone as one.

Thea lay back on the blanket of grass, watching as the day waned. When she sat up, her chest hitched; she was suddenly surrounded with wild flowers. Crocuses and lilies and delicate little bluebells in the palest purple-blue. Wild flowers that shouldn't have risen until spring had awakened, tilting their faces to her as if she was the sun. And beside her, watching her with the same regard, was Jasper, propped up on one elbow. 'You're cold,' he said.

Thea smiled at him. 'It was worth it.'

He smiled back at her. It brightened his entire face, until Thea couldn't look away. The wild flowers tipping their blooms towards her were wrong; it was Jasper who was the sun. He just spent most of his days overcast. He plucked a single violet from the bevy of flowers and slid it into Thea's hair, tucking it above her ear.

CHAPTER

Nineteen

WHEN THEY ARRIVED back at the apothecary, Thea slid from the back of Eclipse and walked in first, still humming with happiness, expecting to see Zofka pacing, keeping up the pretence that she was concerned about Thea's whereabouts. She did not expect to see Malek standing behind her counter, flipping through her Compendium of Magic.

'Malek?' she gasped, hearing Jasper enter behind her.

Malek snapped the Compendium shut and strode over. 'Are you all right?' He gave her a once-over. 'You appear . . . out of sorts.'

A kind way to allude to her bedraggled state. 'I'm fine,' she said, subtly removing the violet from her hair and slipping it into her pocket. Guilt surged up her throat, unsettling her stomach. It had been the most peculiar day and she didn't know how to process it all. She was desperate to curl up in bed with Cinnamon, a book, and a big bowl of something comforting. The apothecary seemed to agree; she was sure she could smell butternut squash soup, the kind that Zofka made; roasted and caramelised with lots of garlic and cream and a kick of spice.

'She's fine,' Jasper echoed.

Malek ignored him, placing a hand on Thea's shoulder as he peered down at her, full of concern. 'Did something happen?'

Jasper muttered under his breath. Thea chose to ignore it, smiling at Malek. 'We fell into a lake when gathering ingredients, that's all. I'm just tired and cold.' A shiver followed, with uncanny timing.

'What can I do to help?' Malek asked, tucking a runaway strand of Thea's hair behind her ear.

'Honestly, I'm fi—'

'That won't be necessary.' Jasper stepped forward, taking Thea's arm. 'I promised I would escort her home, and I mean to stand by my word. Good day, Pan Jaromir.'

He marched Thea into the backroom and upstairs. 'Was *that* necessary?' she hissed at him. 'He's going to think—' Her cheeks heated, imagining all the things that Malek might possibly think, in full vivid colour. The worst of it was that he would be right while Malek had been nothing but kind and considerate towards her. *What had she done?*

Jasper glanced down at her with interest. 'Yes?'

'You shouldn't have done that,' Thea said instead. She was still conflicted when they reached her door at the top of the stairs. Before she could bid him farewell, Jasper opened it.

'Ah, you found her!' Zofka's gasp of delight was too loud and Thea cringed, hoping Jasper wouldn't pick up on how contrived it sounded. 'I was so *worried*.' Zofka stood, shaking crumbs from her skirts with one hand and folding the leaf of Thea's book she'd been reading with the other.

Thea cast a sad little look at the bookmark lying beside it, forgotten.

Jasper regarded Zofka, perplexed. 'Indeed.'

Zofka straightened under his look with a gleam of intrigue. 'Why are you both bedraggled?'

'We took a swim in a cursed lake.' Thea's mood was eroding, fast. She hadn't expected to face Malek so soon after she'd ... dallied with Jasper, and now Jasper was acting as if he was her personal protector, and gods knew what Malek thought. Zofka widened her eyes a touch, filled with silent question. There was an apology floating in there, but grudges were little ghouls: if you held them close, they would haunt only you. Besides, thanks to Zofka's misguided attempts at engineering another kiss between Thea and Jasper, that *thing* hiding at the bottom of the lake hadn't gobbled her alive, and she'd come out of the encounter with the exact ingredient she needed to complete Malek's key. When Thea gave her an imperceptible nod back, Zofka looked relieved. It was chased with burning curiosity. 'I'll explain everything soon,' Thea said in a hurry, before Jasper read the truth from Zofka's expression. 'But I need to . . .' She gestured at her tangled hair and ripped dress. Cinnamon hopped over, patting a hanging hem with a curious paw.

'I'll go and check on Gretel, then. She was meant to be keeping an eye on my stew but that woman's got the memory of an earthworm,' Zofka said fondly. 'I've left a pot of soup in your stove,' she added, making herself scarce, though not before giving Thea a suggestive wink that thankfully Jasper did not see.

'Well, thank you for bringing me home,' Thea told Jasper, taking her cloak off and blushing furiously.

'You need a bath.'

'Excuse me?'

Jasper had the sense of decorum to look appalled. 'I meant before you catch a chill. That water was freezing, and you sustained a great shock. And then we—'

Thea's blush deepened.

'Stayed too long outside,' Jasper finished decorously. 'It was most ungallant of me. I felt you shivering behind me on the ride back.'

'You were never ungallant,' Thea said softly. 'But I can assure you I know how to take care of myself. I've been doing it for at least seven years now, perhaps more.'

Would the loss of her past ever stop stinging? How could Jasper know her history, when she did not? Her voice sharpened with the unfairness of it, her words biting at him as if she could make him feel the same pain.

'The moment you take your leave, I shall get changed.'

Unless he was inclined to stay, a little voice whispered. One of her more unbidden thoughts. She swallowed hard.

Jasper's look was rife with something left unspoken. 'Very well. Then I shall fill your bath for you – you ought to warm up quickly before you take ill.'

'That's not necessary.'

Thea's protest slipped off Jasper's back as he took her pail and walked out of the door. Several journeys to the Quarter's crooked well later, Jasper had filled Thea's copper tub. Then, taking the large, flat stones left warming in her fireplace, he slid them into the water with a hiss.

'It would have been quicker if you'd asked a weather-witch,' Thea pointed out, hovering in the kitchen.

Jasper blanched. 'Weather-witches are a flighty sort. I can't get close enough to one to ask.'

Thea slid him a considering look. 'Perhaps if you came to one of our Quarter meetings, they'd stop fearing you as much. You don't help matters by stalking around after dark and scowling at everyone.'

'No,' he scowled, filling her bathtub with a bottle of scented oil.

'You're impossible.' Thea's teeth chattered harder as steam rose from the tub. Then, because she was hungry and tired and unable to control her raging thoughts, she asked, 'Why haven't you kissed me again?'

Jasper froze. It would have amused Thea had she not been mortified.

'Do you want me to kiss you again?'

He looked like a winter storm, like thunder rolling across the sky at night. He looked like every bad idea Thea had ever had, and still she couldn't stop dwelling on their kiss. On how she had come undone at his touch and how he had looked at her as if she was the sun.

'Perhaps,' she admitted.

Jasper crossed the small space of Thea's home, stepping between stacks of books, plates of forgotten biscuits and Cinnamon's paws. He didn't stop when he reached Thea, sending her pulse scudding like clouds fleeing a storm. Lowering his head, he whispered in her ear, 'Until that answer is yes, and until you deal with that man who insists on courting you, I will not be touching you again. When I next kiss you, I want to know that you have been dreaming of my, and *only* my, mouth on yours.' His breath whispered against her earlobe, warm and sweet and irresistible. 'I will not kiss you again until you beg me to.'

Thea's head whirled. Malek was sweet, and understanding, and kind: the right choice for her. But Jasper's words set her aflame.

Jasper searched her eyes, looking for something he couldn't find. Something she could not give. 'You smile at everyone,' he said. 'Everyone except me. Today was the first time I have been granted a single smile from you.'

'Fine words from someone who looks like they've never smiled a day in their life,' Thea retorted. 'I do believe if you actually smiled, it would kill you.'

Jasper laughed. It was full-bodied as a rich red wine, and warmed Thea more than she'd admit. She'd spent years provoking Jasper, secretly delighting in each frown, each glare, each dark mutter she'd coaxed from him. It had felt like winning a small prize each time, like, if she had enough of them, it wouldn't matter that Jasper held her heart and memories. But that would always matter. So why did she now crave his laugh more than her petty vengeances?

'Why did you come for me today?' she asked, trying to harden herself against him once more. To remember where her loyalties lay.

'The thought of you, wandering through the forest alone.' Jasper drew in a tortured breath. 'I could not bear the thought of something happening to you.'

'I can't alter my habits simply to make you more comfortable,' Thea said, clinging onto her resentment, trying to ignore the way he was looking at her. How she'd felt when he'd sighed into her ear, admitting *I have been dreaming of this.* She relented. 'But I have the final ingredient I needed, and I am grateful you saved me from that thing in the lake. I won't go near the Crossroads by myself again.'

Jasper exhaled. 'Good. The forest is dangerous, Thea. You are not equipped to handle the dangers that stalk those trees. We saw but a shadow of what lurks in those depths today, others are far more awful – things that would see you as prey, that would hunt your scent, stalk you through the streets of Prague after nightfall.'

Cold fingers danced down Thea's spine. 'You're afraid,' she realised. What prowled through the forest that was terrible enough to strike fear in the heart of someone as powerful as Jasper? 'What are you not telling me?'

He shook his head. 'I have said too much already.' He made for the door, but Thea reached it first and stood in front of it, her arms stretched out. 'You know something about the Magic Quarter, don't you? Do you know something about those fate-weavers I overheard? Why they are meddling with our Quarter?'

'I do not.'

'What about that threat that was nailed to my door?'

'I am still—'

'Looking into it,' Thea finished for him, giving him a suspicious look. 'Just like the wards. I'm starting to wonder if you'll ever figure out either.'

Jasper flinched. 'Believe it or not' – he ran a hand roughly through his hair – 'I do not have all the answers. But I am not the only fate-weaver interested in this world. You may have certain . . . opinions about me, but know there are worse out there. Old enemies of mine that, should they come to light, would threaten everything.'

Thea twisted her mouth, unsure what to make of that. 'Those old enemies of yours,' she asked carefully, 'could they be the culprits behind the failing wards?'

Jasper tilted his head back, considering. 'I am not inclined to believe they are.'

'But you're not sure?' she pressed.

'Take your bath, Theodora,' Jasper said. 'I shall lock up the apothecary tonight.'

She knew when he had closed a conversation; he was every bit as stubborn as she. Dropping her arms, she stepped aside. Just in time, she remembered to call out, 'Isabella?'

His soft, 'No,' echoed up from the stairs.

CHAPTER

Twenty

'I CAN'T DO THIS.' Thea stared up at the duck-egg blue sky and the shivering trees. She had woken to frost, laced over the cobblestones. The first frost in the Magic Quarter – the cold snap that had stuck birds to branches and blown out all the street lamps after the blizzard didn't count; according to gossip, that had been a failed attempt to repair the ward by one of the weather-witches. Thea held onto Biscuit's box for another minute. His presence soothed her and she was still frustrated with Jasper this morning; he knew something about the attack on the Magic Quarter and its wards, she was sure of it. Worse, she'd dreamed of their encounter in the forest last night, reliving every second of it until she'd woken tangled in her bedsheets.

'Of course you can.' Zofka impatiently bit into one of the cinnamon buns she'd brought for breakfast, sweet and steaming in the frigid hour before the shops rolled up their shutters and unlocked their doors. It had been a few days since Fleur's defence had chased Pan Novak and the Hunters from her modiste, but judging by the stare Pan Novak had given Thea as he'd walked away, it would not be the last they heard of him.

The witch light gourds were gone, replaced with golden stars strung between the street lamps and trees, which glittered when someone happened by. Their resident pixies seemed fond of them, judging by the trilling laughter that had danced into Thea's open windows last night.

Talibah, in a berry-red headscarf, wrapped extra snugly around her neck, nodded in agreement. 'It's time. Biscuit belongs with the other messenger ravens and the sky, where he can stretch his wings.'

Thea knew all of this. It didn't stop her throat from aching as she stroked Biscuit's beak one last time. He gave a soft caw, rustling his feathers. 'I've loved having you stay with me,' she told the raven. 'Come and visit sometime, I'll keep your jar of worms ready.'

Zofka pulled a face.

'I didn't know witches were squeamish,' Talibah teased.

'Kitchen-witch,' Zofka amended primly. 'I deal with pastry, not invertebrates.'

Thea set Biscuit's box down. He hopped free and with a flutter of his wings, flew down the street to the Crypt, with its crooked turret stuck on its roof like an awkward additional limb.

'Well done.' Talibah interlinked her arm with Thea's.

Thea watched until Biscuit's dark plumage vanished into one of the tiny windows in the turret, where the messenger ravens dwelled. Until the lump in her throat had hardened into a rock. She was going to miss that bird.

The following week presented itself like a gift: Thea's headaches did not return, all seemed quiet in the Magic Quarter, with not a peep from Pan Novak, and the magical folk began returning to the tangled streets and alleys as the wheel of time shifted further into winter.

The resident weather-witches decorated the streets with cascading snowflakes and bewitched the frosted windows to paint wintry scenes of sleighing and snowpeople, and everything smelled like baking.

'I don't like that he's missing.' Zofka was whirling round her kitchen like a winter's gale. A cinnamon-sweet scent emanated from the stove, and with the addition of iced gingerbread biscuits hanging from the windows and beams, it was starting to become believable that Christmas would be here in a few short weeks.

Outside, a snow was falling that the weather-witches had nothing to do with, and Thea was spending the evening with Zofka after opening Stiltskin's early to serve a waiting line. The most welcome sight she'd seen in days, even if half her customers had been inflicted with colds. She was running dangerously low on fire-ginger now. But the Magic Quarter was coming back to life and Thea had fallen in love with it all over again. Here, books and coffee and magic and kittens were a way of life, and a slice of enchanted cake could put a smile on your face like nothing else.

Thea perched on Zofka's scarred table, nibbling a gingerbread person she'd liberated from the nearest window, brewing her own potion under Zofka's supervision. 'Who's missing?' she asked, grinding the lake spirit's fingernail and last pair of the silver spot-dabbles into a shiny grey paste.

'Pan Novak and his pack of leeches.' Zofka glanced out the window. 'It feels nefarious, like he's planning something.'

'I agree,' Thea sighed, 'But when I raised it with Rose, she seemed inclined to believe that the weather-witches mended the wards—'

Zofka snorted. 'I love the weather-witches, but it's going to take more than some ice to fix those wards. It's complex magic, you can't just' – she gesticulated wildly, scattering sugar everywhere – 'patch it up with a bit of ice and expect that to solve everything.'

A spirit drifted through the wall.

Thea almost fell from the counter.

'Sorry to startle you,' the spirit said, rather pleasantly. 'My name is Radim; it's a pleasure to make your acquaintance.'

Zofka pointed to Radim with her wooden spoon. 'My spirit.'

'So, I guessed,' Thea said dryly. She smiled at Radim, making a concerted effort not to glance at his medieval vestments, which were stained with blood, nor his neck, which bore the kind of wound you could not survive. 'I'm Thea.'

'Ah, the apothecarian.' Radim gave a knowledgeable nod. 'Terrible business with the wards, isn't it?' he tutted. 'What are you making?'

'It's meant to be a potion, but I'm not quite sure it's coming out right and I don't have any spare ingredients.'

Zofka cast an expert eye over it. 'That needs thinning.'

'With what?' Thea asked.

Zofka snatched something off one of her many shelves without looking. 'Pop a bit of rose water in there. Anything watery will thin it, but rose water will improve the smell.' She wrinkled her nose.

Thea did as advised. Sitting next to a hot stove was chasing the chill away, but she couldn't shake the feeling that something terrible was waiting around the next corner. She agreed with Zofka; she'd seen the intricate wards – patching them together with *ice* of all things would have done nothing. Which meant Pan Novak was planning something more nefarious. And none of the patrols had unearthed any hint of any fate-weavers or Hunters, which made her very nervous.

Zofka wrapped dough around a wide stick with slick, practised movements as she formed the signature shape of the *trdelník*. 'Now you can add the fairy's tear.'

Thea carefully uncorked the tiny shimmering vial and tipped a single tear into her bowl. It bounced, once, twice, then sank into the mixture like a stone.

'And stir it all together until its silky.' Zofka shooed Radim away from her own bowl, brimming with sugar and spices, and began scattering her pastry – and half the flagstones. 'Jasper was in here the other day, ordering one of these.' She nodded to the *trdelník*, now cooking on a stick over the flames. She rotated some of the others in the line.

Thea stirred her potion. 'Oh?' she asked, curious despite herself. She hadn't seen him in days, but her body still ached from his touch. She wouldn't beg him. She wouldn't, she vowed, telling herself that was the truth, even as she tasted the lie. But yesterday, when the night had been at its blackest point, swollen with stars like ripe hanging fruits, her heart-spell had thumped at the thought of never feeling his lips on hers again.

'Though he may not be dead, the man is haunted,' Radim commented, peering at Zofka's dough.

Thea paused. 'He lost his daughter some years ago,' she told them.

'Oh.' Zofka snapped upright. 'How sad. No wonder he always seems so . . .'

'Grumpy?' Thea suggested.

'Lost,' Zofka declared. 'He looks lost. And no wonder, being a widower, too.'

'He is? Why didn't I already know that?'

Zofka wrinkled her nose. 'I presumed you did.'

'Who was she? What was she like?' Thea resumed stirring, reminded again that Jasper was not grumpy, he was lost in grief. It was too easy to villainise him as a heart-thief, a fate-weaver, but he was just another person muddling through this strange and wonderful existence. And maybe he was even lonelier than her, for at least she had friends and a community. Jasper was all alone.

Zofka shrugged. 'Nobody knows. He doesn't speak about it, Paní Dagmar just happened to mention it in passing one day when she was collecting her bread.'

Thea pursed her lips. She couldn't picture Jasper with a wife, something about the image made her feel uncomfortable, like lacing into a too-tight gown.

'Now plop the dead man's finger bone in,' Zofka said, with no little excitement.

Radim cringed. 'Please excuse me.' He floated away.

'He doesn't like the *d* word,' Zofka winced. 'I should have been more sensitive. I'm sorry, Radim!' she yelled, before turning to Thea. 'Do you think he heard that?'

'I think half the Magic Quarter heard that.' Thea drew the bone from her pocket, cleaned since the last potion, and dropped it into the bowl. 'Please don't be a disaster.' She could not afford to hunt down another lake spirit or water demon or whatever that horrible thing was that had almost drowned her.

'It'll need to brew for at least a day and a night, more if you can spare it,' Zofka told her. 'Then it'll be perfect for you to do your thing.' She wiggled her fingers.

Perfect timing for the Winter Ball. Provided it worked this time.

A raven tapped on the window with its beak.

'Hello there, Biscuit,' Thea crooned on letting him in. Biscuit nudged his head against her hand and she laughed, petting him as she untied his note with the other. 'Oh, it's Malek, he's replied.'

Offering Biscuit a chunk of leftover gingerbread, of which she always had an abundance, Zofka leaned against her counter, trying to see the note, too. 'Read it out, read it out,' she chanted like an incantation.

'*Dearest Thea,*' Thea read aloud, '*I am cheered to hear of your good health and swift recovery. I look forward to attending the Winter Ball with you on my arm. Do be assured, I am not threatened by other men.*'

Zofka groaned. 'What did you write to him?'

Thea glanced up guiltily. 'I just wanted him to know that there was nothing . . . untoward happening when Jasper made a point of escorting me back to my bedroom.' Though there had been earlier. Her guilt thickened. She liked Malek and he'd been good to her. . . Surely he was the sensible choice for her?

Zofka swatted her with a floury cloth. 'You daft pigeon, you shouldn't draw attention to these things!'

'Well, I'm not exactly practised at courting!'

'What else did he say?'

'*Though if you bore any doubts as to my intentions, here they are: I intend to win your heart. Yours, Malek.*'

Thea let out a slow breath.

Zofka copied her. 'That was . . . good,' she admitted. 'As much as I'm rooting for Jasper—'

Thea shot her a curious look. 'What?'

Zofka waved a dismissive hand, 'You're not ready to hear that yet.' She gestured to the note. 'That was good though. Are you all right? You've gone pale.'

Thea grimaced. 'I have no heart to be won.'

'You don't need to have a heart to be in a relationship with someone,' Zofka said gently. 'Isn't that what you decided? That you didn't want to be by yourself any longer?'

Thea worried at her lip. 'Maybe.' Something white fluttered past the windows. 'Oh, look, the weather-witches have been experimenting with snow again.' Thea jumped down from the counter and went to look outside, followed by Zofka.

When they stepped out onto the street, Thea was first to realise. 'That's not snow.'

'They're notes,' Zofka exclaimed.

Hundreds of notes, folded into the shape of birds, were whirling through the Magic Quarter, coaxing its residents outside. Talibah emerged from the Lantern. On spotting them, she hurried over.

The white paper was luminous against the black skies, drawing the attention of a couple of pixies, who flitted from cobblestone to cobblestone, trying to catch one. More than one note set alight when its paper wings flew too close to the witch light street lamps, scattering the evening with embers.

Rose peered out of her window, already in her sleeping cap, vanished, then reappeared with a Venus flytrap, sending it spiralling up. The plant's jaws clamped around one of the notes and shot back to Rose, who shut her window and vanished again.

The notes settled onto the cobblestones like snowflakes.

Thea bent to retrieve one.

'Take care.' Zdenka, the fortune teller, materialised in robes of violet satin. 'They're a portent of doom.'

Thea tightened her hold on the note, unfolding it in a hurry. When she glanced up, Zdenka had vanished again.

'Ignore them,' Zofka said, 'They like to rustle up drama.'

But Thea had already read the note. She handed it to Zofka with an unsteady hand. 'They're not wrong.'

'*I'm coming for you, Theodora,*' Zofka read aloud. When her gaze rose to meet Thea's, it was filled with fear as dark as night. The witch light street lamps flared, emerald-green flames licking higher, as if they could burn away the threat.

Talibah began picking up other notes, unfolding them one at a time. 'They all say the same.' She started collecting handfuls, then armfuls, and still the notes kept coming, flying down into the Quarter on sharply folded paper wings.

The words ricocheted through Thea's bones. 'You were right,' she told Zofka bleakly. 'Biscuit being nailed to my door, that note . . . I was the target all along. What if I'm the reason that someone attacked the wards and sent Pan Novak in against us? What if—' She grabbed

Zofka's arm. 'What if I came to Jasper looking for a deal because I was in hiding?'

'You could be.' Zofka squeezed Thea's hand. 'But as valued as you are to me, I doubt you are the reason that Hunters were sent in to cause chaos in the Quarter.'

Thea did not relax. 'Perhaps. But someone's sending these threats.'

Ignoring the witch light, more notes nosedived down onto the three women. Thea yelped and covered her head with her arms, shielding her face as they ran into the apothecary.

Talibah yanked the door shut as another volley of bird-notes slammed into the wood. She slid the bolts firmly across.

'Who would want to threaten me?' Thea watched the notes pile up against the window like drifts of snow. 'And why?'

'That's what I'd like to know,' Talibah said grimly.

Thea rested her head against the glass. 'My customers have just started returning. If they hear of this, they'll be frightened away for good.'

'They won't.' Zofka nodded to the window. 'The Magic Quarter protects its own – look.'

Thea looked up.

Rose was shuffling by, holding flower baskets stuffed with notes, feebly flapping their wings as she shoved more in. Zdenka was gathering more at her side. A quartet of the widest gowns Thea had ever seen waltzed past by themselves, their skirts sweeping up more notes like opulent brooms. In their wake, walked Fleur. Even Wojslav had joined their ranks, though he looked less than pleased about it. The skulk of vulpine shape-shifters were running around in their fox forms, using their tails to brush notes into a heap, which a flock of weather-witches then razed to ash with witch light. And Paní Dagmar seemed to be waving her hands around, conducting notes to fly straight into that witch light.

'Maybe she's a weather-witch after all?' Talibah pondered.

'Could be,' Zofka mused.

*

It wasn't until Talibah and Zofka had left for their own homes that fear overshadowed Thea once more. Somebody was targeting her. But who? The more Thea discovered, the less she knew. Except for one thing: she couldn't delay in asking Jasper for a new deal any longer. It was time to get her memories back.

CHAPTER

Twenty-One

LIGHTING CANDLES TO chase away her worries, Thea made herself a large cup of hot chocolate. Adding a plate of iced biscuits, she settled down on her bed in a nest of yellow blankets and looked dubiously at her newest book. Cinnamon nibbled the edge of it. 'I know, I'm not sure about it either,' Thea sighed, cracking *Falling in Hate with his Lordship* open to the second chapter. Her other unfinished books stared accusingly at her from her bedside table. 'Maybe the Lord will be as arrogant and commanding as Jasper and remind me why I'm never letting him kiss me again,' she told Cinnamon, who perched on his hind legs, tilting his head to one side as if considering the matter.

Despite her misgivings, Thea soon lost herself in her book. Until a loud crash jolted her back to the present. With a squeak of alarm, she leapt off the bed. Cinnamon ran under her blankets and hid. He'd knocked over Thea's tallest stack of books. 'It's all right,' she told him gently, kneeling on the floor to pick them up.

Her door burst open.

Jasper stood there, eyes darting around Thea's home. Until he noticed the violets she'd painted behind her bed, and his gaze stuck there. She was surprised he hadn't noticed them last time but now, he couldn't look away.

'What are you doing?' she demanded, standing. 'You can't just break into my personal space.' Clearly he was unimpressed with her decorations but she didn't care if he was precious about his property;

she lived here now and she wouldn't shrink her personality to keep it as pristine as she'd found it.

'I apologise.' He sounded as if he'd run up the stairs. 'I was looking for you downstairs when I heard something. I was concerned you had fainted or were under attack. I had no intentions of startling you or invading your privacy.' His cheeks turned the faintest shade of pink. 'I saw the notes outside, and I thought—' He shook his head. 'I will take my leave now.'

'No, it's fine.' Thea set the fallen books down on her bed. 'I need to talk to you, and I suppose we may as well do it here, where it's warm.' Now her cheeks were warm; she was standing in front of her bed, surrounded by candlelight. It didn't help that she was now intimately familiar with his touch, his taste, the way his voice had deepened and roughened when he'd told her *I know exactly what you want. What you need.* When he had later proven that he did indeed know what she hungered for. He'd woken an appetite within her that she hadn't realised she'd held.

Jasper removed his coat and hat, silently hanging them on a hook as Thea bustled around her little kitchen, making more hot chocolate. When she sneaked a glance at him, he had settled into one of her armchairs, stroking Cinnamon, who was reclining on his lap. Thea turned back to her stove. Pressing her hands to her cheeks, she ordered them to calm. This would not give her any ideas, she told herself strictly. This temporary truce was only necessary to ask if he would forge a new deal with her.

Handing him a cup of chocolate, she settled into the other armchair.

Jasper met her gaze. Under the candlelight, his hair was as dark as Biscuit's feathers, his widow's peak prominent. 'What did you wish to discuss?' Though he took pains to keep his face impassive, she caught a whisper of intrigue, a brush of hope.

Thea curled her legs up, watching Cinnamon's eyes close as he fell asleep on Jasper's lap. *Traitor.* Though she knew from experience how warming Jasper's touch was. She set her cup down, dragging her focus back to the matter at hand. 'After the first threat, you said you were going to investigate the matter. Did you find anything?'

'I did not.' Jasper's face shadowed. An almost imperceptible change, but Thea had learnt the shifts in his mood the way she'd learnt the phases of the moon. She'd butted against another of his secrets, then. Interesting. 'But I do have news.'

'Tell me,' Thea said at once.

'You were right,' Jasper said, though his voice was filled with a foreboding that brought Thea little comfort. 'Another fate-weaver has launched an attack against the Quarter. I spotted her skulking around the vicinity. Testing the boundaries of the wards. They might be fractured, but she seems to be biding her time. For what, I do not know, though I fear she fractured the wards herself, in which case, we need to stay vigilant in case she tears them down altogether.'

Thea looked uneasily at him. 'Who is she?'

'An old enemy. You must stay within what remains of the wards now, Thea. She will be able to recognise the shape of my power within you. If you were to become a target on my account . . .' His hand tightened on the arm of the chair. 'I should not be able to forgive myself.'

'You need to inform the rest of the Magic Quarter,' Thea said quietly. 'They cannot be left defenceless if the wards worsen or, gods forbid, fall.'

'I will.' Jasper heaved a ragged sigh. 'I shall send a raven to my contact in the Quarter and they will spread the word. The more eyes we have out there, the better.'

'What does she look like?'

'Heloise is a fate-weaver, she can change her appearance on a whim. But the last I saw her, she was in her true form: short blonde hair, green eyes and a tall frame.'

Thea's hot chocolate melted on her tongue like satin. A small comfort against the great unknown, looming at their doors with threats and Hunters and whispers from other worlds. 'I'll keep a lookout for her. What happened between you? Why is this Heloise after you?'

'We have a long history, but I do not know why she is targeting the Quarter.' Jasper toyed with the fabric on the chair. 'I can only suppose that her anger has grown over the years, and now she wishes to destroy anything connected to me. Including Stiltskin's Apothecary and the Magic Quarter itself.'

Thea grimaced. 'You're going to be even less popular around here after that.'

Jasper inclined his head. 'I am aware of that.'

'Is there anyone in the Quarter who isn't afraid of you?' she asked. 'Do you have friends here?'

Jasper finished his chocolate, balancing his cup on the arm of his chair, seeming reluctant to move and dislodge Cinnamon, who was happily sprawled out, his paws twitching as he dreamed. Jasper tapped his fingers against the cup. 'That's a story for another time.'

'Fine.' Thea filed it away to ponder over later. Talking to Jasper was like speaking to a wall where each stone was a secret, all stacked with such care, such balance, that to remove one would cause the entire façade to crumble. Thea wondered what that would look like, what was behind it all. Who he was he behind the shadows and smokescreen.

Jasper glanced down at Cinnamon, idly stroking his fur. 'You're thinking so hard I can practically hear it. What did you need to talk to me about? Is it to tell me that you are attending the Winter Ball with Malek?'

Thea ripped her attention away from Jasper's hand. Their cosy scene was lulling Thea into a false sense of security, into trusting the one person she knew she could not. No matter how she hungered for him. 'How could you possibly know that?'

'I can see the invitation.' Jasper glanced at the said invitation, propped up against a bowl of apples.

Thea's face burned. 'No, it wasn't that.'

'Talk to me, Thea.' Jasper's voice was a command, veiled in silk.

'I wanted to ask you something.' Her stomach twisting, she stood, taking both cups over to her little kitchen for the excuse of having something to do. She dropped them into her pail of soapy water.

Jasper gently scooped up Cinnamon and deposited the sleeping rabbit on Thea's bed. 'What is it?'

Thea pushed herself off from the kitchen counter, drawing herself taller. 'Before you deny me, I want you to listen.'

Jasper's furrows deepened.

Thea's heart-spell pulsed harder. 'I wish to make a new deal with you.'

Jasper tugged his collar up, his frown vanishing, along with any hint of emotion. He'd retreated to that place where Thea couldn't touch him. Couldn't find the man who had ridden into the forest to save her. Who had kissed her like he might have died if he didn't.

She stood her ground. 'If these threats were the reason I fled my previous life, I need my memories back. I need to know what's coming for me. Neither Pan Novak nor this fate-weaver you have history with have any reason to threaten me personally: so there has to be someone else. Someone the wards were keeping out.'

Jasper's face was immovable, revealing nothing.

'I am prepared to pay any price. Jasper, I *need* my heart and memories back. Without them, I can only ever live half a life. Please, there must be something else I can give you in their place.' She ignored the fear sliding down her neck. 'How many years of life is my heart worth?'

Jasper stiffened. 'I will not allow you to shorten your life.'

'You can't need my heart and memories this badly,' Thea cried out. 'So what else is there? Are you truly that desperate to keep me indentured to the apothecary?'

'I could do without you in a heartbeat if I wasn't concerned you'd run off and do something foolish and make everything worse,' Jasper snapped.

This time the warmth flooding Thea's cheeks had nothing to do with surreptitious glances at Jasper's mouth, his hands, the echoes of her dream staining her thoughts. It was anger. 'What does that mean?'

Jasper stormed to the door and pulled on his coat. Each detail was immaculate, from the folds in his neck ruffle to his crisp hems. 'I do not renege on my deals.'

'You're keeping secrets from me,' Thea accused.

Jasper tugged sharply at his coat. 'I do not renege on my deals,' he repeated.

'If you won't return my heart, will you at least tell me why?' Her throat thickened. 'Why did I give it all away?'

Jasper shook his head, turning his back. 'You know I cannot tell you that.'

'Jasper.' His name was a command, a plea, a cry for help. He turned back, wary. 'Am I in danger?'

'You are safe here, Thea.'

'Do not call me that. It is not my name.'

A tense silence squeezed the air until Thea was suffocating, buckling under the weight of everything. 'I think you had better leave.'

Jasper hesitated on the threshold. 'You do not need to fear these threats,' he said. 'You've made this apothecary home; the Magic Quarter rallies around you. You are adored here.'

'I don't care what you say,' Thea whispered. 'The one thing, the only thing I have ever wanted or needed, you're refusing to grant. Anything else is meaningless.' Jasper held a power greater than she could imagine. Yet he refused to use it to help her. Their tryst felt like it had happened in another lifetime now. How could she have surrendered herself to him so willingly? 'One day I will find a way to reclaim my heart,' she declared. 'And I will not forget how you took pains to keep it from me. I will not forgive you for this, are we clear?'

'As crystal,' Jasper growled.

Two knocks sounded. They took a moment to permeate the thick atmosphere curdling between them. 'That's the back door,' Thea realised aloud. 'Someone needs help.'

CHAPTER

Twenty-Two

JASPER OPENED THE door. 'I'll deal with this.'
'I can do it.'
Jasper ignored her, running lightly down the stairs.

Thea threw up her arms in exasperation before following, shooting daggers at his back.

A man was pacing back and forth, visible through the back window. When Jasper let him in, he looked between Jasper and Thea, nervous energy radiating from him that did not match the deep bags scored under his eyes, his shadowed jawline, too sharp, gaunt. His patched shirt clung to his thin frame, too insubstantial for winter settling in outside. 'I heard you could help me.' Thea didn't recognise him from the Quarter; he was non-magical, then.

'We can,' Jasper said. 'Please, sit down. Tell us what you need.'

'I am sick,' the man began, refusing the chair. 'I saw the doctor tonight and he told me . . .' He resumed his pacing, tugging at his hair. 'He told me that death would come soon. That I would not see next spring.'

Thea lowered her eyes in sympathy. Hearing these stories never got easier.

Jasper addressed him. 'We cannot cure you, but we can prolong—'

'No.' The man stopped pacing.

Thea and Jasper exchanged a wary glance.

'I am leaving four children and a wife behind,' the man said quietly. 'I am here to ask you to provide for them. Make me rich before I go.

Then I won't have to . . .' His voice broke. Thea closed her eyes, aching for him, for his family, unable to imagine the path that lay before them. 'I won't have to worry,' he finished.

'Done,' Jasper said, making the man near collapse in relief. 'That will be two months.'

The man gaped at him. 'I . . . What?'

'Two months of your life if you wish me to help you,' Jasper said calmly.

The man looked to Thea as if she could do something. 'Two months,' he repeated faintly, shock surging through his face. 'That's too much, I would lose so much time, I . . .'

'I'm sorry,' Thea whispered.

Jasper yanked the chair out from beside Thea's workbench. 'Sit down,' he ordered the man, who obeyed as if he was a small child. 'I can't tell you what to do, but this is your choice, so think on it carefully.'

The man looked up at Jasper, as lost as Jasper had been that night in the forest, out of his depth, bereft. 'What would you do?'

Jasper hesitated, his back to Thea so she couldn't see his expression, couldn't guess at his thoughts. 'I cannot tell you.'

'Fine. Do it. Do it now.' The man exhaled shakily. 'I might lose time with them, but if I can secure them for a lifetime, I will have done right by them.'

'That is a good decision,' Jasper said softly, resting a hand on the man's shoulder for a beat.

Thea blinked hard, staring at the wall. Grief swirled in the room, a saltwater scent rolling through the apothecary as if the walls themselves were crying. In her growing space, the trees had fallen quiet apart from a steady rustle, which she suspected was her apple tree. It was rhythmic, like it was sobbing to itself.

Jasper rolled up his shirtsleeves, revealing his strong and supple forearms. Thea averted her eyes. Rubbing the back of her neck, she tried to forget how it felt when he'd lifted her effortlessly onto the back of his horse. How he'd kissed her like he was claiming her. Now was *not* the time, she instructed herself strictly.

'Are you well?' Jasper asked her in an aside.

'Yes,' Thea half yelped, caught unawares.

His gaze turned shrewd, then knowing.

When Jasper unveiled the skeins of fate, his power set it aglow bright enough to light the entire apothecary up from within. All that power, and still he refused to help her. Anger rattled her bones.

Jasper amended the man's fate swiftly and confidently, taking the months of his life as if he was plucking a single hair from his head. Afterwards, when the man had left, silence stretched between them.

Jasper broke it first. 'As long as there are people in this world, they will have their problems, and they will come to us to amend their fates. It's what we do.'

'I am aware of that,' she said. 'But the day I find it easy to look suffering in the eye is the day I worry who I have become.'

'Good. Never lose a single piece of yourself to this. You're too important for that.'

Thea frowned as his words sank past her anger. 'Are you . . . complimenting me?'

'And when those people regret the prices they have paid, we do not indulge them. Fate is not to be treated lightly, it must be wielded with respect. We do not deal with remorse.'

Thea's anger crept along her veins. Growing and building and swelling.

When she refused to respond, Jasper handed her a slip of paper. 'I couldn't help seeing this on your table earlier.'

She took it, knowing what was written before she skimmed over it:

Abigail, Edith, Annmarie, Jane, Bridget, Georgina, Amy, Helen, Eleanor, Gillian, Mildred, Ruth, Shannon.

Another list of names. They were scattered over her home like dust. Most were used as bookmarks. Some had been chewed by Cinnamon. Others were in Zofka or Talibah's handwriting, when they'd offered their own contributions. All of them forever searching for the right name, the name that would be the golden key, unlocking Thea's past.

'The answer is no,' Jasper said softly. 'This is not your name.'

'Which one?' Thea couldn't help the bitterness seeping into her tone. She knew her stare was icy, but she had made her feelings towards Jasper clear: she would not forgive him for this.

'Any of them.' Jasper pulled his coat back on for the second time that night and took his leave.

Thea spent the following day checking on the key. The Winter Ball was tonight, and her potion was still brewing. She distracted herself by alternating between loathing Jasper and wondering how she was going to discover who was behind these threats without having access to her memories. Several visitors stopped by. Zdenka, who offered their services with their crystal ball again, which Thea politely declined, again. The skulk of shape-shifters arrived in a pack and vowed they would now patrol three times per day. Paní Dagmar, who gifted her a protection stone that she'd found in the back corner of her haberdashery. 'It's a hagstone,' she'd told Thea, cackling. And Sarah, who'd popped round with an armful of kittens, all black with white socks, who'd bumbled playfully around the apothecary and cheered Thea more than any of the others combined. Nobody mentioned a mysterious fate-weaver and she sent Jasper several ravens, asking when he would warn the rest of the Quarter, or if she ought to. He had yet to reply and she hoped that signified he was out hunting for more information first.

A second gown arrived. Golden as starlight, it moved like poetry and whispered musical notes with each rustle of satin.

It was incandescent. And when wearing it, Thea felt incandescent too. Radiant. How reassuring that Malek had ordered such a delectable gown: not for the expense, but because it set off the shine on her golden hair, brought out a deep glow in her skin, coaxed out the gilt in her hazel eyes, like pieces of honeycomb. He was coming to learn her. Had paid attention to her. She had been right: he was the better match. She had no need for a man who frustrated and confused and beguiled her. Not when she had Malek.

'This is becoming somewhat of a tradition.' Zofka's eyes wrinkled with pleasure as she laced the thick silk ribbons of Thea's stomacher. 'Maybe you should hire a lady's maid, someone who understands where all these frills and ruffles go.'

Thea laughed at the notion. 'A few gowns, gorgeous as they may be' – she stroked the thick fabric with reverence; it chimed a little harmony at her – 'do not make me a lady.'

'You'd make a finer one than most, though,' Talibah added, straightening Thea's skirts over the pannier.

Thea caught Talibah's eyes. 'You have that look again.'

Zofka shot up from behind Thea. 'She does?'

'She does,' Thea confirmed.

Zofka pointed at Talibah. 'Tell us everything. Right now.'

Talibah grimaced. 'It's impossible to keep anything from you two.'

'So, where are you hungering to visit this time?' Thea persisted.

'Switzerland has been calling me of late.' Talibah's gaze turned faraway. 'I've been dreaming of snow-capped mountains and little towns nestled between them. But I will not leave until this threat to the Magic Quarter has passed and I know in my bones that the two of you are safe, do you hear me?' She directed the last words to Zofka, who sniffed and nodded, before flinging her arms around Talibah's neck.

'When Jasper was here yesterday evening, he informed me that he'd spotted an old enemy lurking around the wards. A fate-weaver who goes by the name of Heloise, with cropped blonde hair and green eyes. He believes she's the one who's been stirring up trouble and setting the Hunters onto us.'

Zofka pursed her lips. 'What happened between them?'

'He wouldn't tell me,' Thea admitted.

'Then we don't know whose side we ought to be on,' Talibah thought aloud.

'Jasper's,' Zofka said automatically. 'This Heloise is planning on decimating the Magic Quarter; we're not on her side!'

'That's true,' Talibah relented.

Zofka resumed dressing Thea.

'What exactly did Jasper say when he refused to make a new deal?' Talibah asked, referencing the ravens Thea had sent them late last night when she'd needed to vent.

Thea pulled a face. 'Stop that,' Zofka admonished, tapping her on the nose with a brush. 'You're my work of art, I refuse to let you ruin the masterpiece I'm creating here.'

'He said that he does not renege on his deals, then later made some vague commentary on how fate-weavers do not engage with remorse or regret.' Thea battled to keep the emotion from her voice.

'I'm sorry,' Talibah said quietly.

'We don't need him,' Zofka declared, waving the brush as if she were conducting an orchestra. 'We have our own power, we're more than capable of figuring this out.'

'It's been seven years, and we haven't figured it out yet,' Thea said bleakly.

'I am sorry I interfered with Jasper,' Zofka said suddenly. 'I still maintain there is something there, but—'

'The fact that I kissed Jasper is immaterial. I have no *romantic* feelings towards him.'

'You do know witches can taste lies, don't you?' Zofka commented calmly.

'Zofka,' Talibah warned, watching Thea's face.

Thea shot Zofka a strong look. 'Fine. I bear *some* small attraction to Jasper – you said it yourself, he's handsome. And something else might have happened between us in the forest after he rescued me—'

Zofka's head popped up. 'What—'

'But he's also arrogant and authoritative and refusing to return my heart and memories,' Thea said firmly, before she could ask anything else. 'I told him I'd never forgive him for that, and I meant it. Besides, I thought you were a kitchen-witch?'

Zofka shrugged. 'Oh, I'm magical in many ways.' She wiggled her fingers. 'Multi-talented, you might say.' Her smile dropped. 'You really said that to him?'

'And really meant it.' Thea fussed with her skirts.

A gentle press of her hand had her lifting her eyes to Talibah, who had reached across the wide swoop of her gown. 'Then it is just as well Malek is the one who invited you to the ball.'

An owl perched in a silvered branch outside Thea's window hooted the hour.

'Is that the time?' Thea picked up her skirts and ran downstairs, through the backroom of the apothecary and into her little jungle. There, the glass-panelled roof revealed a star-spangled sky, each constellation a curiosity she'd never seen before. But there was no time to sit and wonder at the stars. Giving her apple tree a quick affectionate rub on its latest creation – a single midnight blue apple that glimmered like a sapphire – Thea bent to the bowl she'd left sitting on her side table.

It glowed like a pearl.

'That looks ready to me,' Zofka said, having hurried along, too.

'Weave your magic,' Talibah added, appearing in the doorway.

Pulling the bone from the silky mixture, Thea inhaled a trembling breath. The potion was clinging to every groove of bone, wrapping itself around the finger like a robe of moonlight.

She drew up the gossamer strings of fate, knowing from Talibah's soft sigh that her second-sighted friend saw it, too. Then, tuning everything out but her intent to make the key for Malek, to admit him into a secret place, to conceal his every footstep, every brush of his hands, every sound, she began knitting threads around the key. Knotting them into place. And when fate clamoured at her for a price, she whispered *not yet, not yet*.

'It's beautiful,' Talibah murmured.

Zofka whipped out a brush and dabbed Thea's forehead. Making the key had devoured a lot of energy, but she wasn't exhausted with it, as she'd feared. She was exhilarated.

'Your carriage awaits, my lady,' Zofka told her.

CHAPTER

Twenty-Three

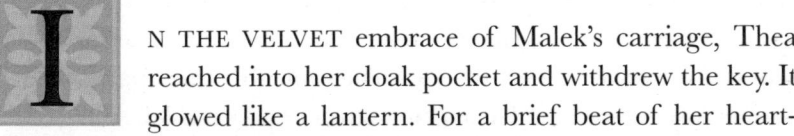N THE VELVET embrace of Malek's carriage, Thea reached into her cloak pocket and withdrew the key. It glowed like a lantern. For a brief beat of her heartspell, its power was so rich, so potent, that it illuminated the carriage with a thousand possibilities of fate, each strand gleaming in different colours, making Thea wonder at this magic that lived and breathed within her. Wishing she had been born to it. Wishing it didn't belong to *him*.

She forced herself to smile across the carriage at Malek. 'I am sorry it took me this long to make; it was a greater challenge than I've embarked on before. I hope your sister fares well?'

Malek received the key with trembling eagerness. 'All will be well now,' he murmured, eyes locked on it. 'I confess, I did not expect it to be beautiful; I always thought of a key as an object with a use, a means to an end, but this . . . Why, it's a work of art.' He lifted his gaze to her.

The tension in Thea's smile eased; even if he could not see the threads of fate rippling through the carriage, he saw the workmanship in the key, her skill that had given it its potency.

'As are you.' Malek's dimple appeared.

And at last, so did the payment that was necessary for this expenditure of power, this working of fate that she had begged and begged *not yet*, holding it off just a little longer, just enough to allow her to savour this moment with Malek. The last moment he would look at her this way. It popped into her head like an intrusive thought: five years of life. Her smile melted from her face. *Five years.*

'What do I owe you for this?' His throat bobbed up and down. 'It must be . . . considerable.'

'It is,' Thea whispered.

Malek reached across the carriage to clasp her hand. 'It's all right, Thea.' His smile was tentative. 'I know what I asked for; for me, no price is too steep for saving my sister from that snake.' He searched her gaze. 'Nor will I think any differently of you for taking it. I invited you to the ball for the pleasure of spending more time with you. Had I not asked you for this key, I still would have sought your company.'

Thea took a shaky breath. Jasper had told her that his power required balance, that she couldn't steal time. But the way that Malek was looking at her, tender and truthful, prepared to sacrifice a slice of his life for his sister, decided Thea. What were a few more headaches, another fainting fit, awful as they had been, compared to five years of Malek's life?

'I will not take a price from you,' Thea said softly. 'Not for this, not when you only wish to do good. It—' She braced her quivering hands on the velvet bench either side of her. 'It doesn't seem fair to me.'

Malek's breath escaped in a single sigh. 'You, lovely Thea, are a gift. I cannot thank you enough.'

His dimple reappeared, giving Thea the urge to move and sit beside him. She gave in.

'Hello, there.' His smile warmed.

The carriage lurched, throwing them both against one side as it swerved wildly, two of its wheels lifting from the street before the coachman shouted to the horses, drawing them to a halt. The wheels hit the cobblestones, the impact juddering through Thea as she clung onto the bench, her gown letting out a single high-pitched scream.

'What was *that?*'

Malek leapt from his seat, opening the carriage door to reveal the far end of the Magic Quarter, next to the Crypt, before the exit that led onto Prague Bridge.

The street had ruptured.

A rift was running down the centre, tearing the liminal space apart. Within the rift was a void, blacker than night, its nothingness a presence all of its own. Mist drifted up. Folks from the Magic Quarter were running out of their homes, exclaiming at the damage, and Thea made to exit the carriage, but Malek grabbed her wrist. 'There's nothing you can do now,' he said, wearing his concern on his face.

'But—'

'Come to the ball with me, Thea. You are Lord Stiltskin's apprentice, are you not?'

Thea frowned. 'Yes.'

'Then the apothecary was never yours. It always belonged to him, will always belong to him. You do not owe Lord Stiltskin, nor this Magic Quarter, your entire life.'

Thoughts squalled in Thea's mind as she stared at Malek. He snapped the carriage door shut and thumped on the roof. It rattled on, exiting the Quarter, skirting the rift and leaving it in their wake. 'I need to check that my friends, my rabbit, the apothecary are safe . . .'

A raven dashed through the carriage window.

Malek started, but Thea half tore the note from its talon:

We are all fine. Go to the ball, this can all wait for a night.
   With love, Talibah

'My friends agree with you.' Thea slumped back against the seat, her golden gown half-heartedly trilling a little melody.

Malek poured Thea a healthy glass of champagne.

As she accepted it, a horrible thought lodged in her brain. One that grew and grew until she couldn't think of anything else. Until it was a single roar. And it bore Jasper's voice: *Fate took its price from you. If I hadn't entered when I did, then I do not know how much more it would have taken.*

Had *she* just broken the Magic Quarter?

*

Carriages wound up to the castle, perched atop a hill like an eagle in its eyrie, overlooking Prague and the Vltava river ribboning through it. Horses stamped their hooves in impatience, tossing their manes and huffing plumes of steam into the cold night as the line of carriages crawled through the Giant's Gate. Thea's dress hummed as she looked out of the window, up at the statues of clashing titans battling either side. Their carriage clattered through a courtyard, then another gate, leading to yet another courtyard; Prague Castle was immense. Thea's nerves returned in force; she should have turned back, gone to help her friends. But they'd told her not to. And Malek had been right: what did she owe the Magic Quarter, really? She'd never chosen it. Or if she had, she possessed no memory of the fact.

'They are giving out masks at the door,' Malek noticed.

'How scandalous,' Thea teased.

'Quite.' Malek smoothed his wig.

Perhaps he was nervous. Thea traced the frost-patterned window as they awaited their turn to disembark. The castle had been left in disrepair since the Bohemian Revolt, until Empress Maria Theresa had got her hands on it and decided to renovate. Thea searched the skies in case she'd been sent another raven, but saw only decorations: candlelit orbs were hung from trees like fallen moons, making the snowy rooftops and courtyards sparkle. On exiting the carriage, Thea spotted tiny lanterns strung everywhere, until the castle shone as brightly as a star itself, lit up against an indigo sky. Trunks sat at regular intervals, with silks and satins spilling from their open mouths like treasure, inviting guests to rummage through their wares.

Thea found a mask in golden silk, a perfect match for her dress. Tying it around her eyes, she turned to Malek. 'How do I look?'

He appraised her through his own mask, a forest green which complimented his tawny eyes, cut to flatter his smile and dimples, and suiting his brocaded suit and breeches nicely. 'You are, quite simply, a vision,' he proclaimed. His dimple lessened. 'Though I had been expecting you to wear the gown I had gifted you, you are radiant in gold.'

Thea stifled her confusion. Who else could have sent her this gown but Malek? But there was no time to ponder that now, as other guests were donning their masks, crowding impatiently behind them. Thea took Malek's arm, allowing him to guide her into the Spanish Hall and the spectacle of the Winter Ball.

As the beautifully carved doors opened to admit them, Thea's intake of breath was audible. Living in the Magic Quarter for the past seven years, dipping her fingers into the pool of fate, had little prepared her for the sight that lay before her.

CHAPTER

Twenty-Four

HE SPANISH HALL, grand in its own right, with its high stuccoed ceiling, large arched windows and golden chandeliers, had been transformed into a frosted vignette. Shimmering white-silver stars were scattered on the parquet flooring like ripples across an enchanted lake. Snowdrops bloomed in an intricate display over the walls, each flower bearing a waxen dewdrop of candlelight, and waiters dressed as fir trees wandered through the hall, offering branches laden with goblets and bewitching treats.

It couldn't have been more enchanting if it had been magical.

'Will you do me the honour?' Malek held his hand out, smiling as he watched Thea take everything in.

She laid her hand in his, ignoring the guilt snarling in her stomach that she was here, enjoying herself, while the Magic Quarter had been cast into disarray. 'Of course.'

An orchestra of musicians played a waltz. Malek led Thea to the centre of the hall, where guests were dancing, their gowns and suits and masks a jewellery box of riches. One woman's cream skirts whirled like a dandelion clock. Another person wore a cloak of feathers. Thea's dress echoed the sweet harmonies of the orchestra as Malek's arm came to rest around her waist, and, with another flash of that wide smile, waltzed her around the hall.

As they danced, Thea noticed a masked gentleman on the far side of the ballroom, staring at her hard enough to make her pinken beneath her mask. He was dressed smartly in black, with silver buttons that shone like icing. Even amidst such a crowd, his wardrobe, his height, his presence, were striking. A star in a room of clouds. Jasper.

Each time Malek whirled her around, Thea's eyes clashed against Jasper's. He watched her over the rim of his glass, in a way that made Thea conscious of the way she moved, of Malek's hand in the small of her back, of how her gown sang out in joy. Perhaps it was risky wearing it to a non-magical place but the orchestra covered it nicely.

'Please excuse me,' Malek murmured to Thea as the dance wound to a close, nodding to someone over her shoulder she couldn't see. 'I shall return shortly.' He gestured at the nearest waiter, heavily laden with marzipan robins. 'I suggest you peruse the offerings.'

'Don't take too long or that might prove to be dangerous,' Thea laughed, covering her unease with a smile. Was Jasper here because he knew she'd failed to take an immense price? Had she really torn the Magic Quarter apart by being too soft-hearted for the power she wielded?

With a press of her hand, Malek departed the dancefloor. Thea went to stand beside one of the windows, watching the dancers couple up as the opening strains to a minuet sounded. A waiter offered her a caramel bonbon. A second cut in with a branch of ruby-red macarons, as if he was competing for her attention. She bit into each so as not to disappoint either waiter.

Jasper materialised in front of her. 'May I have this dance?' His voice was cut from velvet as rich as his mask and every bit as dark. She didn't need bonbons or macarons when the words falling from his mouth were silken as chocolate.

'No.' She glared at him. 'You have some nerve asking me after the last time we spoke.'

'Theodora.' Jasper's throat tensed. 'Forgive me, I couldn't resist. You are exquisite in gold. A rare gem indeed.'

Thea's heart-spell thrashed behind her ribs. Jasper's remark on learning Malek had sent her a gown echoed through her head: *You should be in gold, as radiant as the sun.*

'It was you! You sent me this gown.'

Jasper said nothing. No, that was untrue. Though he did not speak aloud, the way in which he regarded her said everything.

'How dare you? I have no wish to be standing here, wearing your guilt.'

Regret wisped over Jasper's face. 'My apologies. I meant it only as a gift.'

'It was inappropriate.'

With Jasper's mask concealing half of his face, it drew attention to his mouth, those full lips . . . Thea's memories scalded her with the knowledge of how they felt pressed against hers. How he tasted. Like the winter wind as it cut through the forest. Her cheeks flushed. Ridiculous, for a woman in her thirties to be blushing like a young girl; she had never felt such awkwardness with Malek. As if hiding a guilty secret, she cast a glance to where she'd seen him vanish. He was nowhere to be seen.

'Dance with me,' Jasper commanded. 'There are things that I must tell you. I came here tonight for you, Theodora.'

Thea hesitated, then placed her hand in his, allowing him to pull her into the minuet.

'It was ungallant of Malek to abandon you at a ball,' Jasper commented.

'I do not need nor want your advice on the matter,' Thea snapped. 'I am not your responsibility.' It mattered not if Jasper danced the way he strode into the apothecary, assured and commanding. Nor if his arm secured her against him as if they belonged together. 'And if I am to wed and have a family of my own . . . I'm running out of time. Malek may be my only option. Besides which—'

Jasper stopped abruptly. The couples surrounding them veered away, flowing on through the ballroom. Jasper stared at Thea. 'You would wed him?'

'If he would have me.' Thea held her chin high, meeting his stare.

A vein pulsed in Jasper's neck.

'You do not know me, Jasper,' Thea said. 'Knowing my true name, the life I gave up, does not mean that you know *me*.'

Jasper's face shuttered. 'Apparently not.' He resumed their dance, plunging back into the stream of dancers to continue the minuet.

'It vexes you, does it not?' Thea asked softly. 'That you cannot choose who I spend my time with, that you have no notion of what I might say or do next.'

'Yes.' Jasper's throat moved up and down as he swallowed, a galaxy of meaning contained in that single word. 'It vexes me.' His voice was throaty, raw in a way Thea was unused to hearing. It gave her pause. It was almost as if he . . . cared. She knew he had admired her: that had been plain from each of their kisses, the way that the tension, the heat had scored deeply through them, sending them crashing into each other's arms. But this spoke of something *more*. His gaze dropped to her neck and caught there, as if he'd become tangled in the necklace she wore. As if he remembered it, when she herself did not.

'What was I to you?' Thea asked.

Jasper reared back, breaking their dance apart. 'I'm sorry?'

'Before you took my heart and memories, what was I to you? Was I just another customer, or did you know me? Did you . . . care for me?'

Jasper went still. 'What could I have possibly done to give you the impression that you meant anything to me? Yours was just another deal. One of the hundreds I have forged in Prague alone.'

Thea's throat thickened. 'Hundreds?'

Jasper inclined his head.

Thea bent closer to whisper in his ear. 'If there are hundreds, why are you always paying such close attention to me? Or are you that wealthy, that you have gowns sent to each recipient of your *deals*?' She stepped back, surveying those dark blue eyes, shadowed with secrets. 'What did you come to tell me?' she asked. 'Though if it's the rift cutting through the Magic Quarter, I already know. It occurred just as we were leaving for the ball.'

'The wards have fallen,' Jasper told her. 'I came to warn you. Whoever has been threatening you will be able to walk into the Magic Quarter now. Heloise will be able to take whatever she wants.

You need to take care. Stay close to Zofka and Talibah until I can figure out a way to reinstate the wards.'

His words sent freezing fog down Thea's spine. Was this her fault? Did he know? She worried at her lip. And where was Malek? She scanned the ball for him, spotting a familiar figure just as the doors opened and closed again, swallowing him. *Where was he going?*

'Thea—' Jasper began.

'I'm not Thea,' she whispered. 'I never have been. And I don't need you, nor your warnings.'

Channelling every last shred of a confidence she did not feel, she sauntered off, her gown humming a rousing aria as if she were a budding heroine in an adventure novel. It was covered by the orchestra so she alone heard, but it boosted her confidence. Still, she couldn't resist glancing back. Jasper had frozen in place, a single hand resting against his heart as if Thea had pierced straight through it with her words. Her satisfaction eroded. It was chased with frustration; she refused to sympathise with her heart-thief.

Dancers engulfed Jasper as Thea navigated towards the doors Malek had slipped through. She left the Spanish Hall, her gown hushing to a golden murmur as she searched for Malek. *There.* His powdered wig bobbed past a window. He was in a large courtyard on the other side of the ballroom. Lifting her skirts, Thea lightly ran outside, chasing his path.

When she emerged in the courtyard, she caught sight of Malek . . . and *Pan Novak*. The pair were walking towards each other with purpose, and as Thea ducked out of sight behind a fountain with an ostentatious ice swan, she caught them exchange a folded slip of paper with a brief nod before passing on.

CHAPTER

Twenty-Five

HEA'S THOUGHTS SHUDDERED to a halt. She'd been spending time with Malek, forgone taking a price for his key, had a vision of their possible shared future. If he was up to something nefarious, she needed to know at once.

She stepped out from behind the fountain. 'Malek.'

He turned, his dimple appearing on seeing her. But his eyes flicked to the side, as if unsure how much she'd seen. 'What did you give Pan Novak?' she asked quietly.

His frown was tight, his smile tighter. 'What are you talking about?' He adjusted his wig. It had slipped on his forehead. Beneath, he was sweating, turning the powder to paste where the two met .

'I saw you pass Pan Novak a note. You must know him, therefore you must know of his actions in the Magic Quarter, in my home. He's been threatening all of us for weeks now.'

Malek's laugh, too, was tight. 'I have no idea what goes on in that head of yours. Let's get you back to the ball . . . Perhaps you need a drink.'

But Thea knew what she'd seen. 'Oh, Malek,' she sighed. 'I'm sorry for this.'

He took a step back, alarmed, but Thea had already sunk her hands into the fabric of the world, sacrificing her memory of reading *Eudora and the Ship's Captain* to tweak Malek's viridian-green thread, compelling the truth from him. A bad feeling was tickling her mind and she needed to know the truth. When it came to protecting her friends there was nothing she would not do.

'Tell me what you're hiding,' she ordered.

A pink spot on each cheek painted Malek with fury, but he was powerless to resist. 'I know what secrets you hide in that Quarter of yours, fate-weaver,' he hissed. 'My father was a Hunter, and so was his father, and his father before that. I am no landowner, I am a councillor of this city and I know all too well the dangers of your kind. Witchcraft might not be a criminal offence any longer, but that does not mean I will allow your kind to cluster in such large numbers. The kind of power you hold is a threat to us all.'

'We want nothing to do with power. We are no threat to you.' Thea's thoughts shuddered with the effort of replying calmly when everything within her wanted to rage and scream. All this time, Malek had been a toad in disguise. The other Magic Hunter the fate-weaver had mentioned in the forest. He'd been hiding in plain sight all along. She pulled on the thread she held. 'Now, tell me what was in that note.'

'I was informing Pan Novak that the last of the Hunters in our network have reached Prague tonight. My lookout sent a messenger to the ball, informing me that my suspicions were correct earlier; your little wards have fallen, exposing your Quarter and its dark secrets to the world. If I had my way, I would burn it down to the cobblestones, but Pan Novak desires to shut it down, instead. He does not have the same Hunter ancestry that I do; his motives are purely political.'

Malek's smile chilled Thea.

'People won't believe you, that magic exists; they'll think you've lost your mind,' she whispered.

His smile sharpened, tasting her hope.

'You do not have the authority!'

'Actually,' Malek continued, 'now that the wards have fallen, your precious Quarter is just another neighbourhood in Prague, and answerable to all its laws and customs. I think you'll find that *you* don't have the authority to conduct any of your businesses there.' He leant closer. 'And happily, the rest of the councillors are in agreement.'

Thea raised her eyebrows at him, burying her fear in the pit of her stomach. 'You were right earlier; an entire Quarter of magic-wielding folk? We are powerful. You ought to stop before you get hurt.'

Malek's smile turned sympathetic. 'We represent generations of Hunters, we know every one of your weaknesses: how to hurt you, where to attack to strike fear into every one of your hearts.'

'Then why attend a ball before raiding the Quarter? Surely you do not need other Hunters' support if you are that assured of your own success against us? Why bother bringing me here?' Malek's smile slipped. She held onto his thread more tightly. 'Tell me the truth,' she ordered.

'You're a fate-weaver,' he said seriously. 'You and Lord Stiltskin are the biggest obstacles in my plan, the thorns in my side. I needed you out the way. After this, I was going to take you back to my house and leave you locked in there.'

Somehow, listening to his betrayal stung anew. She could have cursed herself if she had broken the Magic Quarter to give him that key without a price . . . She jolted. If Malek had lied about everything, it was not a stretch to imagine his sister was fictional, too. *Then what had he requested the key for?* 'Why did you need that key? Was it to sneak past our wards before they ruptured – *what?*'

Malek shot her an anguished look. 'I shared intimate details of my sister's life with you, Thea. I cannot believe you would question that.'

'What—'

His grin was genuine this time. Just as Thea registered that her hold on his threads had slackened, he bolted across the courtyard, darting out of sight before she could quiet her anger enough to grab onto them again.

Thea shook her head angrily. She needed to get back to the Quarter, *now*.

But perhaps there was something she could do here first, if she could get her hands on Malek again.

An explosion rocked the courtyard.

Thea hurried for cover behind a nearby topiary tree, her heart-spell-pulse skittering like a frantic squirrel as a second volley of gunpowder exploded in the courtyard. No, not in the courtyard, above. She looked up as the first masked guests rushed outside, murmuring in delight, not fear, faces tilted up to the lights that crackled across the sky in a blaze of greens and purples and blues. They were chased by a sulphurous bite and the acrid tang of smoke: fireworks.

This was her chance to find and compel Malek, while Pan Novak and any other potential Hunters were distracted.

Thea's dress let out a shrill peal of alarm. She whipped round.

A woman was standing behind her, watching Thea with keen interest. Sleek and pantherine in a vivid blue jacket and breeches, her blonde hair slicked back: could this be Heloise?

Anxiety screamed through Thea's head. 'Do excuse me.' She smiled politely, making to step around the woman.

'Do you take me for a fool?'

Thea recognised her voice as the fate-weaver she'd overheard telling someone of her plans in the forest. The same fate-weaver who'd sent the ravenous *bludička* chasing after her. Who'd boasted of being the puppet master who'd orchestrated the entire attack against the Magic Quarter.

Thea's smile fell, but she continued to feign ignorance. It was the only way she might get out of this trap, find Malek and compel him not to send his Hunters marching on the Quarter. 'For me to do that, surely I would have to know who you are.'

Another volley of fireworks fizzed and spat above, shooting indigo and violet rays across the courtyard. Each explosion eroded Thea's nerves a little more.

The fate-weaver's green eyes sharpened with intrigue. She prowled closer, surveying Thea as if she was an exhibit in a cabinet of curiosities. 'You truly don't know who I am, do you?' she murmured. 'How . . . delicious.'

Thea shrank back from her, discomfited. She had the feeling Heloise – if Thea's presumption was correct – was referring to something other than her name. Something Thea had missed. Her golden gown jangled a discordant note. 'If you'll excuse me, I had better take my leave now.' Her heart-spell rattling against her ribs, panic sliding sweat down her stays, she turned and walked briskly away. When she glanced back, the fate-weaver was still watching Thea, that almost-smile toying with her lips.

Thea pushed through the crowds in the courtyard. Above, crimson birds flew on sparkling wings and cobalt flower buds spread their petals. Each grand, glittering firework making the night sky their plaything. Searching the crowd for Malek, Thea halted when she came across Jasper at the far edge, watching the dazzling performance.

She sidled up to him as emerald-green trees sparkled over the snow, making everything gleam in shades of green, as if they all stood beneath the forest's canopy. 'Malek's a Magic Hunter,' she told him quietly. 'I just caught him passing word onto Pan Novak and compelled the truth from him. They already know the wards have fallen, and Hunters have gathered from across the continent to back them up. They're planning on shutting down the Quarter tonight.'

As Jasper listened, the hint of a smile that had appeared when he saw her was consumed by a growing shadow. That same darkness swallowed her heart-spell, leaving despair in its path.

'I need to return to the Magic Quarter at once,' she said. 'But I was going to find Malek first and see if I could compel him to call the whole thing off, or lead the Hunters astray. . .' She shook her head, frustration eating her voice. 'He slipped out of my hold and fled, but before I could take chase, a strange woman appeared. I think it was Heloise. I recognised her voice from the forest. She matched your description – green eyes, light hair and skin. She's wearing a rich blue suit – have you seen her?'

The trees, flowers and birds dissolved from the sky.

And Jasper became a haunted man. 'Not tonight.' Scouring the courtyard, he lowered his voice as if she might appear at any moment. 'Did she speak to you?' he asked urgently.

Thea nodded. 'It was most peculiar.' Snow drifted onto her curled hair, her gown, chilling her for the first time that evening. Secrets were piling up everywhere she looked, but she was just half a person, missing her heart, unable to piece everything together.

The last guests were vanishing back into the ballroom now, chattering about the fireworks.

'Tell me,' Jasper ordered. 'Quickly.'

'Her eyes were a beautiful shade of green, though when she looked at me, they seemed hard, vindictive—' A memory of those eyes suddenly surged back.

Jasper's face drew tight. 'What is it?'

Thea gripped his wrist without thinking. 'I've seen her before.'

Jasper's expression flickered, his stare searching hers. 'You – you have?' A strange note was woven through his voice, one that Thea's gown echoed gently.

'Yes, at the start of autumn, on Prague Bridge.' Thea frowned to herself. 'She saw me open the secret passage to the Magic Quarter, must have seen me vanish in plain sight. Did she – did she recognise me? No, that isn't possible . . .'

'She recognised that you'd entered a warded place,' Jasper said quickly. 'Perhaps she recognised my power within you, too, and knew I was close by.'

'But now the wards have fallen,' Thea realised with a growing horror, dropping her hand.

'We need to return to the Quarter at once. Heloise is notorious for her ambition and her scalding cruelty, feared even among her – our – own kind.' He blazed with intensity. 'If ever you have hated me, then know that she is a hundred times worse. If she has set her sights on you, then you must remain out of sight.' His stare hardened. 'Promise me.'

'I will do no such thing,' Thea sputtered.

'Godsdamn it Thea, why won't you understand?' Jasper groaned. 'I cannot lose you!'

'That does not give you the right to order me about,' Thea informed him, ignoring how her heart-spell had spasmed. 'Your feelings are immaterial. Though I am sure that you would have me simper and bat my fan at you like a lady at court.'

'I would have no such thing,' Jasper snapped. 'I would have you exactly as you are.'

Thea's lips parted. She shook herself. 'We are wasting too much time! I need to go.'

'Go. I will try to catch Heloise before she leaves. Delay her from heading to the Magic Quarter. If I see Malek, I'll *persuade* him to take his Hunters elsewhere.'

Thea's breath hitched. She wanted to tell him to leave with her rather than endanger herself, but Jasper was the only one who could take on Heloise and survive. She had to let him go.

'Take my carriage,' Jasper commanded, searching her face. 'Eclipse is pulling it.'

'No. You'll need that to join us in the Quarter. Come as soon as you can, we're going to need you.'

'Thea—'

But she was already breaking into a run. She wished she could send a raven, but they could only be summoned from within the Quarter itself.

She'd almost cleared the courtyard when it suddenly altered. She could see it in the way the air thrummed with energy, how it took on that sheen, that glisten of thousands of threads, cobwebbed together in patterns only a fate-weaver could discern. Somebody was weaving. She knew even before she glanced back that Heloise was responsible. She caught a trail of Jasper's dark hair, tied back, as he ploughed through the last guests meandering through the courtyard, rushing towards the central fountain. Where Heloise was standing, watching his path towards her.

The castle grounds contorted as Jasper unleashed the full force of his power. For the first time, Thea glimpsed the true power beneath his mask.

The castle shuddered, its stonework groaning as it struggled to contain the force that Jasper wielded. No, that Jasper *was*. He leapt onto the fountain edge with arms outstretched, a fistful of threads in each hand as he lashed out at Heloise.

She stumbled back, losing her grip on the strands she'd been knotting together. Just as she reached back to reclaim them, Jasper attacked again, his power hitting her like a runaway carriage.

Thea seized her window to leave without Heloise noticing. Fleeing into the main courtyard, she ran through the maze of carriages, her heart-spell slamming into her ribcage as she hoped and hoped – *there*.

Malek's carriage was still awaiting his return. For a moment she wondered if she ought to return to the ball and attempt to find him, but she dispelled that instantly; it was far too dangerous with Heloise battling Jasper in the courtyard. Heloise was the true enemy here, the reason Thea needed to get back and warn everyone, in case Heloise slipped through Jasper's defences and headed straight for the Quarter.

Decided, Thea marched over to Malek's distinctive ochre carriage. His coachman was laughing nearby with a gaggle of others, far enough away that Thea managed to sneak onto the driving seat and take up the reins without him noticing.

'Go horses, go,' she whispered, pulling on one side of the reins to steer them out of the line of waiting carriages.

'Hey!' The coachman had noticed. 'What do you think you're doing?'

'Go faster!' Thea urged, unsure how to take charge of a pair of horses. Before she could attempt to fate-weave her way out of there, the horses took charge themselves and gathered speed, cantering out of the courtyard and through the gates.

CHAPTER

Twenty-Six

MALEK'S CARRIAGE RATTLED violently in its frantic dash downhill, away from the castle.

Thea clung onto the reins, attempting to steer as the carriage veered from one side of the street to the other, forcing other carriages to dash out of their way, their coachmen swearing loudly.

She rushed over Prague Bridge, the Vltava glinting far below like a knowing eye. When St John of Nepomuk came into view, Thea stiffened. The statue was broken. 'No,' she whispered. She pulled on the reins. The horses reared up, the carriage swerving into the side of the stone bridge, its wheels screeching.

Thea leapt from the carriage without a second thought, holding her gown in both hands. St John had been torn in two, much like the void speared through the heart of the Magic Quarter, though instead of revealing an infinite blackness, it revealed the staircase down, yawning open to anyone who happened by. They were truly defenceless now.

Thea ran through the broken statue, navigating the stone and rubble. It was a rocky crevice, unpassable for anything larger than a horse. It crackled with the remains of the disintegrating wards. When Thea threw a look back, Malek's horses were trotting on, their breath silvering the frozen night. She slid into her power, searching through the skeins of fate to try and hide the entrance to the Quarter, but the remains of the wards were such a tangled web, she didn't dare interfere any more. She'd already done enough damage.

Thea fled through the Magic Quarter as fast as her heeled shoes and wide skirts would allow, her breath like ragged feathers as she avoided the rift, its shivering inky darkness seeming to watch her path. Witches and shape-shifters and pixies congregated on either side of it, muttering blackly and conjuring various attempts at repairing it. A makeshift bridge, made entirely of ice, traversed its narrowest point, but nobody seemed keen to cross it. Not when it rumbled with shadows that felt like death.

Thea ran past them all, her guilt driving her onwards. She still wasn't sure if her refusing to take a price from Malek could have caused *this* to happen, but even if this wasn't her fault, leaving for the ball was.

Stiltskin's Apothecary came into view. The gilt letters shone under the gaze of the street lamps, as did the weathervane, which almost stilled Thea in her tracks: since her departure it had transmuted into a dragon with a colossal wingspan. Its wings sheltered the entire roof of the apothecary and its jaws were unhinged in a silent roar.

Thea hurried towards it, her heels clattering. She needed to warn Zofka and Talibah what was coming. Malek and his Hunters, including Pan Novak – and Heloise. A veritable army of enemies had the Quarter in their sights. If the weathervane was any indication, it sensed what was coming their way, too.

Candlelight spilled from windows and as Thea neared home, she spotted Zofka and Talibah bathed in the apothecary's welcoming glow as they stood outside, considering the rift.

Thea reached them gasping for breath, her hair falling loose from the elaborate curls Zofka had arranged, her face paint slipping. Revealing the fear beneath.

'What happened?' Zofka demanded, as Talibah's concern unfurled across her face.

'I found out that the last of the Hunters have reached Prague,' Thea managed to get out, clamping a hand onto the stitch in her side.

Zofka craned her head down the street. 'Where's Malek? What happened?'

'Oh, he's fine,' Thea said through gritted teeth. 'He's from an old line of Hunters – I caught him passing a note to Pan Novak and compelled him to tell me the truth. They're orchestrating an attack on the Magic Quarter tonight. They're going to shut us down.'

'Shut us down?' Zofka exclaimed. 'Then we're not safe here any longer.' She crossed her arms over the comfortable velvet dress she wore.

'We need to warn everyone, now,' Talibah urged.

Thea nodded grimly. 'Let me call the ravens—'

Hooves beat against the cobblestones, growing louder and louder.

Zofka grabbed both Talibah and Thea and tugged them inside the apothecary. All three women peered out of the window. 'Is it the Hunters?' Zofka asked with a tremble in her voice.

'I don't think so, I see only one horse—' Thea trailed off as Jasper rode into view on the back of Eclipse, his hair in disarray, his collar crooked. He must have ridden furiously through the city to catch up with Thea. Leaping from the back of his horse, he strode over to the apothecary.

Zofka yanked the door open.

'Good evening, ladies.' Giving a quick bow of his head, Jasper shut and bolted the door behind him. 'Forgive the intrusion.'

'Are you all right?' Thea asked, fretting anew. 'What happened with Heloise?'

Jasper looked self-conscious under the scrutiny of all three women. He tugged his collar back into place.

'Heloise . . . the fate-weaver you warned us of earlier?' Talibah's amber eyes glinted warily.

'Yes. Heloise appeared at the ball. Jasper was fighting her before I fled back to you . . .' Thea turned to Jasper. 'But you seemed more powerful than her; is she really that much of a threat?'

Jasper's voice was ice. 'I am her match. I was lucky tonight; she seemed . . . distracted. But I am incapable of eliminating her myself. She is also far more devious and does not hold the same morals I do. She cares not for who else might be decimated in her path; she will use anyone to achieve her means, and she is *not* to be underestimated.'

Pan Novak, Malek and the Hunters are all inconsequential in comparison. We knew from what you overheard in the forest,' – Jasper nodded to Thea – 'that a fate-weaver has been involved in this from the beginning, stirring up chaos for their own purpose.' He shook his head, glaring fiercely out the window. 'Heloise and I clashed some time ago, and she has been clamouring for vengeance since.' He looked darkly at Thea. 'This apothecary and you are both marked with my power.'

Thea suppressed a shiver.

'Heloise is notorious in our world. She craves power above all else and the Magic Quarter is the ideal place to take that power. I believe she intends to seize it all for herself in the name of revenge, though envy would be a better fit.' Jasper scowled. 'She was manipulating the Hunters to throw us into turmoil, to mask her presence, but I do not know what her end goal with them is. To her, they will be nothing but another plaything. It amuses her to toy with people's lives.'

'What did you do to earn her wrath?' Zofka whispered, a little in awe at the chaos Jasper had unwittingly caused.

'I defended another of her targets.' Jasper sighed. 'They were innocent, and did not deserve her ire. I should have known she'd come for me one day.'

'Why did she bother hiding then, if she's so powerful?' Zofka asked. 'Why send Pan Novak and Malek sniffing around first?'

Jasper scanned the street outside the window again. 'She likes her little games. Once she fixes on a target, she'll stop at nothing to decimate every last bit of their life, their livelihood, everything.' When he turned from the window, his face was overcast. 'I am sorrier than you'll know that you have become entangled in her web.'

Zofka and Talibah offered their sympathy, but Thea's thoughts were running down another track. 'I thought these threats I'd received were from someone involved with the Hunters,' she began tentatively. 'But could they have come from Heloise? I think she saw me on Prague Bridge. Sometime near the start of autumn. I remember how shocked she looked. At the time I thought it was because I'd vanished, but now I wonder if she recognised me . . .'

'I think it far more likely that was another of Pan Novak's little games,' Jasper said firmly. 'You galled him from the start.'

'Those notes falling into the Quarter were magical,' Talibah pointed out. 'Pan Novak is human.'

'Unless he recruited someone else to send the notes on his behalf,' Zofka gasped. 'Maybe it was one of the weather-witches.'

Thea sighed. 'That feels unlikely – he hates magic.'

Jasper turned thoughtful. 'Would it surprise you if he were a hypocrite? If he used magic for his own purposes, while hammering down on it elsewhere? We are an obstacle in his way, nothing more. And Heloise has somehow managed to identify Pan Novak as our greatest threat and capitalise on the entire thing for her own good. She is playing the puppet master.'

'Perhaps,' Thea said. 'But I saw the way Heloise regarded me.'

'Heloise won't attack while I am here, not yet at least.' Jasper leant against the wall in a manner that seemed too casual for him. His white shirt was torn. The smell of lemons, sugar and sunshine began washing through the apothecary, as if it had noticed its owner's exhaustion, the fatigue bruised beneath his eyes. 'She's weakened after our clash today, but that will not last for long. I have exerted too much energy to confront her again now, otherwise I would tear the city, the forest, apart searching for her, if it ensured your safety.' Jasper looked intently at each of them in turn. 'The rest of the Quarter will not listen to me the way you have. I urge you to plead my case: we need to send ravens to everyone, telling them to stand down tonight so that we might regroup and form a plan for when Heloise decides to make her move. The Magic Quarter can and will survive being closed for business by the Hunters. It will *not* survive Heloise.' Jasper sighed. 'You need to call for an emergency meeting.'

'Are you . . . planning on attending that meeting?' Thea asked after a beat.

'Unfortunately so,' Jasper said.

Talibah snapped into action, running upstairs for paper and a quill. 'I'll send ravens out at once.'

'Good.' Zofka yanked the apothecary door open. 'I need to fetch Gretel; I don't want her alone if that creepy man is coming back, there's safety in numbers. I'll warn everyone I see along the way.'

As the two women split in different directions, Jasper pulled Thea aside. Deeper into the apothecary, where the moon was in her waning phase, and the lemon and sugar scent turned buttery. 'Are you well?' he asked, scanning her face, as if expecting to find something troubling there. 'I was worried after you fled the ball.' A vein pulsed in Jasper's forehead.

'I'm fine,' Thea said, absent-mindedly looking across the apothecary at the crack threatening to split their ceiling in two. It echoed the deeper rift outside. It had been there, warning her all along, but she'd refused to see it. 'Jasper, I . . . I have to ask you something.'

His gaze turned wary.

'I made a mistake,' Thea whispered. 'I didn't take a price from Malek for the key I crafted him.' She swallowed nervously. When Jasper said nothing, waiting for her to continue, she ploughed on before she lost her nerves altogether. 'It was. . . a large price, and the moment I refused it, the Magic Quarter, it . . .' She trailed off, unable to force the words out over the guilt, wedged into her throat like a blade.

'It broke,' Jasper finished for her.

Thea closed her eyes. 'Did I break the Quarter?'

Jasper ran a hand over the back of his neck. 'Honestly, I had my suspicions over the crack in the ceiling but when you told me Wojslav's antique shop had broken first, I dismissed it. Then I thought fate had sought to balance the scales through your health instead.' He shrugged. 'I have no idea what happened to Wojslav's windowpanes, but yes, I do now believe it was you all along. The timing of the large price and the rupture of the Quarter is too coincidental.'

Thea's stare turned incredulous. 'Why are you taking this so lightly? I have ruined everything!'

'You made a mistake, Thea,' Jasper said gently. 'You're not the first and you won't be the last.'

'Everyone's going to hate me for this,' Thea whispered. 'I've endangered them all.'

Jasper gave a single shake of his head. 'They will understand.'

'Why are you being so understanding? You told me that you weren't nice, but this is suspiciously nice behaviour.'

'Because I can't keep up this pretence any longer.'

Thea's anxiety sharpened. 'What have you done? If it's about my memories—'

Jasper's voice lowered, turned guttural. 'I can't keep pretending I feel nothing for you when I live with you inside my heart every day.' His face was stripped bare, not a hint of a frown to be seen as he waited for Thea's reaction. The hollow of his throat pinkened. A reaction she usually associated with their barbed exchanges, but tonight it seemed to be . . . nerves? Thea watched it in fascination. Did she make Jasper nervous?

'Are you going to let me in on any of those thoughts?' Jasper asked, his flush creeping up his jawline.

Thea sighed. 'You infuriate me. The things you've dared say to me, the way you've refused to cut a new deal with me to return my heart, how you still insist on keeping my memories locked away, though my past could be the key to everything the Magic Quarter faces today—' Heloise had *recognised* her. Thea was beginning to suspect that her own past was why she was being threatened, why the Quarter was being attacked. She needed to remember it urgently now.

Guilt flashed through Jasper's gaze. Still, he said nothing. She half wished he'd argue back: it would make things less confusing.

'But I broke the Magic Quarter,' Thea whispered. 'I've been slowly breaking it all along, and you haven't judged me or criticised me for making a mistake. I know you're hiding something from me, but curse it all, you've stolen inside my thoughts, my dreams, and that afternoon we shared in the forest hasn't stopped haunting me. The way you kissed me—'

Jasper strode towards her, the same way he had in the forest. Thea's head tipped back as he bent over her. Her golden gown hummed in excitement and she tugged at its material, making it silent before it revealed every feeling racing through her head, her quickening heart-spell. 'You need only say the word and I will give you everything you need, and more,' he said hoarsely. 'But I will not, I cannot kiss you again, knowing that you hate me. That you resent my presence in your life. I want this to be real.'

The ferocity in his dark blue gaze halted Thea's thoughts. Channelled them into one singular roar. 'Kiss me,' she gasped.

He reached forwards, his hands sweeping up her neck, into her flowing curls, and placed a single kiss on her cheek. 'Not yet.'

Heat coiled in Thea's stomach. 'Don't play games with me.' She rested her hands on Jasper's forearms, holding him in place, his fingers splayed in her hair.

'I would never,' he vowed, his breath coming faster as he kissed her other cheek. 'You don't realise what that afternoon in the forest meant to me. What *you* mean to me. Until you do, this is all I can give you.'

'Please.' Thea moved her head to the side, seeking his mouth with hers, desperate to feel that warmth, that softness, an easing to their unbearable tension. 'It meant everything to me, too,' she half cried, her gown falling silent as she became overwrought, unable to pick out a single emotion to sing out.

His hands tightened in her hair as he pulled back to consider her.

'I felt seen,' she said simply. 'Now kiss me, Jasper Stiltskin, because nobody in this life has ever made me feel the way you do. It matters not if I hate you or love you, only that it feels as if I might die if you don't kiss—'

He kissed her.

She'd expected that same passion that had swept them into its current in the apothecary when they'd shared their first kiss, in the forest when they'd charged into each other's arms, but this was sweet and soft and tender in a way that brought tears to her eyes. She blinked them away, sighing as his arms fell to her back, embracing her as he deepened their kiss, tasting her.

A sharp whistle screeched outside. Puncturing their moment with a fresh threat.

Jasper tore his mouth away and strode over to the windows.

'What was that?' Thea asked breathlessly.

Zofka and Gretel burst through the door as one. Footfalls sounded on the stairs as Talibah reemerged. 'I sent the ravens out and received just as many back; we're standing down tonight.'

'Your weathervane just roared.' Zofka braced her hands on her knees as she fought for her breath back. 'Didn't you hear?' She gave Thea a curious look. Thea smoothed her hair down, hoping her lips weren't reddened. What a time to have succumbed to her passions; she'd always been dubious of the romance novels she'd read where the characters had declared their love for one another in the midst of danger. Now she doubted them a little less. It was the nerves, the threat of what was to come, the uncertainty of it all. It invited strange behaviours. *Like begging the secretive fate-weaver whose apprentice you are to kiss you.*

'It's the Hunters,' Jasper said grimly, observing from his vantage point. 'They're here.'

CHAPTER

Twenty-Seven

THEA'S HEART-SPELL PALPITATED.

Stepping away from the window, Jasper steadied her. His fingers were strong and tender as they wrapped around her elbow, anchoring her. 'I will handle this,' he told her.

Despite all her instincts for self-preservation, his touch was lightning.

Zofka and Talibah's rapt attention was hot on the back of her neck.

'I do not require your assistance.' Despite begging him to kiss her, she would not yield her independence to him, and now was not the time to invite suspicion from her friends. She slipped out of his hold, opening the apothecary door and striding towards the commotion. After a beat, she heard him follow.

Pan Novak was striding down the centre of the Magic Quarter, flanked by an army of Hunters, careful to keep far from the shivering black void bisecting the street like a cruel gash. Smoke seeped from its edges.

The witches, shape-shifters and pixies who had been flurrying around, attempting to shore up the Quarter, had vanished back into their homes. Doors quickly closed as Pan Novak paced past. Faces appeared behind frosted windows, then vanished, as the occupants of the Quarter reacted to the Hunters' presence. Most held tight, as urged by the unkindness of ravens Talibah had sent out on Jasper's bequest. Some could not be contained.

Jasper's faint sigh was audible only to Thea as Rose marched outside in her nightclothes, brandishing a sharpened trowel in one hand, a watering can in the other. Thea didn't want to guess at its contents.

A row of shops' candles extinguished in one breath as their residents wisely decided to hide.

Zofka whispered something Thea didn't catch. 'It will be all right,' Gretel murmured to her at Thea's side, wrapping an arm around Zofka's waist. 'I'm here and I won't let anything bad ever happen to you.'

Pan Novak cast a dour look in the direction of Fleur's, neighbouring the Rose Basket to the other side. Fleur emerged in a beautiful nightgown in cerulean silk, joining Rose and raising a pointed eyebrow back at Pan Novak. A row of petticoats rustled menacingly behind her. Thea's nerves rustled in tandem; Rose and Fleur needed to stay strong and not provoke Pan Novak, not yet, not now. Fighting fire with fire was never wise, and either way, they needed to bank those flames for their true enemy, hiding behind her Hunters. She cast a look around, but didn't spot Malek in their ranks. That was . . . worrying. She didn't trust his absence after the vitriol he'd spewed at the castle.

Pan Novak drew in line with Stiltskin's Apothecary. And halted. The tilt to the corner of his mouth, that glint he did not bother to disguise, set Thea's stomach writhing. This was a man who took pleasure in the misfortune of others. Slowly, he turned his head and smiled at Thea. A smile that did not reach his eyes.

She glared back at him.

'Easy,' Jasper warned at her side.

Less than half the inhabitants of the Quarter had crept outside, huddled in the doorways of their shops and homes, bracing for the news they all knew was coming.

Pan Novak took his time before addressing them, his army of Hunters marching to each corner of the Magic Quarter, unfolding like a show of force. But they were only human. And the magical folk of the Quarter knew that. Thea caught a few exchanging glances, tension rippling through their ranks.

'Witches are not like fate-weavers,' Zofka told Thea, speaking across Gretel. 'We are not scales, bound by birth to balance fate. Our power, our magic, is innate – but not infinite. If this Heloise, who Jasper believes has orchestrated all of this, is biding her time, waiting for the right moment to strike, she may have deliberately planned this.'

Thea frowned to herself. 'Are you saying that if the witches defend the Magic Quarter tonight, they won't be able to defend it at a later point?'

'That's exactly what I'm saying,' Zofka finished grimly. 'If we use a lot of power now, it's going to take time and rest to recover before we can use our powers again.'

'Witches burn bright and fast,' Jasper said at Thea's other side. 'We need their fire for the coming battle.'

'What about you?' Thea fretted. 'You've already battled Heloise once today—'

'A fate-weaver channels their power instead. We would have to channel an almost inconceivable amount of energy before our strength failed us.'

Pan Novak's brittle voice sounded as if it might snap when he raised it. 'I hereby announce that this Magic Quarter is closed. No business, nor trade is to be conducted here, by order of the Prague City Council.'

If he expected an outburst, he was to be disappointed; the residents who'd braved the void and the Hunters to stand outside, stared at him in a silence that was eerier, more disquieting, than their outrage would have been.

He cleared his throat, forging on. 'Furthermore, we have been granted permission to search your establishments and homes for any harmful magic that has been ruled a danger to the citizens of Prague and the House of Habsburg.'

Jasper stiffened.

Thea's dress warbled in panic, fast and shrill, as a handful of magical folk bristled at the suggestion.

'He's deliberately provoking us,' Talibah said, her height enabling her to see above Thea's head.

'Absolutely not.' Rose brandished her sharpened trowel at Pan Novak. 'I refuse to allow you entrance into my home.' Her nightcap sat crooked on her wispy grey hair, and her slippers were embroidered with sword-fighting roses.

One of the Hunters looked at her and laughed.

The silence of the Quarter grew an edge. Rose might be an interfering wretch, but she belonged to them, hissing roses, eavesdropping and all. Fleur grabbed Rose's trowel-wielding hand and spoke in a flurry of fast, furious French.

The Hunters shuffled, unsure if she was verbally assaulting them or arguing with Rose.

Thea's teeth sank into her lip as she fretted.

Wojslav caught her eye from the other side of the street as she drew blood.

'Don't mind him,' Zofka whispered. 'He's been on a diet since he was caught eyeing up Sarah's litter of kittens.'

But Zofka's words hardly registered as Thea watched Fleur and Rose. Jasper's fingers spasmed at his side, catching her dress, which let out an indignant hum. She caught his hand, ignoring the way he tightened at her side, his attention pooling on her face. 'Don't compel them with fate,' she whispered out the corner of her mouth. 'We want the Quarter to trust you, remember? Using fate against them, to stop them from fighting back, won't do that. They need to make this decision themselves. They have the right to free will.'

He grumbled something incomprehensible. But when she let go, his hand recaptured hers, keeping her close.

The tension sharpened like a dagger, everyone drawn to the same point of focus: Fleur and Rose, the tip of the blade.

Rose batted Fleur away. 'Fine, search my home,' she told Pan Novak, giving him a slow, venomous smile that Thea did not trust one bit. 'Search all our homes, our places of work.' Her smile turned wicked. 'But you mightn't like what you find there. Don't be fooled by the rift tearing our beloved Quarter in half: this is a magical place. And magic doesn't like being threatened by weasels like you.'

Pan Novak was silent as he listened. Then he lifted one hand. 'Search it all,' he scratched out. 'Detain anyone who objects.'

Fleur took the opportunity to drag Rose away.

Jasper ushered them all back inside the apothecary and shut the door. 'You were right,' he told Zofka. 'There's safety in numbers.'

Zofka and Talibah exchanged a wary look.

'Close the shutters,' Jasper ordered.

Thea jerked to attention, her, 'Me?' on the tip of her tongue, when the shutters all obediently snapped shut.

Gretel looked faintly impressed.

'Candles,' Jasper barked out next.

The apothecary flared with candlelight. More candles than Thea had seen flickered alive, new ones appearing on each step of the spiral staircase and along the mezzanine railing, stuck in place with melted wax.

'Are you sure you're not a witch?' Zofka half grumbled to herself.

'It's my apothecary,' Jasper told her. 'It listens to me.' He patted the nearest wall fondly.

Zofka snorted.

Thea glanced at the rows of towering shelves, each one home to weeks and months of her work, using the Compendium to research new potions, searching out the magical ingredients for her concoctions, brewing them over long periods of time. 'If everything you've said about Heloise is true, then Pan Novak is just her puppet.'

'The rest of the Hunters too,' Jasper added. 'And your Malek.' He sidled a look at her that intimated if they hadn't been interrupted, he would have shown her all the ways she'd never been Malek's.

'He's not *my* Malek,' Thea fired back, knowing from the looks on her friends' faces, particularly Zofka's, that they would be requiring more details when they were no longer under threat.

Hiding his smile, which was entirely too self-satisfied, Jasper conjured glistening strings of fate, which he looped over and around the apothecary, cloaking it from sight. It cut off any sound from the Quarter outside, leaving everything muffled and dim. As if they'd retreated into a cave.

'I thought we didn't want to provoke the Magic Hunters?' Talibah asked, watching him.

'I'm not just removing it from view, I'm removing it from their memory. Just for a little while.'

'Can you cloak the café, too?' Zofka popped up, fixing Jasper with a hopeful stare.

He gave a slow shake of his head. 'I would cloak the entire Quarter if I could, but there are limits to my powers.'

Thea hurried about, pouring cups of her most soothing valerian and nightingale-song tea, and making everyone comfortable as their group congregated in her little jungle. Guilt snarled in her stomach that they were hiding while danger prowled through their Quarter. Zofka and Gretel squeezed onto a single armchair, Talibah claimed Thea's rocking chair, next to her poor anxious apple tree, whose leaves had flailed when they'd all retreated there. And Jasper silently took a seat on Thea's planting bench, among all the herbs and potted flowers. A bevy of lavender flowers were tilting their heads towards him, curiously tickling his arm with their buds until he frowned, and they fled to the other side of their generous pot.

Thea knew, even with her back turned to him, that he was watching her. Her hand shook as she overfilled Gretel's cup, almost scalding her. 'Sorry,' she winced.

Zofka, whose magic had immediately caught the escaping tea like an invisible saucer, missed nothing. 'What's wrong?'

Thea gestured at the walls, which were thick with plants and errant stacks of books she'd left downstairs, sheltering them while Pan Novak and his Hunters marched on the rest of the Quarter. 'I feel bad we're holed up safe in here, while outside . . .' She gulped.

Gretel took the shiny red teapot from Thea and pressed her down onto a nearby footstool as she poured her a cup. 'Sit, drink,' she said kindly.

From the outside, it might have appeared as if they were passing a pleasant spell of time, nestled in Thea's lush sanctuary, making their way through several cups of tea. If it wasn't for the guilt swirling through Thea that they were safe while she'd endangered everyone else.

Until Zofka looked at her, narrowing her eyes. 'What are you not telling us?'

Thea nodded to herself, avoiding Jasper's gaze. Jasper, who had calmly listened to her confession without judgement. She'd promised never to forgive him for withholding her heart, leaving her ill-prepared to face whoever had threatened her, but his dark blue eyes shadowed her thoughts, haunted her dreams. Deep with feeling in the forest, brimming with hunger the night of the blizzard, when he had surged forward and taken her mouth. The look in them before he kissed her tenderly when the Hunters had marched on the Quarter.

'It was me. I broke the Magic Quarter,' she said bleakly.

'You did *what?*' Rose's voice broke into their conversation as the garden-witch stepped out from behind the apple tree, which shivered nervously.

CHAPTER

Twenty-Eight

OW DID YOU get in?' Jasper snarled.

Rose bristled. 'I will not be spoken to so rudely by a fate-weaver of all things!'

Jasper stood. 'This is my apothecary.' His voice glittered with menace. 'There are protections in place to prohibit entering uninvited, magically or not.'

Rose patted the apple tree fondly. 'I have my ways.'

They all looked at the apple tree. Its single midnight-blue apple wobbled.

Thea's heart-spell lurched in her chest. 'Nobody look at my apple tree!' she shrieked, panicking on its behalf. It had been proudly growing that apple for the past month and she couldn't bear it falling from fright. Standing between Jasper and Rose, who were still glowering at each other, she lowered her voice to a whisper her tree wouldn't hear. 'You told me this apple tree was a welcome gift, not that it was a portal you could sneak through whenever you felt like it.'

Rose gave a haughty sniff. 'Well, I wouldn't have had to if you'd answered a single raven. Most of the Hunters have left, we're all waiting for to see what *he*' – she poked Jasper in his chest – or at least, appeared to aim for his chest, but being significantly shorter than the fate-weaver, ended up poking him in the stomach – 'has to say for himself after ordering us all to stand down.' Her glower turned fiercer. 'We all had to suffer the injustice, the indignity of watching the Hunters search our homes while you ran away and hid.'

Talibah and Gretel remained silent. Zofka was rapt. Thea's heart-spell pattered weakly as Jasper drew himself to his full height, glaring down at the garden-witch in her nightie, her nightcap hanging on for dear life.

'And did they take anything from anyone?' he asked, his tone sharper than broken glass. 'Or did you all conceal anything of worth with spells and charms and carefully placed distractions?'

Rose scowled.

'As I thought,' Jasper said.

'Gloat away, fate-weaver.' Rose leant forwards, jabbing Jasper with that same finger. 'You'll have to answer to the rest of the Quarter now, and they're every bit as peeved as I am. Our Quarter is endangered and it's time to step up and save it.'

When Jasper uncloaked the apothecary, they were greeted with an unkindness of ravens lining up to deliver notes. Rose gave Jasper a pointed look, which he ignored. 'If she pokes him again, I think he's going to break her finger,' Zofka whispered seriously.

Thea nodded. The main street of the Quarter was thronged with most of the magical folk who lived there, congregating in gossiping huddles. A few were casting spells at the void, which deflected any magic tossed its way. It gave an ominous growl. A pair of Hunters were stationed at the far end of the Quarter, preventing anyone from leaving.

Talibah's hand found Thea's. 'However it came to happen, what you told us you did, nobody will hold it against you,' she told her.

Guilt dredged Thea's stomach. She stared miserably at the void. Something deep below crackled and gurgled. It was an open jaw, threatening to devour the Magic Quarter in one hungry bite. 'I think they just might hold it against me.'

Zofka scoffed. 'I've set half the Quarter on fire, and nobody cared. Twice.' She nudged Gretel, 'Right?'

'Right,' Gretel answered, her gaze flitting uncertainly between Zofka and the gaping chasm.

Rose's voice boomed out across the street, silencing everyone.

A nearby weather-witch startled into action, throwing up a quick fog to obscure and muffle Rose from the pair of Hunters watching at the end of the street.

'My fellow witches, shape-shifters, pixies, gifted humans and spirit,' Rose began, speaking into the tallest sunflower, plucked from one of her window baskets.

Wojslav cleared his throat pointedly.

'And vampire,' Rose added. 'The time has come to fight back. Some might say, we had the opportunity to vanquish our enemies already tonight, but we were assured that was a foolhardy plan,' she looked at Jasper. A couple of weather-witches cast distrusting glances at Jasper. A shape-shifter on the other side of the void backed away on noticing his presence. Thea sighed inwardly. 'Whether or not that will be seen to be true remains,' Rose continued. 'However!'

'Goddess take me away now; I cannot listen to another of Rose's soliloquies,' Zofka groaned.

'However!' Rose resumed, 'We must work together to defend our beloved Magic Quarter. We can't swat this danger away as if it poses no more threat to us than a particularly stubborn fly – we must form a united front, or it will be our undoing.'

'I agree.' Zdenka, the fortune teller, stepped forward. Their hair was wrapped in indigo silk, and they'd bundled up in an oversized cloak. 'It's time to fight back. Where are we having our proper meeting?'

'Can't it wait till morning?' Wojslav grumbled.

'What, when you'll be sleeping safe and sound in your coffin?' Rose's voice boomed out. 'No, you're not getting out of this one, you old bat.'

'Takes one to know one,' Zofka whispered into Thea's ear. Thea smiled weakly, unable to think of anything but what awaited her. Her confession to the rest of the Quarter.

'The Crypt has plenty of furniture,' Zdenka began, before catching Wojslav's look of abject horror and falling silent.

'You are all welcome at the Gingerbread House again,' Gretel offered. She laid a hand on Zofka's arm. 'We have enough space for you all, and it's the warmest place in the Quarter.' She cast a dubious glance at the Hunters, peering at the magical fog with suspicion. 'We need to get inside, where it's safer.'

'And cake?' Rose piped up, eyeing Zofka with eager speculation. 'Have you got any leftover treats? I smelt you baking all morning, and we haven't had many customers . . .'

Zofka scoffed. 'Of course I have cake.' Thea and Talibah shared a smile; Zofka was a feeder.

As the crowd made their way to the café, some crossing the ice bridge over the void with squeaks of alarm – and one full-throated scream of terror as it let out an ominous creak – Jasper went to retrieve his horse. Thea waited for him to return. 'I found her behind the Rose Basket,' he chuckled, patting Eclipse's onyx neck. Buttery daffodil petals clung to the horse's nose. Thea's eyes widened, unaccustomed to seeing Jasper's softer side. Soft like the way he had kissed her, slow and feeling. With a start, she gathered herself.

Jasper left Eclipse outside. 'Keep an eye on those Hunters,' he whispered to his horse, who huffed in response. He cast a dark look at Thea. 'Make the most of this; you won't witness it again.'

'I'm too nervous to enjoy your first Magic Quarter meeting,' Thea confessed, worrying at her lip again.

Jasper pressed a thumb to her bottom lip. 'Stop,' he said gently. 'You're making yourself bleed.'

'I've spent the past seven years trying to make myself fit here, forcing myself in where I don't belong.' Thea's chest squeezed tight, her emotions a dam threatening to break loose. She shored them tighter, desperate not to reveal any cracks they might pour through. 'Now I'm going to walk in there and prove that I don't belong, to all of them.'

'I thought you didn't wish to belong here?' Jasper's gaze was a dangerous thing. It drew her in, despite herself.

'I have nowhere else to go, Jasper.' Thea leant against the gingerbread door, glancing down the street. The whimsical decorations sparkling through the Quarter were jarring against the void. 'For all intents and purposes, I have no choice but to make the best of this. Make a home here.'

Bending down, Jasper placed his hands on Thea's shoulders. 'You are the bravest person I have had the honour of meeting, and you can do this.' This time his glare was fierce on her behalf. He offered a pained smile. 'Do not forget, you will be entering at my side, and I am much more hated than you.'

Thea brightened a little. 'Well, that's true.'

The Gingerbread House was crammed with almost everyone who lived in the Magic Quarter. As usual, Rose was holding court at the front, while Zofka handed out huge slabs of gingerbread cake, sticky with cinnamon frosting. Snow was piled in drifts against the glazed sugar windows, slowly melting into puddles. A nervous energy hummed through the café. Smoke curled up from the void, and the Hunters had inched a step closer, as if they had been ordered to keep tabs on what the Quarter was up to before Heloise made her grand entrance. Thea swallowed thickly. They were running out of time.

Gretel waved Thea and Jasper over. She and Talibah had saved them seats at their table. A thick slice of cake already waited at each of their spots. Her stomach grumbling a reminder that she hadn't eaten for hours, Thea took a hungry bite. 'Don't . . .' Talibah began, too late, as the spiced gingerbread warmed Thea. When she opened her mouth, steam hissed out. ' . . . eat it in one bite,' Talibah finished, laughing with Gretel as more steam coiled out from Thea's nostrils. Jasper chuckled, declining his slice.

Thea shrugged off her cloak and took a more cautious nibble as Zofka flumped down in the other empty chair beside her. 'What did we miss?' Thea asked, glancing at the melting snowdrifts. 'We were right on your heels.'

Talibah adjusted her headscarf, forest green tonight. 'Not much. It snowed inside for a minute until Rose made a pair of weather-witches go home until they could control their emotions, then Zofka handed out her gingerbread cake to warm everybody up.'

A couple of vulpine shape-shifters growled as they noticed Jasper's presence. If they'd been in their fox-forms, their hackles would have stood on edge. The resident pixies had all migrated to the opposite side of the café. But Rose was the loudest in her mistrust. 'You,' she said, pointing at Jasper. 'Will you now deign to tell us why we weren't allowed to prevent Pan Novak and his worms from storming through our homes? My begonias might never recover from the shock.'

'An old enemy of mine has targeted the Magic Quarter,' Jasper said, remaining seated, though he raised his voice an increment. The café hushed, everyone craning closer to hear, despite themselves. They needed to know they'd been targeted, that a dark fate was marching to meet them. 'A fate-weaver, one who is very powerful and very dangerous, and yet craves the power and magic we have collected here.'

'You don't even live here,' Zdenka pointed out.

Jasper canted his head. 'That you have all collected here, then. Her name is Heloise and it has only tonight come to my attention that she has been the instigator behind these incursions into the Magic Quarter. Pan Novak, Ma— the Hunters,' he amended, glancing at Thea, 'have all been dancing on her strings. She is the real threat and the one which we need to prepare to meet. We need to hurry, ready ourselves to defeat her. An attack will be coming soon, and though you needed to hear this, we do not have time for discussion—'

'How can we trust a word he says?' Zdenka exclaimed. 'For all we know, you are in league with this fate-weaver, this Heloise, and you were the one who destroyed the wards to allow her to target us!'

The gingerbread door creaked open. Paní Dagmar shuffled inside, squeezing herself through the crowd until she reached Thea's table. She was as tall as Jasper, though he was seated. 'Don't listen to them dear,' she said, giving Jasper's hand an affectionate pat as everyone in the café stared at her. She stared back. 'You're all forgetting that it was a fate-weaver who erected the wards in the first place. Jasper will have them popped back up in no time. I say, is that gingerbread cake?' She squeezed onto the same chair as Gretel, who slid a plate of cake towards the elderly witch.

Zdenka and Rose's disbelief was visible. 'It seems a very big coincidence that the wards were completely destroyed the same night you attend your first meeting,' Rose pointed out.

Thea stood. Her dress screamed in fright, echoing her damp palms and trembling voice. 'Actually, that was me.' She made her way to the front. Time was drizzling away like melted honey, leaving her more and more anxious. 'You all know I'm apprenticed to Jas—Lord Stiltskin and his apothecary.' More cutting looks slashed in Jasper's direction. He calmly ignored them all, leaning back in his chair as Thea continued. 'For some time, I . . . I stopped taking a price to alter fate.' She twisted her dress in her hands. When it chimed unhappily at her, she let her hands drop. No, that was too awkward. What did one usually do with their hands? She slid them into her pockets. 'I didn't realise it was taking its toll on the Magic Quarter. When Wojslav told us that his windowpanes had gone missing before I stopped taking prices, I presumed the timing was a coincidence and something else was at play—'

'Er, actually.' Zdenka coughed into a fist. 'That was me.' They lifted their palms as the vampire glowered at them across the café. 'On Rose's behalf,' they added quickly, shooting an apologetic look at Rose, whose lips had thinned so much they'd vanished. 'You were quarrelling at the time and Rose thought it would be funny since you're afraid of the ravens—'

'Disliking a creature does not mean I fear it,' Wojslav snapped.

'Anyway,' Thea said loudly, clawing the attention back before any bloodshed and they bickered away what remained of their time. 'I hadn't realised I was to blame. When the apothecary ceiling cracked, the Quarter was already starting to give way so I reassured myself it could not have been my fault. I don't know what happened with Wojslav's windowpanes but when I refused a price for someone I thought I was helping, the street ruptured.' The café fell deathly silent. It gave her chills. Even the group of noisy pixies sharing a slice of cake had gone too still, too quiet.

Rose eyed her sceptically. 'Was that when you dashed off to that fancy ball of yours?'

'Yes,' Thea whispered. 'But I wasn't sure that it was my fault—'

'Pish posh,' Rose said. 'You knew. I can see the guilt shining out of you, girl.'

The café was heavy with stares.

'Who's the oldest here?' Rose demanded, eyeing the tables with speculation. 'One of you must know if it was a fate-weaver who put the wards in place.'

'Oh yes, it was,' Paní Dagmar nodded. 'Jasper saw them, too. Five hundred years ago now, wasn't it?' she asked cheerfully.

'Something like that,' Jasper said gruffly.

Rose did not point out that she mistrusted Paní Dagmar's memory or that she could be five hundred – *five hundred?* – years old, but her pinched mouth did.

Thea reeled, giving Jasper a speculative look. His glance back at her was knowing, making her blush despite herself.

Zdenka pointed to Wojslav, who was standing at the back, next to the gingerbread door, which he shot a longing glance at. 'Were you here five hundred years ago, Wojslav?' Zdenka asked, tightening their purple satin headwrap.

Everyone pivoted their stares to the vampire, whose sigh was audible. 'I was not,' he said. 'Why not ask the spectre?'

The crowd looked around, giving Wojslav enough time to dart out of the door. It swung shut behind him. 'He made it ten minutes longer than the last meeting,' Talibah noted, impressed.

Radim floated through from the kitchen as if he'd been conjured. 'I believe someone called me?' he asked politely, smoothing his medieval vestments as if it could be ignored that they were covered in blood. His hair was long beneath a short cap, and his smile was generous, though as it widened, more blood appeared, crusted around his neck.

'Goodness,' Rose exclaimed. 'However did you die?'

Zdenka pressed a hand to their chest. 'You should *never* ask a spectre how they died.' Zofka nodded in agreement.

'I heard you were discussing the wards?' Radim asked, swiftly changing the subject.

'Yes.' Thea seized hold of the conversation before it charged in another direction again. Keeping everyone's attention was as impossible a task as corralling Sarah's bundle of white-socked kittens. 'How long have you, er, been around for?' she asked diplomatically.

'Just a short three hundred and thirty years,' Radim mused, sinking onto – and into – a gingerbread chair. 'I have only had the pleasure of visiting this corner of Prague recently.'

Jasper unfolded himself from his chair. 'I think I've heard enough.' He strode to the front of the café, where he stood next to Thea. 'Whether you believe me or not is immaterial: Heloise *is* coming, and she is not to be underestimated. While I am greatly sorry that an enemy of mine is threatening this Quarter, I cannot defeat her alone. Our only hope is our combined powers. We are running out of time and we must act swiftly.'

'If a fate-weaver made the wards, surely you could just fix the wards and prevent her attack?' Rose's beady eyes targeted Jasper.

'They are complex. I've been attempting to fix them for some time now, but there are many pieces to this puzzle. Some of which I have at home and are almost ready. I wager I could have the wards repaired in the next few days, but there is no guarantee. The damage is considerable.'

Thea's gaze dropped to the floor.

Something nudged against her little finger. Jasper's hand. He didn't, wouldn't take it in public, not when it would invite so much more debate and distrustfulness, but knowing he stood beside her eased her turmoil. When she glanced up, he was wearing his concerned frown. 'I will take care of this,' he said, addressing the café, though he looked at Thea. 'I only require some assistance.'

Rose sighed. 'What can we do to help?'

Suggestions fired through the air like arrows, turning the café into a battlefield of half-formed ideas and nonsense. It could be argued some ideas, such as the weather-witches forging weapons of fire and ice, were good. Others, like the shape-shifters forming their own army of claws and talons and teeth, were also productive. Others were not.

'Has anyone seen a fate-weaver fight a vampire?' Zdenka cried out. 'Somebody get Wojslav back in here!'

'A vampiric fate-weaver's *worse* than a regular fate-weaver,' Rose groaned in response.

When they'd exhausted their options and organised a plan of attack – or rather, defence – Jasper looked as if he'd aged ten years. And Thea felt as if she were a hundred. But at least now maybe they stood a chance at defending their homes.

'I shall take my leave now; I need to fetch some things to repair the wards, but I will return shortly,' Jasper said, already striding through the café. 'Send me a raven if there is any sight of Heloise.'

The gingerbread door slammed shut after him. Seconds later, he rode past the glazed sugar windows, Eclipse's hooves pounding against the cobblestones as he urged her faster. Fast enough that the Hunters didn't attempt to stop his exit.

'Thank you everyone,' Thea said, giving them her warmest smile. 'I am so grateful that we're all coming together like this.'

Rose pointed a crooked finger at Thea. 'You have some courage standing up there and presenting yourself as a hero when this has all been your fault all along. You were the one who ripped down our wards, giving these so-called enemies of ours – who sound like enemies of *yours* – an opportunity to enter our lives and throw them into disarray.' Her voice was unrecognisable, filled with judgement and disapproval. Long gone was the nosy yet grandmotherly garden-witch next door in a nightcap. This woman had teeth, and she wasn't afraid to bite. 'You invited this upon yourself, upon all of us.'

Thea ran cold. The Gingerbread House fell silent once more, save for the gentle brush of snow against the iced roof, as everyone stared at her. She reddened under their scrutiny. 'I made a mistake,' she began.

'I'll say,' Zdenka muttered, frowning to themself.

Thea's cheeks were so hot she worried they'd catch fire. 'I'm sorry. I should never have refused one price, let alone multiple prices, and I should never have gone to the ball with Malek . . .' Something new occurred to her. *Malek*. He had yet to reappear, though his Hunters had made a move on the Quarter earlier. He'd fled from her at the ball, and she was certain he was up to something . . . Their previous interactions dashed through Thea's head, one after the other. But several stuck there, lodging in place: *Does Lord Stiltskin reside near his apothecary? . . . No, he doesn't even live in the Magic Quarter.* She reframed their conversations, Malek's questions about Jasper's address, her catching him looking through her Compendium, his *key* that he'd requested for a sister who bore unusually similar circumstances to Thea herself.

She all but ran out of the café. Outside, it was still snowing from the weather-witches' outburst, and she welcomed the cold. It made her head clearer, more concise.

Zofka and Talibah emerged on her heels, cloaks in hand.

'I think Malek asked me to make that key to go after Jasper,' Thea told them breathlessly. 'The wards might be down, but they were just the barricade, never the determent. It was Jasper and his power that's been protecting us, all of us, all along. He's not just Heloise's target – Malek is after him, too. And I played right into Malek's hands, presenting him with the perfect weapon. A key,' she said bitterly. 'A key that can admit anyone anywhere. Even into a magical fortress. He's going to break into Jasper's house.'

CHAPTER

Twenty-Nine

HEA ROLLED HER urgent warning to Jasper into a little scroll, opened her window, and whistled for a raven.

Biscuit flew through the window, dusted with flakes of snow. 'Oh, hello there.' Thea smiled for the first time in hours as the familiar raven landed on her counter and clacked his beak in greeting. 'Look at you, all better now.' Biscuit preened as Thea stroked his back. 'I'm so glad it was you who came,' Thea told him. 'And I just so happen to have some worms left over from your stay.' She retrieved a jar of the promised worms from beneath her counter.

Biscuit ruffled his feathers in delight.

'You can have as many as you like when you come back to me,' she told Biscuit. 'But I need to warn Jasper. Bring his answer back to me, please.'

After Biscuit had flown away, Thea struggled out of her gown and panniers, pulling on a scruffy, comfortable dress as she awaited her raven's return. In muted tones of brown and grey-green, it was more suitable for scrambling through the forest than the finest streets of Prague; when she'd pulled it from the bottom of her armoire, it had had muddy hems, and pockets stuffed with acorns and horse chestnuts, suggesting that this was precisely when Thea had last worn it.

Biscuit did not return.

After staring out of the window for longer than she could bear, checking that the street remained empty of any threats, Thea sent two further quick ravens, letting Zofka and Talibah know she was going after Jasper.

Thea marched towards the exit to the Magic Quarter, outside the faded Gothic exterior of the Crypt. Wojslav would cross the street to avoid a conversation, but whenever he found himself caught in one, would inevitably lament the time when the Magic Quarter had been host to just one or two shops and far, far quieter. Thea had once asked if he'd had more customers back then, not being entirely sure when 'then' was, to which Wojslav had replied, 'Not when the doors were locked.' Now, golden star-lights were strung over the Gothic exterior, undoubtedly against Wojslav's will, clashing against the macabre gash through the Quarter, still bleeding smoke.

The Hunters snapped to attention as she neared. Thea slowed; they raised their pistols. 'If you come any closer, we have been authorised to shoot,' the nearest one warned.

Thea's lungs shuddered with panic. She needed to leave and warn Jasper *now*.

Wojslav stepped out of the shadows. 'Good evening, gentlemen,' he said smoothly. 'I understand that you've been . . . deposited here to prevent anyone from leaving. Unfortunately for you, the wards are broken.'

The Hunters exchanged unsure looks, tightening their grips on their weapons.

'Which leaves me free to do *this*.' Baring his fangs, Wojslav lunged towards them.

As they screamed, Thea averted her eyes from Wojslav dragging his prey away, and hurried past. She spared a glance for the Crypt's turret, spotting the shiny beaks and feathers of the messenger ravens nestling down for the night. Biscuit still hadn't returned. A dark foreboding crept through her thoughts. She broke into a run.

'Wait!' Talibah materialised.

Thea halted, frowning at her friend's ensemble. 'What are you doing?'

Talibah was used to long, globe-crossing expeditions on a ship filled with mostly men: she knew how not to draw someone's eye, and between her dark dress and headscarf, she was a living shadow. 'We're coming with you,' she told Thea. 'Zofka should be along just – ah – here she is.'

Zofka rushed towards them, side-stepping the thinnest part of the street, where the void loomed like a malevolent creature, its seeping smoke like prowling fingers.

'The aim was not to draw attention to ourselves,' Talibah sighed, on seeing what Zofka was wearing: a mourning dress that might have been fashionable several decades past, somehow severe and ornate at the same time.

'Your raven said to wear dark colours.' Zofka indignantly smoothed down the macabre lace trimming around her neckline. It refused to obey, sticking up in odd places.

'Don't you own anything dark and simple?' Talibah gave the taffeta and satin monstrosity of a gown a bemused look.

'This was my mother's!'

'We don't have time for this!' Thea cried. 'I'm sorry, you know I care for you both dearly, but I have imperilled us all, and now Jasper could be in imminent danger – and I can't reach him.' She sucked in a deep breath. 'I cannot ask you to come with me, not for this.'

'We are coming with you,' Talibah said firmly, Zofka nodding at her side.

Thea opened her mouth to argue but Zofka was faster. 'We're not giving you a choice.' She yanked on her ruffled neckline. 'We're a sisterhood, united for good and bad alike. Now let's go and hunt ourselves a toad.'

The waning moon peering over their shoulders, they filed out of the Magic Quarter in silence and dashed across Prague Bridge. River mist twisted across it, but the street lamps sent golden light splashing onto the cobblestones like puddles of melted butter. Shadows huddled in closer, as if keeping watch over Thea's shoulder. The back of her neck prickled like someone was watching, and now and then she cast a wary eye back, half expecting a figure to emerge from the mist.

'There are no carriages to hail this time of night? Morning? I don't even know any more.' Zofka's sigh was feathered white. She shivered, clutching her cloak tighter around herself.

'We'll go on foot unless we spot one.' Thea forced her legs to move faster. Malek had bolted away *hours* earlier; he could already be inside Jasper's house by now. Guilt tasted bitter, like the blackest chocolate Zofka tempered. If only she hadn't made the key for Malek. If only she hadn't refused his price. If, if, *if*. The word rolled round and round her head like a ticking clock. It wasn't until they were halfway across Prague Bridge that she realised that the prickling at the back of her neck was no lie: they were not alone.

'We're being followed,' Thea murmured. Under the baleful glow of the street lamp they were dashing past, she registered Zofka's quiet focus, and Talibah's softening of her gaze as both women tapped into their gifts.

'They're not human,' Talibah whispered.

Thea's blood turned as cold as the night they were sneaking through. She stole a look back.

Cropped blonde hair caught the gleam of a street lamp they passed beneath. A woman, following their every step.

'That's Heloise.' Thea's whisper sounded too loud on the silent bridge. She drew on Jasper's power, but fear crept through her thoughts, poisoning them. Her power failed. 'I can't do anything,' she told the others in an undertone that tasted like panic.

'I could cast a spell to put her off, but I don't want to rile her up,' Zofka whispered.

Although Zofka was a kitchen-witch, there was a certain groundwork of spells, castings and workings that all witches learnt first, and since the days when witches being burnt was a common occurrence, basic self-defence belonged to that category. But she was right; surprise was their greatest weapon, and the use of magic would remove that.

'I have a dagger strapped to my ankle,' Talibah admitted.

Zofka tripped over her frilly hem. Thea grabbed her arm before she fell flat on her face. 'I'm sorry, what?' Zofka demanded.

'For emergencies,' Talibah continued. 'I found it in a souk in Tehran, it's enchanted never to miss—'

'*No.*' Horror slinked through Thea's veins at the notion of Talibah confronting a fate-weaver with nothing but an enchanted dagger.

Heloise laughed. It sent panic shooting through Thea like someone had dragged nails down her back. 'I know you know I'm following you, Theodora,' she called out, her voice a whip-crack in the dark.

Thea's breath caught. Zofka, still clinging onto her arm, clung harder.

Heloise knew Thea's name.

'You can tell your friend she has no need of that dagger, I am here only to pass on a warning.'

Dropping Thea's arm, Zofka wheeled round and cursed at the fate-weaver, conjuring a bundle of witch light in her palm.

'Zofka,' Thea hissed. 'Don't aggravate the situation.'

Heloise leant against one of the statues on Prague Bridge, kicking out one heeled boot at a jaunty angle. 'Yes, little kitchen-witch, I would think twice before winding me up.'

'What do you want with me?' Thea asked levelly. 'I assume you're the one who's been leaving me threatening notes the past few months.'

'Oh, very good.' Heloise's grin stretched wider. 'And here I thought you were just a poor lost thing, missing your memories.'

Ice filtered through Thea's body, freezing her in place. 'How do you know about my memories?'

Heloise wagged a single digit at her. 'You're asking the wrong questions, *Theodora.*'

'What are the right questions?' Talibah asked, inching closer to Thea's other side.

Heloise arched an eyebrow. 'Your friends are foolishly loyal.'

'What is my real name?' Thea asked. 'And who are you? What do you want with me and the Magic Quarter?'

Heloise smiled. A vicious, cutting smile. 'What's the matter, Theodora? Don't you recognise your own sister?'

Thea staggered back.

'*No*,' Zofka whispered.

'Yes.' Heloise's sharp attention swept over each of their faces. 'And I want to bring you back home. Where you belong.' She feigned a sad pout. 'We all missed you so very much after you ran away.' Lifting a hand to inspect her nails, she continued, 'Dear Jasper is such a bore. Aren't you tired of him yet?'

'You're lying,' Thea said. 'I don't know why, but you're lying.' She hardened her voice, finding her last shred of courage. 'You want to take me somewhere? I'm standing right here.' She stepped free of Zofka and Talibah, spreading her arms wide. 'Go ahead.'

That insouciant smile that Thea loathed returned to Heloise's lips. Kicking off from the statue, she unfolded to her full height. She was taller than Thea, slimmer and more angular, eyes green rather than brown, but her hair . . . it was the same sunshine-golden shade. Thea's certainty wavered.

'How sweet of you to offer, but not tonight.' Heloise lowered her voice. 'I've already given the orders for your dear moody Jasper's execution.' She gave a mock wince. 'He ought to be bleeding-out in his townhouse just about now.'

Thea's legs threatened to give way. Something in her reared in horror at the thought of harm befalling Jasper. She cared more than she dared admit, even to herself.

'You see, I don't want to take you now. I want to raze your precious Magic Quarter to the ground, and drag you screaming away from your friends' corpses.' She surveyed Talibah and Zofka, and shrugged. 'Two corpses just don't have the same panache.'

'Something is very wrong with you,' Thea whispered.

'We'll never let you take our Thea away,' Zofka said hotly.

Heloise strolled down the bridge towards them. 'Your time is running out, *Theodora*. Enjoy your last night while the Quarter still stands.' She held up a finger. 'One night of mourning Jasper.' She drew to a stop just in front of Thea, bent to whisper in her ear. 'My gift to you, sister to sister.' Heloise turned her face and kissed Thea on the cheek. 'One last night. Then I am coming for you.' She wove her fingers too quickly for Thea to see the tapestry of fate, and vanished.

Talibah slid her dagger out of sight. 'At least now we know who's been threatening you,' she said grimly. 'Knowledge is power; it gives us something to work with. We'll deal with her soon, but one thing at a time—'

'That woman cannot be my sister!' Thea ground out. '*I am coming for you*; that's what the messages said. She's taunting me. Even tonight; Jasper said that she was weakened after they fought, that's why she's biding her time, not to give me time to mourn . . .'

Zofka's witch light sputtered and died.

Thea grabbed Talibah's hand. 'We need to get to Jasper,' she said urgently. She broke into a run, Talibah and Zofka on her heels.

Snow painted the spires and domes of Prague into a wintry fairytale. It was a crisp night, the Vltava silvered with ice, the sky sequinned with stars. The women sprinted deeper into Prague, wending through Hradčany with the castle standing sentry on the hilltop above, blanketed in snow.

They hurried past empty palaces, each one devoid of light, as the Czech aristocrats who owned them had relocated to court life in Vienna. Past churches and sculptures encased in frost. Thea was still struggling to pay attention to anything other than her own guilt and worry and fear rattling around inside her skull – until they stopped in front of Jasper's townhouse.

It looked even older than she'd remembered. Low and wide, painted butter-yellow with countless windows staring out like eyes, the flicker of candlelight or a fire, banked low, visible through some, its roof sugared with snow. A thin plume of smoke leaked from the chimneys.

'How will we even know if Malek's inside?' Uneasiness gnawed at Thea's bones. 'The key I made hides the holder from sight.'

'We go in and locate Jasper.' Zofka shrugged. 'And stay alert to anything . . . suspicious.'

Thea's unease swelled, threatening to devour her. She marched up to Jasper's front door and eyed the brass knocker mounted there. It was a creature shaped like no animal she recognised, with talons and batwings and a protruding horn. With frozen fingers, ignoring the creature's glaring eyes, Thea tried opening the door. It didn't budge. 'It's locked.' She hadn't entered when she'd popped by to consult Jasper around five years ago and she worried she wouldn't be able to now.

'Try it again.' Zofka shuffled from foot to foot on the top step in a bid to keep warm. Each time she moved, the heavy skirts of her mourning gown grew in volume like an inverted umbrella.

Talibah examined the door. Impatience rolled through Zofka. 'We didn't think this through; surely there's magic at play here to ward against someone breaking in.'

'Yes, Jasper's power.' Thea slowly smiled. 'His power, which runs through me.'

'Smart thinking.' Talibah moved aside for Thea. 'Jasper's wards should recognise his power – in the guise of you – enough to let you through, and then once you're on the other side, you can let us through as well.'

'Great. Then we can figure out how to defeat an invisible enemy.' Zofka blew into her hands to warm them. She blew a little too hard, with a little too much warming magic, and the air crackled around them. A nearby street lamp shattered, shards of glass tinkling onto the cobblestones like broken ice. 'Oops.'

Thea softened her gaze, until the world looked as if she was viewing it through a frosted window. Until fate sparked to life and she could see possibilities twisted through the fabric of the world like many, many strings, each one leading to a hundred more. It was the work of seconds to locate the knot outside Jasper's front door and unpick it, whispering a quick promise to do no harm inside, to take nothing that was not hers. Paying with a nightmare she would never miss.

The creature on Jasper's door blinked. Thea blinked back at it, wondering if she'd imagined it, or if it was the knot, the source of Jasper's power bound up in a protective ward on his property.

The door swung open. Without giving herself pause to think – to overthink, as she did everything – Thea leapt over the threshold.

Nothing happened. Holding the knot she'd unpicked in her mind, her fingers stretching through the world's fabric of fate, Thea kept it open. 'Come in, now, quickly,' she whispered.

Zofka and Talibah rushed inside. And Thea released her grip on fate. The door swung shut, relocking itself.

'That wasn't ominous at all.' Zofka stared at the door.

Talibah tilted her head to one side, considering Thea. 'Can you sense the key? It was your magic that made it; perhaps you can locate Malek through the key he's carrying?'

Thea closed her eyes, releasing the swarm of thoughts that flitted through her head like angry bees, the fear snarled in the base of her spine, the worries churning her gut. She let it all go, calming her breath until all she heard was her own pulse and the faint thump of a grandfather clock somewhere in the house, measuring time like a heartbeat.

She opened her eyes. 'I can't sense anything. Can't hear anything but that incessant clock ticking. But if Malek made his way here after the ball, that was hours ago. I hope I'm wrong and he hasn't been waiting here all this time, but I have a horrible feeling . . .' she trailed off. 'We have no reason to trust Heloise; she wanted to strike fear into us.'

Zofka looked sceptical. 'Not that I trust her, but should we consider—'

'Let's start looking and quickly,' Thea interrupted, before Zofka could finish that thought. *One thing at a time*, she promised herself. 'I don't know why Jasper never replied to me, but that doesn't mean that he's dead. Malek had a key and the advantage of surprise, but he's still only human.'

'Agreed.' Talibah set her hands on her hips and her sights on the foyer they stood in.

Thea was on the verge of suggesting they go upstairs when a distant creak on the floorboards emanated from the right. Holding a finger to her lips, Thea crept through a low, interconnecting arch that led into a burgundy panelled room, hung with paintings. Nothing seemed amiss. A suit of armour glared at them from a corner. Zofka liberated the suit of its sword with a murmured, 'Just in case.'

Talibah glanced at the hilt. 'Careful with that thing; it looks like it could have been from the Crusades.'

Zofka wielded it as they wound through two more rooms, one plush with carpets, a crackling fire and settees in embroidered sage and olive tones, the other boasting a dining table set for one. And the largest, grandest fireplace Thea had ever seen.

Where Malek was poking around.

Thea gasped.

'What? Do you see something?' Zofka whirled round, sword tip pointing out.

Soot billowed out from the fireplace as Malek startled at their entrance.

'Got him,' Thea said, watching Malek stand and brush the soot from his breeches and stockings. 'I take it neither of you can see Malek standing in the fireplace?'

Talibah shook her head. 'No.'

Malek stiffened, caught like a deer before a carriage. 'You can see me?' His tawny eyes swivelled between the women, filling with alarm. 'I thought that you wouldn't be able to see me.' Stunned into admission, Malek stared at the key he held in his hand – the key that had cost Thea days and days of work, the key that she'd let go unpaid, ripping apart the Magic Quarter as fate claimed the balance that was due. The key that he had lied and lied for.

She glared at Malek, expecting to feel a gathering sadness that this man she had thought might be the right one for her had been the worst toad of all. Instead, she was numb.

'What are you doing in that fireplace, and what have you done with Jasper?' she demanded, spreading her hands, ready to command fate at a moment's notice.

'I haven't done anything,' Malek argued, giving her hands a fearful look. 'I was merely lighting this fire.'

'You're lying,' Thea said. There was a lot of that wreathing around tonight, like a noxious smoke strangling the city. Shrouding the truth from sight. And she was lost in it, set adrift without a lamp.

'Thea,' Talibah murmured. 'Look.'

Thea wrenched her attention away from Malek long enough to glance at where Talibah was looking: the bottom of the fireplace was moving. It was a trapdoor. And it was opening.

Malek spun round, withdrawing a dagger in the same breath and brandishing it.

'No!' Thea yelled, tensing her fingers and snagging fate's threads.

Jasper emerged from the trapdoor, looking down at something glimmering in his palm. Malek lunged for him just as Thea encircled his life's threads, swiftly knotting them in place as she surrendered her memory of reading *Falling in Hate with his Lordship*. Malek's arm halted, his blade stopping just shy of Jasper's throat.

Jasper pushed it aside as he stepped back up into his dining room, his frown more severe than Thea had witnessed in some time. He scanned the four intruders, his face set in stone, and when he spoke, his voice grated like an ancient rock. Hard and immovable. 'What exactly is going on in here?'

Thea's knees gave a threatening wobble.

With a happy chirrup, Biscuit soared into the room and settled on Jasper's shoulder, giving his ear an affectionate nip.

'Someone's playing favourites,' Zofka whispered to Talibah, narrowing her eyes at Biscuit's attention-seeking.

'You never received my note,' Thea realised. Her throat was thick, cloying with emotions as she stared at Jasper and his infuriating, beautiful face. He had stolen her heart. And maybe it had felt like he'd seen into her soul when they'd clashed in the forest, perhaps he had kissed her as if she was the most precious thing in the world, but he'd also refused to cut a new deal with her.

Thea needed her memories. She needed to understand. She glanced around the room; her heart could be close by. Zofka caught her eye, raising her eyebrows in a silent question. Thea's eyes slid down to Zofka's borrowed sword, wondering if they could do anything to buy a little more time.

In silence, Jasper unrolled Thea's note. His gaze lifted to Thea. 'Consider me warned,' he said dryly, pocketing it. His gaze locked on Malek. 'Malek Jaromir. I took the liberty of having you investigated before you took Theodora to the Winter Ball. Would you care to inform me what the head of the Bohemian wing of Magic Hunters is doing trespassing in my home?'

Malek was a mouse in an owl's talons. He stammered something unintelligible.

Quicker than a hunting snake, Jasper liberated Zofka of her purloined sword, bringing the blade to rest at Malek's throat. 'Not good enough,' he growled.

'I presume he's pointing the sword at Malek?' Talibah asked in an aside and Thea nodded, holding onto the threads she'd used to tie him in place.

Jasper pressed the sword harder against Malek's throat. 'This may be rusted, but I would wager I can still slice your head off with it.'

Trapped by Thea's threads, Malek couldn't evade the blade. 'Fine, fine, fine,' he yelped. 'I asked Thea to make me a key so that I might enter your property without your or anyone's detection. Pan Novak thought I invited Thea to the ball for my own satisfaction, but I knew you wouldn't be able to resist attending if I took Thea.'

Thea chanced a look at Jasper. Their glances collided like passing stars. A flash of feeling, too powerful, too brief.

Malek gave a dry laugh. 'I might have been a scoundrel to use you for your power, Thea, but you were using me, too. It was plain to all to see where your heart truly lay.'

Zofka let out an outraged gasp.

'How dare you?' Thea yanked harder on his threads, forcing him up onto the balls of his feet. 'We are not the same. I wanted to like you. I held only the best intentions—'

'You're too sanctimonious for your own good.' Malek laughed again, though this time it was hard, mocking. 'Too bound up with feeling sorry for yourself that you're blinded to everything you have. That *power*—'

Jasper's hand slipped on the sword, cutting into Malek's throat and cutting off his words. 'Continue your story,' he growled.

'I knew the raid on the Quarter would be the perfect chance for me to uncover your secrets,' Malek managed to gasp. 'Give me enough time to find your hiding places. I had expected more creativity than a trapdoor in the hearth.' He had the audacity to dart an accusing look Thea's way. 'What I didn't consider was that the key you spent so long making might not work.'

'Thea's power forged that key.' Jasper answered the question before Thea could find the words, outrage painting her cheeks red. 'Of course she is exempt from its effects. That is an object borne of her; she will be immune.'

Still Malek looked sceptical. 'Then why can you also see me?' he questioned Jasper.

'You are not in the position to be asking questions,' Jasper snarled, snatching the key from Malek's hand.

'Hold on.' Talibah seemed half lost in thought. 'You entered Stiltskin's Apothecary before the wards were first damaged. How did you sneak through them?'

'I needed a potion to fix my insomnia.' Malek stared at the key Jasper was pocketing, hunger etched through his expression. 'And I had a request. Any ill will I held was purely towards you, and you weren't living in the Quarter.' He aimed his words at Jasper. 'I've been hearing whispers about you and your kind's power for years. I know you're practically immortal; there are rumours about the magical artefacts you have hidden here. Stiltskin's Apothecary might be popular with people in the know in Prague, but you – you are the source of all that power.'

Anger ripped through Thea. Malek wheezed, those traitorous lips Thea had kissed mottling blue. Almost as if . . .

'Not that I'd mind if you killed the toad,' Zofka said mildly, 'you know I'm the kind of friend who'd help you bury a body, but it does sound like you're strangling him, Thea.'

Thea loosened the threads she held with a start. 'You were working with another fate-weaver. With Heloise. Why didn't you target her instead?'

Malek gasped for air, his cheeks flooding with returning blood. 'She doesn't live in this world, and—' His words rasped against his throat.

'And what?' Thea snapped.

'And she paid me,' he admitted. 'She paid me to summon my wing of Hunters here, to ally myself with Pan Novak, the other Magic Hunter living in Prague, and his weaselly efforts to get noticed by myself and the rest of the councillors that rule this city.'

Zofka snorted. 'How surprising that you didn't have an original idea in your head.'

Malek glowered at her. 'The key was my idea.'

'And lying to me about a sister that desperately needed rescuing, was that your idea, too?' Thea asked, her voice dripping with cold anger.

Malek smirked. 'That story worked like magic on you, didn't it?' He shrugged. 'I can't claim credit for that one though, that came from Heloise.'

Jasper towered over Malek, the deep shadows beneath his eyes etched in fury, each word a searing cut. 'You are fortunate Thea has spared you today.'

Malek exhaled, slumping against Thea's threads. She released them, letting him fall to the stone floor. He hit it with a pleasing smack.

'That's my girl,' Talibah murmured.

Malek began scrabbling backwards, fighting to get to his feet as Jasper handed his ancient sword back to Zofka. Jasper seized Malek's collar and hauled him to his feet. 'I will not be so forgiving,' he whispered.

Thea swallowed apprehensively. She was angry at Malek. Jasper was angrier.

Malek's pale face whitened on registering Jasper's words.

Moving with that same preternatural speed he'd displayed earlier, Jasper flipped his trapdoor open with one boot and threw Malek down into it.

Thea gaped at Jasper as he shut and bolted the trapdoor, drowning out Malek's scream as he fell into gods knew what. 'What's down there?'

'My vault. It's unreachable, an underground fortress.' Jasper dusted his hands. 'My apologies that your raven could not breach it; it was not my intent to concern you. Now, I have everything that I need to reinstate the wards, shall we—'

Zofka swung the ancient sword wildly through the air, hitting Jasper's head with the blunt side of the blade.

He fell to the floor and did not move.

CHAPTER

Thirty

'WHAT WAS *THAT* for?' Thea demanded as Talibah bent to one knee and assessed Jasper.

'He'll live.' Talibah stood, joining Thea as both women stared at Zofka. 'He's just unconscious.'

'You asked me to. Message received.' Zofka blew her sword as if it was a pistol smoking gunpowder.

'I only looked at your sword,' Thea said.

'With intent,' Zofka supplied. 'Now, we need to hurry.' She turned serious. 'We're in Jasper's townhouse – *find your heart.*'

'I don't know if I can, if it's even here and not in that secret vault . . .' Thea staggered back a step.

'That's right,' Zofka whispered. 'You can hear it, can't you?'

Jasper's townhouse creaked with age, crackled with candlelight, and ticked with the steady beat of a grandfather clock. A beat that she couldn't shake, couldn't stop tuning into, until it pounded through her head, her chest. 'It's not a grandfather clock.' She pressed a hand to her mouth. 'It's my heart.'

After Thea fate-wove a blanket of knots around Jasper, knowing it wouldn't hold him for long after he came to, the women rushed through the rest of the downstairs.

'How did he manage to put together such a large collection?' Talibah marvelled as they entered a library. Walled with floor-to-ceiling bookshelves, each one was double-stacked with leather tomes in

Czech, English, German, and more languages, spanning not just this world, but others, too, judging by the tongues even Talibah failed to place.

'Well.' – Thea opened a trunk at the base of one of the bookcases – 'He's at least five hundred. I wonder how long he's lived before he came to the Magic Quarter?' That single setting at his long dining table haunted her. 'It must be a lonely life,' she said softly.

Talibah helped her search the trunk. 'Not all of these are from this world, either.' She pulled out a hunk of stone that had been cut to reveal crystal inside, a crystal that looked purple at first glance but was clear as glass, with plum-bruised clouds and the occasional ribbon of lightning. If you squinted, you could see tiny figures walking through the storm.

'Yes, yes, it's a treasure trove,' Zofka said, rummaging through the other trunk in the room. 'But we don't have time. When Jasper wakes up, he is *not* going to be pleased I whacked him with his own sword. Not when Heloise is coming to raze the Quarter down.'

Thea cringed. 'Am I being selfish, risking everyone by taking time out to search for my heart?'

'No,' Zofka said immediately. 'Heloise has singled you out, we need to know why. And finding your heart will return whatever memories you might have of her.'

'We need every weapon we can get,' Talibah agreed.

'Then let's keep looking,' Thea said. 'Because I am ready to remember and fight back.'

As time seeped through their fingers like water, they ran upstairs. 'Can you hear it any clearer here?' Talibah asked.

'No, it still sounds distant.' Thea pushed her hair back. She jerked her head at a second staircase, thinner and steeper. 'Let's search the attic next.'

The attic was low, dim, and stacked with crates.

Talibah pulled a face. 'It's going to take us too long to search all these.'

Zofka popped one open with her sword. 'Then the faster we get started, the faster we'll finish. Let's hope those threads were thick as ropes.'

Thea cringed; they were fighting against time itself, their capture imminent and unavoidable. Though it was her own heart they were looking for, she couldn't stop picturing Jasper's face when he awoke and realised what they were doing. She knew well the power that she channelled from him, and if that was only a bit of his power siphoned off, she couldn't imagine how powerful he could be. Nor how it would feel when he opened his eyes and witnessed Thea's betrayal. Well, he had betrayed her first.

She pulled out the topmost item in the crate she'd just opened. 'Oh,' she breathed. It was a dress, with long billowing sleeves and wildflowers dancing along the neckline. Simple and lovely. A quick peek through the rest of the crate revealed more dresses, all in a fashion Thea hadn't seen before, each one more beautiful than the next, though their silhouettes were clean, needing no stomachers nor panniers, nor assistance in fastening laces and buttons and pins. She closed the lid, shutting out her guilt. 'Maybe they belonged to his family.' A sudden wistfulness overcame her at the idea of the woman who Jasper had loved wearing these dresses for him.

'I have more of the same.' Talibah closed another crate. 'We ought not to look through these.'

Thea nodded. It was bad enough they were snooping through Jasper's home while he lay unconscious downstairs; she held no interest in searching through his personal belongings. It was disrespectful. And it gave her the strangest feeling that she couldn't quite pinpoint.

'I feel like this should be easier,' Zofka grumbled on the stairs back down to the second level. 'Are you sure you can't hear your heart any louder *anywhere*?'

'Very sure,' Thea replied, more than a little tersely. Creeping around Jasper's house as he was poised to wake any moment and dawn pinkened the sky outside unsettled her. Not to mention that she'd been awake the entire night, as had Zofka and Talibah.

'Where *is* it?' Thea raked her hair back a few minutes later, after they'd raced through the second floor, which was mostly empty bedrooms and a dusty music room. 'We've looked everywhere, even the attic. The sun's already rising, and we have to get back to the Magic Quarter; we've risked everything by leaving it undefended.'

Zofka pointed her sword towards Jasper's bedroom. 'Actually, there's one room we have yet to search.'

'Why would he keep my heart in his bedroom?' Thea whispered.

Zofka looked enthralled. 'I keep telling you that the man wants you, Thea. When are you going to wake up and realise his feelings for you?' She poked Thea's arm with the blunted sword tip. 'You have to admit, it would be awfully romantic for him to sleep guarding your heart.'

'Thea!' Jasper suddenly roared out from downstairs.

Thea bit her lip. 'Oh, no.'

'I'm with Zofka,' Talibah said. 'We have seconds left, come on. One last look.'

Zofka raised the ancient sword in triumph.

Thea pushed Jasper's bedroom door open and ran inside, her friends on her heels.

Jasper's bedroom was cosy with firelight, more books, and a journal on his bedside table that Zofka immediately gravitated towards. She picked it up to examine it closer.

'Zofka, that's intruding,' Thea hissed, unable to not feel protective over Jasper while he was in such a vulnerable position, tied up with fate as they crept through his bedroom.

'So is taking your heart,' Zofka shot back, but she replaced the journal without peeking inside.

Pursing her lips, Thea looked through his books. Some history, some philosophy, a couple of novels – including one in Chinese, that Talibah read as titled, *Journey to the West*, though she warned them that her Chinese was rustier than she'd like. Nothing stood out in Jasper's bookcase, no margin notes that could be clues, no scraps of paper tucked among the pages. Thea moved onto an antique dresser, painted with dragons. It was getting harder to cling onto hope. Impossible to imagine her heart beating in her chest, her memories surging back. That she'd ever remember what her name had been before she'd been Theodora.

Sometimes she wondered if she'd miss being Thea, or if Zofka and Talibah would. There might be others though, friends and family, that knew a different woman by a different name – perhaps a different version of herself was already being missed elsewhere. Thea's head spun. She forced herself to concentrate. She had seconds left. It had to be here, otherwise . . . No. She refused to finish that thought. It simply *had* to be here.

The dresser was filled with small boxes. Sliding out the first, Thea opened it, her hope soaring up to the vanishing stars outside before plummeting back to earth. Gold and silver and jewels twinkled back at her. She picked up a necklace without thinking, holding it up to look at the heart pendant. Writing scrolled across the gold on the back: *I am yours until the end of time.* Thea's heart-spell quivered.

The staircase creaked.

Thea froze, necklace dangling from her hand. Talibah, over by the mantelpiece, and Zofka, rifling through a chest beneath the window, stilled in place, all three women exchanging a look. 'He's coming,' Thea mouthed. Panic slickened her palms, threatening her grip on the necklace as they returned to their search, quieter and faster.

Sensing something, Thea reached past the boxes, to the back of the dresser, and felt around. There was something there, something she couldn't quite reach . . . because she could not see it. Closing her eyes, she cleared her mind, searching with Jasper's power until she slotted into that other awareness.

On reopening her eyes, she saw it: a heart-shaped box, tangled in three knots of fate, rendering it invisible to the naked eye. Untouchable. Like it resided neither here nor there, but in the between. Thea began unpicking the knots.

The door slammed open.

Thea's heart-spell shuddered in her chest, Zofka yelped in surprise, and Talibah quickly adjusted her headscarf, which had slipped lower over her hair.

Jasper stood in the threshold. His frown, his glower, were notably absent, his face unreadable. 'And here I thought you were all wiser than to challenge me.'

Zofka stood, raising her sword.

'I'll be taking that back now.' With a twist of his fingers, Jasper tweaked fate, faster than Thea could comprehend. The sword vanished from Zofka's hand, reappearing in Jasper's instead.

Hurrying to unpick the remaining knots, Thea's fingers shook. A web of red threads encircled the box, keeping it hidden from sight.

'Fine. I don't need a weapon when I *am* a weapon.' Zofka summoned a ball of witch light in her emptied palm.

The heart-shaped box materialised, visible once more. Thea's heart-spell trilled, as if threatened, on seeing it. She pulled it out of the dresser. 'I found it,' she whispered, staring at the dark red velvet box. Zofka and Talibah turned to her, responses dying on their lips as they watched Thea reach out a trembling hand to open the box, to reclaim her own heart.

'No!' Jasper cried out, leaping across the room before she could blink. 'I beg of you . . .' Jasper's eyes met Thea's with the power of a hundred storms whipping through the woods. 'Do *not* open that box.' His voice cracked and blistered.

'Stay back,' Zofka commanded, raising her witch light.

'Open it,' Talibah whispered. 'Open it and take your heart back.'

Her head swimming, her nails digging into the velvet after Jasper had half scared the life out of her, Thea opened the heart-shaped box.

Inside, on a bed of plush satin, lay a golden ring.

It was old, evident from the warp of the metal, worn lace-thin in places. Simple, too. Seeing it brought a lump to her throat, at the woman who must have been married for so long to have worn her ring thin. She lifted it to show Talibah and Zofka. Disappointment rushed over Thea, so acute it was like being back in that cursed lake, her lungs filling with water. She could have drowned in it.

Talibah's expression cleared, murky confusion giving way to comprehension. 'Oh,' she said softly.

'Oh, what?' Zofka frowned at her, but Talibah gave her a small shake of her head, her amber gaze softening with concern as she glanced at Thea.

'I don't understand.' Thea gave a dry laugh. 'Where is my heart?' She licked her lips as if that would make the words come easier. 'Why wouldn't you want me to open this box? Have you . . . Have you lost my heart?'

'Yes,' Jasper whispered, giving her an anguished look. 'I lost your heart.'

Thea breathed in sharply. 'What? How could you—'

'You need to tell her the truth,' Talibah broke in. 'If what I suspect is true, you need to tell her the truth. Now.'

Jasper ground the heels of his palms into his eyes. 'I never knew loneliness could cut so deep,' he admitted, looking at Thea again.

Frowning, Thea stepped back, afraid to hear whatever came next.

'Each night I go to bed alone. Each morning, I wake alone. I am living a cold and meaningless existence without . . .' His voice roughened. 'Without you.'

The box dropped from Thea's hands, sending the ring rolling across the polished floorboards, onto the Persian carpet, where Jasper stood at the foot of his bed. Meeting his boot, it stopped; Jasper bent to pick it up. 'The one thing that has brought me some semblance of life, of light, has been visiting you. Allowing myself to see you again. The person I would die a thousand deaths for. My twin soul. My everything.' His voice rubbed the words raw. 'Even if you look at me with distrust, with dislike, the love lost from your eyes, the memories stolen by my own hand, it is worth it all just to spend a heartbeat in your presence.'

'My dreams of you,' Thea whispered.

Jasper looked like a lost man. Like he'd fallen into a pit of grief he could not claw himself free from. 'Fragments of the past clinging on.'

Zofka was still staring at the ring Jasper was holding like a delicate wild flower. 'Do you mean to say that that's Thea's *wedding ring*?'

'No. No,' Thea whispered, shaking her head. 'I thought you were a widower.'

Jasper's hands tensed at his sides, as if he yearned to reach out and catch her, to stop her free-falling through time and space. 'I mentioned losing my wife to Rose, once. She took it to mean my wife had died, but you were just lost to me. Unreachable.'

Thea reeled. 'No. I don't want . . . whatever this is. I have a beautiful life, even if it's a little lonely sometimes, and I've made some mistakes.'

Pain bled across Jasper's face. His eyes were soft and sad, a lighter blue than Thea had seen before. As they rippled like a shallow pool, she realised why; they were filled with unshed tears. 'I never intended you to find out this way,' he said hoarsely. 'I never thought I'd have to be the one to tell you, not like this.'

'Did you ever mean to tell me at all?' Thea demanded.

His silence was answer enough.

She nodded bitterly. 'That's what I thought.'

'I want you to know that I do not expect anything from you; you do not need to fear me, nor my involvement in your life,' Jasper told her. 'If you are . . . happy as you are, then I have no wish to change that.'

He seemed genuine. Though Thea could not trust Jasper, let alone picture herself wed to him, she could not deny the depth of emotion playing through his face, the truth searing his words. 'Return my heart and memories,' she said. 'I deserve to know the entire truth, and I need to know it now.'

'I never took your heart.' A tear escaped Jasper's eye, but he ignored it. 'I could never have done that to you. It is only a trick of fate, a looped thread, that makes you believe so.'

Thea clamped a hand to her chest. 'I've spent seven years believing it wasn't there. Not being able to feel it.' She still couldn't feel it, wasn't sure what to think. 'My memories, then. Give me back my memories. Heloise is coming for me, and I must know if her other claims are true. If she is indeed . . . my sister.' Her head whirled. All the past seven years, she would have died to know a single relation. Now she'd gained a sister and a husband in a single night . . . if she believed either of them.

Jasper sat heavily on the end of his bed, lowering his gaze to the floor. 'I cannot.'

'You cannot? You *cannot*?'

Jasper did not raise his eyes. 'No.'

Thea's chest spasmed. 'How convenient,' she said. Jasper's head jerked up in confusion. 'That you never intended to give my memories back, that you've ensured I will never know when you are lying, never know the truth for myself.' Her thoughts darted to and fro like a flock of frenzied birds, the noise in her head intolerable. She needed to leave, couldn't stay here a second longer – even the sound of the fire sputtering in the grate was too loud, too much. She backed towards the door. 'You can't keep my memories hostage forever. One day, I will find a way to reclaim them myself, and then I'll find out exactly what you're hiding from me.' If anything he had told her was true, or if they were lies stacked on top of lies, like Thea's impossibly high piles of books, destined to topple over.

Jasper lurched up. 'Thea, wait! It's not safe out there, Heloise—'

But Thea refused to hear another word. Flinging his door open, she ran downstairs, through the foyer and out into the street, where she kept running, towards the river.

Thea fled back over Prague Bridge and through the gaping entrance cleaved straight through St John of Nepomuk, who no longer guarded the Quarter, though what was left of his face seemed to give her a concerned look, just as Zofka and Talibah came skidding into view as she glanced back.

'Wait!' Zofka cried out, battling her mourning gown as Thea bolted down the spiral stairs leading to the Quarter. The Hunters left guarding it were long gone, as was any sign of Wojslav. Perhaps he was sleeping off his feast.

She skirted the edges of the void, which was now rumbling hungrily, refusing to stop until she reached the apothecary, where she hesitated, glancing up at the gilded sign swinging outside. The one with Jasper's name on it: *Stiltskin's Apothecary*. How could he be her *husband*? She refused to believe it, even as something niggled deep down that there was something between them, had been all along. That their kisses had been their most truthful exchanges.

The weathervane creaked a sorrowful tune, cut in the shape of a solitary magpie, the falling snow lending it a white nightcap that looked uncannily like Rose's.

Zofka and Talibah caught up.

'I appreciate you both coming with me last night, but I am not ready to discuss this yet,' she told them before they could speak.

'No,' protested Zofka, gasping for breath. 'Don't shut us out, let us be here for you.'

'It's all right.' Talibah rested a hand on Zofka's arm. 'This has been a big shock, she needs time to process it all.'

'Fine.' Zofka eyed Thea speculatively. 'But I will be making sure that you're eating enough,' she threatened, bringing the faintest smile to Thea's lips. Zofka launched forwards, wrapping her shorter frame around Thea's and holding her fiercely. 'I'll be back to leave breakfast on your doorstep,' she promised. 'Make sure that you eat every last bite of it; you need to keep your strength up if we're to battle this fate-weaver.'

'My sister, you mean?' Thea said darkly.

'We don't know that yet,' Talibah pointed out. 'Something tells me she would say anything if she knew it would disturb you. Keep you wrong-footed. Muddling up truths and untruths is a good tactic to unnerve you. Keep you unsure. And Jasper did not confirm it.'

'That's true.' Zofka added. 'She was a conniving one. Can't trust a word out of her mouth. I'll make you something special to eat and you'll feel more like yourself again. Then we'll all be ready to take on whatever that fate-weaver flings at us next. She didn't know what she was taking on when she targeted us, but we'll make her regret it.'

Thea already knew that breakfast would be bursting with magic. There was nothing like someone in distress to coax out Zofka's best kitchen-witchery. Even if nothing would stop that roar in Thea's head drowning out everything else, as if she'd had too many glasses of *svařák* and the world was twisting around her.

When Zofka reluctantly relinquished her hold on Thea, Talibah swept in. 'We will be here for you the moment you need us,' she vowed.

Thea nodded, supressing a sudden burst of tears. When her friends, her true sisterhood, had prised themselves away to return to their respective homes, she locked the apothecary door behind them.

Then she closed the shutters. The folk residing in the Magic Quarter were a curious lot and she didn't want anyone peering in at her with accusing eyes as the void still rumbled and smoked outside. As the Hunters waited somewhere out there, as Heloise bided her time.

But first, tea.

CHAPTER

Thirty-One

‘I CAN'T BE JASPER'S wife,' Thea told her trusty old teapot, painted a bright cherry-red with its cracked handle that hadn't yet given way. The teapot steamed. But all the lavender and camomile and soothing fairy's tears she'd crammed into it couldn't ease her relentless mind. She poured a second cup, then a third.

Sitting in a little rocking chair in the furthest corner of her growing space, between her anxious apple tree and a couple of cherry trees that crept closer, bouncing in their pots when she wasn't looking, Thea rocked and sipped tea and stared up at the snow falling onto her glass roof.

Perhaps she was better off not knowing what she'd forgotten. Maybe life would be happier that way. Thea stopped rocking.

Jasper had told her that his daughter died and she knew from Zofka that he was a widower but Thea was very much alive. Though if she had been Jasper's wife, she supposed with her missing memories and lists of names that didn't belong to her, she was lost enough to him.

She put her teacup down on the nearest table. It missed, shattering on the floor. The cherry trees curled their leaves away, the apple tree shaking in panic, but Thea scarcely noticed. Had that been *her* daughter?

She surged to her feet. Enough was enough: she was sick of Jasper's half-truths, of battling her own cursed mind. It was time to get her memories back. And if Jasper refused to do so, she would simply have to find a way around that. Luckily, he was not the only fate-weaver she happened to know.

Dipping a quill into her favourite sapphire ink, she penned a quick note to the person she wanted to speak to least. The person that might just hold all the answers. Maybe Thea could save the Quarter herself, right the wrongs she'd caused when she'd broken the wards. And if she was the reason that the Quarter was being threatened, if she learnt *why*, maybe she could fix that, too.

I wish to speak with you.
Meet me on Prague Bridge, after sundown.

After whistling for a raven, she tied the note around its ankle. 'Take this to Heloise. Do not enter the Crossroads, but wait for her outside, do you understand?'

The raven croaked in acknowledgement and flew out of the window.

Waiting for a response, though she was not sure one would come, Thea wandered upstairs, where she seized her Compendium of Magic, searching for anything she'd missed. Anything that might help save the Quarter. Her eyes fell on the last entries of the love story penned into the margins:

The walls of my life are closing in on me. I am beginning to fear I shall never evade them. The sole time I feel free, I feel myself, is with him. My love. We traded rings today, wisps of gold that encircle our fingers. When I wear mine, I feel his heartbeat.

She snapped the book shut. It was just a coincidence. Taking it upstairs, she made herself some hot chocolate, even though she'd already drunk enough tea to send her running to the chamber pot every other minute. Clasping the warm cup in both hands, she sat on the edge of her bed, looking at the Compendium. It stared back at her. She flipped it back open and reread the last entry penned by the mysterious previous apprentice of the apothecary:

*

We ran away together. We had no choice, but if I had to make a choice, I would choose him, always and forever. A thousand times over, I would choose him.

Thea knocked her hot chocolate over one of her yellow knitted blankets. Cursing, she mopped it up with a shaking hand before forcing herself to read on, ignoring how the words seemed to echo Heloise's when she'd confronted Thea on the bridge. *We all missed you so very much after you ran away.* Sensing her disquiet, Cinnamon hopped onto the bed and nestled into her side.

Our first home together. Could there be any more beautiful words in any language? I think not. It is smaller, simpler than what I am accustomed to, and yet I think it the nicest place I have ever seen. We are inseparable, day and night. He cooks for me. I collect bunches of wildflowers until our cottage blooms. These woodlands that surround us are quieter than the wild forests where we met, yet they possess a certain elegance. Here, nature is not a force to be feared, a magic to tame, but a quiet walk beside a frothing brook, hand in hand. The hedgehogs and badgers and foxes I feed each twilight. The blossoming violets outside our windows.

Only the people are strange. But we have each other, and that is all we shall ever need.

Thea couldn't finish her hot chocolate. She turned on her side and lay on her bed, words and thoughts floating around her like clouds. Too insubstantial to hold onto, to understand, but thick enough to disorientate her.

Zofka sent breakfast. Then a mid-morning snack, which was shortly followed by lunch, with a mid-afternoon snack arriving not an hour later. Thea collected each one to prevent the kitchen-witch from fretting, though she didn't have the stomach to eat. The reprieve that Heloise had given them was running down the clock. The apothecary's shelves rumbled as if it was hungry, enticing Thea with scents of warm sugar biscuits, fried cheese and potato dumplings, hot toast puddled with butter, and rich hot chocolate by turns. It only coaxed her into her kitchen when she caught Cinnamon sniffing, his whiskers trembling. When she got up to fetch him some vegetables, cutting carrots and broccoli into a bowl for her rabbit, she noticed that Talibah, too, had sent her goodies: a new stack of romance novels waited on the doorstop. She brought them inside, though she still had plenty to read; with the whirl of threats and danger and business that autumn and now winter had brought, she still hadn't started *Eudora and the Ship's Captain*.

A note poked out of the cover of the topmost book:

> *Jasper has called everyone together this evening, to start our counter-attack. I'll let you know what the plan is if you don't come.*
> *With love, Talibah*

Thea retreated upstairs in case Jasper happened by the apothecary, though she doubted he'd dare. She had no wish to have everyone blaming her for the demise of the Magic Quarter. Especially since they were right: the void was a raging reminder of her biggest mistake. Besides, she had her own plans for how to save the Quarter, and as soon as the sun went down, she would act. Curling up on her bed, with Cinnamon's head resting on her stomach, Thea slept at last. When she next woke, sunset was bleeding across the sky. Heloise's reprieve was over.

Thea lurched up. Her head already filling with noise instead of memories, with questions and worries that howled like a hunting wolf. She'd always believed she worried so much, thought too hard, because her mind was overcompensating for her lack of memories, her missing heart. Now she wasn't sure what to believe. Perhaps she was like Zofka, who couldn't keep still, only it was her thoughts rather than her body that refused to calm.

A flurry of shadow cut through the snowfall, manifesting at Thea's window. She hurried to let the raven in. She didn't want to read anything anyone might have sent her, especially if it came from Jasper, but she'd never leave a raven out in the cold.

Biscuit cawed happily as he fluttered through the window and landed on the bedside table, folding his wings back and lowering his beak for gentle scritches. Thea relieved him of his note as she rubbed his stomach with a knuckle:

> *I am sorrier than you'll ever know that I cannot give you the answers you need. Stay home, I shall re-forge the wards under the light of the full winter's moon tonight. I will not allow Heloise to enter the Quarter, you have my solemn vow that I shall do whatever it takes to keep you safe.*
>
> *Forever yours,*
> *Jasper*

More ravens crowded behind Biscuit, bearing notes from Talibah and Zofka, appraising her of their plans to fight back against the foe that Thea had exposed them all to. Heloise's words whispered around her skull, haunting her: *I want to raze your precious Magic Quarter to the ground, and drag you screaming away from your friends' corpses.* No matter what past she might have once held, Thea would never ignore that Zofka and Talibah were her present-day family, and she couldn't risk their lives. Nor could she allow Heloise to march on the Quarter and decimate it; regardless of how Rose, Fleur, Zdenka, Wojslav and all the others felt about her, she'd grown fond of them over the years.

Thea would face her so-claimed sister herself.

She pulled on her forest-green velvet cloak and stole out into the winter's night like a wraith, ignoring Jasper's note.

A pot had been left on her doorstep with strict instructions to *Eat me!* in Zofka's looping script, but there was no time to take it inside now. She needed to hurry before she lost all nerve, her decision, her desperation for the truth weighing her cloak and soul down. The future of the Magic Quarter rested on her shoulders now.

She hurried up the street, keeping to the shadows, far from the void that seemed to be widening by the hour, devouring a little more of the Quarter bit by bit. Crunching a path through the snow, she kept her hood low, evading the weather-witches that were monitoring the void, the pixies sitting in the lowest branches of the oaks, keeping a watchful eye out, and *Jasper*.

He stood beside the Crypt, with its turret of ravens, the dark-winged birds flying in and out like inky quills. His back was turned to her, he seemed to be commanding a group of magical folk as he held that same gleaming object he'd removed from his vault.

Thea dived behind the nearest oak. Peering around its trunk, she watched as Jasper began to weave fate. He seemed to be tackling the void first: its black depths shuddered in response, leaking smoke like blood. She darted from tree to tree, taking a meandering path to avoid being seen. When she cast a final look back at Jasper, she glimpsed Stiltskin's roof over his shoulder. A lone wolf howled back at her from the weathervane.

Shivering, Thea tightened her cloak.

She fled the Magic Quarter.

Too many carriages rattled past on Prague Bridge, bright with street lamps and laughter at this hour, shoppers with festive packages and the odd child, staying up late to play in the snow. Thea wandered up and down, waiting for Heloise to appear. If Jasper was to be believed, there had never been a spell in place of her heart, no reason that she could not fall in love. But perhaps she'd struggled finding a great love because her traitorous little heart, hiding away in her chest, had already had its sights set on Jasper and refused to consider another man. Kept her chasing after toads as a distraction.

Five minutes passed, then another five. It was arctic, and the river below wore a thick crust of ice. Snowdrifts were piled high on its banks.

She possessed little hope that Heloise would meet her as requested, but nevertheless, Heloise would have to walk past her on the bridge to enter the Quarter, and Thea would not let her go without a fight. Her fate-weaving was weaker than Heloise's, but Thea would do anything to protect her family. Even if she only bought them a little time, distracted Heloise while they launched whatever offensive they had planned, it would be worth it.

Another figure exited from St John of Nepomuk and strode towards Thea with a familiar gait. 'What are you doing here?' Jasper asked.

'I could ask you the same question.' Thea frowned at him. 'How did you know I was here?'

Jasper's brow furrowed. 'You think that I do not sense you? Wherever you are in this world, across all the worlds, I will always find you, Thea. Your heart calls to me.'

'I suspect your power helps,' she said dryly. When he set his mind to it, there was little Jasper could not achieve.

'Zofka has sent me eight ravens over the past day—'

'She had no right,' Thea hotly interrupted.

'—fiercely scolding me,' Jasper continued.

That sounded like Zofka.

'As the ravens kept coming, her fierceness faded to worry as you didn't take the dinner she'd cooked for you.'

She knew she should have taken that pot inside.

'Then fear, as Talibah spotted you leaving the Quarter tonight. I also received ravens alerting me to your exit from Rose, Fleur, Zdenka, and Paní Dagmar, among others. Even Wojslav sent me a raven, and he's terrified of the creatures. No less than thirteen people, including myself, saw you attempt to sneak out of the Quarter in that ridiculous cloak of yours.'

Thea glanced down, frowning. 'What's wrong with my cloak?'

'It's far too figure-hugging,' he ground out, looking anywhere but at her. 'And entirely too thin for winter.'

Her cheeks betrayed her; she just knew they were pinkening gleefully at his attention, even though she absolutely, certainly, did not want her possible past husband and current employer to be noticing her in that way. 'I thought I was very subtle . . .' she began, trailing off when Jasper made a noise that sounded suspiciously like a snort.

He searched her gaze, his voice softening. 'Everyone was greatly concerned that you failed to attend today's meeting. In fact, it was discussed to such an extent that I am still not certain if anyone paid attention to my orders. They mentioned that it was the first meeting you had not attended since you moved in?'

Thea's eyes were too dry in the freezing evening. She blinked hard to ease their prickling. 'I didn't realise going for a walk wasn't permitted,' she choked out.

Jasper's eyes darkened as he continued to survey her. 'They know you are hurting.' He sighed, turning to brace himself against the stonework of the bridge, looking at the frozen river below, the birds skating over it. 'You know I told you to stay put. Which begs the question, what you are doing here? Though I suspect I already know the answer.'

'I needed some space,' Thea lied, glancing over her shoulder, half-expecting to see Heloise materialise on the bridge.

When she looked back, Jasper was watching her, his frown tinged with regret. 'You may be in denial, but I know you. I know you better than anyone else who has ever existed. I know the way you think, how you struggle with unwanted thoughts, unbidden and unrelenting—'

Thea jolted, looking at him anew. She had never told him how her own mind plagued her. Unless she had . . . but didn't remember doing so.

'Which is why I know you came here hoping to confront Heloise on your own,' Jasper continued, a vein pulsing in his neck as he attempted to corral his anger, to hide it from her. 'You always were a gods-cursed hero, too eager to sacrifice yourself for the greater good.'

'I will not let her unleash herself on my friends,' Thea told him, raising her voice.

'I was this close' – Jasper stood, towering over her as he brought his thumb and forefinger together – 'from repairing that void, from restoring the wards.'

'Good, go back and carry on then,' Thea told him. 'Protect them all.'

Jasper looked done with attempting to hide his anger. It was strangely reassuring; this was the Jasper she knew, this push-pull between them familiar and comforting. Thea half-smiled to see it, which only seemed to incense him more. 'Not without you,' he growled.

Thea folded her arms. 'That is not your decision to make. I don't know who I was before, or what we were, but I know who I am today, and I will *not* budge from this bridge.'

Jasper glared at her. 'I am trying to keep you safe.'

Thea glared back. 'And I am asking you to save everyone I love. It is the least you can do after having lied to me time and time again.'

A sudden sound bellowed out over Prague Bridge, sending birds fleeing to the skies.

Jasper grabbed Thea's arm, steadying them both as the bridge shook, the icy river cracking into a patchwork of floes. One of St John's stars snapped from his halo.

'That came from the Magic Quarter.' Giving Jasper a panicked look, Thea bolted towards the source of the sound.

CHAPTER

Thirty-Two

HAT WAS THAT noise?' Thea gasped as she ran round and round the stairs, back down into the Magic Quarter. 'Are we under attack?'

'It was your weathervane.' Jasper's voice was steady as he ran at her side.

'Surely it's *your* weathervane.' Despite knowing that they may be about to meet their fate, that was the detail Thea's mind snagged on.

Jasper's small sigh almost went unheard. Almost. 'Actually, it's yours. It was a gift. It used to be a nuisance, but I suppose it makes for an effective warning system.'

Thea fell silent as the spiral staircase ended, spitting them out into the Magic Quarter. The – *her* – weathervane was the first thing she saw. It had reclaimed its dragon form, though it was much, much larger than it had been last time, its wings stretched out across half the Magic Quarter as the apothecary roof groaned under its weight. 'Are we under attack?' She clamped a hand to her side, bracing against the stitch needling her there. She'd been doing far too much running of late.

Jasper eyed the Quarter, vacated of all magical folk in the half hour since Thea had departed, the void crackling and hissing down the centre. 'Not yet, but I would say it's coming.'

'What does Heloise want with me?' Thea turned to Jasper. 'Now would be excellent timing for my memories to return. Am I Claire? Nicola? Alicja?'

He gave a single, sad shake of his head.

Thea blew out an aggravated sigh.

'*There* you are!' Zofka had cracked open the door of the Gingerbread House and was peering out. 'Hurry up and get inside.'

As it happened, *everybody* was inside the Gingerbread House. A sea of faces turned as Thea entered, Jasper bringing up the guarded rear. She tensed as Rose marched over, her eyes narrowed into fierce slashes. 'You worried us half to death,' Rose accused, yanking Thea into a crushing hug. 'First you skipped out on the first Quarter meeting you've ever missed, then you bolted up the apothecary and wouldn't let any of us inside, and then you skedaddled out of the Quarter itself!' She gave one of her disapproving sniffs, which was rather too loud, pressed against Thea's ear. 'What makes you think you can get away from us that easily?'

'I . . . I broke the Magic Quarter,' Thea said, looking around in bewilderment as Rose released her with a squeeze. 'The wards and the void—'

'Adds a bit of excitement.' Zdenka grinned at her.

'Once I had two jealous lovers duel over me,' Paní Dagmar said fondly. 'Many a witch was caught in the crossfire.'

'And I've nearly burnt half the street down twice so far,' Zofka reminded her, brightening as if she was proud of the fact, Gretel shaking her head at her side.

Rose patted Thea's hand. 'The point is, we all make mistakes, dear. Even Wojslav has been known to feed off the occasional pixie.'

The nearest pixies fluttered away from the vampire in the corner. He picked his elongated teeth delicately. 'We all have our vices.'

'I don't know what to say,' Thea forced out through the lump in her throat. It felt like she'd swallowed a toad.

'Well, don't you worry a bit about this battle,' Rose continued. 'We've got our marching orders and . . .' She lowered her voice, giving Thea a devious little smile. 'It's been half a century since I've had a good fight; I can't wait to take down this Heloise. Sister indeed.' Another sniff. 'The only family you need is us.'

'Hear, hear!' Zofka called out, nudging Talibah with excitement as both women hovered nearby.

Thea sat at the last available table with a bump. All this emotion was wearying. Talibah, Zofka and Jasper joined her, squeezing in tight.

'It's like we've always told you.' Talibah's amber eyes gleamed with something Thea had spent so long looking for in other places – in men that had turned out to be toads and among the pages of her romance novels – that she'd underestimated how the best thing of all was seeing it reflected from the eyes of her friends, the family that she'd cultivated by herself: love. 'You may not have sought this out as your home, but look at what you've built here.'

'Home is where you belong,' Zofka added, 'And you've belonged here since that first night the three of us sat down to eat dinner together.' She grimaced. 'And I even let you cook! Though how you burn goulash, I don't—' She stopped talking when Gretel nudged her.

Thea wasn't even pretending not to cry any more. 'I love you both more than you could ever know.' She turned to Jasper. He was already watching her. She was not ready to forgive him for keeping the truth from her, but she didn't have the energy to continue hating him when he looked at her as if she was the sun. He seemed more lost than Thea had ever been, living alone with his secrets and a past she might have once shared with him. She reached out a tentative hand and touched his. He jerked, his gaze shadowing as he looked at her hand. After an extended minute, frozen in place, he responded, interlacing his fingers with hers. Once more, she was struck with how warm he was, how tender. How that heat licked between them, almost chasing her thoughts clean out of her head.

'I know that you look at me and see a history, an entire past between us, but I have spent the last seven years with a different family, and—' She swallowed hard, looking to Zofka, to Talibah. 'I don't need to be whoever I was then. Because I am happy here. I love the community I've built, the friends I've surrounded myself with, and my cosy little home with Cinnamon. Everywhere I look in the Magic Quarter, I see my home.'

Jasper's throat bobbed up and down as he gave an unsteady nod. 'I understand,' he said in a gravelly tone.

'So, I am not going to guess my name any more,' Thea whispered. 'Because who I am, who I want to be, is *me*. Exactly as I am now. My name is Theodora and this is my home.'

Jasper closed his eyes as he gripped her hand harder. A single tear chased down his cheekbone. 'Oh, Thea,' he whispered. 'I have never been happier to hear you say that.'

'I . . . What?' Thea asked, catching his words.

When Jasper opened his eyes and looked at her, something in her head *gave*. She clapped her hands to her temples, her heart quickening.

'Thea?' Zofka and Talibah stood as one, as Jasper clenched her hand harder.

Her heart quivered and shook, insubstantial as a moth wing as the world shuttered around Thea.

And her head filled. Not with thoughts, worries and anxieties, but with *life*, in all its facets. Joy and grief, love and loss. It beamed through her as an entire lifetime of memories surged back.

Suddenly she was seven again, skipping through the forest around her home, picking lilac flowers to wear in her hair, when the world burst to life with a thousand threads in every colour she could name, and more she could not. Each one fizzing at her fingertips with possibility. Her parents had warned her this would happen one day, that she would have the power to play with fate, but that fate was a balance, and she was not its ruler, only its scales. Still, she couldn't resist, reaching out and brushing her fingertips against her own thread. It was a bright, shiny pink, her favourite colour. Rubbing closely against it was a second thread, a soft sage green that she instinctively knew belonged to Heloise, her little sister. Thea frowned, annoyed at how Heloise's thread seemed to be suffocating hers. Heloise was five and wouldn't stop pestering Thea, following her around and stealing all her playthings. Thea had skipped into the forest to avoid her, but she knew their mother would scold her later. Her cheeks pinkening with frustration, Thea flicked Heloise's thread away from hers.

Another ten years, and Thea had grown into her power. Heloise's had sputtered reluctantly to life, but was a weaker echo of Thea's. And if Thea felt guilty for pushing her little sister away, that guilt eroded when Heloise began looking back at her with jealous eyes. Manipulating their parents into turning their backs when Thea tried to warn them that Heloise hungered for more, that her ambition bordered on cruelty.

Another few years, and the forest was Thea's refuge. It crackled with magic, though never more fiercely than the day she met Jasper. He gave her his cloak to collect flowers; she ended up giving him her heart. When the storms hit that year and Thea was barricaded inside, hiding from Heloise's little tricks and mind games, she fell in love with Jasper through the notes they managed to exchange. And when the storms ended, they fell into a love deeper and truer than she'd thought possible, a love to shake the stars from the sky. A love that saw her sister for who she was when nobody else cared to.

It had been a blustery evening in the forest, the white-eyed deer turning their gazes to the twin moons rising, when Heloise sprang her trap. It was a simple loop of fate that had Thea believing Jasper was in danger from the tricksy demons who lived in a cursed lake on the other side of the forest. She had charged off to rescue him without a second thought when he had snatched her out of the trees and informed her what Heloise had done. How her sister had bribed the lake demons to strip Thea's flesh from her bones and devour every last slick of marrow until nothing remained.

Another flash of memory, this time exchanging the sweetest promises with Jasper under two swollen moons in a field of wildflowers, their scent clinging to her hair and skirts, even after they fled through the Crossroads into the human world.

A few years later, and a searing rip of pain and a second love, fierce and new and all-consuming as she birthed their daughter. Violet. Named for the purple flowers unfurling around their cottage.

Thea's memories plunged further ahead, into the deep darkness she'd been dreading, that hole at the centre of her life that had made her believe she'd lost her heart. Because she had. Death and fire and a loss so prolific it had robbed Thea of her breath. Made her incapable of seeing anything beyond her own suffering as Violet had been violently taken from them at a tender age. Burned on the altar of human ignorance and intolerance for the witchcraft they suspected Violet possessed.

Jasper dragging her to safety once more, though she was so lost in her ravaging grief she begged him to strip her of her memories, to make her forget it all. At the cost of forgetting him, too.

And Jasper, who had loved her enough to oblige her.

Thea's heart-spell ceased its flutter as she felt her true heart beat once more. At last, she was whole, the two parts of herself reuniting, the Thea of the last seven years meeting who she had been before. Who she *was*. She was Theodora Stiltskin, and she was a fate-weaver. Flexing her power, knowing it was hers, had been hers all along, was never borrowed – she felt it soar to answer her. Like honey through her veins, a loving caress, a playful kiss on the tip of her nose.

She opened her eyes and stared at Jasper. Her husband. At that face she'd believed had been scored into the very fabric of herself. Impossible to forget. At the person she had loved for hundreds and hundreds of years, and would continue to love for evermore.

'Thea?' he gasped, his hands rushing up to her face as he searched her eyes, mistrusting that gleam of recognition within them. After all, it had been seven years.

Tears slipped down Thea's cheeks, falling onto Jasper's hands. 'I remember,' she said, their loss stealing the breath from her lungs, making her heart spasm with grief. 'I remember it all.' When fate-weavers wed, their powers mingled, making them stronger together. Binding them together in a shared fate. It was why she had been able to enter his townhouse. Why he'd been immune to the key she'd forged for Malek.

'What about me?' A sudden voice asked at Thea's other side. 'Do you remember your beloved sister?' Heloise wiggled her fingers from the seat she'd materialised in, opposite Thea. 'Hello, Theodora. Did you miss me?'

CHAPTER

Thirty-Three

EFORE THEA, BEFORE Jasper could react, Zofka moved first. 'You don't deserve to call her *sister*,' she snarled, hurling her arms up and out.

Thea had seen Zofka's magic before; as a kitchen-witch, anything that came from her stove, her ovens, was deliciously bewitching. She had a way with flour and sugar that could cure a cold, ease a heartbreak or alter a mood. Thea had even seen the way ingredients responded to Zofka; she could reverse the direction of a spill with a flick of her fingers. But Thea had never seen her channel magic like *this* before.

The Gingerbread House, being a café built entirely from enchanted panes of gingerbread biscuit, responded to Zofka's magical outburst.

It exploded.

The glazed roof blew off, sending gigantic sugar-plums rolling through the street, half of them going until they dropped down the void. With a rush of air, as if the café had sucked in a breath, the sugar windows shattered.

Jasper lunged at Thea, knocking her chair over backwards as he braced above her, protecting her from the flying shards of sugar, each one dagger-sharp. 'Thank you,' she gasped, drinking in his dark blue gaze as he stared back at her. Wondering. Wanting.

All the magical folk that had crammed into the café fled, diving out of the gaping holes where the windows had been. Shape-shifters that could fly and jump shifted forms to exit faster.

The walls of gingerbread creaked and groaned as the tapestry of fate manifested around Thea. 'Oh, no you don't,' Jasper said grimly, rolling off Thea as he began his own working, severing threads as quickly as Heloise knotted them. Preventing her from escaping.

Zofka threw up her arms and the gingerbread walls snapped. With a grunt of exertion, Zofka sent them charging towards Heloise, the biscuit crumbling as Zofka reshaped her walls into smaller panels. Panting under the effort, Zofka clenched her fingers into fists, making the panels reform around Heloise, containing her in a gingerbread prison.

Thea sat up.

Jasper swiftly knotted a tangle of fate around the construction. 'That should hold her for a short time.'

'Zofka, sit down.' Gretel sounded more overwrought than Thea had ever heard. Thea and Talibah whirled round to see Zofka wobbling in place, an exhausted smile on her mouth. She allowed Gretel to push her down onto a chair.

Thea stared at the ruins of the Gingerbread House. 'What did you do?' she whispered, horrified.

Piped icing dribbled across the floor, melting into a small river that carried broken gingerbread chairs and tables out into the street.

Zofka flapped a hand, seeming remarkably unconcerned. 'It's fine, we were due for a remodel anyway.'

A low rumbling sounded. It heralded Rose, who stuck her head around the last remaining piece of the Gingerbread House: its front door. 'That nasty little worm's back, and he's brought his friends with him.'

Pan Novak marched through the Magic Quarter, surrounded by Hunters, enough to render himself unreachable. They were an army walking into battle, pistols loaded, swords raised.

Once, witnessing this sight would have terrified Thea. Now, in the wake of her returned memories, she saw Pan Novak for who he really was: insignificant. He might have been handling the commercial side of the Quarter's demise, but Thea had spent enough of her adolescence being manipulated by her sister to see Heloise's work behind this. Pan Novak was merely dancing on her strings.

'I see you've got your memories back.' Paní Dagmar appeared in front of Thea, peering into her eyes with a smile that buried her eyes in wrinkles. 'Didn't I tell you that your name was Theodora?' she cackled.

Snapping from her reverie, Thea laughed, embracing the ancient witch, her dear friend in Prague when they'd lived here, the first time around. Some five hundred years ago. 'Of *course* – you were Jasper's friend still living here in the Quarter! All those times I thought you were just pestering my customers for spell ingredients.' She shook her head, wondering.

Paní Dagmar cackled again. 'Well, I had to keep an eye on you.'

'Though you can't blame me for doubting you . . .' Thea frowned. 'Why do you keep calling Rose "Daffodil"?'

Paní Dagmar lowered her voice. 'Why else? She *detests* it.'

They laughed together before Thea sobered. 'What are you doing out here? Go inside, it's freezing and—' She fell silent as Pan Novak threw up a hand and his army halted.

'You have all been found in breach of the law,' Pan Novak said. His smile was most unpleasant. It was no surprise he'd allied himself with Heloise; they bore the same sick satisfaction from others' misfortune. Once Thea had watched from behind a tree as Heloise had toyed with a frog's threads, making it contort and shudder in pain. She could imagine Pan Novak inflicting the same poison on a vulnerable target. 'You are harbouring dangerous magic that presents a threat to the good people of Prague. I come bearing warrants for each one of your arrests.'

A second ominous rumble sounded.

Pan Novak stood fast, even as a couple of the Hunters shuffled, casting uncertain glances at each other.

'I warn you, if you resist, we will shoot to kill,' Pan Novak finished.

Thea spread her fingers, ready to reach for the threads of fate, to take out Pan Novak first, but there were too many Hunters, their weapons pointed at the people she loved most. Zofka and Talibah and Paní Dagmar, and Gretel and Rose and Zdenka and Fleur and even Wojslav. And Jasper. Who had been forever at her side, protecting her even when she did not remember him. Even while she loathed him and courted another. 'Not yet, hold for the plan,' he murmured, at her side, always. Her fingers itched to entwine with his, to stand with him as one, as they always had. Until she had broken, and he hadn't been able to fix her. Now her heart was raw, but it was no longer an open wound.

'Now!' Jasper yelled.

Figures appeared through the dense snowfall, standing on rooftops like statues. They flanked each side of the street. Weather-witches. Raising their arms as one, their magic whirled through the Quarter as Pan Novak and the Hunters eyed them with increasing suspicion.

The temperature dropped. Ice ran along the street, crackling as it devoured everything standing in its path.

Zofka and Gretel leapt back, behind the Gingerbread House doorway to avoid the ice. Zdenka, over by the Rose Basket, was too late, and lost one of their boots. Three of the Hunters were later, and the weather-witches took advantage: ice rushed up their shoes and stockings, freezing them in place.

'Enough.' Pan Novak's voice knifed through the chaos. 'Any more of this shall be met with a prolonged interrogation in a cell.' He flashed that thin-lipped smile for the first time that night, sending a chill over Thea. 'And I will personally ensure that it will not be ... pleasant.'

'We refuse to yield to you,' Jasper said calmly.

Thea was wondering what else he and the other magical folk had concocted in the meeting she'd skipped, when she heard a deep intake of breath. She glanced back at Zofka, who was an alarming shade of milk after she'd blasted her own café apart, supported by both Gretel and Talibah, but it hadn't sounded like any of them. Her gaze travelled higher and higher still. Up to the apothecary rooftop, where her weathervane dragon had grown again since she'd last noticed it. If it wasn't night-time, it would have cast half the Quarter into shadow. *It was your weathervane,* Jasper had told her just an hour earlier. *It was a gift.* She hadn't believed him then, but she remembered now.

Guessing what was coming, she grinned at Pan Novak.

Paní Dagmar gave a dark little chuckle. Rose and Zofka and Thea herself had often wondered what kind of witch Paní Dagmar was; her haberdashery offered no clues, and much of what she said was passed off as eccentricities. Including her age. Of course, now Thea remembered meeting Paní Dagmar five hundred years ago, and the weathervane she'd gifted Thea as she'd come into her rare, complex strain of magic: transmogrification.

The weathervane was linked to Thea's moods. And right now, she was feeling defensive and very, very angry.

A colossal roar seized the entire Magic Quarter and shook it to its bones. Long and loud and filled with the promise of teeth and talons. If anyone made a sound, Thea couldn't hear them over the sheer volume of her weathervane dragon. But it was not magic the residents of this Quarter feared.

'Aim your pistols,' Pan Novak shouted when it drew to a close.

Thea and Jasper braced, strands faintly glowing around them as they fell into that shared vision. Thea had quite forgotten what it felt like, to wield power together, to work as a unit rather than fight against it. No wonder she had always struggled when she'd believed herself human; surrounding herself in a fog of distrust and suspicion had muted her power.

A guttural growling sounded. It was chased by a metallic creaking, like a carriage axle that required oiling, only louder. Pan Novak and those Hunters who were not frozen in place wheeled around, searching for the threat. One slipped on a patch of ice, delivering him straight to the mouth of the void. His scream lasted mere seconds, cut the instant the void claimed him.

A couple of Hunters began shooting in a panic. Thea wielded fate, paying with little dreams she'd once had, small memories she didn't mind losing, felling half the bullets. Her power came quicker and quicker, with the kind of speed she'd once envied from Jasper.

Now she outwove even him, relishing in reclaiming that lost part of herself. Other bullets were intercepted by weather-witches flinging up a wall of ice, thick enough for the bullets to lodge there instead of in the magical folk ducking behind. Paní Dagmar caught the last ones, turning them into metallic moths that swarmed the Hunters, flying into their faces and attempting to crawl into their mouths.

Nobody looked up.

Until a great cleaving noise came from above. Like an ancient oak pulling its roots free. Thea's eyes widened despite herself. Stiltskin's Apothecary rocked in its foundations as the weathervane dragon broke free from its mount and took its first heavy, juddering step over the roof.

The blood drained from Pan Novak's face. A couple of Hunters' pistols fired as they jumped back, their bullets pinging into the cobblestones, into the void.

Creaking as it did on a blustery day, the weathervane dragon uncoiled its immense neck, rolling its head down to look at Pan Novak.

'Is it going to *eat* him?' Zofka whispered.

The head of the dragon slunk down, its neck close enough that Thea could have raised a hand and touched its sleek iron scales. Its head came to a stop directly in front of Pan Novak, a hair's breadth away. Pan Novak glared back at it, though his legs were trembling. 'You do not frighten me,' he said in a low, dangerous voice.

The dragon roared again. Louder, longer, more venomous than the last roar. It shattered the ice coating the street, making icicles drop from branches like daggers. Thea threw up her arms, pressing her hands against her ears like everyone else, and still it deafened her for one blistering moment – until the Quarter distorted and the roar turned soundless.

Jasper's fingers were moving quickly, knitting together threads only he and Thea could see as he protected the magical folk's hearing.

Magic Hunters dropped to their knees in rows, like toy soldiers being knocked over.

When the roar ended, their hearing returned. A crimson bead ran down either side of Pan Novak's face. He calmly wiped the blood from his ears, as several lines of Hunters staggered away.

The weathervane dragon shrank down, its iron bulk vanishing before their eyes until it could have fit on Thea's palm. She dashed to picked it up. It was a robin with beady eyes and feathers so intricate, she could hardly believe it was made from metal. Then again, it was not from metal alone. 'Thank you,' she told both the robin and Paní Dagmar, who looked frailer now; it had not been Thea's mood alone that had caused her weathervane to launch a counterattack.

With a metallic chirp, the robin spread its wings and flew back up onto the apothecary roof, where it perched atop the weathervane.

'You have no idea what you have just done.' Pan Novak's voice was flat, his eyes lifeless as he stared at the magical folk still thronging the Quarter either side of the void, watching the remaining half of the Hunters like prey.

'Oh, no,' Jasper muttered darkly, casting a concerned glance at Thea. 'Heloise's bonds are—'

The gingerbread prison collapsed, and Heloise stepped free.

CHAPTER

Thirty-Four

ELOISE'S CROPPED BLONDE hair was ragged, her fury evident as she glowered at Zofka, tugging her sharply tailored suit back into place. 'You are growing rather tiresome.'

Gretel pushed Zofka behind her as Thea splayed her fingers, preparing to take on her sister, but Heloise's words were directed at Pan Novak. With a twist of fate's threads, Pan Novak was immobilised.

Heloise sauntered over to him, grasped the back of his collar and yanked him up onto the toes of his boots. His coat flapped, his wig and sides of his cheeks bloody from his burst eardrums.

'What are you doing?' Thea asked, her heart quickening. She never knew what Heloise would do next and that uncertainty, that quiet fear, had always left her unsettled. Now, amidst the people she cared for most, it was downright terrifying.

'He is my puppet,' Heloise said. 'Would you like me to make him sing for you?'

Thea shook her head.

'What's the matter, sister mine?' Heloise asked. 'Do you not like my new toy?' She smiled. 'I thought you liked playing with him.' She drew a nail down Pan Novak's bloodied cheek. 'Or did you play with him too hard?'

'Leave him. Leave this Quarter and talk to me in the forest, just ourselves,' Thea offered. 'I remember now, and I know I pushed you away when we were children.' Guilt coloured her tone. 'I am sorrier for that then you'll ever know, but let me make it right; we've both made mistakes, done things we regret. It's never too late to make amends.'

Heloise's smile widened, scenting blood. 'How unlike my perfect sister to admit making a mistake. But you're wrong. It *is* too late.' She gave a bored sigh. 'I'm done playing now.' She shoved Pan Novak away, sending him careening over to the void, where he teetered on the edge. His eyes were the only part she had not bound in threads, bulging wide as he confronted the black nothing before him.

By chance, he stabilised, and Thea let out a sigh; she had no wish for violence, even for those she detested most. But she'd forgotten the golden rule when it came to her sister: never show your emotions. Heloise kicked out a heel, sending Pan Novak straight into the void. He fell, long and slow and silent.

'Oops.' Heloise giggled.

The remaining Hunters fled.

'Good riddance.' Heloise stalked towards Thea. 'I'm ready for the end now. When I say the end, I mean the end for you, your precious Jasper and all your little friends.' She sneered at Talibah and Paní Dagmar, since Gretel had forced a still-weakened Zofka back from the fray.

Paní Dagmar surveyed her calmly. 'Well, you're a nasty one, aren't you? I can see why you ran away from home, Thea.'

Heloise ignored her, stealing closer and closer until she came to a stop, facing Thea.

Thea stared at the sister she'd once fled from. 'I'd often wondered what seeing you again would feel like,' she mused. 'I pushed you away, but it was your choice to turn that distance into cruelty. We could have grown closer again, been allies against the coldness of our parents. Instead, you were colder and crueller than they ever were.'

Heloise smiled to herself.

'The truth of it is, I pity you,' Thea said quietly. 'You'll never know what it feels like to be surrounded by people who love you, who would stand in a broken street, surrounded by your own missteps, and fight for you. You'll never know true love, and for that, I feel sorry for you.'

Heloise's smile flickered.

'That's why you were so desperate to destroy me here, in the Quarter, wasn't it? You wanted to shatter all the things I have that you never did. Destroy the home, the family I built for myself. Your envy is your greatest weakness.'

Heloise reached out and grabbed Thea's necklace. 'Wrong,' she snarled, tossing it down onto the iced cobblestones and stamping a heel on it. 'I wanted to destroy you here because your gods-cursed husband warded you. I've been wondering where you disappeared to for centuries. Imagine my surprise when you suddenly popped up in Prague and vanished into a protected hiding place. I tried to follow you down here, but I couldn't, of course. So, I paid off a couple of shape-shifters to investigate for me. Tell me everything about your new life and your little apothecary. Oh, and your new beau. Malek.'

Jasper stiffened, raising his hands to weave fate at a second's notice. 'You can do this,' he growled. 'End her, Thea.'

Thea reached for fate, but too much emotion was surging through her as she stared at her sister's face again for the first time in hundreds of years. And Heloise took advantage. Spinning her own web, she sent Thea flying back.

Gasping for breath, flinging her hands out to break her fall, Thea realised she'd been bound: her hands refused to answer her call.

The street rushed up too quickly. Thea met it with force. She lay there for a moment, winded, unable to move, to speak, to breathe, even as she heard Jasper's roar of vengeance and saw the familiar tell that someone was weaving: the air undulated. He appeared at her side seconds later, fury shining out of his eyes as he unpicked Heloise's knots, freeing Thea.

'Thank you,' she gasped as he yanked her back up to her feet. Just in time to see Heloise rising, too, a gash across one cheek where whatever Jasper had done to fling her away had hit its mark.

Heloise widened her eyes at them. 'How curious that you took it into your own head to begin *courting* Malek.' She sidled a glance at Jasper, lingering on the tightness of his jaw with no little amusement as she wiped the blood from her face. 'I knew then that it was the opportune time for my revenge. That something had happened between the pair of you, severing that once indestructible bond and leaving you, dear sister, all helpless and alone.' Her voice tightened on the last word. She raised her arms to attack once more.

But Thea had been watching her intently. And she'd heard her sister's weakness, the moment Heloise had revealed herself. 'I am never alone,' she said. 'Even without my memories, I found a home, a family. Even when I didn't know myself, didn't love myself, others knew and loved me.' She leant in closer. 'You could have killed me on the bridge two days ago,' she whispered. 'When I was still missing my memories, my heart, and couldn't fight back. Perhaps then you would have achieved your vengeance. Instead, you let your jealousy win. You were watching my life from outside the Quarter, never permitted inside, hungering for what I had yet again. You can lie to yourself, but I see straight through you.'

Heloise's fingers twitched in a familiar pattern, but Thea had rattled her, she knew from the way her sister's hands fumbled.

It mattered not. Thea was stronger. Thea was faster. And she'd spent the past seven years believing her power hadn't belonged to her, that it was smaller, less consequential than she'd liked. Now she knew otherwise, she flexed that old familiar muscle and threw up the skeins of fate, shining brightly all around them. Her thoughts and fingers a blur, Thea located Heloise's thread before her eyes spotted it, something within her knowing where it would be, instinctive and primal. It would be all too easy to toss a couple of years away and snap that thread, cut Heloise's life off at the strings like a collapsed marionette.

But Thea was not cruel. Instead, she configured an advanced knot, ensuring it would be impossible to pick apart, and leashed her sister, banishing Heloise back to her realm, to Orion. Where she could never leave again.

Heloise gasped, her hand flying to her throat as she stared at Thea, a sliver of disbelief, of doubt, betraying that confidence.

'You'd better hurry back to the Crossroads,' Thea told her. 'Before your time runs out.'

Heloise attempted to snag her own threads, reaching for her own power. But they slipped through her fingers.

Thea smiled at her. 'That's not going to work any more. You are banished from this realm, from any realm other than yours. If you want to use your power ever again, if you want to be able to *breathe*, I suggest you go home and leave me, and everybody in this Quarter, alone. Forever.'

Rasping for breath, Heloise pivoted on one heel and staggered in the direction of the Old Town.

The magical folk watched her leave before they erupted in glee.

Thea bent to one knee and picked up her necklace. Smashed by Heloise's heel, it revealed the pictures inside. She'd been wearing a locket with Jasper and their daughter's miniatures inside for the past seven years without realising. It was the first time she'd looked on Violet's face since her memories had returned; she'd always loved how her daughter looked like Jasper but now she realised that Jasper's dark blue eyes and raven hair would serve as a constant reminder of Violet. Jasper's hands closed around hers as she stood. 'I shall have it mended for you.'

She did not release her hold on it. 'I have no other pictures of Violet,' she whispered. That grief she'd pushed down, refused to acknowledge while battles were being fought, suddenly broke free, overpowering her.

'I have.' Jasper's hands were solid and warm and reassuring as they slowly took the locket from her. 'I will fetch one now, if you like?'

Zofka and Talibah and Pani Dagmar all hovered, kindnesses on the tips of their tongues, but Thea shook her head, tears running down her cheeks. 'First, I need to do something.'

Heloise might be banished, Pan Novak lost to the void and Malek locked down in Jasper's secret vault – Thea frowned, making a mental note to inquire exactly what Jasper's intentions were there – but the Magic Quarter's wards were still broken. Leaving the magical folk vulnerable to whoever decided that someone a little different from themselves made an excellent scapegoat. Or to whoever looked at their power with jealous eyes. And she would not let anyone else be hurt or taken from them the way Violet had been.

Jasper had not been able to resurrect the wards because he had not been the fate-weaver who'd forged them, five hundred years ago.

It had been Thea.

On a winter's night in the late 1200s, two things had occurred. The first: Thea and Jasper had arrived in Prague and immediately fallen into an exhausted sleep in their newly purchased apothecary shop. Secondly, a young witch had banged on their door, accidentally turning it into a small bear, which had bumbled around the apothecary, knocking things over until Thea woke. At which point, the witch had begged Thea to help. Her two lovers were duelling in the middle of the Magic Quarter and innocent magical folk were getting entangled in the violence. Jasper had removed the lovers' memory of the witch, much to her dismay, but Thea had then acted in precaution. It wasn't safe to be a witch, and the witches that lived in this Quarter peddled their wares only behind closed doors; it masqueraded as a simple shopping street and nothing more. The incident reminded her that it wasn't enough to relocate and hide from her sister. Thea needed to make sure that Heloise could never take a step inside, along with anyone who wished to persecute magical beings.

So Thea had warded the Quarter. Ensuring that nobody could enter unless they bore no ill will towards its inhabitants. Magic had thrived in response. No wonder that seven years ago, Jasper had decided this would make the ideal hiding spot for Thea herself. How ironic that it was the misuse of her own power that had brought the wards tumbling down.

She stepped forward. Her power was already making itself known again, unfolding like a sleeping giant, roused at last. And she was ready to roar. Thea threw her hands up and wove fate in a lacework of intricate patterns, the skeins glimmering like pixie dust, like distant constellations, as she channelled all her anger, grief and sorrow into forging new wards. She embroidered hundreds of colours of threads into one protective bubble, stronger than before, around the entire Magic Quarter. With room to grow, if they so wished.

'They're beautiful,' Jasper admired, his fingertips skimming Thea's shoulder as he made to touch her before thinking better of it, curling his fingers away. They had not yet had time to talk, to address everything that ran between them, as deep as that infernal void, smoking and rumbling in the centre of the Quarter, but Thea ached for him. She always had: even when he had been lost to her, when she'd been determined to loathe him, something within her had loved him fiercer than ever. Had been desperate for him to kiss her just one more time. Her heart, slumbering within her chest, had always beat for him alone.

She turned her attention to the Magic Quarter. To the icy, cobblestoned main street, framed with weathered oaks and those glittery stars that hung crooked after tonight's battle. To the void cutting straight through the heart of it. Digging back into the threads she had not yet released, Thea began stitching the void together, sealing the wound.

'Thea,' Jasper's voice came sharper than before. 'You're overdoing it now.'

Her energy too focused to speak, to reassure him, she forged on. Paying with days of her own life, with mundane memories of books she'd read, with nightmares that had plagued her every day for a year. With beats of her heart. She had broken the Magic Quarter; she had to fix it.

A wetness trickled from her nostril, tickling her upper lip. It smelt like blood.

'Thea!' Jasper cried out in alarm, attempting to stop her, but she clung harder to those threads, knitting the Quarter back together again, sending that unseeing chasm back into the nothingness it had come from. Her friends' voices began to clamour, but she saw them all as if from a great distance. Like she was perched on top of some mountain, and they were all tiny figures waving from the ground. She smiled to herself. How funny. The words grew into indecipherable noise, the nose-trickle into a flood, and everything turned hazy.

The last bite of the void, the last, lonely wisp of smoke, drew together and closed.

The void was gone.

Panting for breath, Thea wiped her bloody nose with the back of her sleeve as she tipped her head back. 'So many stars,' she said, wondering at the pinpricks of light sequinned across the dome of the world.

Zofka's voice came from one side. 'It's snowing – what are you on about?'

That was when Thea realised that when she moved her head, the stars moved too. 'Oh, are they not real?' she said stupidly.

'That's it, I'm taking her home.' Jasper's voice came from the other side, dark and gravelly and delicious. She wanted to lick it. She was just about to tell him so when the world lurched beneath her as he swept her up into his arms. And then everything faded, faded, faded, as she fell into her own starry void.

CHAPTER

Thirty-Five

HEA SLOWLY BECAME aware of voices. Too many voices, fussing and bickering. She was too exhausted to listen, letting them wash over her like bubbling waves. She was melting in an ocean of stars. Now and then, one permeated the ebb and flow of her consciousness. 'This is too many pillows,' one said darkly, followed not long after by a ragged sigh and, 'How many blankets does one person need?'

Somewhere inside her own head, she smiled.

Light dotted the inside of her eyelids. Prising them open felt like chiselling stone. Hard and laborious and ache-inducing. Through the flutter of her eyelashes, she glimpsed Jasper stirring something at her stove; Jasper feeding Cinnamon; Jasper wetting her parched lips with a little water.

'If you'll just let me feed her this cake—'

'Absolutely not. She needs to rest and recover. She has expended a colossal amount of energy—'

'I know, I was there. That's why this cake—'

'Stop arguing,' Thea croaked.

'Thea? Are you awake?'

'Don't try to talk too soon—'

'For goddess' sake, stop *fussing*, Jasper!'

Thea opened her eyes just as Zofka finished snapping at Jasper. The pair of them were glowering at each other from either side of the bed. Talibah locked eyes with Thea, her amber eyes warm with amusement. 'Welcome back,' Talibah said. 'It's been a few days. How are you feeling?'

Jasper and Zofka immediately turned to Thea.

'Thea!' Zofka exhaled, pushing back her rambunctious ringlets, which were in greater disarray than usual. 'We were so worried.' She waved a slice of cake in her direction. 'I baked some restorative cake for you, but someone' – she shot another glare at Jasper – 'wouldn't let me feed you it.'

'She was unconscious; she would have choked,' Jasper ground out. He gazed down at Thea, his voice softening. 'Are you all right? I – we – have all been concerned.'

'Some of us have been fussing like a deranged mother hen,' Zofka muttered, drawing another murderous glance from Jasper.

Thea sat up, resting back against her pillows. 'This is exactly the right amount of pillows.'

Relief shot across Jasper's face. 'And your memories?'

'All present, as far as I know.' Thea glanced at her bedside table. There, sat a portrait of Violet. Her delicate face was framed by Jasper's raven hair and set with the same dark blue eyes. Thea used to tease that she'd given birth to a copy of him. Looking at her lost daughter's face hurt. A deep, merciless hurt that would always be a part of her – and she would never wish that to be different – but she no longer felt as if she was drowning.

When she looked back to Jasper, he was watching her keenly. Searching for his wife. Her heart quickened in response. Reassuring Thea that it was there and present. 'We have much to discuss,' he said softly.

'Not before breakfast,' Zofka interrupted. 'Witches before britches.'

'That doesn't make any sense,' Talibah said, exchanging a look with Thea. 'Anyone can be a witch, anyone can wear britches—'

'I didn't have time to think it through, but you get the spirit of it,' Zofka said indignantly, shooing Jasper away. 'Thea needs to eat and drink and get changed before you two have your big reunion, or she's just going to pass out again.'

Jasper reluctantly tore his attention away from Thea. 'You have one hour.' It sounded more like a threat than a promise. Seizing his coat, he paused at the door. 'And then not even a legion of weathervane dragons could keep me away.'

When Zofka was worried, she baked. When she was stressed, she baked. When she was seething with fury, she baked. And apparently, during the past two and a half days since Thea had collapsed in Jasper's arms, she had baked a *lot*.

'Where did you even manage to do all this baking?' Thea wondered as Zofka crammed in yet another dish to their picnic, spread out across her bed.

Talibah gave her an agonised look. 'Zofka and Gretel are staying with me for the time being, until their remodel is finished.'

Thea smothered her laugh.

A trio of gingerbread people danced over the bed, dodging between plates of vanilla cake, generously smothered in buttercream, mugs of hot chocolate steaming on a tray, slices of thick, yellow butter sliding across toast, bowls of plush berries, and pastries shaped like stars and moons, dusted with warming spices and sugar.

After drinking two glasses of water, Thea nibbled at the slice of cake Zofka had been waving in her direction since she woke up. She had little appetite since her grief had returned with a vengeance, along with her memories, but she was ready to start living again. Those six months between Violet's death and Jasper taking her memories, she'd been little more than a ghost. Her stomach growled, reminding her that she did indeed need to eat.

'So?' Zofka asked, when her impatience finally ran down the clock.

'So . . . what?' Thea asked between bites of hot, buttered toast. Really, was there anything better on a winter's afternoon? Especially washed down with hot chocolate. Cinnamon flopped over, allowing her to pet his stomach.

'Well, you still sound like the Thea we know,' Zofka gestured at her. 'But you have your memories back, you've lived this whole other life that we know nothing about and I'm dying to know all about it.'

She seemed to remember Thea's great loss and reined herself back in. 'If you want to share, of course.'

'You don't have to tell us anything,' Talibah amended, sipping her own hot chocolate. 'Only if you feel like sharing, and that doesn't need to be today or soon.'

'And apparently you're *ancient*?' Zofka continued, slipping off her reins, as if she hadn't heard Talibah. 'I knew fate-weavers were older beings, but . . .' She whistled between her teeth. 'What's that like?'

'It feels normal.' Thea grimaced. 'Though please don't call me ancient again.' She couldn't believe she'd spent the past year fretting about being thirty-five when she was closer to *seven hundred*. It was strange, the two lives she'd lived, nestling up together.

'Sorry,' Zofka said, without a trace of remorse.

Talibah laughed, throwing a cushion at Zofka.

Sometimes Thea had worried that if she'd found a way to return her memories, it would alter the friendship between the three of them – what if she reverted to being a completely different person? But she needn't have concerned herself with that. She had always been herself; she'd lost her memories, not her personality. And when it came to the three of them, they were eternal. She sat back, surrendering her plate. 'What do you want to know first?'

For once, it was Talibah who indulged her inner curiosity. '*Everything.*'

So, Thea told them everything.

About her childhood in the forested, stormy realm of Orion, where she'd been tormented by her younger sister and misunderstood by her parents. Where she'd fallen in love with Jasper Stiltskin. How he'd saved her from Heloise and swept her away to their own little cottage in England, with ivy clambering up the walls and a garden of wildflowers that swayed to the gentle breeze, a world apart from the storm season they'd had to hunker down through every year back home. How sometimes they travelled this new realm, opening apothecaries in different cities to fund their long lives together. Paris, Firenze, Prague. Yet they always returned to that first little cottage, leaving their apothecaries safely entrusted to their apprenticed workers; other people who had needed a respite from their own lives for a spell. How eventually they had borne a beautiful baby girl, a daughter, with Jasper's dark blue eyes and near-black hair, and they had thought themselves the luckiest people in all the worlds. Until whispers of suspicion were thrown on them like a net they couldn't escape. They'd thought themselves untouchable; there were few fate-weavers living in this realm. But Violet was young, too young to have learnt how to manage her great power, passed down from her parents, at only twelve years of age. So, seven and a half years ago, when she was caught playing with fate in the market square and dragged away by overzealous villagers, she couldn't defend herself from the hatred and flames. Burning witches was outlawed, but in pockets of rural life, superstitions still ran rampant. People looked the other way. Freak *accidents* occurred. And Thea had been too late. Jasper had arrived in time to haul a hysterical Thea away before she was condemned to that same fate, bundling her onto a ship bound for the continent that night.

'That's horribly sad,' Zofka sniffled between tears, holding onto one of Thea's hands.

Talibah held the other. 'I can't imagine what you've been through.'

'We lived in the townhouse here in Prague for months, but I was a shell of myself,' Thea admitted. 'I begged and begged Jasper to take my memories, to remove the pain, and eventually he gave in.'

'What brought them back?' Zofka wondered. 'Why build in the failsafe that your own name would return your memories?'

'I believe that Jasper wanted me to recover – as much as one can recover from something like this – before I returned to myself,' Thea said quietly, blotting her eyes with a handkerchief. 'That I wouldn't be able to reclaim my memories until I'd recovered enough to be happy being myself again.' When she'd lost Violet, she hadn't seen a way forward and though that path was still shadowed, it was there, it existed. She was happy being Theodora again. 'Our contract bound me to this apothecary so that he would stay in my life, watching over me from afar.

'I knew I was right to root for the two of you all this time.' Zofka blew into her own handkerchief.

They sat in silence for a spell. Thea stroked Cinnamon, sleeping on her lap. Eventually the knife edge of grief dulled a little, enough to speak of other things.

'When did you get another rabbit?' Talibah asked.

Thea blinked as Talibah bent to scoop up a second rabbit. This one was tawny brown. 'I didn't?'

'Oh, can I name this one, too?' Zofka reached to stroke the rabbit. 'I think Nutmeg suits him nicely.'

Talibah peered closer at the rabbit's unusual markings: a single splodge of white fur sat beside its twitching nose, just big enough to fit the tip of Thea's finger. 'Did Jasper ever tell you if he was going to release Malek from his vault?'

'No, we haven't had a chance to speak yet.' Thea looked at the rabbit. 'He wouldn't have . . .' She trailed off uncertainly.

Zofka grinned. 'Someone doesn't know her husband as well as she thinks.'

Thea tossed a pastry at her.

Laughing, Zofka held her hands up. 'I'm not judging; Malek suits being a rabbit far more than he ever did being a human.'

Thea shot a scandalised look at Talibah, who shrugged. 'Perhaps it's a coincidence.'

They chatted some more, speaking far longer than the hour Jasper had allotted them before he made his return. Zofka and Talibah left, leaving more cakes and gingerbread and pastries than Thea could eat in several lifetimes, making her promise to send a raven the moment they could visit again.

And then it was just the two of them. As it had been for much of the last five hundred years.

Thea stood, revitalised after her long rest and Zofka's kitchen-witchery. She'd changed into her favourite sage green dress with wildflowers embroidered up the stomacher. It had been Jasper's favourite, she remembered. That was why she'd always been so fond of it.

Jasper hung his coat up in silence.

'I feel foolish,' Thea cried out.

Jasper jerked round, already frowning. 'Whatever for?'

'That I didn't know who you were these past years. Seven years, Jasper, and I . . . I never knew. All those times you glared at me, you . . . you looked at me like you hated me, like—'

Jasper crossed the distance between them. 'Like the way you hated me.'

'Yes,' she whispered.

'My feelings for you are not an easy, gentle thing, Thea. They're fierce and rough and all-consuming . . .' He drew a rattled breath. 'It is not something I found easy to hide. If I had left my mask slip, even for one second, then you would have known—'

'What?'

Jasper's gaze melted into hers. 'That I am impossibly in love with you.'

'Can you ever forgive me for leaving you alone with that grief? All those times I wondered if you were lonely . . .' Her voice cracked. 'I abandoned you. You must have been angry.'

Memories of their sweet daughter overwhelmed her. Good and bad, beautiful and terrible. It was too much to sort through, but she'd come back to herself enough to want to embark on that journey with Jasper. To remember Violet together. Heal together. If he wanted to, after she'd left him.

'Oh, Thea.' Jasper took her hands in his. 'I was lost, broken when Violet was taken from us, but you – you were unreachable. I lost you too, that day. How could I be angry when I saw you smiling again? Saw you coming back to life? Violet will always be a part of me, of us, but grief is a long and tiring journey and I just want my wife back again.'

'Then kiss me, Jasper Stiltskin,' Thea told him.

He surged for her like he was ravenous, his hands sweeping up her neck, into her hair, as their lips met and she kissed her husband, knowing who he was again, at last, for the first time in years.

She kissed him back, every bit as starving as he was, until his arms fell to her waist, and he gathered Thea in his embrace, lifting her to shower her mouth, her neck, with kisses. When she wrapped her legs around his waist, she felt his contented little sigh brush against her mouth.

He ripped his mouth from hers, to sweep a frantic gaze over her. 'How are you feeling?' he asked, in that gravelly tone she adored. The one that had made her blush when he'd stopped to inquire about the dream-buds she was gathering in the forest when they'd met . . .

She narrowed her eyes at him. 'Did you alter my handwriting in my Compendium?'

'Of course.' He gave her a baffled look. 'I couldn't very well give it to you with your own handwriting inside, could I?'

'You' – she kissed his cheek. 'Are very' – kissed the other cheek – '*sneaky.*' She fell onto his lips again. All this time, she'd been consulting the Compendium, believing Jasper had given it to her because he couldn't stand teaching her magic himself. Instead, he'd given her their own love story to read. And it was still her favourite one.

When he hoisted her higher, holding her tighter, she deepened their kiss, seeking more of him, never wanting to stop kissing him. They toppled against the bed together and Jasper pushed her dress and petticoats up to her thighs, before stopping and looking panicked. 'I'm sorry, I assumed . . .'

Thea held his face in her hands. 'Let me make things very clear to you, Jasper. I am hopelessly in love with you. Then, now and always. Even when I hated you, my heart belonged to you. Since the day I met you, it has been your name imprinted on my heart, and even when my memories were lost to me, I could never love another. It is you, only you, for as long as I live. It always has been, and it always will be.'

Jasper inhaled roughly.

She pulled him back down onto her. 'Now, assume away, because I want everything you've got to give me, and more.'

His dark blue eyes glinted. 'Careful, those are dangerous words.'

She grazed his neck with her teeth before whispering, 'I've spent the last seven years reading a *lot* of romance novels.'

With a growl of approval, he unlaced her stomacher, unwrapping her like a gift he was impatient to see.

'Aren't the pillows comfortable?' Thea asked afterwards, when they lay on her bed together, Jasper's arms wrapped around hers as if he was afraid to let go.

'Yes,' he said begrudgingly.

'I've seen that bed you've been sleeping on, and it looks as hard as stone.' Thea stroked his arm lightly, biting her lip as she awaited his response. They hadn't discussed living together again but surely, surely . . .

'I'll sleep with a thousand pillows if you're in my bed.'

Thea smiled.

'I love it when I make you smile,' Jasper said, pulling her closer.

'You can't see my face,' she accused.

'I don't need to see it to know when you're smiling.'

An indignant caw interrupted them. When Thea looked up, every one of her windowsills were lined with ravens. She sat up, clutching her blankets to her chest. 'What's happened now?'

Jasper kissed her bare back. 'You happened. I think everyone in the Magic Quarter has sent at least one raven since you collapsed in front of them all.'

Thea groaned, burying her head in her blanket. Cinnamon hopped over, nudging his head against hers. 'I suppose I'd better get up and start answering them all. Maybe I should call a meeting just to assure them I'm fine now.'

'That might be a good idea,' Jasper said seriously. Too seriously.

Thea shot up from the blanket. 'This is the second Quarter meeting you've agreed to. Why?' She eyed him suspiciously.

Jasper's hand, running up and down her back, paused. 'Well, if we're going to live here together, they might as well start getting used to me.'

'Live here. Live *here*?'

Being a man who frowned more than he smiled, Jasper's smiles were all the more treasured by Thea. His smile now made her feel like melted caramel. 'You found a community here, Thea. Friends and family that helped heal you. Why would I ever want to take you away from that? No, I think we ought to live here together.' He glanced around Thea's apartment, with its windows overlooking the snowy oaks and winter-blue sky, its stacks of books and heaps of blankets and two rabbits meandering about. 'Yes, I think this will make a fine home for us both. Once we've made it bigger, of course. I shall have to build some bookshelves for you, too; I don't know why your books are all over your floor—'

Thea kissed him. Long and slow and soft.

When they finally drew apart, Jasper was holding the heart-shaped box in his hands. 'Would you do me the greatest honour of being my wife once more and forever, Theodora?'

'Always,' she whispered.

He slid her old ring onto her finger. It felt as if she'd never taken it off.

Acknowledgements

Just like the Magic Quarter in *A Remedy for Fate*, it takes a village to survive writing a book.

For my agent, Thérèse Coen, for always having my back. I couldn't do this without you! I think you might be secretly magical.

It has been a dream come true to work with Hodderscape, who I've long admired from afar, especially having the wonderful Molly Powell as my editor. Thank you for taking my heap of cosy vibes and ten different plotlines and helping me craft an actual story out of it! Working with you on this novel was a joy.

I am also grateful to Sophie Judge and Aiysha Nazir on the editorial team for helping me whip this book into shape as well.

For Daisy Woods, who must be some kind of cover-designing witch because look at that cover! Thank you to Laura Bartholomew, Matthew Everett, George Biggs and the rest of the Hodderscape team for everything you do.

Huge thanks to all the amazing bookshops, booksellers, book bloggers, booktokkers, bookstagrammers and booktubers and READERS for all your love, enthusiasm and support. This author's heart is full to the brim that I get to keep writing books because of you all. Special thanks to my local haunts: Waterstones Nottingham, and Wonderland Bookshop, for always going above and beyond.

A Remedy for Fate is about a cosy community, filled with found family and I couldn't have written such warm and loving friendships without my own tribe: Amy McCaw, Rory Croucher, Ben Humphrey, Jane Kelsey, Aidan Littlehales, Polis and Chris Louizou-Denyer, Jonathan Norman, Alicja and Jake Shellard. Thank you isn't enough for how you've lifted me up and supported me during one of the toughest years of my life.

Writing books can be a solitary existence but I am grateful for my gorgeous author friends who always have time for me, especially Serena Patel, Donna David, and the rest of the Swag Lifeboat.

Thank you to my Shakespearean Sisters, Christine Spoors-Kenny, Sarah Hackmann, Evangelos Palaiologou, Vic James, Alex McGahan and the rest of my friends. Much love and appreciation to my family for everything, especially my parents, Joe and Marion Kuzniar, Hannah Kuzniar, and Michael Brothwood.

About the Author

M. A. Kuzniar is the bestselling author of *Midnight in Everwood* and *Upon a Frosted Star*. Before she became a full-time writer, she spent six years living in Spain, teaching English and travelling the world. She lives in Nottingham, where she spends her time reading, writing, playing board games, and dreaming of magic.

RAISING READERS
Books Build Bright Futures

Dear Reader,

We'd love your attention for one more page to tell you about the crisis in children's reading, and what we can all do.

Studies have shown that reading for fun is the **single biggest predictor of a child's future life chances** – more than family circumstance, parents' educational background or income. It improves academic results, mental health, wealth, communication skills, ambition and happiness.[1]

The number of children reading for fun is in rapid decline. Young people have a lot of competition for their time. In 2024, 1 in 10 children and young people in the UK aged 5 to 18 did not own a single book at home.[2]

Hachette works extensively with schools, libraries and literacy charities, but here are some ways we can all raise more readers:

- Reading to children for just 10 minutes a day makes a difference
- Don't give up if children aren't regular readers – there will be books for them!
- Visit bookshops and libraries to get recommendations
- Encourage them to listen to audiobooks
- Support school libraries
- Give books as gifts

There's a lot more information about how to encourage children to read on our website: **www.RaisingReaders.co.uk**

Thank you for reading.

---

[1] OECD, '21st-Century Readers: Developing Literacy Skills in a Digital World', 2021, https://www.oecd.org/en/publications/21st-century-readers_a83d84cb-en.html

[2] National Literacy Trust, 'Book Ownership in 2024', November 2024, https://literacytrust.org.uk/research-services/research-reports/book-ownership-in-2024